THE CASTL

'You must be beaten properly, Jana. You shall not know what it is like to be whipped with the *azakha*, but we may come close.'

Jana was powerless to prevent her assailants from turning her on to her back. She felt her legs being spread wide and strong cords binding her ankles and wrists to the sides of the bed. She twisted her neck to look up in the moonlight, and saw Mokka and Cassie standing one on either side of the bed. Each woman held not just one, but three canes from the rack Netta had thoughtfully provided. The canes were bundled together.

'No . . .' she murmured. 'Please . . .' But she knew that her moist sex belied her words. She wanted the punishment, longed for Mokka to beat her.

THE CASTLE OF MALDONA

Yolanda Celbridge

This book is a work of fiction.
In real life, make sure you practise safe sex.

First published in 1997 by
Nexus
Thames Wharf Studios
Rainville Road
London W6 9HT

Reprinted 1998

Copyright © Yolanda Celbridge 1997

The right of Yolanda Celbridge to be identified as the
Author of this Work has been asserted by her in
accordance with the Copyright, Designs and Patents Act
1988.

Typeset by TW Typesetting, Plymouth, Devon

Printed and bound by
Caledonian International Book Manufacturing Ltd, Glasgow

ISBN 0 352 33149 6

Contents

Prologue

The heiress Jana Ardenne went from her pampered London life to become Mistress of the female Order of Maldona, in its remote Spanish castle. Only the toughest or most beautiful women could survive the Order's regime of stern discipline and harsh punishment. Some ascribed Jana's supremacy to her skill in personal combat, some to her cunning, to her endurance of corporal chastisement, to her rumoured magic powers, or to her beauty alone.

She proved herself, and did so again by creating the second Maldona on a windswept Greek island, vanquishing the sorcery of Maldona's enemies, and discovering the fabled lost treasure of the Knights Templar.

From there, she determined to visit the forests and mountains of eastern Europe, and would meet her ultimate challenge in the savage landscape of the Balkans.

From the Rule Book of Maldona

Punishment of Virgins

The following Punishments are deemed appropriate for Virgins, according to the degree of imperfection which has incurred Chastisement. The Punishments, except for a Lady's Beating, are also appropriate for Prefects, Adepts and Housemistresses, save that they have the right to be tried by their peers before sentence. Prefects, Adepts, and Housemistresses may receive only a Grand or Noble beating. A Parfaite is only beaten by another of her Parfaite Sisters, and has the right, according to the rules of the

Auberge des Parfaites, to defend herself against any charge by wrestling her accuser.

Lady's Beating

This is administered in private, by a Corporal with a Prefect in attendance. The imperfect Virgin shall attend her Prefect without undergarments of any kind. She shall be instructed to lift her robe and position herself with fesses lifted. She shall then be caned on the bare, normally with seven strokes, but up to fourteen with the Prefect's permission. A Prefect may administer a Lady's Beating of fourteen strokes, or, with a Housemistress's permission, twenty-one. If a Prefect discovers an imperfection committed by a Virgin outside the territory of the Auberge, then she may administer a Lady's Beating of up to seven strokes on the bare in front of all who may be present. A Prefect may also administer seven strokes to an imperfect Corporal, without causing her to lose rank.

Grand Beating

This is received by the imperfect Virgin in a state of complete nudity. The Grand Beating is taken indoors, and must be witnessed by six other Virgins. It is given by a Prefect, with whip, tawse, or cane, or alternate use of all three, and the imperfect Virgin may be whipped on the back as well as the fesses. The whip may have up to four thongs. Occasionally the birch may be used instead of the above Good Instruments. The Grand Beating consists of at least fourteen strokes, or twenty-one with a Housemistress's permission. The imperfect Virgin may elect to be securely tied to receive punishment, if she wishes to be sure not to commit the further imperfection of losing control. In this case she shall be caned seven times more on the fesses, and whipped seven times on the back.

Noble Beating

The Noble Beating is generally taken indoors, and must be witnessed by the whole assembly of the Auberge. The imperfect Virgin is brought to refectory, carrying her restrainer before her, and wearing her best uniform. She is stripped naked by the Prefects, strapped to a whipping-frame by ankles, waist, and wrists, and then gagged with the *bolus sacer*, or steel ball. Her restrainer is inserted *in fundamento*. The beating is given with the *flagrum*, which generally has no fewer than six thongs, and not more than twelve. It is taken on back, shoulders, fesses, and thighs, and after the first stroke has been given by the House-mistress, each Prefect gives a stroke in turn. There is no limit to the number of strokes in the Noble Beating. The number is determined by the Housemistress alone, though it is customary for her to consult the opinion of her colleagues on the Council of Adepts. The Library of Maldona contains punishment books kept since foundation on the orders of the original Maldona, Jana Ardenne of Northumberland. There are records of Virgins who have taken Noble Beat-ings of one hundred strokes for the imperfection of being caught in a lie, and afterwards proceeded to the most illustrious careers as Adepts or even Parfaites. One Virgin took three Noble Beatings of sixty, seventy-five, and one hundred strokes, within a four-month period, and in due course became Deputy Superior. There is also the instruc-tive record of one Housemistress of the Auberge d'Angleterre, who had caught a Virgin in a lie and ordered a Noble Beating of one hundred and fifty strokes. She rejected the advice of her sister Adepts to limit the beating to one hundred strokes, and administered the one hundred and fifty she had ordained. Shortly afterwards she was heard to commit the imperfection of boasting that she knew better than her sisters; was tried by her peers; sentenced to, and received, a Noble Beating of one hundred and fifty strokes. Before receiving punishment, she was publicly stripped of her rank and reduced to a humble Virgin.

Parfaite's Beating

The Parfaites are responsible for obedience and discipline outside the Auberges, that is, within the general body of

Maldona. The Parfaites have their own rule book, which is known only to them and upon whose contents it is forbidden to speculate. Any Virgin, Corporal, or Prefect summoned to the Auberge des Parfaites for the gift of Chastisement is forbidden to speak of what beating they have received, and the scribe of this book, like all others, may not know what form such a beating may take. The Sisterhood of Parfaites are their own law, and this, like all other rules, has been ordained by Jana Ardenne the first Maldona, for all eternity. Also by her *ordonnance*, any slave of Maldona, be she Virgin, Prefect, or Adept, who in the midst of chastisement wishes the chastisement to cease, on crying 'I go down' shall be immediately released from her bonds and her chastisement shall cease. She may then leave Maldona forever. The library has no record of any chastised slave ever crying 'I go down'.

Adore Maldona.

1

Shipboard Discipline

Jana Ardenne, Mistress of Maldona, looked down from the guardrail of Caspar's ship and saw her naked reflection shimmer in the turquoise water of the Aegean. Her long blonde mane cascaded over her bare breasts and the golden forearm on which she rested, while her other arm lay across the body of her slave Cassandra, stroking the full peaches of her bottom, which was scarcely covered by her skimpy black panties. Jana's caress was a gossamer touch as she felt the firm muscle beneath the silk that adorned Cassie's croup. Jana's blonde tresses twined with Cassie's lustrous dark locks, their hair an artful union of black and gold, which in Jana's mind symbolised the love of Mistress and slave. Each woman's neck was graced with a twirl of gold necklaces, and Cassie wore a golden slave bracelet around her bare ankle. Otherwise, both were naked save for their silken panties, Cassie's black ones in counterpoint to her Mistress's shiny thong of a gold as bright as her hair. Their bodies gleamed wet with sun-welcoming oil, and both were barefoot on the polished oaken deck.

'The sea will be our last mirror for some time, Cassie, sweet,' mused Jana, 'so make the most of it. Tonight is our last night on board – and there is to be a fancy dress party to wish us on our way. I do love fancy dress parties.'

'Mmm,' said Cassie. 'I so wish you would tell me our destination, Mistress.'

'It is a surprise,' said Jana. 'You will learn soon, when I have made my plans complete. In the meantime, just think of your wildest fantasies, and go beyond them. You shan't

1

be disappointed, sweet slave.' Jana's fingers idly slipped inside the waistband of her slave's panties and touched the bare skin of her buttocks; she felt pleasure as her palm caressed the smooth globes.

'Our rules are wise to forbid the vanity of the looking-glass,' said Jana. 'We must be slaves of Maldona, not of our own beauty. Womanhood – beauty – must come from love of Maldona and joy in submitting to her rules.'

'And, Mistress, joy in accepting her wise punishments,' murmured Cassie. 'You have no need to remind me, for I was the Mistress of Maldona. I was Maldona herself, until you vanquished me in the most savage *pankration* wrestling I have endured in any arena.'

'You schemer!' cried Jana. 'You *let* me win!'

Cassie tossed her head, making her hair sparkle like a sea of black diamonds, and chuckled mischievously.

'You can prove nothing, Mistress,' she retorted. 'Your skill at wrestling is greater. You challenged and fought me fairly, according to the rules, and I surrendered as was my right, making you Mistress of Maldona. With my blessing, I might add, were it not imperfect for a slave to offer blessing to her Mistress.'

Jana sighed in contentment at the wash of the sun's rays on her bare body, and at the beauty of being naked with her slave and companion. Her finger slipped casually into the cleft of Cassie's buttocks and, almost imperceptibly, her stroking grew a little more than casual. Cassie purred as Jana's forefinger touched the base of her spine.

'Your bottom's all wet and slippery, Cassie,' Jana said. 'The silk of your panties is so thin and soaked with sweat.'

Cassie murmured that she thought it was more than sweat.

'Oh, how I long to know our destination!' she added.

'In good time,' said Jana. 'I like to tease you with surprises, for the unexpected is the spice of pleasure.' Unbidden, Jana moved a silent hand down between her slave's thighs, which parted gently at her touch, and found the lips of her sex. They were swollen and moist with oily secretions and, as Jana's finger touched her vulva, Cassie

2

smiled broadly and quickly kissed her Mistress on the cheek.

'Now you know my guilty secret, Mistress,' she said playfully. 'I'm all excited, because your touch, your perfume, your very presence make my fount wet with love.'

'My perfume!' laughed Jana. 'I'm oily and sweating!'

'Your sweat is the moisture of beauty,' said Cassie. 'I should like to lick every drop from your perfect body, to cleanse her utterly.'

Jana now placed her palm firmly on her slave's shaven *mons veneris*, marvelling at the full smoothness of the creamy hillock. Cassie, as her personal slave, was privileged to shave her entire body; ordinary Virgins, Corporals, even Prefects – anyone below the rank of Adept in the complex hierarchy of Maldona – were obliged to keep a full pubic mink. Cassie was silent as Jana lightly ran her fingers up and down the soft skin of the hairless mount but then she sighed, for Jana, her belly fluttering, allowed the nail of her forefinger to brush the bud of Cassie's nympha, which was stiffening to her touch.

Cassie shuddered at the pressure of Jana's fingertip on her clitoris, and it was not long before all Jana's fingers were caressing the wet fount-lips. Her own quim was moist now and she could feel the beginning of a hot trickle on the soft skin of her inner thighs.

'That remark was rather impudent, Cassandra,' she said as formally as she could. Cassie nodded solemnly, but smiled.

'Indeed. The perfect Mistress of Maldona cannot be cleansed by a mere slave. I suppose I should be punished.'

Jana saw a way to deflect further questions about the planned journey and at the same time take a little pleasure. There was no reason why Cassie should remain in suspense, but Jana did like to tease her. The exercise of power, she thought, is one of the sweetest addictions.

'Yes,' she murmured 'I suppose I shall chastise you.'

Jana thought briefly that she had intended nothing more than a contemplative half hour before luncheon, gazing at the water, but that thought was soon far from her as she felt all four fingers glide into Cassie's soaking hot slit, and her palm and thumb press sternly against the pubic bone, holding the woman's body in the most tender of locks. Her four fingers wriggled like hard fishes inside the warm ocean of Cassie's sex, and her tightly squeezing palm massaged Venus's soft naked hillock. Silent, Cassie shivered in delight and trembling apprehension.

Jana suddenly reached with her free hand and took the waistband of her slave's wet panties. Then she jerked the panties down Cassie's thighs and, swiftly bending, slid them to her ankles. With a smile and a swift movement of her muscled calf, Cassie kicked off her panties and was completely naked for her Mistress.

Jana pulled down her own garment, stepped out of it, and, holding her moist panties on her outstretched thumb, placed a fingertip on the wet petals of her own fount. She parted her swelling cunt-lips, showing Cassie the pink flesh glistening inside her secret place. Then she pressed her oily finger to Cassie's mouth. Cassie kissed her Mistress's finger, and Jana thrilled as she felt her hot tongue licking her love juices, and her pleasure increased as Cassie took the gold panties and held them to her face, breathing deeply of Jana's perfume with a joyful smile.

'Mmm,' said Jana softly, 'you are an impudent slave indeed, and must be chastised for it.'

Cassie's eyes sparkled more brightly than ever.

'Touch your toes,' said Jana curtly. She removed her fingers from Cassie's fount, causing Cassie to make a moue of disappointment, then licked them carefully as Cassie rubbed herself where Jana had entered her. She stroked her engorged clit, as though taunting her Mistress.

'You mean bend over?' she answered.

'I mean bend over and keep your legs spread wide, and thrust your bottom well up towards me. Both hands firmly on the deck.'

Cassie obeyed, pouting, as she had to remove her hand from her clitoris and cunt-petals in order to support her weight.

'Wider,' said Jana. Cassie spread her legs until her thighs

4

and arms were at right angles, and Jana told her mockingly that she looked like a crab.

'And you are merely going to spank me! A crab has a hard shell, Mistress,' said Cassie impishly, 'and can take any little spanking almost without feeling it. A cane or whip – well, that would be another matter.'

'A spanking can hurt just as much when delivered on the bare, and when your bum is wet,' replied Jana, and with one hand began to stroke Cassie's upraised bare fesses, while the other dived once more between the outstretched thighs, and began, vigorously, to massage Cassie's wet, engorged damsel. Cassie began to tremble at this merciless pleasuring of her clit, and Jana felt the girl's already moist cunt become a river of beautiful hot juices. Cassie's love-oil flowed over her hand, and she cupped her palm to store the precious fluid. When she had sufficient, she removed her hand and began to rub Cassie's oil into the naked skin of her fesses. Jana repeated this frottage until Cassie was trembling with desire, each stroke of her clit making her moan deep in her throat while Jana, constantly ordering her to be still, continued to rub the juice into her quivering buttocks until they were soaked in the moisture and gleamed as brightly as the sea beneath them.

'There!' said Jana. 'Now you are properly wet, and your spanking will hurt all the more.'

'Oh, Mistress,' sighed Cassie. 'You make me so wet, I – Oh!'

Her words were interrupted as Jana raised both her arms and brought her palms down with fierce vigour, to deliver one fierce slap on each of Cassie's fesses. This was followed almost immediately by another, harder one, and then by another.

'Hurt much?' said Jana, after Cassie's bottom had taken a good dozen of the fiercest blows.

'Oh, Mistress, yes, how it hurts,' whimpered Cassie. 'Please do not punish me any more, I beg you.'

Jana smiled at Cassie's expert game-playing, for she knew that a woman who could grin as she bore twenty-one strokes of a many-thonged whip – her beloved *flagrum* –

5

or a four-foot willow cane, would shrug off a hand-spanking as a mere tickling. She told Cassie as much, but entered into the spirit of the game, and added that quantity was very often a substitute for quality.

The sun caressed Jana's back and bare buttocks, burning her as the spanking visibly coloured Cassie's own fesses. Jana's arm rose and fell rhythmically, each time delivering the same fierce crack to the reddening globes which quivered so beautifully at her touch, until she was pleased to see that Cassie's naked fesses distinctly bore the crimson imprints of the hands that spanked her. Jana was silently keeping score of her hammer-blows.

'You are marked, Cassie,' murmured Jana as she continued to spank with all the strength of her muscled arms. 'Have you had enough?'

'No, Mistress,' Cassie answered, her voice quavering. 'From your hand, never enough ... Oh, but I never thought a mere spanking could hurt – I mean, hurt so much. With both your sweet hands – how cruel, how beautiful! *Oh!* That one *really* stung! I must have taken dozens, hundreds. I can't count! My bottom's on fire! You are so strong and so pitiless, my lovely Mistress! Please, be gentle. Not so hard! Oh! *Ooh!*'

Jana sensed that Cassie was no longer playing a game, but was genuinely hurting now, for her body had begun to shudder at the impact of each spank. Jana's own body was flowing with the sweat of her exertion, and between her thighs her perspiration mingled with her love-oil, whose trickle from her swollen fount had become a rich warm flow. For the Mistress of Maldona, too, it had ceased to be a game. The tingling in her fount and belly, the throbbing of her nympha, and the exultant feeling of her power over her slave made her wish to inflict real punishment on Cassie's naked body. Now, between every third or fourth stroke, she was obliged to rapidly wipe the sweat that blurred her vision and made the slave's body shimmer and dance before her. Yet the strength and rhythm of her blows did not lessen. Jana found that the speed of her exertion did not tire her or sap her strength, but that the tempo, almost hypnotic, gave her new energy and new ferocity. Her harsh breath followed the rise and fall of her arms, and she felt herself to be godlike and pitiless in the punishment of the naked, abject slave. Cassie's breath now came in sharp gasps as though in agonised astonishment at the force of the blows to her croup, and each breath was followed by a long whimper:

'Oh, Mistress . . . Oh . . .'

Jana had no time to reflect on what she was doing: under that sun, time seemed to have no meaning for her. All that existed in the world was that reddened croup beneath her, and her own pumping arms that flailed the skin. She knew in her heart, and exulted in the knowledge, that as any punishment progressed, the very submission of its victim inflamed the chastiser to a very real anger, and to a desire to make the punishment as fierce as possible. It is, she felt, as though I am punishing Cassie precisely for being so obedient. I want her to beg, plead, implore; I want to reduce her to a quivering pool of pain. Yet I know her quim is flowing with desire at each blow, just as mine flows. How the submission of this worm infuriates me!

Now she began to vary the target of her strokes, applying the force of her hands to the soft, tender skin of the inner thighs, which made Cassie squeal in genuine anguish. Still using both arms at once, she adopted a leaning position, and delivered her blows aslant, the top hand catching the underside of the fesse, and the other landing on the thigh-skin. She began to vary the beating, switching back and forth from the two-handed slap on both buttocks to the stinging blow on the thigh, and occasionally – for Cassie's legs were spread suitably and uncomfortably wide – turning her hands palm upwards to deliver two sharp blows right in the crack of her buttocks, her fingertips lashing Cassie's anus bud and coming perilously close to the thickened lips of her fount itself. Cassie's reaction was almost a frenzy, and as she squirmed her croup, her whole body jerked and went rigid from the pain of the blows to her most tender place. Jana began to rain those cleft-strokes harder and faster, the sight of Cassie's shuddering body flooding her quim with the juice of her excitement and sending shivers of desire through her belly. Her nipples and clit were hard, and her spine tingled until she could bear it no longer.

'I've made you scuttle enough, my little crab,' she panted, lowering her arms.

'Oh . . .' sobbed Cassie, between gasps. 'I never thought a spanking could be so hard, Mistress. So beautifully hard.'

'You took a good two hundred, Cassie,' said Jana in a steely voice. But I'm afraid your punishment is not over.'

She ordered Cassie to kneel on the deck. Cassie obeyed, and bowed her head, but Jana told her to look up. Her slave's face was streaming with tears, and through the tears she smiled.

'Permission to rub my fesses, Mistress?' she said. 'How she smarts! I feel like a girl at Rosebush who's had to take her knickers down and get a brisk spanking for slacking at her work, then have all her friends clustering to inspect her sore bum.'

'Permission denied,' said Jana curtly. 'You will say sorry for being so impudent by kissing my feet.'

Cassie bowed low and Jana felt her lips licking and caressing her toes, the tongue flickering deftly into each crevice, while the slave's hands stroked the backs of her calves. At her touch, Jana's mood of power and punishment changed to a glow of melting love. Softly, she ordered Cassie to leave her feet and worship her elsewhere, but Cassie needed no orders, for no sooner had Jana spoken than her slave was kneeling upright, her head pressed to Jana's fount, and her hands tightly clasping the taut globes of her Mistress's bare buttocks. Cassie placed her lips full on Jana's cunt-petals and kissed her there as she would kiss her mouth. Jana moaned with pleasure, and she felt Cassie delve with pursed lips right between her swollen labia, pecking at the tender pink flesh with little kisses, and sucking Jana's flowing love-juice into her mouth. Between kisses, Cassie let her tongue rhythmically lick the quim's wet interior as Jana, giddy with pleasure, began in her turn to whimper. She stroked Cassie's dark moist hair then

8

found her earlobes and tickled them – she knew that Cassie was particularly sensitive there – so that Cassie, with a soft lowing moan of abandon, moved her lips and positioned her mouth directly above Jana's throbbing nympha.

Cassie's ruthless yet tender lick of her Mistress's distended clit was expert. She flicked the hard bud of desire with her tongue-tip until Jana's giddiness quite overwhelmed her, and she disengaged from Cassie's embrace to sink to her own knees.

'Punishment over, Mistress?' said Cassie breathlessly, her eyes saying it must not be. Jana shook her head, and saw her own face reflected in Cassie's, the lips reddened and the eyes heavy-lidded with desire and pleasure. She hugged Cassie around the shoulders and kissed her on the mouth, tasting the oily perfume of her own sex-juices and swaying her body so that their breasts moved against each other. The feeling of Cassie's hard nipples brushing her own made Jana moan long and deep in her throat and gently she made Cassie lie down beside her on the deck, where they continued their embrace, breasts, bellies and mounds pressed tight in their loving fever. Then Jana rolled away from her slave and turned around to place her quim against Cassie's mouth and her own lips on Cassie's wet fount.

Cassie writhed like a shining dark serpent as her Mistress began to pleasure her, her tongue relentlessly licking the stiff nympha. Jana tasted Cassie's love oil, and felt her belly shudder with warm spasms of joy as Cassie renewed her caress of Jana's own swollen clit. The silence was broken only by the sobs of pleasure from the throats of the two women, and the soft lapping of the wavelets on the sea below. Jana knew that she was near her plateau, that her orgasm was not far away, and could tell from the trembling of her slave that her body too was about to flower with joy. She stroked Cassie's buttocks, hot from her spanking, and murmured, between wet kisses to the cunt-petals:

'You poor lamb. Oh, your poor bum. She must be so red and smarting. Did I hurt you awfully?'

'Oh, yes . . . Mistress, it was lovely.'

Jana parted the cheeks of Cassie's croup and ran her

finger up and down the cleft. 'There, too,' she said, touching Cassie's protruding anus bud and letting her fingertip rest on the puckered skin.

'Mmm,' moaned Cassie.

Jana slipped her finger inside Cassie's anal opening, just the tip at first, then, as the writhing of Cassie's loins grew almost frantic, she pushed it deeper inside, feeling the tender membrane alternately resist, then relax, at her insistent pressure. Then suddenly the whole channel gloriously yielded and opened to her finger, which sank right to its hilt inside Cassie's secret place, as though being joyfully welcomed home. Cassie's moans became a squeal of delight, and to Jana's satisfaction, she returned the caress. Now it was Jana who felt a squeal rise in her gorge as Cassie's finger caressed and penetrated her anus. It hurt at first, and she felt her bud resisting the intruder, try as she might to relax her sphincter muscle. But then in a joyous rush, her anus yielded passage as Cassie's had, and her tight channel seemed miraculously oiled as Cassie filled her. Jana could no longer resist, and cried out helplessly as she felt herself shudder in the warm flood of orgasm. Moments later, Cassie reached her own spasm, and the two women cried out in sharp, breathless howls as they clung to each other, melting together in a love-whipped ocean.

Jana's eyes were closed: she lay there for what seemed an age, sighing and smiling. Her belly still tingled with the fires of her orgasm and she knew what it was to be utterly content. Pursing her lips, she bestowed a very soft and chaste kiss on Cassie's cunt-petals.

'Thank you,' she whispered. 'That was lovely.'

Cassie responded with a similar quim-kiss.

'It is I who thank you, my Mistress,' she said.

They sat up, grinning and making sheep's eyes.

'It must be nearly lunchtime,' said Jana, then laughed. 'I suppose that sounds a bit silly.'

'No, Mistress. It *is* nearly lunchtime,' answered Cassie. 'And all of a sudden, I'm hungry. As well as hungry to know our destination, that is. But maybe you shouldn't tell me . . . let me enjoy my lovely fantasies about our journey.'

10

Just then they heard the tinkle of a miniature gong, and looked up to see a statuesque black man approaching. He was carrying the gong, stroking it with his fingernail, and his arrogant, finely chiselled face wore a sardonic grin. An officer's cap was perched jauntily over his brow, and otherwise he wore a spotless white T-shirt and razor-creased jeans with a designer label prominently displayed on his tight bottom. His feet were bare and his toenails, as well as his fingernails, delicately manicured.

'Good morning, Captain Damien,' said Jana gravely, 'or afternoon, I suppose.' She smiled mischievously at him, suspecting that he had been observing them throughout the entire proceedings, and amusing herself inwardly at the prospect of exacting some light-hearted revenge in return for his imperfection.

'Luncheon is served at your convenience, Mistress Jana,' said Captain Damien, with a bow. Technically, he was not obliged to address her as Mistress, for he was an employee of Caspar's like the rest of the crew, and not a slave of Maldona. Nevertheless, he always extended this courtesy, tinged though it was with slight sarcasm. Jana thought that he probably longed to be a slave of Maldona. Most men did.

'We shall attend shortly,' she answered. Damien nodded and looked at the deck, which was now glistening with rivulets of sweat and the oils which had flowed from the women's founts. His eyes took in their naked bodies, and their sodden, discarded panties. A smile spread across his lips, and his big sleepy eyes widened under their long, surprisingly girlish lashes.

'Dress is informal as always, my ladies,' he drawled. 'Except of course for myself. Caspar has kindly permitted me to be steward, knowing how much I love to serve ladies . . .'

The double entendre was not lost on Jana, who vividly remembered Damien's filmed coupling with Caspar's wife Netta, in one of Caspar's more surreal productions. Damien turned to go.

'In your case, ladies, panties are optional,' he added.

11

2

The Luncheon

Whatever Captain Damien said, Jana and Cassie always
went in finery to the dining-table, although panties were
generally ignored. Jana enjoyed wearing the briefest of
mini-skirts, and crossing her legs mischievously to let the
servants glimpse her shaven mount and pink petals beneath. Cassie sometimes chided her with a look for this
cruel teasing, but Jana would respond with a shrug or a
raised eyebrow. Men were there to be teased, she would
explain, and to be teased by the Mistress of Maldona was
the greatest honour and the greatest supplice a man could
imagine. They liked being teased, just as the knights of
Maldona secretly relished being robed as women by their
Mistresses. It was a sign of humility and of the servitude
they owed to women, but also a chance to express the soft,
female side of their nature which they had been accustomed to hide under a wearisome façade of gruff maleness.
As Mistress of Maldona, Jana had found that males were
often delighted to obey at last instead of pretending to
command. Women commanded . . .

After showering and cleansing their bodies of sun oil,
Jana and Cassie took a long time in selecting what they
should wear at luncheon: they knew that the meal could
not start in Jana's absence. Eventually they entered Caspar's main stateroom. Jana looked splendid in a long,
bottom-hugging white silk skirt, and matching bolero
jacket, which she left unfastened to her navel, so that her
breasts were almost wholly revealed, and her nipples were
clearly visible as the silk caressed them to a delightful

12

tension. A ruched red cummerbund was fixed tightly around her waist, narrowing her already flat belly and throwing her full breasts into prominence. Cassie, slightly more decorous, had opted for a tight black mini-skirt and a red blouse which matched her Mistress's cummerbund. Her blouse was open to the third button, revealing a gold necklace inset with black and red stones, in pleasing harmony with her gold neck chains.

Panties being optional, according to Damien's sarcastic advice, they wore them just to spite him, and had swapped: Cassie wore Jana's gold slip, invisible under her black skirt, but her black panties, stretched tightly on Jana's fesses, were visible under the white silk skirt – a deliberately jarring note which drew attention to the otherwise perfect harmony of Jana's costume and made her feel deliciously sluttish.

Both women were grinning as they took their places. The dining-table, crisp with starched white linen and shining with burnished silver, was impeccable, and in piquant contrast to the lazy luxury of the stateroom's intricate Persian rugs, velvet cushions, jewelled hookahs, and paintings and statuettes depicting the ornate writhings of naked gods and goddesses. Caspar was not wearing his usual Grecian skirt, the one Jana liked as it softened the jutting maleness of his features and gave him a pleasantly androgynous air. Instead he sported a gleaming white mess jacket with a black satin frilled shirt, and tight trousers of dark red with gold piping. Jana found that his heavily muscled body, shaven head and harshly jutting cheekbones were flattered by this finery, and she murmured that he looked every inch an officer. As she said 'every inch', her eyes strayed not quite unconsciously to his groin, where the tight trouser-cloth did little to conceal the arrogant bulge of his cock. Caspar smiled as he noted her glance and Jana was alarmed to feel the hint of a blush on her face. She smiled too: Caspar noted everything.

Caspar's wife Netta was wearing a tight black latex sheath dress which accentuated every sinuous curve of her tall, slender form. She wore this often, and also favoured

13

exotic corselages of straps, chains, and buckles, or else nothing at all save for an ankle bracelet and nipple chain, but such was the grace and ripeness of her body that Jana could think of no costume which would fail to enhance her mature, willowy beauty. And Netta possessed a seeming infinity of costumes, along with all the myriad bric-à-brac and exotica which she tirelessly collected. Decoration, furniture, artworks and apparel, for herself, Caspar, slaves and servants, were her province. Of the couple, she was the hoarder and lover of things, while Caspar, the film-maker, was the lover of ideas and images. Jana thought of them according to the doctrines of *feng shui* – he was the soaring blue dragon, she the white tiger, scouring the Earth for treasure.

Caspar said that since they were to arrive at their destination that very night, or perhaps in the small hours of the next morning, he thought a certain formality was in order. Jana was glad, though, to see that this formality was not overdone. Netta's dress was slit to well above her hips, allowing a tantalising glimpse of her red rubber garter belt, suspenders, and matching panties. Netta's love of rubber was matched only by her penchant for leather, and Jana often wondered if her rubber underthings were not too uncomfortable in this hot climate, before reminding herself that such discomfort was part of Netta's pleasure. Most women, their minds unopened, were content with the titillating constraint of a bra and panties worn a little too tight, but Netta relished the full satisfaction of garments which intricately bound her body in order to free her spirit. Caspar, as an afterthought to formality, wore at his belt a dainty miniature riding crop, only a foot long, of braided red leather. Jana thought that a sweet touch: the unforeseen harmony of red, black and white in all four diners pleased her eye and taste for symmetry. She was pleased, too, at Netta's choice of uniform for the crewmen who now bustled in to serve them.

The young Greek crewmen wore only black leather breeches very tight. Their muscled olive torsos were bare, as were their feet, and their long hair was fastened into pony-tails with red ribbon. It was typical of Netta's conceits that their chests were medallioned, and studded leather straps were fastened around their wrists, the number of straps according to their rank, in a charming parody of a naval officer's gold braid. In addition, their fingernails and toenails were lacquered in the same red as their ribbons.

Serving at table was a privilege for the sailors, and Netta made her selection from the prettiest: the work of the ship went on in the bowels of the engine room or the bridge, where Damien's chief officer supervised their course amid fumes of ouzo and cigar smoke. The servants got to help themselves from succulent leftovers, and Jana supposed it made a change from their usual diet of ship's biscuits or whatever it was seamen ate.

Little dishes of hors d'oeuvres were brought: quails' eggs, spiced meat in vine leaves, taramasalata, an array of salads, and a dish heaped with oysters. There was white wine to drink, and before beginning the meal, Caspar toasted the health of Maldona and all her slaves, and the success of Jana's journey, wherever it might take her.

'But you know, Caspar,' blurted Cassie in a cross voice. 'You all do, and you are keeping it from me! It isn't fair!'

'To tantalise is always a pleasure,' purred Caspar, spearing an oyster and sprinkling it with pepper sauce. 'And besides, our Mistress has ordained it so. You shall know very soon, for tonight we should be in port.'

'It is rare to see you in trousers, Caspar,' said Jana, hurriedly changing the subject. 'I must say you look quite splendid.'

'Thank you, Mistress. The matter of male or female garb is a curious one. Trousers, to the ancient Romans, were fit only for barbarians, slaves and women.'

'Who were frequently one and the same,' said Netta, her mouth full of vine leaves.

'A gentleman wore a skirt, or a toga, some robe at any rate, as do our Arab friends today, with their djellabahs. Underwear of course was unknown.'

'That is why Arabs are so sexy,' added Netta.

15

'Quite,' said her husband drily. 'The fashion for trousers only caught on when the Imperial capital was moved from Rome to Constantinople, next door to the *sexy* barbarians. But how many thoroughly normal males long to robe themselves as women, to wear skirts and frilly knickers and so on, and yet even in our post-Victorian days do not dare, except by appearing on stage in amateur theatricals and the like? It is curious that in the annals of crime, almost every famous desperado has boasted of his prowess in evading capture by adopting female disguise. Since it is so beautiful to *be* a woman, who can blame a male for wishing occasionally to dress as one?'

'There have been plenty of female desperadoes,' said Jana. 'They dressed as men! There was Annie Oakley, Joan of Arc . . . even a female pope.'

'I would not call Joan of Arc a desperado, exactly,' answered Caspar, 'though a pope might qualify. At any rate, the principle is the same. In all males there is a female spirit and in all females a male. It is wilful suppression of one's other side which results in disorder of the personality. To thine own self be true, as the saying has it. And the androgynous way is often the true way.'

'Or complete nudity,' added Netta. 'The absence of all artifice.'

'Perhaps,' said Caspar. 'But human beings feel the need for adornment. Where would you be, my sweet, if we were naked all the time? With your warehouse full of delicious baubles and toys and costumes?'

'It isn't quite a warehouse,' said Netta crisply.

'Clothing,' Caspar continued, 'reminds us of our nudity, so that the splendour of our eventual nakedness is felt and displayed all the more keenly. Female attire is tantalising, a constant reminder of sexuality both to wearer and observer; male clothing is a uniform, its function to cover rather than reveal. It was not always so. Men too were vain and coquettish, and thirst for those compliments on their clothes and bodies which women take for granted. Just as women like to wear uniforms, and carry whips.'

There was a pause as they busied themselves with eating,

16

until after a while Cassie said, 'Mmm, these oysters are good. An aphrodisiac, of course.'

'Why, yes,' said Netta. 'Unfortunately, their aphrodisiac qualities are not revealed by eating them. They are of little value when dissolved in the stomach juices.'

'Please explain,' said Cassie, puzzled but eager.

'The healthful substance must be absorbed directly into the bloodstream by contact with a mucous membrane,' said Netta with surprising coyness. 'There is the nose . . .'

Everyone laughed.

'Women are fortunate in possessing two other suitable membranes,' Netta continued rather primly, 'while men, poor lambs, must content themselves with only one. I'm quite serious! Here, I'll show you.'

With that, she lifted her skirt high above her waist, and pulled down her rubber panties to below her knees. Then she spread her thighs wide and pulled open the lips of her fount. All watched in excited curiosity as Netta gravely took three of the gleaming bivalves from their shells and pressed them to her cunt-petals, then pushed them gently right into her slit. The oysters disappeared and she pulled up her panties again, then smoothed her dress and resumed eating as though nothing unusual had happened.

'There!' she said brightly. 'Quite simple! Another ten minutes, and I should begin to feel a little . . . mmm! But where is our sweet captain? He is supposed to be head waiter; he asked specially to bring us the *pièce de résistance*, lobsters in lemon butter! I'm hungry!'

At that moment, the doors to the galley swung open and Damien made his entrance, wheeling a trolley that carried four silver-domed dishes. Jana and Cassie stared in pleased astonishment at his aspect. Jana thought that there was something so delightful, so piquant, about a man as virile as Damien – she remembered every inch of his proud body from Caspar's 'surrealist' film – who dared to be different and to flout foolish convention. Although, she reflected, perhaps Damien was obeying some convention of his own, just as strict though not as foolish.

'The *pièce de résistance*, ladies and sir!' intoned Damien.

'Oh no!' responded Jana, 'I declare that you are the *pièce de résistance*, Damien. How lovely! How thoughtful . . .'

Damien was dressed in a French maid's uniform. As he moved, he bounced with frilly lace and black flounces, worn over fishnet stockings and dangerously high-heeled shoes. He wore a heavy silver necklace and earrings, but no paint or powder, in fact no *maquillage* of any sort. All the diners joined in a round of applause.

'Splendid!' enthused Caspar. 'Damien has indulged himself in his fantasy, with my permission of course. You see how happy he looks as he performs his menial task in the proper uniform, but see also that he is not trying to pass himself off as a woman. No one could mistake Damien for anything but the very acme of virility. If anything, his charming uniform actually draws attention to his . . . attributes.'

Jana saw that Damien's frilly black skirt indeed did nothing to veil the menacing bulge of his thick manhood, which swayed beneath it to the rhythm of his sinuous movements as he served them their dishes. She saw, too, that Netta's eyes were fixed there, ignoring the food which steamed before her.

'A whole lobster!' cried Cassie. 'Mmm!'

The fragrant aroma filled the room as the diners eagerly set to their meals, all except Netta, who toyed with her plate but whose attention was occupied by the person of their befrocked head waiter, whose face was wreathed in a smile of happiness at his enthusiastic welcome. Netta's hand strayed as though absent-mindedly to her groin, and she began to rub herself there in a way that Jana knew was not the slightest bit absent-minded. There was a lull in the conversation and the room echoed to the cracking of shells and the tinkling of forks and spoons, as the succulent lobster-flesh was prised out and devoured. Then, suddenly, Netta reached out and took hold of Damien's penis.

'Come here, my sweet,' she cooed. 'Mmm, how nice.'

Jana stared in amazement, as did the others. The startled Damien had no choice but to obey Netta, as she had a firm hold, and he inched towards her curiously. She smiled.

18

'I have you by the balls, as it were,' she murmured. 'Now let me see them. Raise your skirt, my girl, and show me your panties.'

She let go of the black satin skirt, and Damien dutifully raised it to reveal his white lace panties bulging with his half-stiff cock.

'Now, panties down,' Netta ordered. Again, Damien did not hesitate, and slid his panties down to his knees, allowing his massive shaft to spring free and in an instant swell to almost its full, massive size.

'Do you like oysters?' said Netta, pointing to the dish which was still well laden and, without waiting for him to reply, she continued, 'I am going to feed you some oysters. Turn round and let me see your bum.'

Damien obeyed, apprehensively, and Netta ordered him to place a hand on each fesse, bend slightly, and spread himself wide. When this was done, the company had a view of Damien's dark anus bud, and Jana suddenly realised what Netta planned to do. Grinning, Netta took two shelled oysters from the dish, and, using a spoon, went to work with an expertise and tidiness that suggested much practice. When Damien had taken the oysters snugly inside him, Netta gave his bottom a playful slap and pulled his panties up tight.

'There!' she said brightly, rubbing her hands with a perfumed towel. 'How does that feel?'

'Well, different,' answered Damien. 'Yes, rather nice.'

'When you come round with our pudding,' said Netta, 'we will see if you still feel rather nice,' and at once attacked her lobster with gusto. Jana was fascinated by her sensual enjoyment of the dish. The way she chewed the tender white meat and licked her lips clean of the glistening butter sauce after each mouthful was positively erotic, as though she were not just eating the poor lobster, but making love to it. Having at first toyed with her food, Netta now cleaned her plate before anyone else.

Caspar proposed another toast, this time to the success of his new film. Wine glasses were duly raised and emptied, to be replenished by the obedient crewmen. Pressed to describe his project, Caspar would say no more than that it was 'very surrealist'. Jana smiled at the memory of the 'surrealist' film Caspar had shown at one of his equally surrealist parties at his Lennox Gardens home. In it, she had observed the fine musculature of Damien as he chastised Netta's bare buttocks with a quirt of seashells plucked from the beach on which they sported, before fucking her from behind in the most powerful of naked embraces.

She remembered, too, her surprise and enchantment that the beach lay on the very Aegean island which she was later to make the Island of Maldona. So, in a sense, it was Caspar and his film which had propelled her to Greece in the first place, just as it was Cassie's trip to Spain which had led her to seek out, and come to rule, the House of Maldona itself. Her heart swelled with contentment at having such tender slaves: my genius, she thought, is to let grateful others nurture and serve the vital force I have from my forebears . . . from the first Jana Ardenne, the first Maldona.

It was no surprise that the film was to be surrealist: Caspar insisted on his inbuilt surrealism as film 'auteur'. Jana had concluded some time ago that by surrealist, Caspar meant 'Greek', which meant 'Dionysian', which meant anything that a mass of ecstatic bodies could do with leather, chains, whips and buckles, copious amounts of wine, and each other.

'A film,' whispered Cassie. 'I would so love to be in it!' Jana felt exactly the same, but her thoughts of the cinema were interrupted as the dishes were cleared and Damien returned with the sweet trolley, a sumptuous display of fruits, gateaux, and a dish of profiteroles drenched in steaming chocolate sauce.

There were dessert wines to accompany these, sweet muscatels and madeiras, but Damien seemed curiously abstracted as he poured them and kept glancing in Netta's direction. When he arrived at her place he became visibly agitated. His hands trembled as he served her, and as he spooned chocolate sauce on to her plate, spilling it clumsily, Jana saw the front of his skirt rise with beautiful suddenness. His penis had stiffened fully! His eyes were wide as he gazed at Netta and there was a flush to his handsome dark face.

Netta's eyes were heavy slits of desire as she ignored her food and swiftly seized Damien's skirt, pulling it up to reveal the bulging panties below. In a savage tug, she ripped the panties from Damien, tearing them almost in half and throwing the shredded cloth to the deck. Damien's cock and balls stood proudly bare, but not for long. Netta murmured in a growling voice that now she had a proper sweet, and with a snap like a leopard seizing her prey, fastened her lips on the swollen gland. At once, she began to suck the massive cock with firmly clamped lips, taking the shaft deep into the back of her throat and furiously bobbing her head up and down like a pigeon's. At each sucking thrust, she made a low animal noise. Damien's hand clutched her hair and pressed her head down towards him while his buttocks and hips began to quiver in rhythm to her fierce caress, so his cock was thrust up into her throat, fucking her mouth as though it was her fount.

Netta's hands were busy; one was fastened hard on Damien's balls, squeezing them fiercely with each bob of her head, as though milking the seed from him. 'Yes. Oh yes!' he moaned over and over, through gritted teeth.

Her other hand had squirmed beneath her rubber panties and with fevered movements she masturbated herself, her wrist flicking frantically while her waist and buttocks writhed as though some *daemon* of lust was struggling to escape, not just from the tight rubber bonds of her dress and panties, but from her very flesh.

The meal was forgotten as Jana, Cassie and even the jaded Caspar watched spellbound. It was not long before the moans of the two grew so loud and anguished that it seemed they could scarcely bear the intensity of their coupling, and Damien's voice rose to a squeal as his cock began to shudder and Netta's throat convulsed in swallowing his sperm. Damien spurted so copiously that a rivulet

21

of shiny white seed spouted from Netta's mouth and shone wetly on both his bucking shaft and her own chin. Then Netta joined her voice to his in a staccato howl that sounded like pain, and her whole body shook in the delirium of her spasm.

'Fellatio,' murmured Caspar, 'a most sacred act. The female submits to serve the glory of the male cock, but in taking his essence, she enslaves him. Worshipped, the male is helpless in the power of the female.'

Jana was still warm with the joy of loving Cassie on the deck, and felt a new tingling warmth in her belly, and a moistening of her fount, as she watched Netta and Damien. Her body glowed with wine and desire. It was not the moment to remark that the proof of the pudding was in the eating, so with a thumping heart, she rose and swiftly knelt at Caspar's feet. He did not resist as she roughly pulled down his fine trousers to reveal his shaven pubis and his cock, which was already halfway erect. At her touch, Caspar's penis became stiff and started throbbing, and with gentle hands he guided Jana's head to his bulb. She fastened her lips around the taut gleaming flesh, and in silence sucked him until the trembling of his shaft and the tightening of his balls told her that he was going to come in her willing mouth.

It was impossible for her not to do as Netta had done. Her fevered hand slipped into her panties and found her quim already wet, the lips swollen and the nympha hard and distended. Caspar began to moan and rock back and forth, his hips writhing as Damien's had. Jana tasted a drop of his sperm at the peehole, and increased the flickering caress on her damsel until she too was moaning. Then Caspar's flood came, washing her mouth with the creamy hot seed as he jerked helplessly in orgasm, and, as she swallowed the last drop of his sperm, her own body flooded once more with the searing delight of her climax, as though it was weightless and being bathed in clouds of molten gold.

'Oh, Mistress,' Caspar sobbed, 'I am your slave forever.'

She did not leave Caspar, though. His penis softened,

but she kept it in her mouth, licking tenderly, and pecking at the peehole with fleeting kisses as she stroked his balls. She knew that males were capable of more than most of them thought. Sure enough, as she caressed the man's flaccid cock, it hardened again until it had blossomed once more into a glorious stiff flower. Abruptly, she removed her mouth, giving the swollen glans a farewell kiss. She decided that now it was Cassie's turn: her slave needed no urging to repeat Jana's action, with the added joy that her own Mistress was suddenly kneeling behind her, peeling her panties down and spreading the cheeks of her naked arse, then busied herself licking the engorged quim lips.

This second adoration of the male's cock took longer to bear fruit, but at last Caspar came, his seed spurting into Cassie's eager throat as she rubbed her own clit and Jana kissed and licked her anus. Cassie, too, shuddered and squealed quite loudly as she was engulfed by her pleasure, and Jana felt the girl's fesses tighten in spasms of joy, squeezing her tongue which probed a full inch inside the slave's elastic anus. Jana continued to masturbate herself gently, not wishing to reach another orgasm but to prolong the tingling afterglow of her enjoyment. Her face was pressed to Cassie's naked buttocks, but from the corner of her eye she saw that Damien and Netta were also repeating their loving fellatio. Covering Cassie's bare croup with kisses, her nose and lips playfully rubbing her anus bud, Jana felt she must look like a pig happily hunting for truffles.

When it was over, and the diners were flushed and exhausted with pleasure, Jana said, 'If only you had your camera here, Caspar!'

'But I have,' he replied with a smug grin, and lifted his hand to show them a remote control device. Then he pointed to the wall: from a recess, Jana saw a purple lens blinking at Netta and Damien like the glans of some all-seeing penis.

'For your film,' said Cassie. 'Oh, Caspar, how I should love to be in it!'

'Why, you already are, dearest Cassie,' said Caspar.

'There are lenses everywhere, even on deck. Your pre-luncheon adventures have been immortalised.'

'But – if Cassie is on film, that means I am too!' cried Jana, secretly thrilled. Caspar shrugged lazily.

'I plead *droit d'auteur*,' he said. 'Of course, if my Mistress decides her *auteur* deserves whipping . . .'

Netta's cries were softening into little whimpers of sated desire, but still she clung to Damien, covering his softening penis and his balls with fervent kisses.

'Oh, how sweet,' she murmured, panting. 'How warm and good, your spunk sweeter than all the chestnut blossom –' she looked up, her face flushed and grinning. 'You see?' she said merrily. 'I told you oysters worked.'

'Agreed, Netta,' said Jana. 'But what did you mean about chestnut blossom?'

'Did I say that?'

'You did, when you were cooing sweet nothings at our lovely French maid, Captain Damien. You said "Sweeter than all the chestnut blossom".'

'It's a figure of speech. It's difficult to explain, but you'll find out when you get to Bulgaria. There are such gorgeous chestnut groves in the mountains.'

'Bulgaria!' whooped Cassie, with a leer of triumph at her Mistress. 'So that's where we are going!'

Netta's hand flew to her mouth. 'Oh dear!' she exclaimed. 'Have I said too much?'

Jana laughed. 'It doesn't matter,' she said. 'I was going to tell you, Cassie, after lunch. We disembark at Kavala, the Greek port, then it's over the mountains to the frontier.'

'So,' said Cassie thoughtfully, as though inviting an explanation, 'we are to go to Bulgaria, are we?'

'Yes, we are,' replied Jana firmly. 'But not just Bulgaria,' she added.

3

Hide and Seek

'Bulgaria!' Cassie exclaimed. 'It is one of the few places I have never been.'

'I told you that a surprise would be waiting for you,' answered Jana. 'We are going to drive back to London, through eastern Europe. There are castles, mountains, gorgeous males in lederhosen . . .'

Cassie frowned. Then she smiled. She said: 'Do you mean –'

'I think you know very well what I mean,' said Jana.

'That big,' answered Cassie with a grin.

'So I have heard,' said Jana, smiling too. 'Now I think it is time for our siesta, Cassie. There is a spirit of place – I think of the castles and mountains of eastern Europe, now – but the sweetest place of all is –'

'Is the castle between a gentleman's legs,' said Cassie.

Mistress and slave slept through the heat of the sunny afternoon, curled in their big round bed like two happy kittens. It was already dusk when Jana stirred, Cassie still sleeping beside her. Jana tried to awaken her slave with a gentle kiss to the naked flesh of her bottom, and Cassie smiled in her sleep but refused to be woken.

Contented, Jana watched the twilight turn to the velvet blackness of the Mediterranean night. She pulled the cord to open the drapes and starlight flooded into the room, complemented by the twinkling lights of the coastline which their craft skirted on her approach to the port of Kavala.

The furnishings of their stateroom were thrown into

relief by the sparkling lights, and Jana thought that she would be sad to leave this pleasant boudoir, with its statuettes of nymphs and satyrs, and countless mirrors, which covered the whole ceiling. There were paintings by Netta's hand which showed scenes of ancient Greece, and by the sight of which Jana was invariably aroused.

There was the ritual whipping of the young men of Sparta, carried out every feast day by the virgins of the city. The whippings took place so that the crops should grow, and the men thus chastised should learn to be victorious in battle.

The men were naked, and the virgins clothed. Netta had written 'Forty!' on her paintings, as the males had been obliged to take forty strokes on the bare buttocks from a vine branch, which had been pickled for forty days.

Jana loved that. In her days as Mistress of Maldona, she had whipped many males, quite severely, and always on the bare. She used the cane or the four-thonged whip on the bare croup of the male and, as Mistress, she found a strange pleasure in the sight of the male's naked buttocks squirming so beautifully under her flogging.

Jana and Cassie had a thick white carpet, and tubular chairs upholstered in soft white leather. The chair-backs were adjustable – Caspar had thought of everything – and at the foot of each chair-leg was a dainty cuff for the ankle or wrist of any lady obliged to bend over for a bare spanking or caning. Cassie had understood the nature and purpose of their stateroom on the occasions when her Mistress Jana did not feel like a siesta. There was even a little rack of canes thoughtfully placed by the boudoir table, itself furnished with every paint and powder Jana could imagine.

The eclectic décor of the room bore all the marks of Netta's touch, her artistic taste, as usual, making no concessions to subtlety. The duvet on the bed Jana shared with her slave was embroidered in gaudy colours, with a representation of Jana dressed in the uniform of a Parfaite of Maldona. On the duvet, Jana was administering a hard thrashing to a trussed and naked Virgin whose bare bottom was splendidly reddened by the four-thonged white whip sacred to Maldona.

After her sleep, the Mistress of Maldona curled up with her slave beside her. Jana had dreamt: her dream left her slowly as she stirred, with Cassie still sleeping beside her. She knew that her dreams were sometimes prophetic, but the sound of the brewing coffee in the bedside machine was somehow reassuring. She looked forward to the fancy-dress party that would celebrate their voyage, and to their disembarkation from Caspar's ship on their way to Bulgaria and eastern Europe.

Jana stretched her naked body and yawned, before drinking a cup of coffee and slipping from the duvet to position herself on the carpet for a set of press-ups. These were accomplished in silence, Jana controlling her breathing until Cassie was finally woken by her Mistress's cry of 'One hundred!'

The two women sat naked on the bed, drinking coffee, until Jana said that, despite the warmth of the room, and Caspar's efficient thermostat, it was time to dress.

'Sweet bare-bummed slave,' said Jana, which made Cassie smile. 'I am, as you know, very fond of coffee, and this one pleases me. An Arab taste, I think, but with Brazilian or African beans, too. The very scent of them brings back memories, as scents so often do. Now, we shall be ashore at Kavala very soon, so we must pack and be ready. Just one holdall each, I think, because Caspar can take care of the rest of our things. Just make sure you pack a coat and some woollies with your pretties. And, of course, the basics.'

'The basics, Mistress?' said Cassie, shyly. 'Should the basics include suitable equipment?'

'The white whip?' Jana answered swiftly. 'Yes. The Mistress of Maldona must not go without the four-thonged whip which has served her well over the centuries. My sweet slave, your croup shall be cared for.'

Suddenly the room was starkly bathed by the beam of a lighthouse flashing through the porthole.

'Oh!' cried Jana, starting, and in her surprise dropped

27

her cup of coffee. Cassie promptly put down her own cup and fetched a cloth to mop up the spilled brown liquid.

'It was my imperfection, Mistress,' she said. 'I must have jolted you.'

Jana put her hand to her brow.

'No, it was the memory of my dream,' she said. 'The bright light just now brought it back to me.'

Cassie said that it must have been a nightmare, and that she was sorry for her imperfection in recalling it to her Mistress.

'It was not exactly a nightmare,' said Jana. 'Puzzling, but pleasant in an eerie way.' She tickled Cassie's chin and laughed.

'Never say you are sorry, slave, because it is against our rules. A female must never apologise. But if you wish to admit imperfection, in the hope of receiving punishment, you have no need to worry. I shall never be short of imagined imperfections so that I may have the pleasure of lacing the sweet peaches of your croup.'

Cassie bowed, and, careful not to ask a question, said, 'To the matter of your dream, Mistress, I am curious.'

Jana frowned in recollection.

'There was a castle,' she said, finally, 'but not like my own House of Maldona. This one was not sunlit, but dark and somehow menacing. I remember green firs and grey rocky mountains shrouded in mist. The mountains seemed to have faces, and were speaking harshly to me in a language I could not understand. At one time I was with you, in a lovely bed like this one, but then men came to take me, and I found myself alone in a cell whose walls were of that grey rock. I was stripped and hung naked, upside down. I was suspended by my ankles, and gagged with a steel ball. When I looked up, I saw that metal hands were clutching me.

'I was surrounded by robed men with metal faces. They whipped me without explaining why, whipped me with my own white thongs. My legs were spread wide, and the thongs lashed me so fearfully, landing with full force near to the crack of my fesses. They whipped me on my belly,

28

on my breasts, and on my thighs. The beating was everywhere and it caused me the most terrible pain, but
somehow I didn't feel the pain, I just knew it was there. I
wanted to tell the men that I was the Mistress of Maldona,
and could take any flogging, but because of the steel gag I
couldn't speak. Being so helpless – hung upside down and
unable to speak – made my fount flow! Cassie, I was so
wet!

'Then I was outside, still naked and still surrounded by
that rock, as I was in some kind of quarry or workplace. I
was chained to other naked women. It seemed that we had
to break rocks on the orders of the men with steel faces.
We had no choice, because we were bound by tiny chains
threaded through our pierced cunt-petals. I did not know
why the men wished the rocks to be broken; it was work
and we had to do it. When I demurred, one of the men
took a piece of rock that I had just cut, polished it, and
made me spread my fesses. He parted my buttocks and I
felt the rock tickle my anus bud, then – Oh! Cassie, I
enjoyed it! – it filled me completely.

'The man went away, taking the polished rock from my
arsehole with such a delicate slippery slither that I wanted
to burst with sadness. But suddenly it began to rain. The
raindrops hurt – they were very hard, like bullets. I saw
that they were metal, and shaped like giant shiny cocks, so
big and so hard, and they began to fuck me and touch me
everywhere. The metal cocks entered my fount and filled
her, filled my mouth and rubbed my nipples and belly and
my back, too, sliding all the way up my spine. Cassie, I
came! My dream gave me the most beautiful orgasm. Oh,
it was so nice.

'Then, as I looked up, I saw that in the sky there was a
woman, dressed only in a very tight metal corset, and with
her legs spread and her fount open. I saw that all these
metal cocks which were fucking me so sweetly fell from the
open fount of this heavenly woman. And, Cassie, this
woman – was she a goddess? I don't know – she had the
face of a man. I thought that at the time, in my dream. I
can't be sure. I suppose it sounds crazy.'

'Dreams are not crazy, Mistress, and your dreams especially have a quality of prophecy. There are those humans who are attuned to the timeless resonances of the Universe, who can see ghostly spirits, see the future, remember the past. Your ancestor Jana Ardenne was one and you are one. I am not, I have other qualities. Why do you think I am willing to go anywhere with you, and why do you think I made sure you became Mistress of Maldona?'

'You lovely silly girl,' said Jana. 'But you are naughty to say such things. You are only a slave, and it won't do.'

Suddenly Cassie embraced her Mistress tightly, pressing her face into Jana's breasts, her lips soft on Jana's nipples. Cassie sobbed, and Jana knew what she must do. She stroked Cassie's hair as she put her down across her thighs. Jana caressed the smooth, taut skin of her slave's fesses with her fingertips as she told her that she must be spanked again for her impertinence and for her imperfection in forgetting that there was something, at this moment, a little more important than ghosts and dreams and the resonance of the Universe. She spanked Cassie again, very soundly, and loved each clench of the girl's bare buttocks as the blows fell to slave from Mistress. This time she did not count, but thought that there were perhaps forty strokes.

'Now that your bum is nice and red,' said Jana, 'what are we going to wear for the fancy-dress party?'

How I wish my bum was nice and red, thought the Mistress. That will come . . .

It was past ten o'clock. The decision on costumes had to be made rapidly, and Jana ordained that rather than await inspiration from the clothing at their disposal, they should decide on their adornment and then find garments to suit. After a little frowning, Cassie said that she would be Queen of the Assyrians, or perhaps a princess of the Empire of the Ottomans of Turkey. Jana said that her slave, being beautiful, would make a splendid princess, for was a princess not the mirror of a slave, just as a male was the mirror of a woman?

30

Jana watched as Cassie adorned herself with every jewel she could lay her hands on. The slave swept her black hair up into an imperial cone, and chose to knot her most magnificent gown so artfully that her slightest movement revealed a chink of bare breast or thigh. At the boudoir table she rouged her nipples and, lifting the hem of her robe, her pink-petalled quim.

Cassie made her eyes as dark as the most velvety night, and painted her cheeks red with the swastika, the symbol of the male essence, and green with the four-thonged verven, symbol of the union of male and female. On her neck were the arrows of Eros, on either breast the Yin and Yang signs, and on her forehead the Sun and Moon. Jana said that she was a true Mistress.

For herself, Jana decided to be just the opposite: reversing her role, she would be an abject slave girl, the plaything of Cassie. She picked out one of her most precious robes, an ankle-length dress in blue shantung silk, and casually ripped it into a tatter of ribbons. Cassie stared in astonishment as her Mistress slipped the fragile garment over her naked body and ripped a deep gash in the neck, so that her breasts were barely covered by the edges of the silk. Satisfied, Jana threw off the dress again and sat herself naked at the boudoir table. She took a selection of pots and began to apply *maquillage* to her whole body. She covered every inch of herself, with every colour of the rainbow, and when she was finished, she rose for Cassie's admiration. She twirled on tiptoe like a ballerina.

'Oh, Mistress!' Cassie cried.

Jana's body was filthy, as though she had not washed. Her blonde hair was matted in greasy wisps and her skin, under its cake of dirt, was a mass of deep pink weals. She bore the flowers of what was apparently a prolonged and recent beating. Her bare breasts and belly were crisscrossed with whipmarks.

'I think it is you who are Mistress,' said Jana softly. 'I am nothing but a slave, although I am good at *maquillage*. Circe the sorceress taught me some things.'

Jana slipped on her tattered robe, over the body of a

chastised slave girl, and knelt to lick the toes of Cassie's sandalled feet. She licked until she knew that Cassie was in pleasure.

'There is one thing lacking, Mistress,' Jana said in a humble voice. 'I must be chained like the humble creature I am. You must lead me in your triumph, my Princess, for it is my glory to serve you now. Please select a cane for my willing fesses, and chain me properly.'

Jana had her silk skirt lifted high over her buttocks, and a chain fastened around her waist. Another longer chain was fastened to it at the front and passed back between her legs so that it pressed hard against her anus and clitoris. The remaining length hung down like a leash, and Cassie allowed Jana's robe to fall down so that it was visible through the shredded cloth above Jana's buttocks.

'Come, slave,' said Cassie contemptuously, as she led Jana on all fours, flicking the cane on her croup. 'We are now slave and Mistress. Our roles are changed.'

The cuts to Jana's bare grew frequent and she loved every one, just as she loved Cassie. But she had to say, before they entered the candle-lit stateroom, that their roles in Caspar's fancy-dress party were not really those of Mistress and slave, rather those of slave and mirror.

Thus, the two women entered the stateroom.

The stateroom had been transformed. The bright, easy lunchroom was now a shadowy grotto dimly lit by perfumed candles. A table was piled with wine flasks and dishes of food. Cassie drove Jana into the room with a swift cut to the buttocks, and, as her slave, Jana scuttled to obey. Their appearance was greeted with coos of delight from the company, who were themselves curiously garbed. Cassie did not bother to look down at her new slave: her whole demeanour was truly that of an empress. Jana, meanwhile, reflected on the transformation that mere robing and *maquillage* could effect on a woman's behaviour.

A drumbeat played softly. From her position on all fours, Jana craned to look up at the other guests and could see a number of figures silhouetted against the candlelight.

Caspar and Netta were easily distinguishable, and Jana assumed that the others were crew members. The tall figure of Damien seemed to be alone in a corner. The centre of the room was decorated with statues of females, clad in items from Netta's seemingly inexhaustible collection of leather and rubber clothing, further adorned with chains, and with whips in their lifeless hands. Jana wondered if these mannequins would come to life, and begin to move, then use the whips. By them stood a squat flogging-frame of polished wood, gleaming with the leather straps which festooned it. Knowing Netta, Jana decided, it would not be surprising if the mannequins were clockwork mechanical creations, who would indeed come to life and use their whips. They were very realistic, some made of metal and some of wood. Perhaps there were real flesh and blood women concealed inside the statues . . .

Jana's musings were interrupted by Caspar, who addressed not her, but Cassie.

'My dear!' he cried. 'Exquisite! A veritable empress! Do tell me, who is this snivelling creature at your feet?'

'Why, my slave,' said Cassie, 'once a princess, now a mere dog of a captive. So turns the wheel of Fortune.'

With that, she delivered not one, but two strokes of her cane, one to each of Jana's fesses, and with such strength that Jana yelped in surprise. Then, feeling oddly grateful, Jana at once bent to lick her Mistress's feet. Like the whipped dog I am, she thought. As her tongue caressed Cassie's painted toenails, she felt the strange power and the joy of her enslavement. She wondered if she would be strapped to the flogging frame later, and found she wanted to be. Her trussed body would be crimson under the lash. Jana's heart beat fast with longing for the freedom of utter submission.

The company began to serve themselves from the foods and wines, and the conversation became animated with laughter. Jana did not get anything.

'May your slave take wine?' said Caspar to Cassie.

'It may,' said Cassie disdainfully. 'Give it a saucer of champagne. It eats too. I may throw it some scraps.'

Jana found herself lapping her champagne as a dog drinks from a bowl. She gulped the wine noisily, imagining that a slave might claim a little latitude in manners. From time to time Cassie threw her a piece of food, either on to the floor from where she had to gobble it, or else making her beg with her mouth open until she dropped the morsel between Jana's lips, usually with a flick of the cane to her croup. Everyone would laugh, and Jana imagined they were laughing at her, the Mistress of Maldona tethered like a beast. Her heart glowing with pride in her obedience, she began to survey the costumed company.

Netta was fetchingly attired in the uniform of a Rosebush schoolgirl, a white blouse and blue pleated skirt from under which peeped a frilly white slip. She wore blue tights, and had tied her long hair into pigtails with blue ribbons. The Rosebush School in Knightsbridge, which Caspar owned, was actually a college for young ladies with certain specialised tastes and, as such, was also a rich source of 'actresses' for his surreal films, and of virgins for Maldona. However, Netta's uniform was not quite demure enough for the streets of Knightsbridge: her mini-skirt was a shade too mini, her stiletto heels and fishnet tights quite unscholastic, and the nipples of her firm breasts, bare under her blouse, could easily be seen pressed like plums against the thin satin fabric.

Jana smiled. Netta's husband had correspondingly dressed as a schoolmaster of the old-fashioned type, complete with gown, mortarboard, frock coat, pinstripe trousers and a starched collar, and carrying a yellow cane. All was in perfect order, except for the huge red codpiece he wore at his loins. As for the crewmen, merry with champagne, Jana thought them quite imaginative, and even rather pretty. There was a harlequin, a Venetian gondolier, a Greek soldier in a pleated white skirt and buckled shoes, a Roman legionary, a monk in his cassock, and, rather daring, a flouncy can-can dancer. Damien seemed to be keeping to his corner, but she saw that he was wearing a long cloak with what looked like a hangman's hood covering his head. She shivered, not sure whether she felt fear or desire.

Cassie threw her the scraps of food, and Caspar kept her bowl filled with champagne. The group talked more excitedly as the wine flowed, and the insistent drumbeat seemed to grow louder with the conversation. Soon, the talk turned to the evening's entertainment. Jana felt well filled by her curious supper but, when she asked Cassie if she might rise, she was rewarded for her impertinence by a sharp cane-stroke to her shoulders and told to keep silent.

Caspar called for quiet, and spoke.

'Now, dear friends,' he said. 'A party is not a party without games. What games shall we play?'

The Greek crewmen were unfamiliar with the English tradition of party games, but entered into the spirit of the occasion, and suggested various activities of stunning lasciviousness which were in fact unconscious adult variations of the old favourites Jana had played as a girl. She was reflecting that perhaps all games are really just one game, when Damien's voice rang out. It sounded booming and strangely metallic.

'We shall begin with hide-and-seek,' he ordered. 'It is the best game, because the loser must pay a forfeit, to be decided by the winner.'

He explained that the player who was 'it' had a start of a count to one hundred, during which 'it' had to find a hiding-place. If discovered within twenty minutes, then 'it' would lose, and would have to pay the forfeit. If still at liberty, 'it' would have the right to demand forfeits.

'Hide-and-seek!' said Caspar mildly. 'Splendid. Who, then, shall be "it"?'

Jana had the impression that he already knew the answer.

'My slave shall be "it",' said Cassie at once, her tone as imperious as Damien's. 'She is already a dog, so she must run like a dog.'

Cassie unfastened Jana's waist-chain and ordered her to stand up. It was then that Damien stepped forward, removed his hangman's hood and shrugged off his cloak.

Jana's heart leapt. Damien shone in bright metal. Only

35

his eyes and lips were visible: his head was encased in a gleaming helmet of Damascus steel, his body in a suit of chain mail, and at his waist hung a huge broadsword. He was a knight in armour – no, a veritable Saracen! The fingers of his steel gloves and the curled toecaps of his boots ended in sharp claws. And at his loins hung not a codpiece like Caspar's, but a huge cock of dazzling steel, as wide as Jana's forearm and longer, every detail of the massive bulb and the heavy balls perfectly sculpted. The cock was not strapped on, but seemed to grow from the armour itself, as though man and metal were one. Jana thought him very beautiful. Damien fixed her with piercing eyes as he slapped his heavy sword against his thigh, the clang of metal on metal louder than any drumbeat.

'One,' he said. 'Two . . .'

Jana looked into the cruel eyes behind the blank mask, and, taken by a sudden panic, turned and ran from the room. She had remembered her dream.

Jana panted as she ran, her bare feet helping her to get a grip on the smooth polished wood of the deck. Her heart pounded; she knew that it was Damien she had to fear, Damien the crisp sea-captain, Damien the pretty, befrilled maid, and now Damien the avenging Saracen in his beautiful but terrifying armour. She shuddered as she thought of that cruel broadsword, and the inhuman arrogance of the huge steel cock. How things are transformed, she thought, as she ran in the moonlight. I am Mistress of Maldona, and now I am running like an escaping slave, running from *something*. My body is in rags, smarting from my Mistress's lash, and I am a plaything in some stupid game. *If it is only a game.*

She careered aimlessly through the deserted decks, the ship now hostile and unfamiliar to her. She emerged, once, on to the foredeck and thought of hiding in a lifeboat, but rejected the idea as too obvious. She wanted to throw herself into the sea, knowing she could stand the cold for twenty minutes, but no – there, also, she would be observed. They would think of that. She had not been counting, but knew that a hundred must soon be reached. She had to go down, down into the bowels of the ship. She made her way into the warm metallic interior and was hurrying down a stairway when suddenly all the lights went out. Oh no, Jana shuddered, it *isn't* a game. A million confused thoughts whirled in her mind as she clambered downwards, towards the throb of the engine room. There they would have to have light, their own power supply. Have I been set up all along? Maybe Cassie has betrayed me, in league with Caspar and Damien. Does it mean she wants to be Mistress of Maldona once more? And this time there will be no chance of wrestling.

Her passage was now lit from the engine room. The most logical thing would be to make for the deck again, and take to the sea. But Jana could not bring herself to believe her fears. It *must* be a game! Suddenly she heard the faint whoops of her pursuers and knew it was too late even to think of the sea. She must find some dark bolthole and hide, curled into a ball like an animal in its cave. She came to a hatchway and twisted it open, and found herself once more in near-darkness, with only a dim light from the engine-room filtering through an air vent. She was in some disused hold, a junkroom piled with sacks and old crates and rusty metal. It smelled of damp and mould and, oddly, of human sweat. Shuddering, she lifted a pile of sacks and crawled underneath them, shutting herself in a womb of shelter. Above her, she heard the voices recede, and her fear gradually gave way to amusement. How silly she had been! Of course it was a game, and the Mistress of Maldona always won at games. She lay still in her snug new home and began to count the minutes. She had reached sixteen minutes and was preparing to return to the party, when she heard the sound.

It was a slow, deliberate scraping of metal on metal. She knew who it was. After her initial shock, her reason took over. She was not to be frightened: the Mistress of Maldona could defend herself against anyone or anything! Even, she added a little doubtfully, that great broadsword. The metal footsteps clanged on the stairway, and the hatchway door swung open. Any girlish fear she might have felt gave way to a woman's cold fury. She flung off her covering of sackcloth and stood, blinking in the wan light that shone through the open hatch. Damien stood in the doorway, blocking it. She could feel his cruel eyes gloating as he surveyed her half-naked body.

'Well, you've found me!' she spat, hands on hips. 'Do your worst, Damien. Or try.'

Damien chuckled.

'Nineteen-and-a-half minutes,' he said. 'You lose, Mistress, and must pay your forfeit.'

Jana was momentarily puzzled. Forfeit! Yes, of course it was the game, after all.

'And what is my forfeit to be?' she said contemptuously, still warily looking for a means of escape, just in case he . . .

'Why, whatever you like, Mistress,' said Damien almost humbly. Jana was taken aback at this reversal.

'Whatever *I* like?' she blurted.

'Of course. You are the Mistress of Maldona, and I am only a servant. How I wish I could serve you, Mistress, as a Knight of Maldona. It pleases me to dress thus – Netta, who gave me the costume to wear, knows me very well. Do you like my costume?'

All at once, everything seemed to have changed. And all at once, Jana understood. Jana saw the naked man beneath this metal carapace, beneath the maid's uniform and his crisp sea-captain's outfit. Damien *was* a servant. She remembered Caspar's film in which Damien had whipped Netta on the beach, with a quirt of seashells. There, too, he was serving her, or acting on Caspar's orders while Caspar's camera whirred. She smiled, because he was no monster, no Saracen, but a man looking for a role. A Knight Errant . . .

She looked at his frightening armour, and shivered. Despite herself, she found it attractive. It was his uniform, and she sensed the naked male brute within.

'Yes, Damien,' she said faintly. 'I like your costume very much.'

His eyes sparkled in the open visor of his helmet, and she knew that she had this male, this mere male, in her power. Her fears had been groundless: she had been frightened of her own solitude.

Damien was trembling as his metal claw hesitantly reached towards her. She made no move to stop him.

'Mistress,' he said hoarsely, 'may I – may I touch you?'

Jana laughed, exultant as her power strengthened her, warming her belly and making her moisten between the thighs.

'Is that the forfeit?' she said.

'If it pleases you,' he murmured. The steel claw hovered at her breast, and she felt her moisture quicken.

'A forfeit should be more than a mere touch,' she replied. 'You may watch me too.'

She gently lowered the thin rag of cloth which covered her breasts, and bared herself to him. Her nipples stiffened as she felt the claws touch her naked breast, then stroke her softly, with the touch of feathers, down her belly to her mount of Venus which was still covered by her shredded robe. Jana let the robe fall. Her breath was deep as the claw fastened on her pubis, and the cold fingers brushed the lips of her fount.

'You are so beautiful, Mistress,' whispered Damien from his steel prison.

'Then beauty demands a beautiful forfeit,' answered Jana, and reached out to touch his broadsword, using her fingertip to test the edge of its blade, which she found to be smooth rather than sharp. Her hand strayed to the huge metal cock and caressed its hardness. She found to her surprised delight that, at her touch, it sprang into the erect position, as though propelled by some hinge or inner mechanism. She thought the conceit delightful.

'Well!' she said.

Damien chuckled.

'Netta told me the armour was made in Italy, in the fifteenth century, for the amusement of one of the more decadent popes,' he explained.

'He's lovely,' replied Jana, 'but such a pity you can feel

39

nothing through him. Have you nothing real and warm
behind that armour? Or are you only a man of cold metal?'

Damien's eyes flashed.

'Do not mock me, Mistress,' he said.

'I mock any man who is not brave enough to show
himself to a lady,' she retorted. 'Take your helmet off.'

Damien obeyed.

'I cannot mock you,' said Jana. 'But I shall command
you. My forfeit – my proper forfeit – shall be paid here and
now.'

Naked now, she unsheathed his broadsword, then kissed
the tip of the blade and handed it to him ceremoniously.
Without another word, she turned and bent over, her
hands around her ankles, thrusting her bared buttocks
high.

'I see,' said Damien. 'Very well, then. But have you ever
taken punishment from the flat of a steel broadsword?'

Jana shook her head.

'It will hurt very much.'

'That is my forfeit, then,' she replied.

The sword reverberated viciously and audibly, as it
thrashed down to land on Jana's fesses, and she was jolted
by the weight and force of the blow. A streak of fire laced
her naked croup; then another, and another, in swift
succession, until after five or six strokes her buttocks
seemed white-hot. The smarting pulsed through her body,
and made her flesh sing with pain. Jana had never felt
anything like it. She seemed to be at one with the metal
which seared her.

'Yes, yes!' she heard a voice moan. 'More, more, harder,
I beg you, lace me to purple, my sweet knight!'

The voice seemed to come from far away, and was her
own.

Jana's quim was throbbing now, and she streamed with
hot liquid.

'I am hurting you,' said Damien anxiously. 'I warned . . .'

'Yes! Oh yes! It is the purest agony! Oh! Oh!', as two
more blows landed hard and cruel in rapid succession, 'Oh!
such sweet agony!'

The beating continued until Jana's croup burned like a lake of molten gold, and then suddenly she heard the sword clatter to the floor.

'There is sweeter,' said Damien hoarsely, and Jana felt his clawed fingers, as gentle as feathers, part the petals of her fount. She knew, she hoped she knew, what was to follow, and allowed herself to descend face down on to the pile of sacks. Now the sacking seemed to her the softest of beds as she spread her buttocks and felt the tip, then the whole shaft, of the metal cock. At first she thought it too big to fit into her trembling wet quim, and cried out, but Damien was so gentle, and she so wet, that he was able to penetrate her to the neck of her womb.

With slow, remorseless, strokes, Damien began to fuck her. The cold steel took on the warmth of her fount so that soon Jana could scarcely tell that she was not being fucked by the man's own cock. Damien turned his fist and began to rub her swelling clitoris with the back of his glove, the mesh of which was surprisingly soft. Spasms of joy shook Jana's body at each flick of the metal on her throbbing damsel and at each powerful thrust of the metal cock in her quim.

'Oh!' she cried. 'I've never been so filled before! It's like being fucked by . . . a tree!'

And then her voice dissolved into staccato yelps of ecstasy as her body shuddered in orgasm. Panting, she felt the immense cock slide from her fount, making her feel suddenly lonely. She turned, and saw the shaft gleaming with her own wetness. She twisted round and grasped the metal penis, and began to lick the fragrant juices from it. Straining against his armour, Damien's real cock stood up for her, and Jana said, with moist lips, that her forfeit was not yet paid. Damien fumbled with his armour suiting, and rapidly wriggled out of the lower part. He wore nothing underneath, and his naked cock sprang to its full swollen height. Jana gasped with pleasure, for his fleshly cock seemed as big as its metallic surrogate. In her fever of lust, she could no longer tell which was his real cock. Hungrily, she knelt before him and took the hot stiff member into her mouth, right to the back of her throat, and began to suck him with rhythmic bobbing motions of her head.

Damien moaned and clutched the back of her head, pressing her to him. Jana tasted a droplet of seed from his peehole, and knew that his climax was not far off.

'Mmm,' she sighed as she cupped his tight balls in her palms and began to squeeze him there, as though to milk him of every drop of seed. He moaned loudly and his penis began to buck. Her throat was bathed in a flood of hot liquid, and as she felt the jet of fluid inside her, she took one hand from the man's quivering balls and placed her fingers on her own throbbing nympha. As the creamy seed bathed her throat, she began to masturbate herself so vigorously that she came to a climax almost at once.

His cock softened and gradually she released him from her mouth's embrace, kissing the tip of his bulb as one would kiss a faithful lover. She licked her lips, still shiny with his seed, then rose to kiss him on the mouth, her tongue probing and exploring inside it while she continued to rub herself.

'Mistress,' he stammered. 'I have a confession to make. I lied to you.'

'What! That is the worst imperfection!' she cried in real anger.

'Yes – more than the twenty minutes had passed when I found you. You should not have paid the forfeit. Now it is I who must pay in return.'

Jana's eyes narrowed.

'And so you shall,' she hissed, furious. 'Down with you, boy! For a taste of your own sword!'

She pushed him roughly on to the sacks and picked up the broadsword, then prodded his bare buttocks teasingly with its point. She spread his thighs wide and, lodging the smooth blade of the sword in the cleft of his buttocks, placed its point gently against his balls. She was pleased to feel him tremble.

'Hmm. I think you can take a good thirty on the bare,' she said evenly.

'Thirty! Oh, Mistress . . .' he whimpered.

'Perhaps more.'

She lifted the heavy sword with one arm, and brought the flat of it squarely down on his croup, which added a nice red tone to his ebony skin. Then, counting, she followed one stroke with another, until his dark globes were positively fiery. A wild desire invaded her; to twist the blade just once, and land a blow directly on the balls whose vital essence she had so recently drunk. But no – it was the feeling of her power that was the true pleasure, the knowledge that she could do so if she wished.

She counted a full thirty before she laid the sword aside, and all the time he made no sound, although each stroke had made his arse squirm so beautifully that Jana had accompanied her one-handed beating with a delicious frottage of her stiff clitoris. Her breath came as harshly as his, and she saw that, under his flogging, his cock had become fully swollen, like a lush dark flower springing from the fertile earth of his ball-sac.

Jana ordered Damien to remain where he was, and then picked up his nether garment. She forced her legs into it, and pulled it right up so that the metal cock hung at her waist. The armour trousers were surprisingly comfortable, although the steel cock was very heavy. The shaft still gleamed with her own saliva and love-oil, and she found that by tightening her sphincter muscle and clenching her fesses she could make it spring into the erect position. She lay over him and tickled the tight bud of his anus with the tip of the cock. Then he moaned softly as she thrust it a little way into his anus, twirling and teasing all the time. Gradually, his passage relaxed and gave way to her insistent probing.

'No, Mistress!' he cried, almost sobbing. 'I've never –'

'Then you must learn,' Jana replied, and now her tickling became a remorseless thrust. She found to her delight that pressing the penis into Damien's arse made its base tickle her own nympha. His anus loosened, and suddenly there was no more resistance: the passage opened to her, and Jana pushed her penis inside Damien as far as he could take it. She reached down and took the bulk of his cock in

43

her fingers, and began to rub it hard while her palm squeezed his shaft. With sharp, powerful motions of her hips, Jana, grinning in triumph, fucked the whimpering male in his tender hole. With each thrust, her nympha throbbed with pleasure and, when she felt herself reaching her plateau, she redoubled the force of her strokes, fucking him rapidly in the African way as her hips danced over him.

She knew that a man could climax just through penetration of his anus, but she wanted them both to come at the same moment. Vigorously, she stroked his cock until she felt the tell-tale drop of sperm at his peehole, and then it was time; slowly, she withdrew her metal penis from his anus. He squealed in ecstasy and, as his silky hot flood soaked her powerfully squeezing hand, she too shuddered and cried out at the force of the orgasm which pulsed through her. They lay still for some minutes, the weight of her body on his.

'Thank you for my punishment, Mistress,' said Damien in a tender voice. He lay without moving, and Jana patted his bottom.

'Well taken,' said Jana softly. 'You have the makings of a knight. Perhaps a Knight of Maldona.'

'Oh, sweet Mistress, thank you,' he replied joyfully.

But suddenly, Jana's attention was distracted by a fleeting movement in the darkest corner of the hold, and a glint of eyes. Frowning, she picked up the sword and approached the corner of the hold. She found that it was stacked with a jumble of crates and planks that resembled a makeshift hut. There was silence, save for the thrumming from the engine room, the breathing of herself and Damien, and the soft but definite breathing of another person. With a swift swordstroke, Jana sent the pile of crates crashing to the deck.

Before her stood a woman of about her own age. She was slim but powerfully built, dark-haired with big lustrous brown eyes, and she looked up at Jana without fear. She wore only a dress, once a fine robe but now smudged and torn, as though she had been living for some time in this filthy lair. Curiously, it was up over her belly, exposing strong, smooth thighs and a lush black mink. Jana saw her quim, and noticed that its pink lips were spread and engorged. Swiftly, the woman pulled down her dress with glistening fingers.

'Who are you?' cried Jana. 'You are spying on us!'

'Please do not give me away,' said the woman coolly, in heavily-accented English.

Jana grinned at Damien. This mysterious female, hidden here for whatever reason, had been masturbating at the sight of their embraces! Jana smiled at her and put the sword down.

'Captain Damien!' said Jana gleefully. 'I do believe you have a stowaway on board!'

4

A Noble Beating

Jana lifted her sword again and placed its tip under the chin of the dark-haired woman, who stared at her sullenly. Her gaze was stony and incurious, even haughty, as though it were Jana who was the captured stowaway. The Mistress of Maldona permitted herself a wry grin, understanding that in her ragged and besmirched condition she scarcely presented a figure of authority. However she consoled herelf with the thought that a drawn weapon excuses all raggedness.

'Get up,' she said. The woman obeyed, and when she had got to her feet, Jana saw that she was very tall, with the legs and arms of a wrestler. She wondered fleetingly if there was a rival to Maldona somewhere, training women in the arts of wrestling, and the sculpture of body and soul.

Jana appraised the proud woman who stood defiantly before her, as a prospective buyer would eye the physique of a slave at auction.

'What is your name?' she asked. The woman did not answer, but glowered at Jana with her sultry eyes. Jana, expressionless, used the tip of the sword to trace a line up the woman's thighs, stopping just short of her fount.

'Your name, please,' she said softly.

The woman tossed her head.

'My name is Mokka,' she said.

'Mokka? That is a kind of coffee,' Jana replied.

'My name is Mokka,' the woman repeated.

Jana shrugged.

'Well, well. So, Mokka, what are you doing here? Why

46

have you stowed away, imperfectly, on our ship? Explain yourself.'

Mokka laughed scornfully.

'I may ask you who *you* are, and what *you* are doing here,' she said. 'Although I think you do not need to explain what I have seen and, I may say, enjoyed. Such games please me.'

Jana did not speak, but pressed the flat of the sword blade gently against the woman's labia and raised her eyebrows.

Mokka frowned, then sighed. Her scorn was gone, and in a muted voice she answered Jana, 'I must get to –'

She stopped as Damien slowly and timorously approached, and made no secret of the interest his person aroused in her. Jana saw a slight flaring of her nostrils, a widening of her eyes, and tapped the sword gently against the tender skin of her captive's inner thigh.

'To where? And why a stowaway?' continued Jana.

Mokka's answer was to take the sword blade in her bare hand and push it away from her skin. When this was done, she knelt suddenly and, to Jana's surprise, bowed her head to kiss Jana's feet.

'Please help me,' she stammered. 'Please do not give me away. I must reach the castle. I had to stow away. I slipped aboard at Corfu, and I have eaten and drunk from the scraps of your kitchen. But in secret – there are those who wish me ill, those who must not know of my passage.'

Jana found herself distracted by the sensation of Mokka's warm lips and tongue on her feet, and took the opportunity to delegate her decision. She told Damien that he was, after all, captain of the ship, and that therefore Mokka's fate lay within his jurisdiction. She saw that the interest in Mokka's eyes for the captain's ebony person was mirrored in his own glances at her proud body. In her crouching position, she revealed a croup so wide and full that Jana thought it quite the largest she had ever seen. The perfection of the smoothly moulded fesses brought a tickle of warmth to Jana's belly, and she felt a sudden pang of jealousy – which she knew to be the most useless of

47

emotions – at the muted but definitely lascivious glances her two companions had exchanged. This feeling, though, was promptly overridden by the healthier and much keener desire to make those impudent, tempting fesses dance under a sound caning.

'Mistress,' said Damien, 'have I your permission to address your captive?' Mokka looked up as Jana nodded her assent.

'You are Mistress?' she said. 'He is not Master?'

'I am the slave of Mistress Jana,' said Damien, 'as is everyone on board. That, or they desire to be so. You will find no enemies here. Nevertheless, you must explain yourself. What castle? What enemies?'

Jana took Mokka's shoulder and made her rise, then ordered her to speak, accompanying the command with a sharp stroke of the sword blade across her buttocks. However the woman, wincing in surprise, only shook her head.

'I cannot explain,' she said. 'I have already said too much. I escaped but now I must return, for a woman cannot truly escape from what is within her. But I beg you, forget me and I shall slip away as quietly as I came. No one need know. I understand that I have been guilty of a crime, that a stowaway is a criminal on the high seas, and so must be chained and put in a dungeon.' She gestured at her shabby confines. 'What is this but a dungeon? My rags and scraps of food are my chains. In a few hours, I can be gone.'

'Nevertheless,' said Jana thoughtfully, 'punishment is in order. Not just for stowing away, but for spying on us.'

Mokka grinned slyly.

'I have seen your way of punishment,' she said, 'and you did not notice me until my excitement gave me away! I am quite a good spy,' she added smugly. 'I am willing to take the punishment, if you feel that you can then free me. In fact, I – I ask you to punish me. Here and now, if you please. It is a very long time since I have been cleansed.'

She looked hesitantly between Jana and Damien, her eyes wide and pleading. Jana smiled.

'Well,' she said, 'I grant your request, Mokka, and perhaps punishment will loosen your tongue. But not here. No, you must come with us to an assembly of witnesses, whose scornful eyes shall make your punishment all the sweeter.'

Jana still could not rid herself of her awareness that Damien's eyes had met Mokka's with more than curiosity. Suddenly, above them on deck, they heard voices.

'They are looking for us, and will find us soon,' she said, 'so we must go back to the party, with a new slave as our trophy.'

Briskly, she ordered Mokka to strip naked, as she did so herself. It did not take long for her to don Mokka's begrimed robe, while the stowaway put on Jana's own rags. Jana picked up two loose lengths of chain from the deck and, kneeling once more, Mokka suffered the indignity of having the heavy links of one fastened around her waist. Damien smiled, until Jana indicated that he was not to be spared his merited humiliation, and must kneel and be chained likewise. He obeyed, and thus the Mistress of Maldona, holding two leashes in one hand and the sword in the other, led her captives up on to the deck and made towards Caspar's stateroom. From time to time Jana delivered gentle pats with the flat of the sword to the buttocks of her slaves as they wriggled clumsily along, and, smiling at the noise of Damien's metal penis scraping on the deck, she triumphantly re-entered the stateroom.

The applause at her arrival was led by Caspar and Netta, and the crew members enthusiastically joined them. Only Cassie seemed taken aback.

'What's the matter, slave?' said Jana curtly. 'You seem nervous for an empress. I ran from here as a dog and, as is proper, I return as Mistress, with not one but two slaves. I lead my would-be captor, Damien, and I lead myself, a woman's body in my own rags.'

'Such is the power of Maldona,' intoned Caspar smugly. 'I knew you would win the forfeit, Mistress. Do grace us with an explanation of your other self – your new slave.'

Caspar, too, knew how to frame a question so that it

was not a question. All eyes in the party were fixed on the abased figure of Mokka, who, from her crouching position, swept the candlelit chamber with her own defiant gaze. Her body shone with an aura of beauty and tamed menace, like a captive she-wolf who threatened at any moment to spring from her bonds. Jana felt herself shiver very slightly, feeling the woman's aura envelop her, and feeling, too, the dangerous thrill of holding such a proud beast captive. Her other self, indeed! The very words had her in their strange, mesmerising, power. Jana unfastened the chain that bound Mokka's waist and, with a flick of her sword, motioned that she should stand.

The stowaway obeyed, uncurling to stand with her legs apart and her hands on her hips, and continued to survey the men whose eyes were fixed on her. She smiled a cruel, leering smile, as though she knew what lustful fancies filled their minds and their loins, and gloated in her power over men's bodies. Jana ordered Damien to remain on his hands and knees, then approached Cassie and touched her belly with the sword point. Cassie trembled but was silent.

'Well, empress,' said Jana, 'I think you did not expect to see your new slave return as Mistress. And as Mistress, it is right that I punish you for your *hubris*, your damned insolence, as I have punished Damien. Now you may join him like a dog. Kneel, slut.'

Jana was surprised at the venom in her voice, and at the very real anger she felt towards Cassie, who, for the briefest moment, had allowed the game to go too far. She wondered if there was jealousy in her, if her emotion at this strange new arrival would be felt equally by the impudent Cassie. Her own belly fluttered in exultation as her slave knelt before her and allowed another chain to be fastened around her hips.

'Now,' Jana continued, 'the games are not over yet. What game shall we play, my friends?'

At that, Mokka tossed her head in derision.

'Games!' she cried. 'I want no games, Mistress. I am a criminal, and must be punished to cleanse me of my crime. Then, perhaps, we shall have games.'

Suddenly, she lifted the ragged remains of Jana's dress and tossed the garment aside, so that she stood naked.

'You shall be punished for insolence, if nothing else,' hissed Jana as she made her sword whistle through the air.

'Still, an explanation of some kind . . .' said Caspar, shrugging as though he expected none and did not really care.

'I shall give no explanation, other than what I have told my Mistress,' said Mokka tersely. 'If that earns me more punishment, so be it. And when I have paid my . . . forfeit, then you shall, if you have any sense, permit me to depart, and shall see no more of me.'

The candlelight made the proud curves of her nudity shimmer as the flames caught the sheen of sweat that bathed her and eerily reflected the bright eyes and expectant faces of the assembly, as though Mokka's naked body was in some way sucking in their own auras, making them her possessions. She moved abruptly to the costumed crewmen and placed herself in front of the can-can dancer.

'A pretty girl indeed,' she said mockingly. In her accented English, she pronounced it 'preety gerrl'. 'Not as pretty as I am,' she added, stroking her bare breasts which were within inches of the man's wide eyes. Suddenly, she drove her hand under his flounced frock, and he jumped in startled apprehension. Mokka's hand had plainly clasped his balls and prick, and from the rhythmic rising and falling of the frock, it was clear that she was putting his virility to the most elemental of tests. Vigorously, her hand moved up and down until the frock stood out as though of its own accord, at which Mokka smiled and nodded in approval, then passed to the next man, the Roman centurion. He too received the testing caress of her hand, then it was the gondolier's turn, and then the priest's, and when every costume was tight and bulging where Mokka had raised the males to throbbing hardness, she turned to Jana and pronounced herself satisfied.

'One of the pleasures of being a stowaway,' she mused, 'is the constant thrill of expecting to be discovered, and then delivered up into the mercy of the raw men one finds

51

aboard ship. The thrill of being apprehended is almost erotic; no, I must say that it *is* erotic, an equal feeling of dread and desire at the thought of being alone and helpless in the power of these men hungry for woman-flesh. And I must admit, Mistress, that it was deliberate on my part to reveal my presence to you. When I watched you and your captain at sport, it was more than I could bear. I had to masturbate, and it was not enough: I knew that I must reveal myself and be taken prisoner, to be justly punished.'

She stooped and took the cane from Cassie's hand, then curtseyed to Jana and reverently handed it to her. Jana nodded in agreement, and gestured towards the whipping frame. She looked at Mokka's perfect fesses, so big and satin-smooth and glistening with her sweat, and felt herself moisten in her quim as she knew she must whip those ripe peaches until they shone the prettiest crimson and Mokka squealed and writhed in her pleading for mercy: a mercy which would not be granted. Jana trembled with desire: she could scarcely wait to begin the lacing, for she knew that in whipping the naked buttocks of the woman, she would, for those precious moments, possess her. She would possess the pain that seared through her helpless body and, in the tender relation of punisher and victim, would actually become her. Just as a man, she reflected, in fucking us, wants to momentarily become a woman, and we, in taking his cock into our wet quims, know that we take his manhood and his vitality, and possess him. Gently, she stroked Mokka's thighs with the cane, then pressed its tip against the fleshy red petals of her fount.

'You have merited a Noble Beating, according to the rules of Maldona,' she said softly. 'For that, a simple cane will not suffice. Caspar, will you please fetch a *flagrum*.'

'I have the scourge you require, Mistress,' said Netta, gravely holding out a flail of black leather, with six blunt-studded thongs, which was nearly three feet in length. Jana took it and drew a sharp breath as she felt how heavy the instrument was; the cane, vicious though she was, seemed a plaything in comparison.

It was as though Mokka guessed her thoughts, for she

grinned impishly and said to Jana and the entire, mesmerised assembly, 'I know not Maldona, nor her rules. But
I am no stranger to rules, and realise my confessed ignorance must be another offence. I have hidden on your ship,
I have refused to explain myself – though for very good
reasons, and in your own interests – and now I confess
ignorance of your ways. How naughty you must think me!'

The lightness in her voice suddenly vanished as she
continued, speaking now as though to unseen listeners far
away. 'I must atone, and re-enter the castle cleansed. But
first . . . I might as well be whipped for a sheep as for a
lamb, as I believe you say in England.'

Mokka returned to her can-can dancer – Jana thought
that the man did seem to be in her possession, now – knelt
before him, and lifted his frock to reveal a naked penis in
its full erect glory. The man smirked proudly, his member,
to Jana's pleasure, rivalling Damien's massive shaft. She
thought the huge penis looked strange, thrusting out from
in between the frilly stocking tops and garter belt. Then
again, she decided, the sight of this man in a garter belt
and stockings was strange enough in itself and his protruding cock just made him look all the more delicious.

Mokka licked her lips and, with the pale pink tip of her
tongue protruding like a scallop from its shell, she began
to lick the engorged, gleaming helmet of the man's cock.
Her tongue flicked delicately around his peehole, and he
groaned, pressing her head towards him. Angrily, Mokka
shook his hands from her hair, and instead made him hold
his frock high up while she sucked the quivering bulb of
his penis. After her tongue had done its work on the
peehole, her lips enclosed the bulb, first for an instant, then
longer and deeper, her head darting downward like a
pigeon's until she had almost the whole shaft in the back
of her throat, the powerful suction intensified by the
movements of her neck. Jana had rarely seen such expert
fellatio, and felt herself becoming quite giddy and wet in
her fount as she unconsciously stroked her own breasts and
belly with the thongs of her flail, in time with the movements of Mokka's sucking lips. Each of the stiff thongs

sent shivers of pleasure through her breasts as the metal studs brushed against her nipples, caressing them into tense buds of desire.

The man upon whose cock Mokka was working such magic now panted hoarsely, his breath interspersed with little moans. As he was about to climax, Mokka took his tight balls in the palms of her hands, stroked them, then squeezed them surprisingly hard, as one would squeeze lemons. Jana thrilled at this, knowing that the man would be at the knife-edge between pain and ecstasy, and loving the power of a woman to bring a male to that edge and keep him there. Suddenly the can-can dancer cried out as his spasm came, his breath quick and harsh as a dog's. Mokka's throat rippled as she gulped his seed and, once she'd withdrawn her lips from the cock's softening shaft, she licked the livid crimson bulb and continued to massage the balls and to rub the base of the helmet with her clenched fingers.

The man began to whimper and begged her not to stop, and then cried out again, his second orgasm causing him to pant almost as passionately as the first. Jana was not surprised: she knew from the yogic doctrines of the *Tantra*, and from her own experience, that a male was capable of a second and even a third climax, the orgasmic ecstasy thereafter maintained almost indefinitely, if the stimulation of the cock was properly and tenderly continued after his ejaculation.

'Oh . . . Oh . . .' the man cried, his voice almost a sob. Then he smiled in utter bliss and murmured, 'I wish we had more stowaways that could suck like this one.'

His reward for that was a firm stroke to the buttock with the flat of Jana's sword. He cried out in shock, and dropped the hem of his dress over Mokka's head as his hands flew to his reddened flesh. Jana snarled, with real anger, that as a mere male he was to show respect to all ladies, even stowaways, and that as a mere crewman he was to speak only when a lady permitted him to do so. But Mokka, emerging from beneath the frilly dress, merely grinned, and gave the man's drained balls a squeeze of farewell before moving to the next in line.

54

She repeated her lustful ritual with each of the men, making no sound but the little purrs of satisfaction as she swallowed their seed. And it did seem to be a ritual: her embrace was not loving, but voracious, as though in giving the males pleasure she was somehow punishing them. Jana noted that she gained particular joy from stroking and squeezing the tight balls before milking them of their sperm, and that her farewell squeeze, as she licked her glistening lips, was harder than Jana thought most males would find comfortable. Yet, mindful of the stinging sword-blade, they kept a respectful silence.

Mokka was almost mechanical in her single-minded and expert fellation of the proud cocks she revealed, and Jana's quim was soaking with desire, her gaze flitting between the woman's pumping lips and the magnificent globes of her bare fesses which seemed to thrust at Jana, for her eyes alone. But, as her belly warmed and her damsel tingled with longing, Jana reflected on her sudden anger, and her sword-stroke to the disrespectful male. It was as though the flippant remark to Mokka, in her abject, captive state, had been an insult to Jana – to Maldona herself – and a feeling of foreboding mingled with her overwhelming desire for the woman. She knew she was being subtly drawn into Mokka's control, just as her act of obeisance to the males' virility was really an act of dominance, of despoiling.

Jana suddenly felt helpless in the sheer intensity of her lust, which was more than merely physical. In desiring to whip Mokka, she longed to know her, body and soul. She wore her dress, and fingered the heavy, silky fabric, sumptuous even in its begrimed state: her fingers strayed to her mount of Venus, and she began softly to rub herself, feeling the damsel already engorged as she watched Mokka's ceremony of lustful homage to the male organ. Homage that was, subtly, more than homage – that was utter control. Mokka's dress was already damp at Jana's quim, from her love-oil which now flowed copiously and, as she frotted herself, she writhed in the dress, sighing with pleasure as she felt the smooth cloth rub against her breasts.

She remembered that Mokka had accepted the exchange of clothing gladly and without protest: she had known that by donning her robe, Jana would enter into her power. Oh God, Jana thought, as her breath came faster, her plateau nearly reached: I wear her clothing, I am in her power, I have become part of her.

Mokka brought the last of the costumed men to orgasm and, as she licked the last droplet of seed from the shining cock, she looked up at Jana and smiled broadly.

As Jana's spasm shook her and her belly was alive with sweet fire, she knew that she wanted to be in Mokka's power, and had to stop herself from crying out with the joy that flooded her.

When she finally calmed down a little, Jana saw that Netta's arm was around Caspar's waist, her hand casually brushing the front of his pinstripes; rewarded with a handsome bulge, Netta grinned mischievously.

'I think, mysterious stowaway, that it is my husband's turn now,' she said simply. 'He is rampant.'

At once, Mokka stood and approached Caspar, but this time she did not kneel. Face to face, she was a good head taller than the schoolmaster, as he was arrayed, and Jana thought that her musculature, if not quite equal to that of the stocky Caspar, would give him a fair fight in the *pankration* arena.

Netta disappeared into the shadows, and the drumbeat started its insistent, menacing rhythm once again. All eyes were on Mokka as she touched Caspar's erect penis through the bulging cloth. Jana, bathed in the afterglow of her orgasm, knew that Mokka was taking control of the gathering. She felt faint and almost delirious with joy and excited apprehension. She scarcely noticed that slight jangling of the leashes she held as Cassie and Damien, uncommanded, rose to view the spectacle. There was no pretence of obeisance in Mokka now: her lip curled in scorn as she looked down at Caspar, whose own lip trembled, betraying a loss of his usual serenity. Yet he stood his ground, and Jana was pleased that he had not forgotten his duty to obey a woman, even though her own role as Mistress had been taken over by the sultry new-comer. When the candles guttered and burned low no one thought to replace them, though the crewmen did at least make sure the revellers' glasses were replenished with wine and, on a signal from Jana, provided her and her two slaves with something to drink.

'So,' said Mokka, 'we have a schoolboy amongst us.'

'He is a school*master*,' said Netta. 'I am a schoolgirl. And he is the owner of our ship,' she added proudly, 'and of the Rosebush school, *and* a faithful slave of Maldona, as am I.'

'Did I ask you to speak, slut?' whispered Mokka with a smile. 'No, I did not. I say we have a schoolboy here. It is well known that in your English schools, masters and boys both wear strange uniforms of servitude, to symbolise the pride and dignity of submission to your rules. So I say we have a schoolboy, a prefect perhaps. Am I right, school-boy?'

Caspar glanced at Jana, who, burning with curiosity, nodded her agreement.

'Yes, miss, you are right,' said Caspar faintly.

'Hmm,' continued Mokka, stroking the bulge of Caspar's erection, 'we all know schoolboys are naughty, and must be punished for it, since they are almost at man's estate. Your shaft is hard, young man, and I am disgusted. You are nothing but a pig, like all men, aren't you?'

'Yes, miss,' murmured Caspar, faintly, after a pause.

'Hand me your belt, pig, then unbutton and remove your trousers,' she ordered. 'Your footwear too.'

Trembling slightly, Caspar obeyed, revealing that his underthings were perhaps unexpected in a schoolmaster, and soon his trousers lay on the carpet, beside his blue silk stockings and garter belt. Mokka fingered the cane he wore at his belt as she inspected the massive cock that strained against the flimsy silk of his panties. Caspar's panties were sky blue with a frilly trim of écru lace and, at his manhood, carried the likeness of a rose in gold thread; a rose now distorted by the massive swelling of his penis.

'Such arrogance to carry a cane,' she said, 'as though

you were a true Master, or even, in your wildest dreams, a Mistress. A golden rose to cover your shame, indeed. Remove your panties, you dirty boy.'

Caspar did so, and his naked cock, far from wilting under these insults, sprang to its full magnificence. Penis and balls were both shaven to complete smoothness, and the absence of a mink made Caspar's bare, thrusting virility seem all the more menacing. Mokka reached down and grasped the bulb of his cock, sharply pulling back the hood and making Caspar wince. Then she began to rub it firmly, at the base of the shining helmet. Caspar moaned softly.

'This is what you males do with each other in secret, isn't it, you pig? You make women of each other, because you would like to be women,' said Mokka, and allowed her fingers to stray to his shaft, squeezing it vigorously before returning to a harsh, tantalising rubbing of his bulb and peehole. 'But you cannot be women, so you are obliged to worship us instead,' she sneered.

'Yes, miss,' said Caspar meekly, between heavy sighs.

Abruptly she released his stiff cock, and ordered him to bend over and touch his toes. He did so, and she stood behind him, holding his own cane between his thighs.

'Legs wide,' she said curtly, with a gentle tap of the cane tip on his balls, 'and tiptoe, if you please, boy. That will stop any silly wriggling and squirming, for you are going to get a thrashing, as you are no doubt aware. She is a silly little cane' – the short yellow rod whipped viciously at the air – 'but she will serve her purpose. Bottom high, now.'

She touched Caspar's naked, upthrust fesses with the cane: it was the lightest of caresses, but he tensed in anticipation of what was to come.

'Well,' she mused, 'how many does he deserve, I wonder? Six of the best is customary in English schools, I believe, but I think this one can take a little more spice. Have the rules of your Maldona anything to say on the matter?'

'The rules of Maldona are for Maldona alone,' responded Jana, summoning a reserve of defiance. 'You are not of Maldona. You are nothing.' As soon as she had said that, she regretted it, and knew she would continue to regret it, unless ... unless she were forgiven for her insolence! Jana was astounded that such an imperfect thought should come to the Mistress of Maldona, but Mokka simply shrugged, and said that six was a nice round number, but seven was the spicier.

'And,' she added softly, 'twice seven is a nicer and rounder number by far. Don't you agree, schoolboy?'

'Yes, miss,' said Caspar in a faint voice. 'I – I very much agree.'

Mokka stepped back five paces, lifted the cane, and ran rapidly at Caspar to deliver a stinging cut to the bare. The cane moved so fast it was a blur, and the loud crack of the instrument on Caspar's naked croup belied its small aspect. Even in the dim candlelight, Jana could see that Caspar's buttocks were well marked. Mokka took her time with the beating, sauntering back from her victim after each stroke and watching him tremble before she chose to run at him for the next. Jana found herself unbearably excited watching the powerful female, naked, her muscles glistening in her passion, flog the helpless male with pitiless cuts: the more so as Caspar's cock stood as stiff and powerful as ever. At last it was over: the fourteenth and hardest cut delivered, Mokka let fall the cane and knelt, clasping Caspar by the legs and pressing her lips in a rain of kisses to his scarlet buttocks. She whispered over and over: 'My poor boy, my lovely man, how brave! Oh, your poor whipped bottom ...'

Netta stroked the woman's hair as she embraced and kissed her flogged husband. Finally, Mokka looked up. Her face was sombre.

'Now, Mistress,' she said, 'it is time, please, for my Noble Beating.'

The proud intruder bowed her head as she allowed herself to be strapped naked to the whipping frame in the room's centre. Her body was stretched tight over the polished frame, her legs and arms splayed. Jana, Cassie and Netta gravely chained her by her wrists, ankles and waist: it seemed fitting, although not a word had been spoken, that the binding was women's work, too sacred to be left to males. When Mokka was trussed, Jana was handed a thick leather gag by Netta, who, as always, was ready with instruments of correction from her stock. Inside the gag was a bright steel ball which filled Mokka's mouth and depressed her tongue: it was impossible for her even to cry out. Jana asked if she was comfortable and able to breathe, and Mokka nodded yes, although firmness, not comfort, was the real aim of this binding.

Next, a pixie hood of soft black calfskin was snugly fitted over her hair, ears and eyes. The prisoner, for such the stowaway Mokka was now, could neither hear, see, nor speak and, in her tight chains, could scarcely move or do more than twitch or shudder. She was ready to receive her Noble Beating from the lash of the Mistress of Maldona.

Jana looked out at the sea and to the sparkling lights on shore, which seemed to her like a mute chorus to the act that must be. An electric silence shrouded her: she could see only the naked orbs of the woman's croup, awaiting her flogging, and it seemed that each stroke delivered would be a stroke of desire and love to every woman, to the female Earth herself. Mokka's fesses were twin worlds, her whole body a naked temple, demanding worship of nature's beauty, tamed and sculpted by the eternal power of the female. A thousand sensations swirled in Jana's mind: scents of flowers and rivers, faces and bodies long remembered, the caress of the ocean waves, and all the beauty she held in her heart seemed to flow from the soft flesh awaiting her whipstrokes. She knew that, somehow, Mokka's arrival was no accident, and that her destiny and the very destiny of Maldona itself were linked to the soul and body of this superb woman. Her breast full of sweet anguish, Jana lifted her whip.

In total stillness, Mokka took a full twenty-eight strokes from the cruelly hissing flagrum before Jana halted the beating. She was giddy with fury, with desire, with a mingling of rage and pity and longing. Her quim flowed with moisture, and she thought she had never been so confused. She knew, though, that she wanted Mokka. She

60

longed to kiss the reddened back, shoulders, fesses and thighs where the thongs of her flail had marked the woman's body.

When Netta and Cassie had removed Mokka's gag and hood, and were unfastening her chains, Jana touched her lips and whispered that she considered her cleansed. Then, loudly, she announced that the party should finish.

'What about the prisoner, Mistress?' said Damien. 'Shall I lock her up?' Jana saw his eyes gleam with eagerness to have Mokka in his power.

'No, you may not,' she replied tersely, and took a deep breath. 'The prisoner shall be in my custody tonight. She will sleep in my chamber, with myself and my slave to guard her. She shall be released in the morning, for she has been cleansed of her impudent intrusion.'

Netta, Caspar, and the crew members, though surprised, bowed in submission to Jana's will. Only Damien looked sad, but bowed also at Jana's reassuring smile. She mouthed a kiss at his dangling metal penis and, to her delight, he made it stand up! Men are such pussycats, she thought.

'It is well that you take me, Mistress,' murmured Mokka as she accompanied Jana and Cassie on deck, 'for I will tell you things. Thank you for cleansing me, but – Oh, I am so afraid! – the best and most loving cleansing cannot last forever.'

5

Mokka's Story

'This is a long way from your squalid dungeon below decks,' said Jana as she led her captive into the stateroom she shared with her slave Cassie. Mokka looked round with mild curiosity, her eyes taking in the large bed, the mirrored ceiling, and the paraphernalia of discipline. Then she smiled.

'Still, it is a dungeon of sorts,' she replied. 'Every room can be a dungeon to a spirit uncleansed.'

'It is a dungeon with a bathroom,' said Jana, and you must wish to bathe.'

'If my Mistress instructs,' answered Mokka. She entered the bathroom and nodded, appraising the ornate fittings with a cool eye, careful not to seem impressed with her new-found luxury – or perhaps, Jana thought, she really was unimpressed. Jana ordered Cassie to prepare a bath.

'Would you like me to anoint your body with oil?' she said to Mokka. 'We have every soothing lotion imaginable, for obvious reasons. Your poor fesses are still glowing like hot coals. Does it hurt a lot?'

'Of course,' said Mokka with a shrug. 'It is necessary. I should like to be anointed, but first –'

She squatted on the Turkish commode in full view of Jana, and with no sign that she was aware of any immodesty. The steam from the filling bath wreathed her and gave her the aspect of an ancient oracle amid her sacred fumes.

'It is late, Mistress,' she said, 'and I have not eaten for a long time. I address you as Mistress, now, and with your permission, of course, but at dawn that shall cease. In the meantime I beg for some food.'

'Of course!' cried Jana, blushing as though guilty of neglecting her duties as hostess. Cassie, having finished drawing the bath, was promptly ordered to return to Caspar's stateroom and to fetch whatever could be fetched from the half-finished buffet. She obeyed, unsmiling, and Jana frowned at her apparent sullenness. Perhaps she was annoyed that the party had been ended so abruptly, without her having had a chance to show off her painted nudity. Perhaps, too, she was jealous of Mokka for having taken the whipping, and becoming the centre of attention instead of herself.

Mokka rose from the commode and wiped herself with the pink tissue which Jana – as though Jana was the slave – handed her, then bent over the washbasin, her buttocks spread, so that Jana could rub the unguents and creams into the raw, crimson skin. Mokka's hands rested on the sides of the basin, and her back was straight, so that she could gaze at her reflection in the mirror. There was untroubled vanity in her gaze, and Jana decided she should order Caspar to remove all mirrors from his vessel, in accordance with Maldona's rules.

As she softly rubbed the woman's flesh, her palms circling slowly as they kneaded, Jana felt herself tingle with warm desire, made gentle and luxurious by the heat of the steamy bathroom and the scent of the healing lotions. She permitted her fingers to linger frequently in the cleft of Mokka's buttocks, even though the whip had not touched her there, and once or twice her fingertip brushed against the tight bud of Mokka's anus, which was surprisingly prominent and jutted, Jana thought, like another damsel. This made her feel moist between her thighs, especially as Mokka did not object, nor even react, to the tickling of her anus. Instead, all the time, she gazed at her own impassive face in the mirror, not seeming to blink.

At last, Jana felt the need to break the silence: there were so many questions. She put away the jars of ointment, and said that it was enough for the moment, although in reality her lustful pleasure in the massage was growing more obvious with each touch of her palm on the firm skin. In an off-hand voice, she said: 'Well! You seem to be no stranger to punishment, Mokka,' hoping that this would draw some explanation.

But Mokka merely grinned into the mirror, and said, 'I think you have a talent for stating the obvious, Mistress. And having begged you for food, now I beg you to join me in my bath, because you, too, are dirty.'

Jana was briefly startled by this abrupt comment, but she realised it was quite true, and was excited by the thought of being naked together with Mokka. In a moment the two women were reclining opposite each other, their feet touching each other's thighs, in the hot water which was slippery with suds and fragrant oils. Both sighed the same sigh of contentment at just the same time, and at that, both chuckled.

'A good night's sleep for both of us,' Jana said.

'Your carpet will be most welcome, if you have a cover for me,' replied Mokka.

'Why, no!' blurted Jana without reflection. 'You are to sleep with us. Our bed has room for three.'

'*Our* bed?' said Mokka, with a quizzical smile. 'Do you order me, Mistress?'

'Yes. Yes, I do,' replied Jana.

'Then,' said Mokka lazily, 'I have no choice but to obey.'

Jana realised how tired she was, and lay motionless in the hot water's caress, allowing the steam, the perfume, and the nearness of Mokka's bare flesh to lull her into a drowsy bliss. She thought that Cassie was taking a long time, although she had not really been keeping track of the time. She decided, too, that she was going to prevent Mokka from proceeding just yet towards this mysterious castle of hers. She was not going to permit Mokka to leave her servitude, at least not until she had learned her secrets, and she was certainly not going to permit Cassie to spoil things with any hint of imperfect jealousy.

The door opened, and Cassie entered, bearing a wide silver tray laden with food, her face radiant.

64

'You look happy, slave,' said Jana, dimly making out Cassie's broad grin through the steam which shrouded her.

'Happy, Mistress? Oh, no! It was awful! Caspar made me *pay* for this food, the beast!'

'Pay? With what? You carry no coin.'

In answer, Cassie carefully set the tray down beside Mokka, turned round, then lifted her dress to show her bare bottom. The naked globes were delicately streaked with red lines.

'That little cane of Caspar's is fiercer than she looks,' Cassie said ruefully. 'Ooh . . . how my poor bum smarts!'

Jana laughed, pleased that Cassie had been graced with punishment at last, and that she was restored to good humour. Caspar, as usual, knew what was what: that a slave of Maldona whose imperfections went unpunished felt unloved.

'How many?' asked Jana.

'Fifteen, Mistress,' said Cassie.

'On the bare?'

'Of course. There is no other way.'

'Well,' said Jana lazily, 'fifteen is not too many.'

'Mistress, they were *hard*! Caspar is very strong,' cried Cassie indignantly. 'The – the beast!'

But her smile of satisfaction belied her words.

'I shall have to sleep on my belly tonight,' she said smugly.

'And that shall be soon,' said Jana. 'We have a busy day tomorrow. After bath, bed. When I have finished bathing, slave, you may take my place and cleanse yourself. Meanwhile, fetch our bathrobes.'

Cassie left the bathroom, and Jana looked to see Mokka hungrily devouring a chicken leg. Mokka waited until her mouth was empty before speaking.

'Water alone will not cleanse,' she said simply, then returned to her food, but without taking her eyes from Jana's. Jana pondered this, and shifted in the bath.

'Yes,' she said slowly. 'I see . . .'

As though casually, her movement brought her foot into contact with Mokka's fount. She felt the lush mink-hair beneath her sole, and the soft cunt-petals at her heel. Mokka did not flinch or move, or give any reaction at all. She fixed Jana with that same unblinking stare as she gnawed her food. Jana yawned and stretched herself, lifting her breasts above the bathsuds and, at the same time, moved her foot slightly against Mokka's quim. Mokka removed the chicken bone from her mouth and smiled thinly, not directly at Jana, but as if in some private dream. Emboldened, Jana began to rub her foot against the open slit in a delicate frottage.

'Where will you go from here, Mokka?' she said.

'Why, to the Castle. I have told you,' was the answer.

'But how? I mean, by what route?' Jana did not feel it was yet time to ask where this castle actually lay.

'To the north,' Mokka said. 'The route, and the mode of transport, are immaterial. I shall get there, because I must.'

She had finished eating, now, and sighed with satisfaction, then lay back in the tub and closed her eyes. Jana continued her frottage, harder now, and felt Mokka's cunt begin to moisten.

'That is better,' said Mokka, rubbing her belly, and Jana was unsure if she referred to her meal or to the caress of her fount. She moved her foot so that her toes were on Mokka's labia, and when she wriggled them against the woman's slit, she felt an oily wetness.

Struggling to keep her voice from trembling, Jana said in a tone she hoped was friendly and conversational, 'We are travelling north, Cassie and I. To Bulgaria.'

'Good luck,' said Mokka curtly. Now she had brought her hands up to her breasts, and was quite openly rubbing her nipples between her forefingers and thumbs. Jana felt her own fount moisten and allowed her fingers to stray to her nympha which was beginning to tingle with pleasure.

'Have you ever been to Bulgaria?' said Jana.

'Yes,' said Mokka in a curiously impatient voice. 'Please, Mistress, do not stop what you are doing with your gentle foot. I think you shall bring me to an orgasm quite soon. I suggest you masturbate yourself at the same time, and we may reach orgasm together, which will be pleasant. Or perhaps you would prefer me to use my foot on your cunt.'

The matter-of-fact harshness of the word jolted Jana for a moment, until she realised that the casual blandness of Mokka's tone excited her. All of a sudden, her fount gushed with love juices, and her idle caress of her nympha became hard and determined. She looked, mesmerised, as her beautiful captive masturbated her own nipples, and felt Mokka's thighs squeezing around her foot. Jana felt breathless with desire, and the slight tingling of her belly and clit became a fire. She gasped in astonishment: she was already on the verge of coming.

'Mokka is a very nice name,' she gasped. 'It is a very interesting name. I should love to know where it comes . . . from. Oh, God, I'm coming. Oh – oh, Mokka . . .'

'Yes,' said Mokka, her voice faint, again as though from a long distance away. 'Yes.'

Her breath was heavy; not coming in gasps like Jana's, but deep and measured. Her hands flickered across her nipples and she began to slap them until they were as hard as plums, gently at first, then harder and harder, until it seemed as though she were spanking her own breasts like soft bare buttocks. Jana felt the woman's love-oil become a flood, and the water foamed as Mokka's belly began to heave. Jana sensed that the woman was coming, but Mokka did not gasp or cry out.

Jana, however, did. She could not repress a little squeal in the back of her throat as pleasure twisted her in a delicious hot spasm.

'Yes, I'm coming . . . Oh, sweet Mokka. I love your cunt! Oh, I'm coming, I wish our cunts were pressed together . . . Oh, it's too late, I'm there! Oh! Mokka!'

'Yes,' said Mokka, and at last, Jana heard her panting. 'Yes, I shall tell you about my name. Yes, do not stop using your foot, I am very wet now.' She said this quite clinically, although her breath was growing harsher and harsher. Jana's belly fluttered with the intensity of her spasm as she heard Mokka thrash the water, heard the frantic slaps of palm on nipple, then heard her say, in a long, drawn-out moan: 'Yes . . . yes.'

After the two women had achieved their climaxes – Jana's all the more delicious for its unexpected suddenness – Cassie re-entered the bathroom bearing robes for each of them, herself included. Jana admired her discretion in waiting until she and Mokka had finished their mutual masturbation, although she grinned as she thought that Cassie had probably been listening, and masturbating herself. Certainly, her face was flushed. She stood with the robes over her arm, and a towel held open, waiting to dry her Mistress. Jana and Mokka both climbed from the bath and stood dripping, their bodies still covered in suds, and Cassie approached Jana with the towel.

Then a curious impulse seized Jana. Suddenly, she felt it would be wrong to precede Mokka in the drying, and motioned to Cassie that she should serve their guest first, even though she was a stowaway – a trespasser and, technically, a criminal. Jana watched as Mokka's proud brown body was dried and robed, and only then was it her turn. It was as though Mokka had taken over control of their quarters; as though she, not Jana, were Mistress. And to Jana's surprise, she found that this subtle reversal pleased her. A warning voice in her head told her that she must not become enthralled by this woman, but her heart was joyful that her caress had been accepted and that with her help Mokka had brought herself to orgasm. She ordered Cassie to bathe, and followed Mokka back into the stateroom.

While Cassie made splashing noises in the bath, Jana indicated to Mokka that she should sit down: they would enjoy a nightcap before bed. But Mokka remained standing.

'Shall I serve you, Mistress?' she said gravely. 'What do you require?'

'Well ... yes,' said Jana, taken aback, for she had intended to go to the drinks table herself. 'A brandy for me, I think. And you?'

'I shall take what my Mistress ordains,' said Mokka, almost scornfully, as though Jana had ignored the obvious. She served the drinks, and awaited Jana's command before

68

taking an armchair. Yet, once again, Jana had the feeling that in her obeisance, Mokka was really in control, just as she had somehow been in control when trussed and gagged for her Noble Beating. They sipped their drinks in silence, and Jana yawned again. She really was very tired, cosy in her warm robe, and looking forward to bed.

'Mistress,' said Mokka, 'if I am to share your bed –'

'You are,' said Jana quickly.

'I have no nightdress.'

Jana laughed. 'Why, we sleep nude,' she answered. 'Surely that does not bother you, Mokka?'

'It is a long time since I was permitted to sleep nude,' said Mokka sombrely, then, her face brightening with a sudden, dazzling smile, 'it shall be such a sweet pleasure, Mistress!'

Jana excused herself and went into the bathroom, where she squatted on the commode while Cassie finished her ablutions in the bathtub.

'What do you make of her, Cassie?' she said.

'An interesting woman, Mistress,' said Cassie. 'I quite fancy her, begging your pardon.' And she giggled.

'Well,' said Jana with a smile, 'there will be none of that tonight. We are all tired, and we have a long day ahead. We have to find a car, get the paperwork sorted out, and everything. If we can do it in a day, I think we won't go very far inland: we'll find a nice little hotel somewhere near the border, on the Greek side. Then, on the morrow, the start of our lovely long drive the length of eastern Europe, all castles and forests and wolves and vampires . . .' She shivered with pleasure.

'As you please, Mistress,' said Cassie, getting out of the bath. She dried and robed herself while Jana remained seated, her elbows on her knees and her chin on her fisted hands.

'She said she was going north,' said Jana.

'I know,' said Cassie. 'Oops!' Her hand covered her mouth in mock fright. Jana smiled, as she knew perfectly well Cassie had been eavesdropping.

'Perhaps we should offer her a lift,' Jana continued,

rising from the commode. Cassie handed her the pink paper and she wiped herself, then rearranged her robe and allowed Cassie to flush the commode. They returned to the stateroom, and Cassie was ordered to serve a last drink, with one for herself. Jana felt gay, happy to be starting another journey, and proposed a toast.

'To Bulgaria,' she said, raising her glass.

'To Bulgaria,' echoed Cassie. They drank, but Mokka did not, and Cassie raised an eyebrow.

'Oh, come on, Mokka,' said Jana. 'To the Castle, then.'

This time Mokka drank, but there was a stony expression in her eyes. When she had drained her glass, she rose, without a word, and doffed her robe, which she folded neatly and placed on her chair. Then, naked, she drew back the coverlet of the bed and climbed in, placing herself dead in the centre, and lay on her back staring at the ceiling. She did not pull the coverlet over herself; Cassie made no attempt to conceal her appreciation of the woman's proud body. Jana was puzzled, and hurried them into bed, where they seemed to have no choice but to lie down one on either side of Mokka. It did not occur to Jana to ask Mokka to move: their positions had, it seemed, been preordained. She dimmed the lamps, and it was only then, in the half-light, that she noticed Mokka's cheeks were glistening with tears.

Suddenly Jana did not feel tired. She lay on her back beside Mokka, breathing in her musky scent, and wondered if she should offer sympathy for whatever sadness had assailed her guest. She knew that Cassie, too, was lying awake, their bed bathed in the moonlight which streamed in through the porthole, each woman alone with her thoughts. Suddenly, Jana felt a gentle hand fasten on to her fount. It was Mokka's hand, and she began to stroke Jana's quim, softly, as one might stroke a kitten. Jana's own hand touched Mokka's fount, but was firmly brushed away.

'No,' whispered Mokka. There was silence for a while, as Jana allowed herself to be lulled by the stroking of her cunt, and then Mokka spoke.

'The orgasm,' said Mokka. 'The French call it "the little death". It is not pleasure nor joy, it is the sublime pain and beauty of life itself. And like life, it passes so soon. Always we seek it, always we hope ... I shall tell you my story, now.'

And with her palm rhythmically stroking Jana's quim and, Jana was sure, the other caressing Cassie's, she began her tale.

'Al-Mukha, the fabled city of Arabia. Nowadays, all people know is coffee, but once, in my great-grandfather's time, and long before that ... Mokka, for so I shall call her, was a jewel of cities, the main port of Yemen. It is from Mokka that the coffee came! And myrrh, frankincense, all the spices of *Arabia Felix*.

'My family was always there, from the old days, the good days, when Sheikh Shadhili brought coffee to Arabia. That would have been in the fourteenth century of your reckoning. In Yemen, they chew the leaves of qat and drink the coffee. The one makes you an animal, the other a god. We were merchants of coffee, perfumes and spices; my forefathers had ships going to India and camel trains going north to Antioch, Tyre and Aleppo. We lived in palaces, and my forefathers had many wives due to their wealth, as well as innumerable concubines in their harems. My forefathers knew the secrets of the herbs and flowers, the secrets of the sea and the earth. Wondrous were their perfumes and oils, their unguents and lotions which they sold to every corner of the world. In those times Mokka was the jewel of the Ottoman Empire, under the rule of Istanbul. But then, in your seventeenth century, Mokka fell to the Arabs. My family were obliged to flee, penniless and disgraced and ... God, I know it as though I had been there myself. The secrets of the herbs and flowers were lost as my family was scattered, and only a dim recollection of those secrets remains. My grandmother told me the stories. But I could never go back.'

As she spoke, her frottage of Jana's quim grew more intense, and Jana knew from Cassie's shifting in the bed that she was, indeed, experiencing the same fevered caress.

'I don't understand,' Jana interrupted. 'You say the Arabs. Surely . . .'

'I am a Turk,' said Mokka, simply, 'not an Arab. Although my grandmother used to say that there was some Arab blood, that we were descended from the great Sheikh Shadhili himself. So many centuries amongst the Arabs, and so many concubines – it would be odd if there were no Arab blood at all. Yet I am Turkish.'

'So you live in Turkey,' Jana ventured.

'No,' said Mokka. She laughed bitterly. 'Turkey is a state of mind. Turkey is an empire that is no longer an empire. The Ottomans were kindly to their subjects; vassals and *vavassours* lived in harmony. The Arabs, sons of the desert, were cruelty itself. The story is that when our palace was sacked, my forefather the patriarch was obliged to watch as each of his wives, and every woman in his *harem*, numbering over seventy, according to my grandmother, was whipped naked. They were first ordered to array themselves in their finest jewels and robes, as they were to be sold at auction. Strange as it may seem, this caused them no little excitement. Does not almost every woman secretly dream of being paraded like an animal and sold into the slavery of a ruthless Master? But it was a trick. When they appeared in their robes, they were stripped and their jewels taken from them. They were indeed to be sold into slavery, but not bejewelled and robed: rather, dirty and naked in the marketplace.

'They took seven times seven strokes each from the *azakha*, which is a fearsome, three-thonged whip originating from Damascus. Then it was my forefather's turn: he was fixed naked to a gallows and flogged every day of the full moon, while his captors laughed, because they forced his wives to perform the flogging, under threat of further punishment for themselves if their lashes were not harsh enough. At last, at the brink of madness, he was sent away, accompanied only by two of his wives: the others, and all the concubines, were taken to dirty Zanzibar and sold into slavery. From then, my family wandered the length of the empire, trading always and using the remnants of their knowledge in the preparation of perfumes and spices.

72

'Cairo, Belgrade, Salonica, Sofia . . . there was nowhere in the empire that my forefathers did not stay, before moving on. Exile enters the blood: a displaced man cannot settle, for he is always seeking an illusory goal, which is to recreate the past. We never ventured into the heartland of Turkey, for to be an exile is shameful. We stayed on the fringes of the empire, for after all that is what we were accustomed to. Dear Mistress, they say that once one is an exile, one is always an exile, and it is true. We did return to Mokka, though, for the Turks regained the city in the middle of the last century, and held it until the end of the Great War. But it was not the same. My family held only a few scraps of their once-powerful knowledge of spices and potions, and the coffee trade had long since withered, when the English and Dutch factors moved away. And there was coffee, now, coming from Portuguese Brazil and Dutch Java.

'My great-grandfather fought in the Great War, as Turkey was on the German side, and when Mokka was once again lost after the Armistice Treaty, he had no home. The wandering recommenced: my grandfather was born in Sofia, in Bulgaria, and when the Second War commenced, Turkey was neutral, but Bulgaria was on the German side, so he also bore arms for the Germans. Always he dreamed of restoring our fortunes, as holders of the secrets of the herbs. My father, too, dreamed of this, but simply to survive under the Bulgarian communists was hard enough, especially for a Turk. It would have been impossible for him to leave the country for Turkey, even had he wished to. It is different now, but in those days . . .

'I am called Mokka because every eldest daughter in our family has been called Mokka, as a kind of magic. We have always thought of Mokka as a woman, as the mother we have sought down through the long centuries of exile. But I have never been there, to Yemen. I could not bear it. The Castle is my mother. Sometimes I rebel against her, but I always return, as one must return to one's mother, and accept my cleansing. Ever since my grandmother told me the story of my distant forefather, I – I have worshipped

73

his memory. I have wanted to be worthy of him. How I dream of the perfumes and beauty and sadness of the past! But dreams are dangerous. There is guilt in me, as though my spirit, unbodied and waiting to be born, did not do anything to save him from his torture, to save the fortunes of our house. Thus it is that I must be cleansed. I must endure as he endured, constantly, and without end.'

By now, Jana's fount was soaking under the relentless pressure of Mokka's probing fingers. She longed to return the caress but was afraid her approach would be again rejected. So she added her own fingers to Mokka's and began to rub her own nympha, longing to swoon into an orgasm that would wipe away the perturbation which the woman's strange story had produced in her.

'Mokka,' she said, her voice trembling, 'you will come with us in the morning. We will take you to your Castle, I promise, whichever country she lies in.'

Mokka laughed hollowly.

'I think not,' she said. 'My, you are very wet in your cunt, Mistress. You are quite insatiable, are you not? And your slave Cassie, also.'

'Oh, Mokka,' gasped Jana. 'You have such a magic touch.'

It was then that Cassie spoke.

'Please, sweet Mokka,' she said, 'do it harder. Bring me to a climax. I'm so, so wet.'

To Jana's surprise, Mokka leaned over and whispered something in Cassie's ear. Cassie made an 'Mmm' of agreement and, to Jana's disappointed surprise, Mokka's fingers were abruptly removed from her quim. She heard Cassie slide from the bed, only to return a moment later. She did not re-enter the bed, but stood beside it, and then Mokka joined her, leaving Jana alone. Jana was about to ask what was going on when suddenly she felt her wrists and ankles being tightly pinioned.

'What . . . ?'

'Slave Cassie and I have both been beaten, Mistress,' said Mokka, evenly. 'But not you. We must right things to maintain a cleansing balance.'

'Damien beat me!' Jana protested. 'You watched, Mokka, and masturbated at the sight!'

'With the flat of his sword,' Mokka retorted scornfully. 'You must be beaten properly, Mistress. You shall not know what it is like to be whipped with the *azakha*, but we may come close.'

Jana was powerless to prevent her assailants from turning her on to her back. She felt her legs being spread wide and strong cords binding her ankles and wrists to the sides of the bed. She twisted her neck to look up in the moonlight, and saw Mokka and Cassie standing one on either side of the bed. Each woman held not just one, but three canes from the rack Netta had thoughtfully provided. The canes were bundled together.

'No . . .' she murmured. 'Please . . .' But she knew that her gushing fount belied her words. She wanted the punishment, longed for Mokka to beat her. Mokka gently stroked her naked fesses.

'I myself have been cleansed countless times with the *azakha*,' she said, softly. 'It hurts more than a woman can imagine. It is pure.'

'Cleanse me, Mokka,' said Jana in a small voice. 'Yes, I beg you. I long for it. Seven times seven. Oh, please. But please give me my leather belt to bite on, so that I do not disgrace Maldona by crying out.'

As she spoke, the oils which washed her cunt became a flood. Her heart raced and her breath was deep and full of yearning in the giddiness of her excitement.

The first cut brought a muffled scream in her throat, so harsh was the lash of three canes together. It was all she could do to keep the belt between her teeth and, fighting back tears of pain, she bit fiercely into the leather. Cassie and Mokka took it in turns to beat her, so that each stroke followed hard and fast upon the last. Tears streamed down Jana's cheeks: she was inured to chastisement, but nothing like this. She thought that, like a good martinet or whipping-slave, she would accustom herself to the pain, but each succeeding stroke seemed harsher. She resolved not to cry out, and she did not, but she was unable to stop herself from jerking convulsively in her bonds, nor from squirming frantically like a tortured marionette as each lash made her naked buttocks smart – no, more than smart! Jana did not think that any language could contain the words to describe precisely what she felt. It was as though molten metal seared her at each stroke of those triple canes. And yet ... through her sobs, she knew that she wanted it. She wanted Mokka to make her shudder with the cruel ecstasy of her pain. She wanted to be cleansed.

At last the beating was over, and Mokka gently removed the bit from between Jana's teeth, then bent down to kiss her seared buttocks with cool lips. She showed Jana her belt: Jana had bitten halfway through the leather. Mokka loosened and removed her bonds, then lay down beside her and kissed her on the lips. Cassie, too, lay down, and now Jana found herself in the centre of the trio. Cradling her in strong arms, Mokka lifted her and turned her to lie on her back. Jana's sobs subsided, and she was left with a wonderful warm glow where the canes had whipped her. The pain was still there, an intense, eye-watering smarting, but beneath the pain was warmth and pride that she had taken her lacing without a murmur. The night seemed to hold the possibility of boundless magic. She knew Cassie felt that too.

No words were spoken. No words needed to be spoken. Mokka lay down with the full weight of her naked body on Jana's, and kissed her long and hard on the lips. Their hands and feet touched, but did not move. All was still. Jana felt the warmth of Mokka's lips and the pressure of the stiff nipples against hers, and sensed the power of the thighs that straddled her. Mokka's lush mink was firm against Jana's shaven fount, and she felt the prickle of the full bush of cunt-hair caressing her own bare skin. Jana's fount moistened and began to flow with juices. She wanted to cry with happiness, helplessly pinioned under the loving weight of her new slave: a slave whom she feared was becoming her Mistress. Yet Jana's heart yearned for Mokka to be her Mistress, longed to worship her. As if sensing this, Mokka quickly rose and squatted on the pillow with Jana's head between her spread thighs. She lowered herself until the lips of her quim were directly on Jana's mouth, and then let her weight sink on to Jana's face. She sat down firm and hard: Jana, ecstatic to be granted her desired act of worship, began to kiss Mokka's wet cunt-petals.

Then she felt Cassie's tongue worshipping her own fount, the agile organ licking and teasing until her nympha stiffened. Tingling pleasure lanced her belly, and she knew that she would not be long in coming. She sensed, too, that the action of her tongue on Mokka's clit would soon bring the Turkish woman to a climax. Then she felt Mokka gesture to Cassie, with the instruction that she should continue to gamahuche her Mistress, but should, at the same time, swivel round on the bed, belly downwards, and, keeping her lips on Jana's cunt, lock her thighs around Mokka's neck so she could gamahuche Cassie in turn.

Jana felt the bed shift as Cassie took up this position, and her excitement caused her licking and kissing of Mokka's fount to become quite frantic. Bathed in the smoky scent of the Turkish woman, and with her fragrant juices flowing into her mouth, Jana felt herself reaching her plateau. Cassie's tongue, too, had become deliciously vigorous on Jana's own clit, and Jana felt her cunt exude a torrent of love-juice which was eagerly lapped up by her willing slave. The three women, in total silence, formed the perfect triangle, a trinity of love. Jana saw their three worshipping bodies as a symbol of ultimate harmony, each woman adoring the sacred fount, and being adored in her turn. As their juices flowed so sweetly, nourishing and quenching, the three females began to moan, their breath coming faster and faster and their moans turning to high-pitched shrieks of joy as they climaxed together in perfect rhythm and with perfect abandon. Jana felt electricity coursing along her spine, from the cleft of her buttocks to her neck, making her tingle and shudder as the warmth seared her belly and her spasm filled her utterly. At last, she sighed a long 'Ahhh . . .', as she felt her body and spirit glow.

Slowly, the triangle of bodies sank down on to the soft bed and they lay down, tightly pressed together, with hands stroking hair, breasts, cunts and bellies, lips wetly kissing, and eyes shining with joy. Mokka broke the silence.

'A mere man cannot satisfy me,' she murmured. 'Woman is sacred. Woman is love itself, and power. Woman is life, the male a mere bringer of seed. But sometimes he is necessary, for the penis is a sacred flower, its honey to be tasted with pleasure. Unfortunately, when I do desire a male, no man is ever big enough, not even Damien! Except . . .'

'Except?' pressed Jana.

'Except for the Master, and he spurns me. I am not yet worthy of him. I am not yet cleansed. But one day . . .'

Her tone indicated that no further questions would be welcomed and, anyway, Jana felt herself deliciously tired, as though floating on a warm cushion of happiness. Arms entwined, the three women fell into a deep sleep. Jana's slumber was dreamless, and she awoke only at Caspar's discreet knock on the door.

'Mistress,' he said softly, 'we are in the port of Kavala, and the sun is high. Breakfast is served when you wish.'

Jana rubbed her eyes and thanked him, saying that they would join him in a moment.

'Come on, slaves,' she said drowsily. 'Today is travelling day. We have much to do.'

Cassie yawned and stretched.

'Rise and shine, Mokka,' said Jana, feeling beside her under the bedclothes. 'It's time to go. Mokka? Mokka?'

But Mokka was gone.

6

Bulgaria

'Well,' said Caspar, as his spoon tinkled in his coffee cup, 'easy come, easy go.'

'You do not seem perturbed,' said Jana crossly.

'I'm not,' said Caspar. 'She was only a stowaway, after all. A lovely croup and a succulent mouth, but there are other females in this world, and less dishevelled. You seem rather taken with her, Mistress.' Caspar's lip curled slyly, and his tone was mocking.

'No ... it's just that – well, yes, I thought her interesting.'

'Ah, a woman of mystery,' said Caspar, lighting a Balkan Sobranie after Jana's nod of permission. 'I dare say you will find plenty of mystery in Bulgaria and all those other dank places you long to visit.' He shivered slightly. 'Myself, I prefer the brightness and warmth of the Mediterranean, the well-muscled satyr and the comely nymph; not barbarians in coarse trousers.'

Jana laughed.

'This is the twentieth century, Caspar,' she said with a smile. 'Everybody wears trousers.'

'And more's the pity,' replied Caspar with a little moue, smoothing his maroon silk tunic. 'On both counts. Anyway, no doubt our stowaway has her own agenda, from whomsoever or whatsoever she is running. You have enough to do in organising your own trip.'

'There is no organising left to do,' retorted Jana. 'We are packed and ready to go.' She looked down at the thronged quayside of Kavala. 'Money, passports, and two small

79

cases each, the rest of our things to stay on board with you. We are travelling light. As they say, if you can't carry it, bury it. All we need to do is buy a car.'

Jana wiped her lips and pushed away her breakfast plate, then lit her own cigarette. The servants speedily cleared the table as she smoked nervously, her heart beating in anticipation and in longing to be on the road. Caspar noticed this, and said that if she and Cassie were ready, it was time to go.

'No long goodbyes,' he said amiably. 'And in any case, it is not goodbye, but farewell. I shall remain in port until nightfall, by which time I shall assume you are equipped and safely on your way. We shall meet again soon in London.'

'No long goodbyes,' agreed Jana.

'But, Mistress, I am curious as to where you are headed,' added Caspar. 'If you have definite plans, that is.'

Jana smiled.

'I thought of staying in southern Bulgaria, going through Kardzali, then Plovdiv and west to the Rhodope. They are supposed to be the wildest and lushest mountains in the Balkans. And as a little diversion, there is the Lamartine Museum in Plovdiv.'

'Ah, yes, dear old Lamartine,' said Caspar. ' "*Un seul être vous manque, et tout est dépeuplé.*" – Just one soul is missing, and all is emptiness. He was a soppy old boy. In fact the line is rather relevant to the story of Rhodope.'

'I know,' said Jana. 'The warrior Haemus and the beautiful Rhodope were lovers, and dared to flaunt themselves as Zeus and Hera. And when the immortal gods found out, they punished the lovers for their impudence by transforming them into two mountains, doomed to be eternally separated.'

She grinned, feeling a little soppy herself.

'Hera is the name of my darling Housemistress, who inducted me into the Auberge d'Angleterre when I was a fresh virgin of Maldona. I love her dearly – she gave me the sweetest Virgin's Beating. Perhaps I wish to pay her a sort of homage.'

80

'There is more in Rhodope,' said Caspar thoughtfully. 'The Mountain of the beautiful Thracian, Orpheus, whose grief on returning from the Underworld without his beloved Eurydice so annoyed the lustful women of Thrace that they tore him to pieces during a Bacchanal orgy. The bits of his body were buried by Mount Olympus, but his head was thrown into the river and floated off into the Aegean: he ended up buried on Lesbos, that island of joyful name! Then the Turks were there for a long time, and many of the Rhodopeians still adhere to Islam, with total submission of the female. There are German settlements, dating back to the Crusades, villages undisturbed by the centuries. Our friends the Templars, too, tarried on their wanderings, and their curious Cathar faith has left its traces. Our delightful word "bugger" derives, most unfairly I'm sure, from "Bulgar", as you know.'

'I do, indeed,' grinned Jana mischievously. 'I think myself less easily shocked than soppy Lamartine.'

'I have no doubt, Mistress,' said Caspar, his face turning sombre. 'But be careful. There are strange corners of old Europe, strange half-forgotten things; stranger things that are struggling to be born. I entreat you, my adored Mistress, to be careful of your most precious being.'

'I shall,' said Jana gaily, and motioning Cassie to rise and attend her. 'Who knows, I might meet my warrior Haemus.'

'You might indeed,' said Caspar, kneeling to kiss his Mistress's feet and hands in farewell. He grinned impishly, now.

'You never know with these Bulgarians,' he said.

Buying a vehicle in Kavala proved surprisingly easy, and Jana was almost disappointed. She had expected a web of oriental intrigue, bribes, false papers, and surreptitious assignations, but the transaction proved almost as simple as buying a new dress in Harrods, or a new whip in Soho. The taxi of a certain Mr Dimitropoulos, who assured them that there was sadly no Mercedes dealer in Kavala, whisked them from the teeming dockside to the 'best car dealer in town', which was a gleaming showroom on the outskirts of the city proudly announcing itself as 'Automobiles de Luxe Dimitropoulos.'

After much male bonding, handshaking and backslapping between Mr Dimitropoulos the taxi-driver and Mr Dimitropoulos the car dealer, they were consigned to the good offices of Dimitropoulos mark two. Jana was pleased enough: the showroom was packed with shiny new vehicles, and she was well prepared to believe the claims of the Dimitropoulos clan. Mr Dimitropoulos the car dealer did not speak much English, but he was able to converse in halting French. His English consisted mainly of the words 'very very good' – not to Jana's surprise, every car in the showroom was very very good – and his French of not much more than '*très très bon*'. This became '*très très très bon*' when he discovered that his customer possessed a distinguished array of credit cards named after precious metals, and wished to pay for her vehicle all at once. Money, Jana was reminded, talks.

A chauffeured car was provided and, after whirlwind visits to the Dimitropoulos Insurance Company and the police station, where a kindly Lieutenant Dimitropoulos provided them with every conceivable document in Greek, English, French, German and Russian, Jana found herself the owner of a luxurious flame-red Japanese four-wheel drive land cruiser. Mr Dimitropoulos the automobile dealer assured her it would be ideal for the rugged terrain of the Rhodope, and Jana had no reason to disagree. Pleased with her purchase, she gunned the cruiser on the Xanthi road out of Kavala, where they passed a huge Mercedes dealership, and a road sign which pointed the way to Route 12 and the town of Drama.

'That would be nice,' said Cassie, wistfully. 'Route 12 to Drama – it sounds like the title of a movie.'

'Well, we're going to Xanthi,' said Jana, firmly. 'Cheer up, I am sure we shall enjoy plenty of drama, if events so far are any indication.'

'You mean Mokka?' said Cassie.

'Yes ... I have this strange feeling that we shall cross paths again.'

Cassie put her hand on Jana's bare knee, and stroked her there, then let her hand pass between her thighs for a cheeky caress of the bare cunt.

'You mean you want it to happen, Mistress,' she murmured.

'Well,' replied Jana hesitantly, 'I hadn't really thought. A stowaway, after all . . .'

Cassie tossed her lustrous mane and laughed.

'Don't dissemble, Mistress,' she said. 'You are wet just thinking of her, aren't you? Unless it is the excitement of a new car. Mmm! I'm excited myself! There is something so erotic about the fresh perfume of a new car.'

Jana grinned.

'A bit of both, perhaps,' she admitted.

They were approaching a bridge over a wide, briskly flowing river.

'Look!' cried Jana, glad to change the subject. 'There is the Nestus! I'm sure that is the river where the orgiast women threw the hacked-up pieces of Thracian Orpheus.'

Cassie made a face.

'It doesn't look very clean,' she said. And indeed, the water was a sludgy effluent-grey.

'It will be cleaner when we see it again,' said Jana. 'In Bulgaria it is the Mesta, and it rises in the mountains of the Rhodope, where I am sure the hacking took place. Bulgaria is Thrace, you know. There, the water shall be crystal clear, and we may bathe in it, naked as the lilies, and giggling like two schoolgirls.'

Jana spoke this last phrase with a sigh, for Cassie's fingers were still tantalising the petals of her bare quim.

'Let us call it Thrace, then, Mistress,' said Cassie. 'You certainly seem to have a thing about it. I wonder why.'

'We'll never get there if you keep on doing that,' said Jana, sighing again. 'I'll have to stop.'

Cassie removed her hand from Jana's wet cunt, causing her Mistress a pang of disappointment, and primly folded her arms.

'That would never do, Mistress,' she said. 'I was hoping we could cross the border before nightfall. I'm a bit tired

83

of Greece; it's not the same as it was. Why, I didn't have my bum pinched once in Kavala!'

Jana laughed.

'People are always a bit dour in the north of any country,' she said. 'It is funny: the northern French are dour, but they are on the same latitude as the jolly Bavarians; the north of Italy is sober, Provence is gay.'

'You are from north England, and that is why you are such a stern Mistress, I suppose,' said Cassie, half-mockingly.

'That is the truth, slave,' said Jana, her tone perfectly serious. 'We shall stop for luncheon, but I agree that we should cross the border before nightfall.' She glanced at Cassie with a grin. 'Only then may you continue your sweet tickling: I think I should anoint my fragrant new chariot with my love-oil only when we have penetrated Thrace.'

They stopped in Xanthi and ate luncheon in a taverna. Cassie washed the meal down with retsina, which she pronounced foul, while Jana, being the driver, had fizzy mineral water. It was a glum restaurant in a glum town: already they seemed far from the sun of the bright South. Cassie opined that she would not be sorry to have a rest from the eternal taramasalata and feta salads and dolmades.

'What do they eat in Bulgaria?' she mused.

'A lot of yoghurt, I imagine,' said Jana. 'Probably a lot of roast suckling pig, apart from the Muslims of course.'

'I hope so,' said Cassie enthusiastically. 'I *adore* roast suckling pig.' Her grin, as ever, was a little more than gastronomic.

Jana judged their meal not bad, but not good either, and they did not linger in Xanthi. The road took them down and along the coast towards where the River Kourou met the sea, and there, in the village of Portolago, they paused for an *al fresco* coffee and admired the wide mouth of the Kourou from their table.

'Portolago doesn't sound much like a Greek name,' said Cassie.

'It's Italian,' replied Jana. 'Founded by the Venetians, no doubt. They were everywhere, in their great trading days. The thing about the Balkans, Cassie my slave, is that everybody was everywhere.'

'Mmm,' said Cassie. 'That sounds rather naughty and delicious. Maybe that is the river into which Orpheus's head was thrown,' she added eagerly, craning to look, as though she might see it floating there.

'I have a feeling you are going to say that every time we cross a Thracian river,' sighed Jana.

'I have that feeling too,' answered Cassie happily.

'Well,' said Jana, rising, 'that is our last stop in Greece, and I don't think we shall be seeing her again for a little while.'

'Until, Mistress, you decide to revisit the Island of Maldona,' murmured Cassie.

'Until then,' said Jana with a smile.

The road sloped gently up again, taking them inland to Komotini, whose nameplate grandly informed them that they were at 50 metres above sea level. The drabness of the town was in contrast to the restrained splendour of the mountain range within whose foothills it nestled. Jana said she thought this was the Tokatzik range, or perhaps the Memkova, or, at any rate, somewhere between the two.

'And the Rhodope is over there to the left,' she added, 'I mean the west. The mountains are higher there.'

At the edge of the town, a roadsign read with grudging simplicity, 'Bulgaria', giving them no indication of how far they had to drive before they reached the border. The road wound precipitously upwards, past valleys bright with flowers, fruit and tobacco, and presently a sign announced that they were at an altitude of 1300 metres. It was cold, the chill seeming to be increased by the gloomy grey massif before them, and Jana switched the car's heater on. There was no sign of habitation in this bleak place, until they rounded a sharp bend and saw a cluster of shabby customs huts with the Greek flag flying limply above them. Beyond was the maw of a dark tunnel.

The Greek customs presented few formalities, although the attitudes of the suitably stubbled officers varied between amity for fellow Europeans and concerned suspicion that they should want to venture 'over there'. The Greeks evidently did not consider Bulgaria to be part of Europe at all, and there was much pursing of lips accompanied by sighs of foreboding. Jana was assured that Bulgarian men all married their sisters, that half of them had tails, and the other half only one eye, in the middle of their forehead. This led, with impeccable Greek logic, to fervent advice that they should change their money on the Greek side and, more specifically, with them. However Jana opined that, currency restrictions or not, this would be less than wise.

'I have plenty of American dollars,' she said, 'and Deutschmarks too.'

As they drove into the border tunnel, Jana observed that her statement had magically affected the Greeks. Their eyes had rolled with impossible yearning.

'Mention a dollar and they almost drool! You would think I had bared my breasts to them,' she said.

'Your bum, more likely, Mistress,' said Cassie drily.

Jana laughed, and watched the disc of light at the tunnel's mouth grow larger and larger until they emerged in Bulgaria. They knew for a fact that it was Bulgaria, as a large new sign proudly told them so in five languages, along with the names and distances of, it seemed, almost every town in the country. The five languages did not include Greek.

Their way was barred by the traditional red and white pole stretched across the narrow road. Jana pulled to a halt, and sat demurely as a duo of Bulgarian officers strolled towards them, trying to conceal their excitement behind masks of nonchalance. They were tall and dark, their scruffy uniforms adorned with rather a lot of braid, and their chins testified to the traditional Balkan disdain for the razor blade. Both stroked their luxuriant moustaches, and Cassie made a shivering noise.

'Mmm,' she said. 'All alone, two females in the middle

86

of the Balkan mountains, with two uniformed thugs for company. Anything could happen to us, Mistress. We could be raped.'

'Is that apprehension or wishful thinking?' retorted Jana. 'Why, I'm sure they are not thugs. English,' she added in a loud voice, winding down the car window. '*Anglaise. Englisch.*'

The car doors were opened, and the officers straightened their ties before beginning to paw the leather seats, the shiny dashboard, the steering wheel, the gear-shift, and everything except the persons of Jana and Cassie. The idea crossed Jana's mind that this might not be long in coming, especially when the handsomer of the two let his fingers brush the hem of her black knee-length skirt. It was as though they had never seen a car, or indeed a woman, before.

The handsome one smiled.

'*Les passeports, mesdemoiselles*,' he said in a thick accent. '*La raison de votre visite?*'

'The aim of our visit is tourism,' answered Jana sweetly, as she handed him the passports. 'We have heard so much about the beauties of your country. The landscape of the Rhodope, the museums, the culture and antiquities . . .'

The handsome one beamed. His fractured French, still the Balkan *lingua franca*, evidently qualified him as a scholar.

'Ah, our museums,' he said. 'We have several, indeed many. Do not miss the Lamartine Museum in Plovdiv.'

'Oh, we shan't,' said Jana, beaming back.

'There is the Great Mosque in Sofia, now the Archaeological Museum. It has many old things.'

'I love old things,' said Jana.

'How I long to be back in Sofia! It is very lonely here. The Museum of Bulgarian Humour in Jambol must be visited. It is very *comique*.'

'I adore Bulgarian humour,' said Jana. 'Jambol shall be at the top of our agenda, after the Rhodope.'

'And you must not forget the very pearl of museums, which is the Museum of Female Costume, next to the

Church of St Nicholas, the miracle-worker, in Varna on the Black Sea. So many things! Gowns and frocks and skirts, corsets, silk stockings and petticoats, the most intimate panties and underthings . . .'

He stopped, blushing slightly, and cleared his throat.

'How did you like Greece?' he continued, still stroking her skirt, as though absent-mindedly. Jana saw a faraway glint in his eye, but knew it was not the glint of lust.

'Far less beautiful than Bulgaria,' replied Jana.

'In Greece, they lack the sense of humour,' said Handsome with distaste. 'They are primitive. In the mountains, there are men with tails. It is true! They marry their sisters! And their soldiers wear skirts!'

'I do not doubt it.'

The other officer grunted something in Bulgarian.

'He says we must inspect your luggage. A thousand pardons, dear mademoiselle, but it is necessary.'

'Of course,' said Jana, and got down from her driver's seat. Cassie did the same. Jana opened the back of the car, and unzipped their four small suitcases, favouring their hosts with a winning smile. The expression on each man's face was beauty itself, as they gaped at the array of clothes and toys with which the women had equipped themselves. They were almost too nervous to touch, and too embarrassed to admit their surprise. Instead, they devoted themselves to a close inspection of the silks, leathers, and satins, breathing with profound longing and pleasure.

The handsome one patted a whip handle and grinned slyly, his other hand caressing one of Jana's red suspender belts.

'Such lovely things you have in England,' he said. 'You are very sophisticated ladies. I should love to buy my fiancée such things, but a customs officer is not well paid here in Bulgaria. You are going to the Rhodope, famous for its spas and mineral waters – primitive, I regret. The Muslim pomaks live there, wearing the baggy Turkish pantaloons, and the Germans, too. It is said that deep in the mountains of the Rhodope there is another museum, for the very discerning visitor, which the Ministry of Tourism does not mention. It is a museum of suffering. We

Bulgarians are famous for our suffering at the hands of so many invaders.'

'Are we free to go?' said Jana abruptly.

'Yes . . . yes, it is in order,' he said with a sad smile, handing back the passports. 'I am trying to remember the name of this very special museum. My fiancée told me. She is fond of Bulgarian suffering.' He looked at her with a puppyish pleading in his eyes, and Jana felt her heart warm.

'I think your fiancée would like this,' she said gravely, handing him a satin blouse. 'And this –' a lacy bra '– and this, too –' panties to match the bra.

'Oh,' moaned the officer, struggling to hide his delight. Jana closed the rear of the car, and the two women climbed back inside it. As she started the engine, Jana felt mischievous.

'Your fiancée is about your size, sir?' she murmured.

'Why, yes, almost exactly,' he blurted.

'In that case,' she said, 'she will just be able to squeeze into these . . .'

She unzipped her skirt and wriggled out of it; the handsome officer gaped at her naked, shaved pubis, framed by a shiny suspender belt and sheer stockings. She kicked off her shoes and unfastened her straps, then unrolled her stockings and gave them to him. These were followed by the suspender belt itself, on which she planted a little kiss before handing it over.

'Thank you, thank you,' he babbled. 'Such an honour! I mean, for my fiancée.'

'The museum?' said Jana pointedly.

'Yes, it is in a German village, now called Nistograd,' he said. 'The peasants there have many secrets, so you must be careful, mademoiselle.' His voice was suddenly low and earnest. 'It is known as The Museum of Correction.'

Jana gunned the engine, and the handsome officer, clutching his treasure, waved a fervent goodbye.

'Welcome to Bulgaria!' he cried, and the two women waved solemnly back, driving straight-faced for a good minute before bursting into simultaneous laughter.

'He did pretty well out of you, Mistress,' said Cassie.

'You mean his fiancée did,' Jana answered.

'What fiancée?'

'Well,' shrugged Jana, 'it gets lonely up here. I'm sure our friend Lamartine would have got a poem or two out of it. Anyway, it's quite nice driving barefoot, and with my legs and fount bare. I believe we can stop for the night in Kardzali, then head west tomorrow, to the Rhodope and, who knows, maybe Nistograd.'

'What about north to Plovdic, and the Lamartine Museum?' said Cassie with feigned innocence.

'When there is the Museum of Correction to be seen? Think of the postcards we can send, Cassie, my lovely tourist. Lamartine can wait,' said the Mistress of Maldona.

Both women were tired as, in the lengthening shadows of twilight, they drove the fifty or so kilometres down towards Kardzali. The road wound on through mountain passes, then, after a few kilometres, the countryside became rolling hills, and they passed lush fields of poppies, tobacco, and strawberries, curiously conical haystacks, and groves of sycamore, pear and apple trees. All stood abandoned and mysterious in the warm dusk, as though awaiting the new day's sunlight for their reawakening.

The town of Podkova sped past; their vehicle was the only disturbance of the tranquil white streets, save for the blue tobacco smoke of the watching menfolk, and the echo of children's footballs. Here, too, a mysterious presence seemed to fill the hazy twilight that was not yet night but no longer day: something not yet born, waiting to take its existence. The bright certainties of the day were gone, and a strange frisson of foreboding touched Jana's heart as she wondered what lay ahead.

Cassie saw Jana frown and, stroking her Mistress's bare fount, murmured gently that they had not yet baptised Jana's new vehicle with their kisses and the juices of their loving bodies. But Jana's fatigue made her smile and say such pleasures were best kept until the morrow. She ordered Cassie to fetch her new raiment, and stopped for

90

a moment to dress herself in a demure long cream-coloured skirt, matching blouse and panties, and sheer tights.

'Might as well begin to look for a hotel,' she said to Cassie with a yawn. 'I'm so tired.' Just then, a bright neon '*МОТЕЛ ВАР РЕСМОРАНМ*' loomed ahead.

That night, they slept chastely entwined, save for the hour before dawn, when Jana's naked body stirred and writhed, and she moaned, in an unconscious mimicry of love's ecstasy. Cassie stroked her Mistress's brow and soothed her back to an untroubled sleep. Jana's dream had come to her again.

7

Chestnut Blossom

Jana and Cassie slept late, and when they entered the motel's garish plastic restaurant for breakfast, it was emptying rapidly. The Germans, being German, believed in an early start, and Jana watched the shiny cars pull out of the lot with a great deal of noisy ceremony. It was as though the drivers – tourists? salesmen? – existed fully only when enclosed in their gleaming metal carapaces, the soft human flesh inside as vulnerable as a snail so easily prised from its shell. She shared this observation with Cassie, who replied sarcastically that men denied themselves the protective comfort of tights and stockings and nice underthings, so they wore cars instead!

Soon Jana and Cassie, too, were on the road and heading west, equipped with an assortment of fading road maps and guides from the motel shop, as well as a kaleidoscope of Bulgarian banknotes and a basket of picnic things. They did not stop in Kardzali, not even to admire the vast lakes which had been dammed by the communists for some obscure hydro-electric purpose. They drove slowly along the snaking, rutted road, through a landscape of towering crags and lush valleys, their lazy progress interrupted only rarely by a thundering truck belching the foul black exhaust smoke that gives the industrial towns of Eastern Europe their acrid perfume. Cassie busied herself with their maps and guide books. 'These are all very old,' she said. 'From the communist days. Look at this phrasebook. "Where is the nearest Party Headquarters?" Honestly!'

'There is a road going up to that mountain top,' said Jana suddenly. 'Let's go up there and have our picnic.' Abruptly, she turned off the main road and on to a rubbled track with no signpost.

'Can you find that on the map? I mean, does it go anywhere? I feel like a wander. The book says the Rhodope is only 300 kilometres long, so we can't really get lost.'

Cassie could not find the dirt road anywhere, and said that she thought the map was no good.

'The communist governments frequently printed their maps to be misleading,' said Jana with a grin, 'so as to confuse capitalist spies like us. I don't think they wanted tourists to visit hilltops, from where they could see too much.'

'The famous hydro-electric dams!' said Cassie. Then, in non sequitur: 'I'm hungry.'

Jana realised she was hungry, too. Even with power steering, driving here was tiring work, and she was thankful when the tortuous dirt road levelled out, and they came to a wilderness patchwork of meadows and coppices.

'Oh! Let's stop here!' begged Cassie, and Jana needed no pleading. They were beside a field of crimson flowers, in the centre of which stood a glade of white-blossomed trees. She stopped, and they unpacked their makeshift luncheon: ham, cheese, tomatoes, bread and honey and wine, with gaseous mineral water. The place was entirely deserted, save for the gaudy butterflies fluttering around them as they approached the sun-dappled grove. Jana sighed with pleasure as she felt the petals of the flowers caressing her bare ankles, and the sun her body. The flowers had a cloying, sweet scent, and she thought, uncontrollably, of Mokka, and wished the strange, tall woman were here with her, leading her into the shadow of the flowering trees. The perfume of their blossom became pungent as Jana neared; she recognised them as chestnuts.

'Well,' she said, 'we were promised chestnut trees in bloom, and here they are.' A crystal stream flowed through the heart of the chestnut grove, which had yielded the banks to a parade of weeping willows. Jana saw swirls of bright fish in the clear water, darting amongst lily-pads.

'Now I think we are well in the Rhodope,' she pronounced. 'Our journey is happily a matter of hundreds rather than thousands of kilometres, although this winding sort of terrain makes it seem longer.'

The sun was high, and both women were sweating even in their light skirts and blouses.

'I wish we didn't have to wear bras and underthings *all* the time, Mistress,' complained Cassie. 'It is so hot.'

'Modesty,' said Jana severely. 'A slave of Maldona must be demure at all times, especially amongst strangers. When appropriate,' she added with a sly grin.

Cassie returned her grin, and said that they were not amongst strangers, since there was no one else around, and therefore no modesty was going to stop her from bathing in the stream. With that, she stripped and plunged naked into the water, which came up to cover her fount. She splashed her breasts and face and shrieked with delight.

'Oh! It's so lovely and cold! Come in, *Mistress*, if you dare! Be immodest like me!'

'You are cheeky too, you sweet slut,' said Jana, smiling. She needed no encouragement to join her slave in the water, and soon they were diving and playfully wrestling as the shoals of fish, having made sure that the naked bodies of the two women did not represent anything to eat, glided incuriously around these new fleshy obstacles. The two bodies were joined as one: wrestling and pummelling gave way to kisses and a tender embrace. Jana giggled, feeling the fish bump against her inner thighs as they swam between her legs.

'I'm so glad, Mistress,' gasped Cassie. 'Glad we came. This moment – the sun, the water, even these nosy little fish – it is so good to be alive, and to be yours.'

Jana felt her belly warming at the touch of her slave's bare, wet skin, but reluctantly she disengaged.

'Come on, Cassie,' she said. 'We are cleansed enough, now. Let's eat: there is still plenty of road to travel.'

Cassie made a moue, but climbed out of the water after her Mistress. As they let the sun dry them, she said: 'That's funny, Mistress. What you said just now.'

'What?' replied Jana with a frown.

'You said "cleansed". That is a word Mokka used a lot.'

'Is it? I wasn't aware.'

'You are still thinking of her, aren't you, Mistress?'

'That is my business. And what if I am?'

Cassie laughed, and kissed Jana on her lips, then touched her fount, as if to brush the droplets of water from the smooth hillock.

'You are all wet,' she said, 'and not just from the river. It is the soft oily wetness of love. For me, or for Mokka? Oh my.'

Cassie wiped the sweat from her brow.

'So hot,' she said faintly. Her breathing was heavy, as the now overpowering scent of chestnut blossoms seemed to fill her. Jana, too, felt giddy. The perfume was not sweet like that of the crimson flowers, but acrid and insistent, and yet the two smells seemed to complement each other. The women selected a tree and spread their picnic at its mossy trunk, after making sure the sward was clean. Then, without a word, both carefully folded their clothing into cushions, as though no lady would dream of an alfresco luncheon unless naked. Jana sat on her red blouse and white skirt, pleased at the harmony with the blossoms around her.

They ate hungrily, Jana permitting herself one glass of the harsh red wine, while Cassie had no need to be so sparing. Wine dribbled on to her bared breasts, mingling with tomato and bits of melting goat's cheese, and Jana said she looked like an artist's palette.

'I suppose we'll need another bathe,' she added.

'You may lick my palette clean, if you like, Mistress,' Cassie taunted.

Jana smiled and said nothing, but yawned. The food, the sun, and the single glass of wine, together with the intoxicating fumes of the chestnut blossom, had induced in her a pleasant feeling of drowsiness, which was warm and satisfying, as though she had just made love.

'Well then!' cried Cassie, pretending to be cross. 'I shall go and pick some flowers for my ungrateful Mistress!'

Jana watched Cassie's lithe brown body scamper into the field, and felt deliciously at peace. Her eyelids drooped, and, leaning against a treetrunk, she gave herself over to a gentle half-sleep. The pungent smell of the chestnut blossom seemed more insistent now, as though her senses had been sharpened by her swim, the food, and her glass of wine. She daydreamed, and in her daydream she saw Mokka as a tall chestnut tree, with branches for arms and with hair, breasts and a fount formed from bouquets of white scented blossom. She dreamed that her lips and nose were pressed to Mokka's quim, the scent of the white blossom intoxicating her.

In her drowsy state, she became aware that her own quim was moistening, and her nympha tingling and sending little warm waves of pleasure through her belly. She began softly to stroke her quim-petals, as she imagined the white blossom cascading from Mokka's proud body on to her own, the caress of each petal making her sigh. Her clit was stiffening as her sleepy excitement grew, and as her massage of the throbbing nympha grew bolder and more insistent. Her nipples, too, were hard, and with sleepy fingers she caressed her breasts, making little noises in her throat as though she were protesting against the onrush of her pleasure. In her daydream, the blossoms sprouting from Mokka's body assumed the shape of a great trembling shaft, which was then used to caress her cunt. Slowly and gently, the stem of white petals penetrated her, sliding softly into her wet opening and up to touch the neck of her womb. Jana was no longer at all sure if she was dreaming, her sensation was so intense.

She opened he eyes and was astonished to see, although her vision was slightly blurred, that her naked body was indeed covered in petals. These petals were crimson. Cassie knelt smiling before her with an armful of picked flowers and was daintily scattering them over her Mistress's skin.

Jana withdrew her hands from her cunt and nipples and rubbed her eyes. She gasped with delight, as she saw, more clearly now, that her body was a mass of red blossoms.

'How lovely!' she cried. 'My sweet, sweet slave!'

'Don't stop on my account, Mistress,' said Cassie impishly. 'It was so exciting to watch. I wonder what or who you were dreaming about. Perhaps my tongue will find out.'

Suddenly Cassie bent down, and Jana felt her wet, firm tongue press against her quim-lips. She moaned as Cassie began to lick her, slowly at first, then faster and harder as Jana's love-oil became a flow. She felt the tongue-tip flick expertly against her shivering stiff clit, sending spasms of pleasure through her belly and spine, and sometimes Cassie paused in her loving work to lick the petals from her Mistress's body. Jana stroked Cassie's hair, pressing the slave's head against her tingling hot skin. The scent of chestnut flowers filled her, the red and white colours of the flowers now joined in a counterpoint of two perfumes.

'Oh, Cassie, what you do to me,' she gasped.

'Let us say I am inaugurating your shiny new car, Mistress,' said Cassie, taking Jana's swollen labia fully between her teeth and biting down ever so gently. 'But your car is a thing of metal, and I kiss you with flowers.'

Jana felt faint with joy and desire, and knew that she would come soon to orgasm. She was at her plateau, the point of no return where the electricity coursing in her belly and spine would brook no stemming of its hot flow.

'Cassie, it's not fair,' she gasped. 'I want to – I must – kiss you, my darling. Wait –'

Jana shifted herself, and lay flat on her back, on the cool moss. She spread her thighs as wide as she could and raised her legs, forcing them up so that her ankles touched her earlobes. Cassie took her by the ankles and gently helped her to stretch further, until Jana's toes touched around the back of her neck.

'There,' she said, 'your Mistress is naked and helpless for you, sweet slave. Take me. My cunt is open, she is yours, if only you will let my lips caress your own fount.'

Cassie positioned herself above Jana, and lowered her full weight on to Jana's waiting lips. Cassie's naked belly squirmed against Jana's hard nipples and, as the two women licked each other's flowing cunts, Jana felt Cassie's deft fingers reach behind her croup to tickle her Mistress's toes! The excruciating pleasure was almost painful, and Jana knew she could hold back no longer.

'Oh, Cassie! Oh, Mokka . . .' she cried, delirious. She felt her quim gush with hot oil as she cried out in the ecstasy of her climax and, with her hips bucking under Cassie's probing lips and tongue, she felt Cassie shudder in her own spasm. Jana's body seemed to melt with pleasure. She shut her eyes, and it was as though the shaft of white blossoms had penetrated her core and was dissolving inside her cunt in a searing flood of joy. When she finally opened her eyes, she saw the crimson flowers all around her, shrouding her like a canopy. Presently, the two women moved and lay in each other's arms, not speaking, but planting soft little kisses on each other's eyes, lips and breasts. As they lay silently together, they heard a strange, distant rumbling noise, as though the Earth herself was applauding their love. If Cassie had noticed Jana's crying out of Mokka's name, she gave no sign. Finally she spoke.

'Mistress,' she whispered, 'it is the perfume of this place which has filled us with such love. These crimson flowers are amaranth, the flower of everlasting life.'

'Mmm,' murmured Jana, 'since you seem to know so much, what explains that gorgeous giddying scent from the chestnut blossom?'

'Didn't you know, Mistress?' said Cassie with gentle mockery. 'That scent was known to the Ancients as a most potent female aphrodisiac.' Jana pursed her lips.

'Wait a minute,' she said. 'No, surely not –'

'Exactly,' laughed Cassie, and, pausing between each word to kiss her Mistress's lips, whispered, 'the scent of the chestnut in bloom closely resembles that of a man's sperm.'

New fragrances filled the car as Jana drove slowly down towards the main road: the back seat brimmed with bouquets of chestnut and amaranth petals, their green leaves making a pleasing contrast to the red and white flowers.

'For good luck,' said Jana playfully. 'And very patriotic – white, green and red, the Bulgarian national flag.'

'Good luck in love,' said Cassie, taking a deep breath.

The sun was now obscured by a thin haze of cloud, although the heat was still intense. Jana said she hoped it would not rain, only to be informed by her slave that they were not rain clouds.

'Still,' Cassie added, 'not ideal weather for wandering, Mistress. Perhaps the Lamartine Museum in Plovdiv?'

'Don't tease,' replied Jana. There is that other museum – you want to see it as much as I do. So look to your road maps, girl.'

Jana rounded a tight corner and abruptly braked to a halt.

'Oh *no!*' she hissed.

The road was completely blocked. Precariously steep scree on either side of the track had slithered down like a small avalanche so that they were faced with a mountain of small grey rocks, as though the two banks had decided to destroy the usurping man-made track and merge into one. Ruefully, Jana remembered her delight at the rumbling sound she had heard in her dreamy post-orgasmic state. So this was Earth's reward! There was no possibility of passage; the only choice was to turn around and proceed up the track, hoping that on the other side of the mountain they could rejoin a proper road.

Glumly they retraced their course, passed their amaranth field once more, and prayed that the track would not peter out. It became more and more tortuous, and the going rougher, as they climbed. The air cooled, and the covering of cloud had now thickened to an ominous grey. Cassie scratched her head in frustration as she pored over the map.

'There *should* be another valley,' she said plaintively.

'We can't be far from the crest of this slope.'

But no crest appeared: instead, the scree banks grew steeper and more threatening, the ruts became chasms, and the vegetation was changing from lush flora to dark conifers and gnarled, scrubby bushes that crouched in sullen elvish masses. They were out of sight of the friendly lowlands they had abandoned, when suddenly they came to a fork in the track. Jana braked. Again, there was no such thing as a signpost, and each bifurcation looked equally unpromising. Cassie shook her head in bewilderment: the map was useless. But Jana smiled, and promptly took the track on the left.

'*Alea iacta est*,' she murmured.

'Oh, *Mistress*,' fumed Cassie.

'The die is cast,' said Jana. 'We choose the left-hand path.' And at once the car clattered with heavy raindrops.

They continued uphill along the ever more twisting track, whose ruts were now turning to mud. A wind had risen in comradely accompaniment to the driving rain. Cassie sighed.

'We shall stop only when we have to,' snapped Jana, reading her thoughts. And then, as if by a miracle, the slope began to level out, and the track widened slightly.

'The crest!' cried Cassie. 'You were right, Mistress!'

Above them towered forbidding grey crags, their lower slopes blanketed with gloomy firs and their summits formed from naked rock. Jana saw sheer cliffs laced with waterfalls: even piles of jumbled scree seemed friendly in contrast to this harshness. She thought of how humans wore their armour on the surface, their clothes and jewels and machines covering their soft animal flesh, while the dark Earth wore her armour hidden. The canopy of flowers and trees was a pleasant front; an illusion: beneath was cold dirt and hard, cruel rock. The Earth *was* armour.

Now the remnants of paving slabs appeared amidst the mud, and continued to do so more and more frequently as the track widened into a passable imitation of a real road. The women were, however, still deep in the forest, with the trees appearing darker and thicker than ever, while the towering crags seemed to sneer over their dark coniferous cluster. The roadway was flat, but they were not in a valley: rather, Jana said, they were most likely to be on a plateau, probably a limestone karst, much eroded by rains like this one. In fact, the rain was turning to a storm, and the trees danced in the wind. Cassie said that her Mistress had chosen the correct fork, because the mud road beneath them would have turned to a swamp by now.

'Where there is a road, there must be dwellings,' Jana said, without much conviction. However she was right: soon they passed broken walls that looked like the ruins of a shack, and then another, and then a third. The sight of this desolation did little to inspire them, until Jana braked suddenly and stopped the car. Cassie asked what was wrong.

'Look!' cried Jana, pointing upwards. There, nestling against the very summit of a grey peak, stood a massive fortress illuminated by a single shaft of sunlight which penetrated the clouds. It was grotesque as much by its unlikely situation as by the twisted crenellations, turrets and buttresses which adorned it, in an inhuman confusion whose very anarchy seemed menacing. And yet, had it not been for the shaft of sunlight, Jana doubted whether she would have seen it at all, as it also blended in perfectly with the grey rock from which it had been hewn. Beside it, a silver river hurtled down the steep escarpment, to become lost amidst the carpet of firs. Jana felt a thrill and wondered if there was a moat.

'This we must see!' she exclaimed. 'Where there is a castle, even one long abandoned, there is a village.'

They continued for another few minutes, the castle looming nearer overhead. Then, suddenly, Jana whooped with glee as they turned a corner and found themselves in the main, and only, street of what was recognisably a village – and only in this dismal terrain could such a forlorn cluster of tumbledown cottages have evoked glee. There was a bulb-domed church at one end, a couple of large buildings, perhaps of some municipal significance, a horse-trough, and nothing that resembled a shop. The only sign of life came from a nameless tavern, where a dim light shone out through the rain, and from the rushing of the river which traversed the main street under a wooden bridge, and slopped water over its banks.

As suddenly as the village had appeared, the paved road

ended, and Jana found herself going much too fast for the quagmire of mud that replaced it. She braked, and the brakes locked. Helplessly, the car slithered across the bath of mud and crashed, with a sickening crunch of metal, into the stone bulk of the horse-trough. Cassie and Jana looked at each other with anguished expressions on their faces, but stoically said nothing. Sighing, they got out of the car and went to inspect the damage. The loud crash had, oddly, attracted no attention from the occupants of the tavern, or of the village in general. Jana surveyed the crushed nearside wing of her car. The wheel and axle were buckled, and the edge of the obstacle had smashed in the wing, crumpling the bonnet and revealing the engine knocked askew. The radiator was shattered, and plumes of steam hissed into the cold air.

There was no use in saying anything. There was no hope of some sturdy rustic wizard affecting a magical repair. Both women shared the same thought, that the work would be complicated and lengthy, and would probably require that parts be ordered from Sofia, or even from outside Bulgaria, perhaps all the way from Japan. In such circumstances, imagination easily turned to nightmare, and Jana told Cassie that a stiff drink was probably appropriate. Fleetingly, she wished she had held out for a Mercedes, but then she shrugged, and nodded towards the tavern.

Jana was prepared for their entrance to arouse excitement, at the very least: two women, clad demurely by London standards, but no doubt highly erotic to Bulgarian eyes here in the back of beyond. The place was bare and grey, lit by only a dim bulb, and smelt of coarse tobacco, spirits, and garlic. Some unlabelled bottles graced a wooden counter, at which presided a squinting man in a shiny shirt that had once been white. A number of sullen and not unattractive young men, with curiously delicate faces, sat listlessly at tables, looking into their glasses, and there seemed to be a preponderance of blond hair and blue eyes among them.

The arrival of Jana and Cassie excited the merest flicker of interest, as though they were no more than raindrops.

They padded over the damp stone floor and came to the bar, where Cassie dutifully opened her phrasebook. As she frowned through its pages, Jana said '*koniak*' and held up two fingers. This got them two filmed tumblers of a liquid that looked, and tasted, like sump oil. Jana coughed and felt it trickle warmly into her stomach, where it performed its fiery duty quite admirably. She ordered refills, proffering a new banknote whose large denomination aroused as little curiosity as their arrival, and was diligently replaced with an Everest of less valuable grubby ones.

'At least they seem honest,' said Jana cheerfully. 'And this may not be Rémy Martin, but it does its work. Now for the hard part.'

Having ascertained that nobody spoke English, she took the phrase book and asked the name of the village, then tried to convey, in Bulgarian, their predicament to Mine Host. His expressionless face conveyed either complete indifference or complete bewilderment, or both, as though such events occurred every day like the weather. Exasperated, Jana tried other languages. When she tried German, ears pricked up: the inhabitants had finally understood her! Perhaps, Jana thought, they could speak nothing else but German. Using, to Jana's surprise, the archaic form of address '*Ihre Gnaedige Hoheit*' – 'Your Noble Highness' – the landlord told them in an equally archaic accent that they were in Enddorf. Cassie searched for it on the map and was unsurprised that it was nowhere to be found. Jana, meanwhile, continued in a mixture of German and sign language and eventually, the landlord picked up an antique telephone from beneath the bar and, still staring woodenly at them, made a brief call. Jana could not understand what he was saying: although the language he was speaking was recognisably German, it seemed to be some dialect of shivering antiquity. How long, she wondered, have these people been lost here?

The landlord nodded at them, indicating that they should sit down. They obeyed, since there was nothing to do but await whoever or whatever the telephone had summoned. They found a vacant table and took their drinks to it. Cassie brushed the dust from the chairs before they sat on them, while Jana lit cigarettes for them. She looked idly at the faces of their co-drinkers: all seemed curiously vacant, their expressions as blank as the grey stone amidst which they lived, as though the Earth had hewn them in half-hearted amusement as gargoyles for her adornment. Jana thought of inbreeding: these people, some lost German settlement, must have been here for centuries. Her imagination wandered, and she thought of the Templars, so bound up with her own destiny and that of her ancestor Jana Ardenne, the first Mistress of Maldona. She thought also of the bloodthirsty madness of the Crusades, and the untutored hordes of the pious who had slaughtered and looted their way across Europe. Perhaps the maniacal Peter the Hermit or the German monk Gottschalk had passed here, and sown their seed . . .

Time passed and the room grew darker, and Jana realised that the day was drawing to a close. She began to wonder about accommodation for the night and reassured herself that, presumably, her pile of grimy banknotes could procure from squint-eye an equally grimy room for them. There was a sudden flapping sound, and a thin shriek, and a bat emerged from the rafters to fly across the ceiling and out through the open transom, into the gathering dark. This caused no stir in the company, and before Jana and Cassie had recovered from their own surprise, the door of the tavern was flung open.

A woman entered. She was as tall and as young as Jana, and shook her head imperiously to cast the droplets of rain from her hair – a shining flaxen mane which framed a strong-boned face with wide red lips and skin as pure as porcelain. She seemed no ordinary woman by any standards, and in the gloom of Enddorf was a vision of almost other-worldly power and beauty. A black leather trench coat clung tightly to the full curves of her erect body, and she was shod in matching narrow-pointed kneeboots, the ankles of which were adorned with silver chains. She saw Jana and Cassie, and went straight to them.

'Darlings!' she cried, raising her arms in a gesture of

sympathy and greeting. 'You must be the English ladies. I saw your car outside. How simply awful! Your first visit to our little domain, and such a poor welcome! You must think us quite dreadful. I came as fast as I could, of course, when Stefan called. I was just about to get into the bath, but I simply dropped everything and *flew* to rescue you.'

Her voice was a husky contralto, and her accent regal, or, Jana thought, the polished Oxford accent that only foreigners could master these days.

'Thank you very much,' Jana said, and introduced herself and Cassie. They stood and shook hands.

'I'm Mimi,' said the new arrival. 'Or, at least, that is what I am known as – my real name is far too much of a mouthful. Well, we must get you out of here. A lady doesn't belong amongst our peasants, charming though they may be.'

Jana explained that they hoped to find accommodation here, and perhaps telephone in the morning, to Plovdiv or Sofia, to see about getting a mechanic to come. Mimi smiled.

'Oh, that will all be taken care of. It is our fault that you're in this pickle: that horse-trough is a hazard and I should have had it removed yonks ago. There hasn't been a horse here since the Second War – they ate them all, you see. You shall be our guests at the Castle! It is humble, but more comfortable than this. Anyway, you couldn't phone from here, since Stefan's line only connects to the Castle. Come! You can have a nice bath and a nap before dinner, and we'll sort out your car in the morning. I'm sure the *Boyar* will be enchanted to meet you, and hear all your news.'

Jana and Cassie followed her brisk pace out into the street, in whose centre stood a gleaming black Mercedes. Mimi helped them fetch their luggage, and insisted on carrying most of it, especially the amaranth and chestnut blossoms, whose perfume she inhaled with a sigh of joy.

'Your car will be quite safe,' she said, 'although you might find bats nesting there. They get everywhere!'

Jana mentioned that they had seen one in the tavern.

'Yes, we have many. They breed as fast as the peasants can shoot them with their catapults. I believe they are very tasty in a stew!'

Mimi's gaiety was infectious, and Jana found her spirits lifted as she sank into the soft leather front seat of the Mercedes. Mimi settled herself, gunned the engine, and they sped off in a whoosh of mud. They crossed the bridge over the overflowing river, then turned left up a narrow but well-paved road that twisted up the mountainside towards the Castle. Its bulk loomed clearly over them, now sparkling with lights.

'A *boyar* is an old Bulgarian word for prince, isn't it?' asked Cassie.

Mimi laughed.

'Of course. How much you know of us already! Well, he is an old Bulgarian prince! I mean, *he* isn't old, but the principate is. Gosh, I'm so excited, you've got me all in a tizzy! One doesn't address him as *Boyar*, of course, that would be too frightfully stuffy. One addresses him simply as Master. Because that's what he is, Master of Schloss Ende.'

'I see,' said Jana, smiling. 'Gosh, Mimi,' she continued, falling, inadvertently into her girlish idiom, 'I imagined it was *your* castle.'

'Oh, Jana, you are silly!' cried Mimi, pleased nevertheless. 'How could it be my castle? I am only one of the Elect, and that only since yesterday! The Master has honoured me! Oh, I've been longing to show it to someone! I know I shouldn't really, but ... Oh, well!' She slowed the car, and lifted the hem of her leather coat, showing the firm muscles of her bare leg. Then the leather slid up further, above her knee, and revealed her thigh. She was naked underneath her coat, and Jana remembered that she had been disturbed at her toilette. Finally, Mimi flicked the coatflap aside altogether, and Jana saw a gold band tight around the bare flesh of her upper thigh, just below her protruding red cunt-petals. She caught only a momentary glimpse of it, but noticed that the heavy gold band represented a snake devouring its own tail; she saw, too, that

106

the luxuriant mink at Mimi's fount had been trimmed into the delicate shape of a flower, with all the hair shaven completely from the quim, so that the woman's fount beautifully resembled a lush orchid.

'Oops!' cried Mimi, accelerating again. 'I suppose you think I'm a bit naughty. But I just had to show you!'

'It's beautiful,' murmured Jana, 'like its wearer.'

'Why, thank you,' said Mimi, blushing deliciously. 'But you haven't seen all of me, you cheeky thing!'

'What is it for?' Jana asked. 'The snake-band, I mean.'

'Questions, questions!' replied Mimi with a grin. 'You *are* cheeky!' With playful affection, she pinched Jana's thigh. 'Maybe you'll learn . . . if you decide to stay with us. We – I – should love to have you, and I'm afraid it will take some time to get your car fixed. Meanwhile you shall be our honoured guests, for as long as you like!'

'Well . . . thank you, Mimi,' said Jana diplomatically. The vast, forbidding bulk of the Castle loomed near. She tingled with curiosity and only caution stopped her accepting the invitation at once.

'Enddorf,' mused Jana. 'An interesting name.'

'It's German, of course,' said Mimi, stopping in front of – yes, a drawbridge, and moat! 'The communists gave it some silly Bulgarian name, but we are awfully conservative and never use it! Hmm . . . I think it was "Nistograd",' she added.

107

8

First Cleansing

They hurried across the drawbridge, through the heavy raindrops which lashed the dark water of the moat. Jana paused briefly to peer into it, but was unable to see if there were any fish there. Their bags seemed heavy, and Jana realised she was tired, and certainly in need of the promised rest and dinner. The red and white blossoms, lovingly cradled by Mimi, seemed to enjoy their drenching. The entrance to the Castle was a huge steel door, with a smaller, spyholed door for ingress. Mimi gave no signal, but this door swung open as they approached, and they stepped inside.

Two young women were waiting by the door, and curtseyed as Jana and Cassie entered, ushered in by Mimi. Jana's eyes widened slightly and a pleased smile of surprise played over her lips. The vestibule was, in contrast to the forbidding exterior of the Castle, brightly lit, softly carpeted and hung with paintings and shining chandeliers. The women, too, were wearing the most gorgeous and delicate costumes, which Jana at once longed to possess.

'Ah! Good! The Students await us!' said Mimi.

Both 'Students' had raven hair, and dark Mediterranean complexions like Cassie's and – as Jana thought with a flutter of longing – like Mokka's. They were tall, and of about Jana's age, and both possessed a striking beauty. One wore her hair long, cascading in lustrous tresses over her full breasts. Her ripe fesses were tight under a clinging silver mini-dress, which left her brown arms bare. Her forearms were adorned with silver bracelets, matching the heavy choker at her neck, and there was a slave bracelet, like Mimi's, around each of her silken ankles. Her sheer black stockings fitted snugly into painfully pointed, painfully high stiletto shoes.

The neckline of her dress plunged well below the soft curves of her breasts, and its hem was so high that it scarcely covered the curve of her buttocks or her plainly swelling mount. Each of her stocking-tops glittered with a band of silver, and black silk garter straps, also edged with silver, disappeared tantalisingly under her skirt. Jana wondered what sort of panties, if any, she was wearing. Without looking, she guessed that Cassie was wondering the same thing. Then, as if the woman had read their thoughts, she moved her thighs slightly to reveal a glimpse of leather G-string.

The other woman's black hair was equally lustrous, but worn short in a stern page-boy cut, which suited her slim, boyish figure. She too wore twin silver ankle bracelets, but hers encircled soft calfskin – a pair of black boots which tightly covered her legs to the very tops of her thighs. A sliver of brown flesh peeped out between each boot and her fount-cover, which was the merest slip of a G-string, a triangle of woven copper thread held to her waist by a chain. Her belly was bare and perfectly flat, with an extruded navel, downy as a little gooseberry, which Jana found quite bewitching.

Her breasts were as flat as a boy's, and covering them were three or four interlaced copper threads, a most primitive form of brassière, wound so tightly that it needed no shoulder-straps. She was so slender that her belly-button was actually larger than her nipples. Her neck and arms too were adorned, not with silver but with heavy jade, which matched her eyes – twin dark green pools that blankly returned Jana's none-too-subtle stare. Jana marvelled that each of the two women could be so differently formed and adorned, and yet, in her own way, exert the same powerful sexuality. Mimi's invitation to spend some time at the Castle was becoming more and more tempting.

With a little smile, Mimi parted the folds of her coat to

reveal her golden thigh-bracelet, and at once the two women bowed low. It was more than a bow: they suddenly jackknifed, pressing their foreheads to their ankles, and forcing their arms up behind their backs with fingers clasped so that their hands were bent backwards. Jana had a sumptuous view of the two arse-clefts: the thin G-strings stretched tightly and, Jana thought, painfully, across the wrinkled pink anus buds. She was reminded of one of the more strenuous yoga positions, until Mimi said proudly: 'They are good Students! That was a perfect bow.'

'I see. Of what are they Students?' asked Jana.

'Why, fashion, painting, sculpture, the art of flowers and scents – the Master is such a profound and many-faceted teacher, as you shall see, I hope!'

Jana followed Mimi's brisk pace down the narrow corridor leading from the hallway, as the two Students carried their luggage. She wished their pace could be slowed, for she wanted to savour all the treasures which lined the walls. There were many suits of armour, and she thought the effect suitably baronial. There were also numerous paintings and statues, some of great antiquity, some apparently new, and the startlingly abstract mingled with the naturalistic. Pots of unfamiliar herbs and flowers hung at intervals, casting their mingled perfumes in a symphony of scent which seemed in perfect harmony with each artefact or painting. Sensing her admiration, Mimi slowed.

'The Master has such talent,' she said with awe. 'Every time I look on his work, I feel quite . . . fluttery!'

Jana herself felt quite fluttery as they rounded a corner – the corridor seemed to become narrower with their progress, or perhaps the paintings were becoming larger – and saw a depiction in oils of a naked man about to enter the vulva of an equally nude female. Her thighs were stretched, and she was holding her toes in her fingers so that her body formed a symmetrical diamond, her torso a bar in its centre. The male, too, was a triumph of geometry, for his hugely erect penis was complemented by another! Jana stopped and stared in awe: the second,

110

slightly smaller, cock sprang from the same massive balls, as though the male's body had been designed for both vulval and anal penetration of his female ... a pleasure machine. The genitals of both figures were shaven bare, and painted in such fine detail that they might have been sculptures: between the female's spread thighs, every fold and crevice of her fount, nympha and anus bud was meticulously portrayed. Jana remarked that there was something architectural about the symmetrical structure of the two magnificent bodies, centred like temples on the sacred nodes of balls and cunt.

'Pretty, aren't they?' said Mimi nonchalantly. 'The Master is indeed the most talented of architects, as you will see. I do hope you aren't offended!' She giggled.

'Delighted, rather,' replied Jana smoothly.

'Nearly at your room,' said Mimi. 'You have heard of the holistic doctrine? It states that the human body is a sacred temple, made for worship, both in her and of her. Like the Earth herself. Well, the Master teaches that temples must be built and, therefore, must also be designed.'

Her eyes strayed over the well-muscled bodies of Jana and Cassie, and she briefly touched the top of Jana's breast.

'I can see that you have done something to build your own bodies,' she said admiringly. 'You have fine pectorals, strong arms and thighs.'

Mimi still clutched the bouquets of chestnut and amaranth blossom, and her face was flushed as she inhaled their perfume deeply. Jana too felt the power of the scent in the confined space. Without mentioning Maldona and her teachings, she explained that she and Cassie practised the art of body-sculpture.

'But that is splendid!' cried Mimi. 'Now I know you must stay! The Master may honour you by asking you to model! And now, here is your room. Oh, just one thing – silly me, I forgot to ask. You don't mind sleeping in the same bed, do you? I mean, there are other rooms free, if –'

Jana looked her calmly in the eyes and interrupted her.

'Mimi, we sleep together,' she said. 'By which I mean we are lovers, or, more precisely, Mistress and slave. Now it is I who hope *you* aren't offended.'

Mimi looked into Jana's eyes, and touched her breast again, this time not at the collar bone, but on the nipple.

'Mistress and slave,' she whispered. 'I sensed you were a Mistress, Jana. No, I am not offended. Quite the opposite.'

Smiling, she opened a gilt-handled door to show them into their room, whose luxury quite took Jana's breath away. There was a four-poster mahogany bed, resplendent with erotic carvings of laughing female faces amidst breasts, buttocks, cocks and quims draped with grapes, peaches and flowers. The carpet had a thick woollen pile, and the tables and plush chairs were also of mahogany. Beside the massive wardrobe, also carved with erotic gargoyles, a doorway led to an *en suite* bathroom. Jana noticed that it contained, in pride of place, a gleaming device of tubes and straps which she recognised as a colonic irrigation machine.

When the Students had carefully deposited the luggage, taken their curious bow once more and departed, Mimi said proudly that these had once been the quarters of a previous *boyar*, a prince of the blood, but – she gestured to the bathroom, telephone, and the electric points – everything had been modernised. Jana expressed her delight, but was unable to hide her tiredness.

'I expect you need a rest, and a bath,' Mimi said. 'I have my own interrupted toilette to attend to. No, don't apologise! It is such an honour to have you here, Mistress Jana. The Master has instructed me to escort you to his table tonight – an honour accorded only to the Elect.'

'We are scarcely that,' said Jana.

'Oh, as guests, you are honorary members of the Elect,' replied Mimi. 'Afterwards – well, we shall see. I shall leave you now, and return at the appointed time. There is just one thing: the Master's dress code is quite . . . formal. You will find a range of attire in the wardrobe, and I am sure you will find something to suit.' Suddenly her hand flew to her mouth, and her eyes widened.

'Gosh!' she cried. 'I must sound improper! I didn't mean to suggest that your own raiment would be wrong! But you are travelling, after all, and I thought that perhaps – oh! Silly me! To tell a true Mistress how to adorn herself! If I were your slave, I am sure I should deserve a bare spanking for my impropriety!' Her eyes shone as they pierced Jana's.

'You are not improper, Mimi,' said Jana, touching her hand, 'unless you feel so. You are very sweet.'

Mimi blushed. She tried to open their wardrobe, but frowned as she found it locked.

'Bother,' she said. 'Never mind, that will be dealt with. There is plenty of time for you to rest first. There is one other thing,' she added as she withdrew. 'You might care to cleanse yourself before joining the Master.' She gestured at the enema machine. 'The Master appreciates that.'

When they were alone, Jana and Cassie hugged each other contentedly, no longer bothering to stifle their yawns. They went at once to the bathroom, where Jana accorded Cassie first use of the porcelain commode. Like the bedroom, it contained lacquered pots of sweet-smelling herbs and flowers; Jana reminded herself to ask Mimi what they were. As Cassie lifted her skirts and spread her thighs to squat on the commode, Jana examined the enema machine and felt a flutter of excitement at its intricate array of tubes, nozzles, pressure gauges and taps.

'Made in Berlin, 1865,' she said. 'I suppose it was state of the art then. Bulgaria was Turkish in those days – perhaps that is why the Germans and Turks were so close, a colonic alliance!'

'It looks like state of the art in any age, Mistress,' said Cassie, rising. 'I'm quite looking forward to using it, and to meeting this hygienic Master of ours.' Jana graciously wiped her with a scented tissue, then took her place on the commode.

'He is not our Master, Cassie,' she laughed as she relieved herself. 'Just as Mimi is not my slave. Not yet, anyway.'

Cassie grinned.

They stripped, then lay beneath the heavy quilts and fell

into a deep sleep. When she was awakened, around two hours later, by a discreet knock on the door, Jana felt much refreshed, and nudged Cassie awake before ordering the caller to enter. It was the buxom slave, who silently placed a gilt-edged envelope on the writing table and, producing a gilt key, unlocked the wardrobe. Then she bowed and departed. Jana supposed that they received her obeisance in their status as honorary members of the Elect, and wondered what one had to do in order to achieve full status. No doubt, as Mimi assured them, they would see.

Jana ordered Cassie to prepare their bath and then picked up the letter. She smelt the rich aroma of the thick cream paper, and was almost unwilling to mar the envelope's perfection by opening it. It was not a modern envelope, but handmade, deckle-edged, and sealed properly with wax and a ring's imprint. The seal depicted a snake, the same snake as Mimi wore in gold around her thigh. At last, as Cassie cooed to her Mistress that the bathroom had every potion a lady could ever wish for, she opened the letter. A flourish of italic letters in neat brown ink greeted her, and she raised her eyebrows as she took the letter into the bathroom.

'Look at this, Cassie,' she mused. 'A droll one, our Master.'

Cassie slipped into the bath beside her Mistress, scanned the letter, then whistled, and began to read it aloud:

'The Master greets to his table his honoured guests, Mistress Jana and her slave Cassandra, and requests that they attire themselves identically, thus:

Waspie corselet laced tightly, constricting the waist by at least one centimetre in depth, with the top two holes unlaced

Strapless brassière, hooked on the inside hook

Silk blouse, with top three buttons open, so that bra and top of corselet are visible

Soft leather mini-skirt, blouse tails to hang outside

Leather garter belt with suspenders, to be worn with sheer silk stockings and no panties

Golden chain G-string, to pass between lips of the vulva

114

and across anus, then between the buttocks, and knotted at side of waist

Above stocking top, gold thigh bracelet of the Elect, with snake's head pointing towards the vulva, linked to G-string at the vulva, by gold chain

Pointed shoes with high heels, and two silver ankle bracelets

Hair pinned back behind the ears, to cover nape of neck

Nipples, mouth and vulva may be rouged

Earrings not more than two centimetres in diameter must be worn.

It is most important that the stockings be noticeably laddered.

My guests may add further adornment at their discretion.'

'Well!' said Jana. 'I wonder what further adornment he could possibly have in mind.'

'I can't wait,' said Cassie dreamily. 'It – he – sounds so exciting.'

Her toe touched Jana's quim-lips, as though by accident.

'Mistress, you are moist,' she murmured. 'We are both excited. Let's look at our new wardrobe.'

'It is not exactly ours,' said Jana firmly, 'and, like good obedient guests, we must take our enema first.'

She climbed out of the bath and began to probe the colonic irrigation machine, and with a frown said that it was not as simple as it looked, especially since the controls were labelled in highly technical and rather sinister German. She had some idea what *Durchauseinfuellung*, *Schnellabspuelung*, and *Heisslufttrockensaugen* probably meant, but was wary of spoiling their welcome by misusing this treasure, whose tubes, she thought with a shiver of naughtiness, had graced the anus of a prince of the blood!

At that moment the telephone hummed, and Jana picked up the bathroom extension. It was Mimi, reminding them that she would arrive shortly to escort her guests to dinner. Jana explained their problem, and soon Mimi was beside them in the bathroom, opening various tubes and nozzles, then expertly manipulating pumps and levers as the machine hissed and steamed quite alarmingly. Mimi's manner was very businesslike. She wore a tight rubber overall which was clinical but rather fetching – and which reminded Jana of Netta's preference for rubber clothing – and explained merrily that it would be a messy business. She ordered them to get out of their bath and towel themselves dry.

Jana and Cassie stood glowing and naked as Mimi explained that the machine could accommodate both of them at once, one on either side. She indicated that they should position themselves standing against a padded belly rest, with their legs spread wide. The machine, taller than they stood, had rails for them to grasp as they obeyed and assumed the position. Attached to the belly rest were straps of thick burnished leather, wide as corsets, with buckles at the end. Mimi lifted the straps and fastened them securely around Jana and Cassie's waists, and Jana's was pinched very tightly, almost as though she were being trussed for a flogging. She found herself curiously excited at the thought of her enema, and all the more so when Mimi strapped their ankles equally tightly to the machine's base. Then she worked a lever which depressed their belly rests until their torsos were horizontal, with their croups higher than their heads. Jana had to stretch her arms high to hold on to the rail, and turned her head to grin at Cassie: both women's faces were flushed with excitement, and Jana felt a stirring in her belly as her quim delicately moistened.

'Bums a little higher, please,' Mimi ordered briskly and, with rubber-sheathed fingers, prised Jana's arse-cheeks apart; Jana started as she felt Mimi's finger inside her anus, almost to the hilt, applying a scented lubricant. Cassie received the same treatment, and both women smiled as they exchanged glances, each knowing the pleasure the other took. Then Jana shut her eyes, concentrating on her own sensation, again aware that she was sharing it with her slave. As the machine filled itself under Mimi's guidance, Jana suddenly felt the thinnest of tubes penetrate her anus in a smooth, almost imperceptible motion, sliding right to her root.

'My, you took that well,' said Mimi. 'Both of you. You

see why you have to be strapped: sometimes Students get jittery, and move about, which spoils the delicate action of the irrigation machine. They are not used to having their bumholes cleansed!'

She laughed, leaving a question hanging in the air. Jana thought she must have guessed that the elasticity of her sphincter was no accident; that she was accustomed to the caress of a cock or dildo in her most tender place.

'Of course, now that you *are* strapped,' said Mimi, gaily, 'I could inflict the most frightful punishments on you, couldn't I, and you'd be quite helpless to resist. A terribly hard spanking on your bare bums, or even worse! Don't worry, though. It is only naughty Students who have to be punished, when they have been improper.'

'And how do they manage to be improper?' asked Jana.

'Oh, lots of ways,' said Mimi thoughtfully. 'Improper dress, for example, or peeking at things the Master forbids their rank to see. Curiosity is impropriety, the Master says, and must be properly cleansed! Anyway, to business. We'll start with some nice soapy water, then there are some special oils for further cleansing: attar of roses, myrrh, sandalwood, musk, and all sorts of Arabian and Persian things I can't even pronounce!'

A steady flow of hot water filled Jana's anus, causing her to squirm and gasp with ticklish satisfaction. Gradually, it increased in speed and volume, the pressure of the liquid making her belly swell as its dancing point spurted against her fundament.

'Mmm,' she sighed, 'that is so good! I feel cleansed already.'

Mimi laughed, rather sternly.

'There is much more,' she said. 'Hold the water in, please, until I tell you to relax.'

Jana's anus felt full to bursting point.

'Oh . . . Oh . . . I don't know if I can,' she gasped.

'Hmm!' snorted Mimi. 'Is that any talk for a Mistress? Well, now for the *Abspuelung* – don't you find German such a pretty language? You may relax now.'

Jana could not answer, for her breath was caught by the

gorgeous evacuation of the liquid from her filled anus. The tube now sucked the fluid from her: on and on the flood came, and she thrilled to imagine just how much liquid she had taken inside herself.

'Yes,' she said, dazed. Her whole belly glowed with pleasure, and she was aware that there was moisture at her fount. Forced, as she was, to support herself with her stretched arms, she was unable to touch herself there, although she longed to. She supposed she should evacuate the tube as well, but no; Mimi quickly told the women to tighten their muscles once more.

'Now a herbal oil solution,' she said. 'Tube number two.'

'I wonder what sort of punishments an improper or curious Student might expect,' murmured Jana.

'My,' said Mimi, 'I rather think *you* are being curious, Mistress Jana.'

She placed her palm on Jana's bared fesses, and began to stroke them very tenderly, almost with reverence.

'What lovely soft skin, and such a gorgeous bum,' she said distantly. 'It would be such a pity if she were marked, but there are those who love to redden improper flesh . . .'

Tube number two was much larger than the first, and slid over it like a sheath. The cleansing flow was repeated, and then again with a third tube, and a fourth. This series of tubes progressively stretched and enlarged Jana's anus, and soon her nympha was throbbing and her fount dripping with her juices for the fourth tube was bigger than any man's cock her bumhole had ever welcomed. She felt so beautifully helpless, and yet very pampered as she let her fesses open wide to receive the cleansing hot oils. The pleasure was maddening, making her giddy with desire, and she longed to touch her swollen nympha, which would send shocks of ecstasy through her belly and spine.

'Oh,' she moaned, as the liquid pumped into her filled belly, 'Oh . . .'

'Am I hurting you?' said Mimi with mild amusement.

'Yes . . . no . . . I mean yes! Don't stop!'

'Good! And now for the last treatment. You might feel a little discomfort,' said Mimi warmly, and without irony.

Tube number five seemed bigger than all the others put together, and Jana's moaning became a groan, and then a melting, fainting shriek of pain and ecstasy, as the tube slid into her, stretching her anus to its elastic limit, and – if only in Jana's fevered imagination – beyond even that. She could not hold back: she thought of Damien's giant metal cock, but this rubber tube was warm, bathing her with the scent of life as she trembled and came, shuddering at the force of her orgasm. It felt as though she were floating in a bath of painful joy, carried by floodwaters of ecstasy that flowed from the firm, gentle touch of Mimi herself.

'Oh! So beautiful! I'm so full, so lovely!' she heard herself moan in the warm afterglow of her climax.

Mimi smiled and ordered Cassie and Jana to make their final evacuation. As the oils cascaded from Jana's anus, she shed tears of grateful joy, and was almost overcome by a longing to bathe her breasts and cunt and lips in the fragrant liquid of her cleansing. She sensed too, from Cassie's sighs, that her slave felt just the same. When Jana's anus was drained, Mimi said that it was time for the 'hot air drying', and a gentle breeze of warm scented air began to flow into Jana's anal opening, soothing and caressing her. She gasped that she had never known anything like it. Very lightly and very briefly, Mimi touched her hair.

'Many a Student experiences joy at her first cleansing,' she whispered.

Mimi released them from their straps, advised them on how they should powder, perfume, and coif themselves, then took her leave to attend to her own adornment, promising to return very soon.

'You have read the Master's note?' she said, strangely shy. 'I hope you were not . . . taken aback.'

'On the contrary,' Jana answered. 'We are most honoured. We cannot wait!'

Mimi smiled and departed, leaving them to their robing. Jana opened the wardrobe, and now they *were* taken aback.

'Oh, Mistress!' cried Cassie. 'How often do we complain

119

we haven't a thing to wear, and here there's everything gorgeous you could think of!'

Feverishly, they selected the required garments, laughing in their excitement. They opened drawers and small cupboards and marvelled at the array of jewels and frocks, and at the wide variety of underthings and corsetry, which included the frilliest, the harshest, and the most revealing of designs. They rouged their lips, nipples, and quim-lips; they tightened their corselets and metal G-strings to an almost uncomfortable degree; they clawed each other's stockings until Jana pronounced solemnly that they looked like true sluts. Then, in a bottom drawer, she discovered a shiny selection of metal artefacts, whose purpose and design she recognised, and her heart quickened at the chilling elegance of the array before her.

'How strange our life is, that beauty can grow from pain,' she murmured, touching Cassie's hand.

Mimi, dazzlingly adorned, and with her stockings fiercely laddered as though a tiger had scratched her, entered just as Jana was admiring a thick double tongue of silver, attached to a thin quim-chain and a buckled leather waiststrap.

'Oh,' said Mimi, blushing, 'I didn't know your room was equipped with – well, you asked about methods of punishment for improper Students. Those are called pacifiers, for naughty girls. They fit – and rather tightly I might add – in the quim and bumhole. You see? Like this.'

Jana nodded as Mimi lifted her short skirt and positioned the pacifier snugly between her thighs.

'Actually – I suppose it's rather naughty of me to tell you – new Students are given pacifiers and have to wear them all the time for their first month at the Castle, just to teach them obedience to our ways, and to remind them who their Master is. They are also used on special occasions, such as when a Student waits at the Master's table; they make a girl walk more elegantly, you see ... How I remember my own breaking! That's what we used to call it.'

Smiling, she rubbed the smooth silver of the pacifier.

'And a beating with pacifier tight in, gosh, how *that* hurts! Of course, you don't have to wear them.'

'But we *shall*,' retorted Jana, her eyes shining with pleasure. 'Just think, Cassie, it is like being at home. Just like new Virgins of Maldona, we have restrainers!'

9

The Master

'You both look absolutely smashing,' said Mimi gaily, as she led Jana and Cassie through the ornate maze of corridors to the refectory. 'And your stockings – so exquisitely laddered! The Master will approve.'

Occasionally they passed a woman, or a pair of women, who curtseyed, nodded, or executed a rapid bow, according to their rank. All were dressed gorgeously. Jana thanked Mimi for the compliment, returned it, and asked casually if there were no men here in the Castle, apart from the Master. Then, suddenly, she thought: could *this* be the Castle of which Mokka had spoken? No, that would be too much of a coincidence. Eastern Europe was full of castles.

'Why, of course there are men!' cried Mimi, laughing. 'You shall see them in due course. They have their uses, you know! But, Mistress Jana, how glad I am that you seem so attuned to our ways. I knew it, psychically, the moment I received the phone call! That's why you have been accorded the honour of dining at the Master's table. The Master is so keen to meet you. He is a perfectionist in painting, dress and adornment, in the high art of cuisine, and in manners, and we sense that you are too, and that you are unfettered by banal prejudices. And that's why you came to our remote village.'

'Well,' blurted Cassie, 'we had heard of the Museum of Correction.' Jana's warning look came too late.

'Oh, you mustn't believe all the stories the peasants tell you,' Mimi responded. 'These Bulgarian peasants are noted for their imagination: for so long, under the oppression of various tyrannies, it was all they had to live on!'

'I do hope the Master approves of us,' said Jana quickly. 'But, Mimi, if he is a perfectionist, why should he demand our stockings be imperfect – I mean, improper?' She noted to herself how rapidly she was falling into the Castle's idiom.

'How well spotted!' cried Mimi. 'Propriety can only be judged and appreciated in the presence of impropriety, and the promise of punishment for it. Thus, we three are attired as proper Mistresses, resplendent at any table. But our stockings are improper! Glaringly holed, so that our true reality as sluts, as *females*, is as obvious as our naked legs. And with that reality comes the delicious knowledge that punishment could be visited on us at any moment, at the Master's whim!'

Cassie pointed out rather woodenly that it was the Master who had instructed them on their dress.

'Aha!' said Mimi, triumphantly. 'The Master may have chosen to instruct but, more important, you chose to obey! Not,' she added hastily, 'that honoured guests could possibly incur punishment.'

'And you, Mimi! One of the Elect?' said Jana.

Mimi smiled proudly.

'As one of the Elect, I must obey my Master,' she said. 'By the way, I hope you like oysters. The Master is very fond of oysters.' Jana expressed her own fondness.

'Hmm,' she murmured to Cassie. 'Remember that as guests, we are honorary members of the Elect.'

Suddenly the corridor turned sharply to the left, with a smaller corridor veering to the right-hand side. Jana naturally turned left, only to be arrested by a tug on the shoulder from Mimi.

'No,' said Mimi, 'we don't go down there. It's a bit confusing, isn't it? The right-hand passage is actually the main one. The left path . . . well, we don't go down there.'

Jana shrugged and they continued down the smaller right-hand path, but Cassie said slyly: 'Would it, then, be improper to venture down the left-hand path, Mimi?'

'Well, yes, it would be improper,' said Mimi, embarrassed.

'And what is there that it would be improper to see?'

'I am afraid,' said Mimi, in even greater embarrassment, 'that the question itself is improper.'

Jana frowned at Cassie to be quiet, and soon they came to the refectory door, guarded by two gorgeously bejewelled and frocked Students, who bowed and opened it for them. The refectory was a small wood-panelled chamber which reminded Jana of Matron's cosy quarters, where she had been introduced to her own House of Maldona in Spain. The floor was of polished flagstones, suitably baronial to Jana's eyes. At the far end a log fire burned, framed in brass by naked nymphs and puffing zephyrs in the baroque style, which Jana thought a little tongue in cheek: the Master evidently had a sense of humour. In the room's centre stood a large round dining table, aglitter with white linen, silver goblets and plates, but, Jana observed, no cutlery. In the open floorspace the guests were already mingling.

Around the walls stood cabinets of walnut or mahogany, on which were laid dainty trays of hors d'oeuvres. These were interspersed with silver candelabras, which were the room's only illumination. At the far end was the bar, a phalanx of bottles, glasses, and iced champagne buckets. The panelled walls were hung with paintings and photographs, and Jana guessed, from their style and subject matter, that they were by the Master's hand, like those she had already seen. Many were fashion views of females in costumes which were at once flimsy, colourful, daring and erotic. Others depicted the totally nude female, although there were many male nudes as well. Jana thought she recognised the two students who had carried their luggage, and Mimi, following her gaze, said that Nadia and Waltraut made fine models. She found the pictures curiously exciting, as all the males seemed to have some slight physical abnormality, though none that she found displeasing, as it was usually to do with the exaggerated size of breast muscles, balls or cock. As she and Cassie were ushered into the company, she had time for only a short look at the paintings high up in shadow. The tableaux

124

themselves were dark, with bright flashes of naked twisted flesh: Jana recognised them with a pleasant shiver as scenes of discipline.

The conversation was already animated, and the guests gestured and laughed, holding glasses of champagne and silver saucers of canapés. Drinks and food were served by a throng of Students – young women dressed uniformly in frilly white lace bustiers over black waspie corsets and stiff black chiffon tutus. These skimpy dresses were lifted high to reveal garter belts, suspenders, and the tightest black panties of roundelled Venetian lace, atop black stockings and perilously high stiletto heels. The breasts of the Student-maids were thrust up and out by their corselages, which gave them the look of hard young plums, beaded with perspiration as the girls moved silently replenishing glasses and plates.

'Wow!' whispered Cassie appreciatively. 'I see *their* stockings aren't laddered.'

'Perhaps they are the lowest of the low, and thus already sufficiently improper,' answered Jana. 'Or maybe perfect stockings are for them the impropriety.'

Jana found the guests' attire no less striking, if slightly more comfortable, than the maids'. Males were splendid in frock coats and gaudy cummerbunds, and some wore medals or even top-boots with spurs, which Jana found a piquant conceit. The females varied from classic dark business suits to outrageous frills, straps and flounces. One was quite naked, save for a gold neck-chain of heavy links with a little padlock, a pleated silken micro-skirt that barely covered her fount, and a pair of large gold nipple rings on her heavy breasts, from which dangled little nude figures of a male and a female, carved in green jade. Jana was amused to see that the female figure held what looked like a lovely miniature cat-o'-nine-tails. Beneath the hem of the woman's skirt dangled another ring, evidently fixed to her quim-lips, and on this was a large bronze key. Her lush red hair hung in an undulating cascade down to her hips. Jana was enjoying herself and also felt strangely reassured by the not-quite-comfortable presence of the pacifier which filled her anus and quim, its oiled, silky metal giving her shivers of pleasure as she moved her thighs gingerly apart.

There were upwards of a dozen guests, and the air was filled with blue cigar smoke and the coo of voices which resonated with the smooth, benign confidence that only charm or wealth can bestow. All the guests were young and sleekly healthy. Jana smiled, reminding herself that spiritual riches can be as charming as material ones. Her musings were cut short by cries of welcome, as names and kisses flew.

'Mimi! How divine! At last you wear the band of the Elect! So good that you are one of us! My darling!'

'Robyn!'

'Gilles!'

'Armintrude! You are serene as always!'

'Mimi, how super you look! And your guests!'

'Jana . . . Cassie. Travellers who have been guided to us.'

'Aren't they scrumptious! Such lovely thighs! And ravishing outfits – the Master has designed you well! What lovely sluts you three are, and what a pretty conceit!'

Jana found herself separated from Mimi and Cassie in the throng, and was assailed with delicate perfumes and the aroma of cigar smoke. Everyone seemed to be an architect, a painter, banker or photographer, and she wondered how she should describe herself, suddenly aware that she was unlabelled, and that even in this unorthodox society, labels seemed to count. Perhaps 'traveller' was enough . . .

Gratefully, she accepted a glass of champagne, and a dish of appetisers, though she wanted a cigarette, feeling it would go well with her sluttish image. She nibbled at little cubes of avocado flavoured with nutmeg, and found the combination strangely pleasant.

'Jana, such a lovely name!' cried a female. 'I'm Robyn!' Jana saw the nearly-nude red-haired woman smiling at her, and smiled back. Robyn's perfume was beguiling, and, close up, the heaviness of her breasts was in perfect hourglass harmony with her extremely narrow waist and wide hips. Her skin was alabaster white, almost translucent, and marred by no blemish: her wide nipples were

126

perfect pink saucers. Jana remembered that redheads could not take the sun. Interestingly, she sprouted thick tufts of hair at her armpits; Jana thought that must be *her* little 'impropriety', and wondered if she wore a mink.

'How clever of Mimi to bring you here,' said Robyn, the figurines at her breasts dancing as she spoke. Jana replied that their travels had brought them to Enddorf, or Nistograd, but Mimi had certainly brought them to the Castle.

'And what do you do when you are not travelling?'

Jana debated with herself. What label?

'Well, I have a certain amount of money: I travel a lot.'

'Poo! We all have a certain amount of money. Money is easy to get, and I should know, I'm a banker.'

'Very well, then,' said Jana coolly, 'I'm a Mistress. That is, I have slaves who obey me. Cassie, there, is my personal slave. There are many others: in Spain, in England, in Greece. We have just voyaged from my Greek island.'

She stopped, not wishing to give too much away. Robyn grinned, and said that she had guessed Jana was a true Mistress, that she always knew.

'And how sweet it is to see a Mistress wearing a Student's pacifier,' she murmured.

'You can tell?' gasped Jana.

'Of course,' said Robyn, placing varnished fingernails between Jana's parted thighs. 'The way you hold yourself. How lovely! I wish I'd worn mine. That gorgeous full feeling in cunt and anus, as though your very soul was filled! Well, *you* know, Mistress Jana, I'm sure.'

'I do. But your dress is already delicious, Robyn,' said Jana, warming to the red-headed woman. *Was* she red-minked . . .?

'Why, thank you. See, I have me here –' she touched the female figurine, and her breast bobbed delightfully, '– ready with my whip, to lash my debtor. And down there at my cunt, I have the key to the vault! It's such a relief after wearing a suit all day at the bank. Although,' she whispered conspiratorially, 'I always wear a short skirt, and always without panties. A little discreet leg-crossing works wonders when one is cutting a deal!'

127

'And do you have such a whip?'

'Oh, *yes*.' She giggled, and Jana asked what bank she worked for, imagining her in a high position in Frankfurt or London. Her accent was not quite English, but comfortably at home in English.

'Oh, you won't have heard of it,' replied Robyn, 'I hope. *La Banque Ottomane et de l'Europe Orientale* ... quite a mouthful. Here, try some of these prawns with honeyed marshmallow. Odd, but delicious.'

Jana did, and they were.

'In Geneva, I suppose?' she said when she had swallowed.

'You guessed, Switzerland.' Robyn made a face. 'Well, at least it's clean. Not Geneva itself – so grey! – but a little place called Le Brassus about 60 kilometres away, in the hills beside the Lac de Joux, which is lovely to swim in. We're just an ordinary house, no smart nameplate or anything. We have always liked to keep a low profile. One can walk over the border into France without going through customs.' She smiled wickedly. 'I don't actually work for the bank as such, though. I sort of own it. And the Masters have always banked with us, in fact we are financing the present Master's whole new construction.'

Jana looked at the males and asked which was the Master.

'Oh, he isn't here yet. He makes a ceremonial entrance, and we have to bow and curtsey, and then we may take our places at the table. You'll see presently. Armintrude will announce it – she's that rather gaunt lady over there.'

Jana looked and saw a raw-boned female, with striking features and auburn hair which flowed down almost to her slim buttocks in a severely knotted ponytail. She wore a plain black strapless dress over hard, mannish breasts, and no jewellery at all. Jana thought that her eyes, burning fiercely in a cruelly handsome way, were jewels enough. 'Gaunt' was perhaps unkind: had she not been so tall, she would have been elfin.

'Construction?' said Jana. 'I'm intrigued. A new Castle?'

'More than that. I just understand numbers, not buildings. Gilles is the architect, he can tell you.'

Robyn summoned a saturnine man, splendidly bemedal-
led in a frock coat, cummerbund and spurs, who bowed to
Jana and kissed her hand. His dark languid eyes stared up
at her and she saw his nostrils flare as he took in a breath.

'Gilles pretends to be a Marquis,' said Robyn gaily after
introducing them, 'but he hasn't a sou to his name, so he
has to look rich and live in a *palazzo* in Venice. I've got
oodles of money, so I have to look poor and hide in a
provincial Swiss backwater.'

'Life is certainly unfair,' said Gilles, showing brilliant
white teeth. He explained briefly that the Master planned
a whole new building, adjoining the Castle – a palace of
painting, sculpture, high fashion and cuisine, all the worthwhile arts, to outshine the great centres of Europe.

'It shall be known only to the Elect,' he said smugly.
There shall be no plebeians, except of course as servants.'

Jana was fascinated, but wanted to know which arts
were not considered to be worthwhile.

'Why, music, ballet, opera . . . They are merely improper
noise, arousing without informing. All these things are
beloved of philistines, high capitalists and low communists
alike, because they contain no thought.'

The rules of Maldona, too, forbade music, save for the
drum, and Jana thought she now understood why. She
asked if the drum, too, were forbidden.

'Why, no!' said Gilles, smiling. 'The drum is not wasteful
music, the drum is the rhythm of *life*!'

At that moment, from outside the refectory, came a light
roll of drums, and a Student opened the door at the far end
of the room. Robyn smiled, and Mimi blew Jana a kiss.

'The Master comes,' said Robyn.

Armintrude, the tall young woman whom Robyn had
pointed out to Jana, imperiously called for silence.

'Honoured Guests and Elect, stand by your places and
prepare to greet our Master and his train.'

'She is Mistress of Electors,' whispered Robyn scornfully, 'but it isn't enough for her, the ambitious cow!'

There was a hush, and the maids guided each guest to

their seat, as marked by a printed card: Jana saw that even at such short notice she and Cassie had them too. Jana was placed beside the Master, with the Marquis Gilles to her left. They stood in silence, and then a svelte, thirtyish man of medium height stepped diffidently into the room. As one, the females curtseyed, along with Jana and Cassie; the males bowed low, and the maids jackknifed their bodies in an even lower bow.

The Master smiled, showing dazzling teeth, as though he had been pleasantly surprised at his welcome. He wore a modest evening suit of dark green silk, but without ornament. Jana looked at his eyes, which were steely and unblinking in an affable, boyishly handsome face. They were directed straight at her, but betrayed no recognition. There was a presence to the Master, and Jana thought of the word majesty, powerful by its very understatement. She could sense that the Master had ineffable charm, but also that he had more than charm: he had power. He moved towards his high-backed chair at the table, and stood, evidently awaiting his 'train'.

'He is a keen hunter, and likes to be attended by his faithful wolves,' murmured Robyn, with a sly little chuckle.

Through the open doors appeared two women, then after them a third. There was a sigh of admiration and contentment around the table, and Jana heard Mimi whisper to her: 'Nadia and Waltraut! Such an honour for them!'

The first two women Jana recognised as their Student baggage-carriers of exotic costume. This time, though, they were not robed. They were naked, on all fours, and walked awkwardly on their splayed fingers and tiptoes, like ungainly spider crabs. Their backs were arched, their bare buttocks thrust high over well-parted thighs, and their heads hung low in obeisance. Both were tethered like animals, on long golden chains held by the woman who followed them, standing erect. She was as blonde as Nadia and Waltraut were dark, but naked like them, wearing only a simple leather strap around her neck.

'That is Freya,' whispered Mimi, 'she is Purified, and one of the Master's Huntresses. Armintrude is so envious!'

Jana was intrigued by this hint, and thrilled at the intricacy of the women's trussing: two leashes of thick golden chain were held by the Huntress Freya, each divided into eight thinner chains just above the small of the wolf's back. Four of these snaked to ankle and wrist clasps, two passed across the ribcage to fasten on to the nipples, and the last two were tight in the cleft of the croup, and secured by rings to each petal of the quim. Jana could not discern whether the nipples and cunt-petals were actually pierced – she suspected they were – but either way the binding was firm enough.

With her other hand, Freya held a small flail of seven nine-inch chain thongs, which had a jewelled handle, and with this she gently flicked the buttocks of her charges. But Jana saw that the women's shoulders and fesses, *and* their tender inner thigh-flesh, already blushed with vivid newly laid whipmarks: they had taken punishment not long before. Here as in Maldona, submission was evidently an honour.

The most piquant detail of the chaining was that Freya's own nipples and cunt-petals were fastened by four chains, which issued from the base of her leash-handle to attach her as securely to her charges as they were attached to her: the Huntress bound to her wolves, the Mistress to her slaves.

The Master's train halted and Nadia and Waltraut positioned themselves one on either side of his chair. A tap from Freya's whip on each bare croup obliged them to squat in a crouching position, and the Master absent-mindedly stroked their heads, as though caressing his pets. Then he nodded, and took his place at the table. This was the signal for all to be seated.

At once, the hubbub of conversation began anew, with much fulsome flattery of the Master, who himself said very little, beyond a polite 'thank you' or 'how kind'. Wines were brought, and Jana marvelled at the efficiency of the gliding Student maids, then, a rapid succession of steaming salvers appeared, laden with hot foods. The guests had plates but no cutlery, and when the Master broke a piece of flat bread and bit into it, Jana's suspicions that this was no oversight were confirmed. They were to eat with their fingers, like the Bedouin.

She grinned and took some bread, then folded pieces of squid, peppers, crab and ratatouille within it, forming it dextrously into a glutinous envelope, which she ate with similar care. Did any specific etiquette apply to eating with the fingers, she wondered. Though entranced by the Castle, she still found its evidently severe rules unfamiliar, and so rationed her intake of wine – what might the punishment be for wishing to visit the bathroom during a meal? She noticed that the conversation was dominated by the males: women, even Robyn and the exuberant Mimi, seemed to say little, or to speak only when addressed by a male. She noticed, too, that the Master, who seemed to be ignoring her, drank little and ate nothing, preferring, with a wry detachment, to study his guests at their messy entertainment. He exchanged a few words with Armintrude; Jana was unsure if the language was English.

Otherwise, the Master was taciturn until a huge platter of steaming hot oysters was laid on table, evidently the *pièce de résistance*. Then he turned to Jana and said in his silky voice that he hoped she liked oysters and that she must eat her fill. Jana noticed that there was a cold look on Armintrude's haughty face, as though she resented the Master paying attention to any female other than her, and in particular to Jana, whose ripe, muscled body contrasted with Armintrude's own pale thinness. The Marquis Gilles whispered mock-solemnly:

'She's jealous. She desires me – all women do! She wants me for her slave, and herself as the Master's only slave.'

'My greedy guests will guzzle the lot,' the Master said amiably. 'They are artists – my friend Robyn is an artist with money, as Gilles is an artist with marble! And there is no one like an artist for emptying his patron's larder.'

She helped herself: the hot oysters were smoky, with a delicious spiced flavour, and she said so.

'Master, I understood that you liked oysters,' she said.

'I do, Jana,' he said. 'And I trust you like our Castle.'

'Most certainly, Master,' she answered happily.

'You shall see more of it,' he said, 'if, as I hope, you stay with us. Our ways and philosophy are different from those of the common herd, but then you and your slave are not of that.' He fixed her with gimlet eyes and Jana felt her heart flutter. Then, softly, he continued:

'The Society of the Castle has been here for many centuries and we have evolved a balance by which we use the outside world, but are not used by it. You will have gathered from Mimi that we have a strict code, which is necessary if proper society is not to crumble. We have a rigid hierarchy: above the rank of Student are the Elect, the Purified, the Cleansed, and so on. You shall learn in due course. This corner of Europe has seen many wars, caused by improper lusts and improper philosophy, and the Castle has always been a bulwark of order and harmony. But to achieve beauty one must take account of the ugly, just as one protects the body from disease by vaccination with the disease itself. False creeds – and by my definition most creeds are false – promise happiness by eradicating the improper, which is not possible: hence the turbulence of this world. The Castle has always been materially and morally self-sufficient and the Master's task is to maintain that beauty.' He paused, and his lips curled in an ironic smile.

'I must not lecture,' he said softly. 'You shall learn. Suffice it to say that improper philosophy puts ideas in people's heads: proper philosophy takes ideas out.'

Jana felt herself transfixed by desire, by curiosity, and by nameless longing. How she hoped that this was Mokka's Castle! It *must* be! And they would find each other . . .

'Why, no, I – I do hope we may have the honour of staying, Master,' she blurted.

He smiled, and then nodded to Armintrude, who issued a brief instruction to Freya behind them. The Huntress unfastened the leashes from her two slaves and, with smart whipcracks to their fesses, made them rise. The full-breasted Nadia was the first to mount the table, where she squatted with her thighs spread and her fount directly over the Master's mouth. Freya stepped forward and took the slender chains that were attached to Nadia's quim-petals and sharply pulled the lips wide apart to reveal the shiny wet pinkness within.

The Master, still smiling, took a sip of white wine and tilted his face up slightly. Jana saw Nadia's belly ripple sinuously and, to her amazement, in the open lips of her cunt appeared a succulent grey oyster. The Master put out his tongue, caught the oyster, and flicked it with the delicacy of a lizard into his mouth. He chewed and swallowed it with a smile of great pleasure and a dreamy look in his hard eyes, then washed it down with wine.

This operation was repeated a full six times, before Nadia's slit was emptied of the steaming hot oysters. Then it was the slender Waltraut's turn. Her cunt was much wider than Nadia's, and from its large fleshy lips she too produced hot oysters, writhing even more than her sister Student as she did so.

'What a wonderful cunt she has!' whispered the architect, Marquis Gilles. 'It is as lovely as a palace. How she deserves a caning! Thin women are always the best, how they writhe and twist, their lovely bones clear and straining beneath the skin, as their bodies squirm.'

'You are rather flamboyant tonight, Gilles,' said the Master benignly.

To Jana's surprise, the rest of the company laughed, all except Armintrude. Perhaps they were used to Gilles and his flamboyance. In fact Jana felt an unaccountable excitement at the spectacle – a glow in her belly, which was from more than wine, and a delicious tingling at the base of her spine, as though a feather were stroking her there. It was as if she had taken the oysters into her own cunt, and she wondered if the students felt the same tingling after thus preparing the bivalves for their Master. Jana longed suddenly for him to be hers.

10

Impudence Chastised

Jana looked again at the Master and felt another wash of desire. He was powerful and strong-bodied, and his face was boyishly handsome but with the added charm of age and mystery. It was a mystery she longed to solve. She wanted to take his penis inside her and milk him of his seed, his maleness, to take his essence for her own. She wanted to take the Castle, the symbol of his male power, and yet at the same time she wanted to be in *his* subtle power, as his – his Student, maid, slave? To attend him and have him eat from her own warm fount . . .

The Master addressed her again.

'Marquis Gilles is a superb artist,' he said indulgently, 'and artists are frequently outspoken. I myself have been accused of bohemianism, which is far from accurate, though I do admit to being a lover of beauty and feasting. Mistress Jana – I may call you Mistress, for now – I am so enchanted with your beauty, and your slave's, that I wish you both to model my dress creations.'

'Oh, yes, Master!' Jana blurted. He smiled and touched her thigh, putting his finger inside the laddered stocking. She thrilled; Armintrude's watching eyes were icy. Breathing harshly, she squeezed her pacifier, hoping it would live up to its name. It did not. She was glowing with desire and her fount was moist, despite her efforts to stay calm. She thought longingly of Mokka, sweet Mokka, which only made her moisture turn to a hot flow of love-juice. Her head whirled. Was her desire due to something she had eaten? The avocado and nutmeg, or the honeyed marshmallow, perhaps – and everyone had eaten them. To what effect? The same, no doubt, as Nadia and Waltraut must feel after holding oysters in their founts.

The atmosphere was becoming gayer as more and more wine was drunk. The air was hot and smoky: clothing was loosened, and touches and kisses exchanged amongst the guests. A sly, silken voice distracted her, and she realised that the Marquis was addressing the table, to great amusement.

'. . . Females torment us, and therefore must be tormented themselves. A female is a slut, fit only for punishment.'

Jana saw Armintrude nod, leering bitterly in agreement. How *could* she? As though denying her own femaleness.

'Why is it that so many of the best-known devices of torture bore women's nomenclature? The iron maiden; the cat-o'-nine-tails; the virgin's kiss, or branding iron of Sevilla; the ball-crushing pincers the Russians call the whore's embrace. I too am a whore, and a slut, but my embrace is kind.'

Jana felt the Marquis place his hand on her thigh, and his fingers explore the hole in her stocking already widened by the Master. His touch was cool and ticklish, and she wanted him to continue higher, towards her wet fount. When he encountered no resistance – on the contrary, her thighs parted, inviting his further exploration – he did so. His fingers deftly found the lips of her cunt and stroked their swollen wetness, and he murmured his approval as he felt the base of her pacifier. Then he found her stiff nympha, the throbbing clit that shivered with joy under his caresses. Jana shifted, squeezing his hand between her thighs. The room seemed to spin and everyone, including the Master, seemed to be watching her, as though they *knew*. She knew she was going to come, and did not care. Dimly, she became aware that similar caresses were being exchanged all around the table, with everyone striving, or, in Robyn's case, not, to maintain decorum.

Robyn had pulled up her skirt to reveal her naked fount, and receive the lascivious stroking of male and female alike; Jana saw that she was in fact completely shaven and, moreover, possessed a vivid crimson tattoo. The lips of her cunt were very prominent, swollen almost to spheres, and above them was tattooed a massive erect penis, the helmet fully revealed, and the whole thing so artfully etched that her cunt-petals appeared to be balls. Her key-ring hung from her pierced labia in such a way that ingress of a real cock would not be hindered.

'Oh,' gasped Jana, as the Marquis's fingers brought her tingling stiff clit to shudders of pleasure, 'you are unfair, dear Marquis. The cat-o'-nine-tails – why, a cat can be male or female.'

'In England, perhaps,' said the Marquis. 'Not elsewhere. In Crete, the divine implement is known as the Medusa, after the goddess with stinging serpents for hair.'

'What do the English know of real punishment?' spat Armintrude. 'A pathetic race, with their spankings and canings and sordid colleges of pretended sodomy. They only play at punishment. Show me an English slut who knows *real* punishment, who can take a *real* whipping.'

There was a silence. The Marquis's fingers ceased their massage of Jana's nympha. All eyes were on Jana, at whom the insult was obviously directed, and then on the Master. It was not long before he spoke.

'Well, Mistress Armintrude, my friend,' said the Master without raising his voice, 'I do believe you have insulted a lady, and an honoured guest.'

'Sir, I have not been insulted,' retorted Jana. 'I can look after myself.'

The Master looked at her with chilling eyes.

'I did not ask you to speak, Mistress Jana,' he said icily. 'I say you have been insulted. My friend Armintrude has committed an impropriety, and must cleanse it. You shall thus correct her, according to your own rules as Mistress.'

Taken aback, Jana looked at Armintrude, who, to her surprise, merely grinned coldly, as though challenging her. The company hushed in awed excitement, and suddenly Jana felt a rush of power which made her already wet fount flow uncontrollably. She squeezed the Marquis's hand with her thighs, and he resumed his stroking.

137

'Very well, Master,' she said in an obedient but trembling voice. 'I take it suitable instruments of correction will be put at my disposal?'

'The Castle contains many things, Mistress,' said the Master, his eyes gleaming, and he gave an order to Freya, who released Nadia and Waltraut from their chains. The two naked females scampered off, then returned bearing a large wooden chest between them. The maids cleared the table, and the chest was placed before Jana and opened. Inside, she saw a glittering array of items, all of which quickened her pulse with their horrid beauty. She swallowed, then, addressing Freya, ordered that Armintrude be stripped and bound. As she spoke, she thrilled at her power, and felt the Marquis's fingers move more and more urgently on her clit.

She could not hold back: feverishly, she delved through the Marquis's silks to find his naked cock. It was already hugely stiff and, as he masturbated her, she rubbed his shaft with a grip of steel, each powerful stroke drawing the prepuce back from the massive bulb to its fullest extent. The Marquis moaned with pleasure, and it was not long before Jana felt his cock buck and shudder, then spray her hand with a hot jet of sperm.

The other guests caressed each other with renewed fervour, cocks and cunts now flaunted quite openly, as though the promise of Armintrude's bondage and punishment had opened the floodgates of lust. Robyn's mane of red hair was swept off her back, now, revealing her magnificent naked bottom, upon which she was also tattooed: emerging from the cleft of her buttocks and stretching halfway up her back was a tail, in the form of a monstrous cock whose balls were her buttocks themselves. As she watched Robyn's body being caressed by probing hands, Jana took her own from the Marquis's still-hard penis and licked her fingers.

Jana sensed that the Master had somehow orchestrated the whole proceedings, so that he might find an excuse for disciplining the haughty Armintrude and instigating an orgy.

138

The chest was a delicious cornucopia of the cruellest art. Glowing with her orgasmic pleasure, Jana brushed the instruments with her hands and sensed that somehow, for this moment, she was in control of the gathering. She rose and nodded to the Master, then deliberately wiped her sperm-soaked fingers on her laddered stockings. The Master purred with approval. Jana turned her attention to Armintrude, who stood defiantly, guarded by Freya. Her wrists and ankles were bound by the thin chains which had adorned the pierced cunts and nipples of Freya's wolf-girls.

Idly, Jana sauntered over to the taller woman, holding a steel-handled whip. With pretended disdain, she paused to inspect Armintrude, trim in her black dress. In truth, Jana found her thinness oddly exciting – a symbol of a powerful will that exerted a healthy control over the body's more excessive appetites, just as Maldona's slaves submitted to the discipline of body sculpture and the building of hard muscle. Armintrude breathed discipline: the male strength of her face was the beauty of power. Jana raised the whip and placed one end of its handle in the bustline of Armintrude's dress. Then, with a swift tug, she ripped the dress open down as far as the navel, exposing the woman's flat breasts and prominent ribs. Armintrude's nipples were surprisingly dark and prominent, jutting out like hard black cherries; the dress clung tightly to her hips and did not fall. Armintrude bristled at the indignity, but was silent.

'Mistress Freya, you will please make her naked,' said Jana slowly. 'And I shall want her properly strapped to a whipping frame, with proper accoutrements. I assume one is available,' she added, giving her victim a thin smile.

Nadia and Waltraut once more scampered off on their errand, as Freya solemnly removed the dress from Armintrude, who wore neither stockings nor panties underneath it. She was, therefore, now naked but for a pair of black stilettos, which Jana decided should remain on her feet. Jana also noted that Armintrude was blessed with a very full auburn mink, as well as heavily-tufted armpits.

The two Students shortly returned, and wheeled in a

139

massive wooden frame a head taller than Armintrude. It consisted of a rectangle of teak blocks studded with straphooks, to which movable cuffs for the ankles and wrists could be attached as was required. Inside the rectangle was a St Andrew's cross, also made of teak, and the entire frame was mounted on a central axis, on which it could be tilted or swivelled to any angle. The whole moved on a trolley, whose wheels could be raised to immobilise it, and at the top was a system of rollers and pulleys, so that the frame and its occupant could be stretched.

'The rack,' said Gilles with delighted awe. ' "The Duke of Exeter's daughter" . . .'

'Admirable,' said Jana. 'You see, we English do know a thing or two.'

She ordered the rack to be positioned where everyone could see it comfortably. Nadia deposited a second chest on the cleared table, and opened it for Jana's inspection. This chest contained the requested 'accoutrements', made of leather, wood and rubber. Jana smiled grimly, seeing some old, and some new friends. She knew that the Master was watching her intently through his hooded eyes: this was her test, and she meant to pass it honourably. She adopted a businesslike tone, hiding her excitement that it would be the first time she had chastised a slave on the rack.

'Well, first we'll have to bind you properly,' she said affably to Armintrude. 'Don't you agree?' Armintrude nodded yes, with as much hauteur as she could muster.

'A gag, I think,' said Jana, stroking her chin. 'We don't want our pleasure to be disturbed by your screams.'

'I shan't scream!' sneered Armintrude, and was rewarded with a lash from a leather whip right across her nipples.

'I shan't scream, *Mistress*,' said Jana. 'You call me Mistress, now.' Armintrude glanced, pleading, at the Master, but he only smiled and nodded.

'Yes, Mistress,' hissed Armintrude. The orgiasts around the table were enjoying the spectacle hugely, and Jana's excitement made her giddy as she heard the swish of clothing raised and the sounds of nibbling and kissing. She squeezed hard on her pacifier, imagining that her vagina and anus were filled by two cocks at once, and felt wetness seeping down her bare thigh to soak her stocking-tops.

Briskly, she had Armintrude bound to the upright rack by her ankles, wrists and waist. Her long hair was swept up and pinned in a bun on top of her head, and her thighs and arms were splayed wide. Jana made sure that her bonds were not dangerously tight, and then turned the racking wheel a jot so that Armintrude was stretched to her tiptoes.

'Of course, you have only to apologise, and I'll release you unpunished,' she said nonchalantly, and received the reply she wanted.

Armintrude spat and cried, 'Never!'

Jana shrugged.

'Very well,' she said, and began to fish in her chest of accoutrements. She found a variety of gags, hoods and blindfolds, and selected a large black hood, to accommodate Armintrude's piled hair, and a thin leather gag, with a spherical steel tongue-depressor. Soon only Armintrude's nose and eyes were visible under the soft leather. She nodded curtly to affirm that she was comfortable; Jana replied that she would soon be less so. She ordered Nadia and Waltraut to bring the chests to within Armintrude's sight, then to begin their task of binding every inch of Armintrude's stretched arms and legs with leather collars. These were to be reversed so that their blunt metal studs would press against Armintrude's flesh.

As Armintrude's bare legs and arms began to disappear under a mass of leather straps, Jana extracted a delicious flail – an ornate whip with six gleaming black leather thongs.

'Mmm,' Jana murmured. 'This, I think.'

She let the thongs brush teasingly over Armintrude's buttocks, then gave her breasts the same treatment, before letting the instrument trail down over her belly to her spread cunt-lips. She lowered it slightly, then pressed the shaft of the handle against Armintrude's exposed pink slit, and smiled as she heard the woman's harsh breathing. Jana knew she was playing a game for high stakes: if she proved herself fearless, she would please her Master, but if she failed to break Armintrude, then the positions could easily be reversed.

'So,' Jana said, with mock solemnity. 'This whip should do for your bum, and perhaps I'll give your breasts just the slightest tickle with it, too.'

Jana knew that her theatre excited the company as much as it pleased her – she had been rather piqued by Armintrude's insult – and, most importantly, the Master was smiling in approval. Armintrude shivered; she seemed genuinely nervous.

'No apology, Armintrude? Brave girl,' said Jana.

The woman's trussed legs and arms were now gleaming tubes of sheer black leather. Jana rummaged in the chest again and found a pair of antique silver nipple clamps, which she promptly attached to Armintrude's breasts, and a restraint belt with two clips shaped like a finger and thumb, designed to stretch the cunt-lips wide apart. When Armintrude's fount-petals were pinned open, Jana took the largest pacifier the chest offered, and slid its twin shafts firmly into the woman's cunt and anus, fastening it in place with an attachment on the restraint belt. Then she gave the rack's wheel a little spin, pretending to put great effort into it. Modifications had been made to the mechanism, so that there was no risk of injury to its 'victim', but Armintrude moaned and trembled as it creaked. Her shining black leather shell was stretched now so that her tiptoes scarcely touched the rack's base.

'Don't complain, Armintrude, a little extra height becomes you. You look almost respectable now, but we'll have to do something about that scruffy mink, and those armpits.'

Armintrude moaned. She was evidently proud of her lush mink, and the nipple clamps at her shivering breasts shook as, having instructed Nadia and Waltraut to fetch her a bowl of soapy water, Jana retrieved a beautiful razor – another antique – from the chest. Carefully, she shaved Armintrude's pubic hair until her mons was as bare and soft as her tender stretched fesses. Jana was also pleased to note that the knob of Armintrude's clitoris which was now visible through the fleshy lip-folds, was standing up stiffly!

'Much better,' said Jana coolly, once Armintrude's stretched armpits had been similarly denuded. 'There may be a few hairs left around your bum, but we can tweeze them out later on. And now we'd better get on with your proper punishment.'

Armintrude moaned deeply, as Jana's hand slid in between her thighs. Suddenly there was a hissing, trickling sound, and Jana felt something warm gushing over her fingers. Armintrude sobbed behind her gag and mask. The leather straps that sheathed her legs now glistened with a cascade of liquid.

Jana grinned in gleeful triumph.

'You messy girl!' she cried. 'Wetting yourself! The punishment for that impropriety will be dreadful!'

At once, she threw down her whip and proceeded to spank the trembling globes of Armintrude's naked bottom.

'You – are – a – naughty – girl,' she chided, punctuating each word with a slap, 'and – in – England – naughty – girls – have – their – bare –bottoms – spanked!'

Jana continued the spanking until Armintrude, squealing and squirming, had taken fifty or sixty hard slaps and her bare fesses were a pleasing crimson. The company roared with wild applause and laughter at Armintrude's humiliation, and the Master touched his hands lightly together.

'There!' said Jana, patting the trembling bare globes of Armintrude's scarlet bottom. 'You may go. I don't think you can take any more punishment for now ...'

Armintrude was released, the process as lengthy and delicate as her binding, and when the hood was removed, Jana saw that her face was wet with tears.

'Did the spanking hurt too much?' asked Jana in genuine concern. Fiercely, Armintrude unravelled her hair and shook her head to let it flow once more down her proud back. Her face was twisted with grief.

'You could not hurt me!' she sneered. 'I felt nothing! So *don't* expect me to apologise, *Mistress* Jana!'

With that, her tears of shame welled up again, and she fled from the refectory. The Master laughed briefly, but his attention had shifted to the games of his lustful and imaginative guests. Jana watched in fascinated desire as the Master's two naked wolves lay down together on the table, and allowed themselves to be pinioned by their wrists and ankles. Nadia on her back, Waltraut on her belly.

Each male fucked them in the anus or the cunt, or drove his engorged member between their willing, sucking lips. Jana saw that some of the males wore restraint belts, and thick anal pacifiers, and all seemed to wear the thigh-band of the Elect. All, too, were busy with their lascivious embraces – only the Master sat aloof and observing. So much was happening, and Jana suddenly felt dizzy. She remembered Armintrude's impropriety, and realised that she wanted to go to the commode. Would it be improper to excuse herself? Surely not, in this slippery tumult of lust.

She saw Robyn, spreadeagled on the stone floor; Mimi was on top of her, wearing a huge double-pronged strap-on dildo, which she was plunging with fierce expertise into Robyn's anus and cunt. Gilles was busy with one of the maids, who was bent over and taking a leisurely flogging with the six-thonged leather whip, with every evidence of satisfaction on both sides. In fact, the role of the maids seemed to be that of whipping girls, for when a male was orgasmically sated, he would playfully rip a maid's stockings and knickers, then redden her naked bottom with an energetic beating, before returning to his lustful pleasure, his penis erect once more. Jana noticed that many of the maids masturbated as they took their beatings, or, when two girls were beaten in tandem, masturbated each other.

'You do not join in, Mistress Jana?' said the Master.

'Why, I – no, I am tired, Master.'

She watched, her belly bursting for the commode, and now saw Cassie and Robyn being pleasured, by Gilles's cock and tongue, respectively, as Mimi whipped their thighs, breasts and bellies with a light springy cane – an ashplant, Jana thought irrelevantly. Gilles was naked but for a restrainer belt and his powerful back and buttocks rippled as he fucked Cassie, with Robyn squatting over him, as over a commode, to receive the homage of his tongue flickering on her stiff red nympha.

He fucked Cassie slowly at first, pulling almost the full length of his massive, gleaming penis out of her, then using the ridge of his helmet to tease her wet cunt-lips for a moment before driving his cock back into her with a single swift thrust. Then his fucking grew faster and faster as his spasm approached, and Mimi's caning arm became a piston as she laid a fierce stroke on his fesses before each thrust. He began to moan as his seed welled, and suddenly Mimi reached down and pulled at his restrainer belt. At his first cry of orgasm, she slowly drew from his anus a huge pacifier of knotted, polished wood, and his cries became squeals of ecstasy. His lips and tongue delved frantically at the squatting Robyn's wet quim, and Robyn, with a grin of delight, committed her own glistening impropriety. Jana longed to join them, but something held her back. She was Mistress – she wanted the Master!

'You have done well, Mistress Jana,' he said, motioning to her to sit down, mere inches away from the writhing bodies. She did so, and crossed her legs so that her clit was squeezed between her labia.

'But,' he continued, 'you should take your pleasure. At a feast, all impropriety is permitted, just as all shall be forgotten in the morning, when your instruction starts.'

'Master, my pleasure is . . . to obey. I should like to retire, when my slave is sated,' she answered. To obey! She had uttered the words, and wondered at herself.

'As you wish. I trust you can find your way back to your quarters?' Jana nodded. 'Just remember that you are free to leave the Castle whenever you wish, but that while you are here you must behave within our rules. Some of them may seem strange, and you may make enemies; in fact you may already have one in Armintrude. Just remember that I am your Master and not your protector.'

An enemy! Jana thought, suddenly, of Armintrude's slim buttocks, and how sweetly they had reddened under her spanking. She had a vision of taming her, flogging her properly with the *flagrum*, before taking a strap-on dildo and fucking her in her anus and cunt, as vigorously as she had seen Gilles fuck Cassie. In her reverie, she saw Mokka, too, their bodies clasped, and their clits and breasts rubbing together in sweet tribadism. Mokka's bottom was upthrust for the cane, her anus bud open to Jana's tongue. She desired Mokka so much, as Cassie knew. And now, Armintrude – Jana truly desired to give her the whipping of her life in retaliation for that insult, but at the same time she wanted to take her in her arms, rub her clit to wetness, and teach her to love. Mokka – Armintrude – so many possibilities to explore – and with Cassie and Mimi they could make a pentangle of love, their naked bodies entwined and garlands of chestnut blossoms at their founts . . .

At that moment Jana could restrain herself no longer. She felt as if the ground would swallow her as a hot flow of golden piss burst from her and cascaded down her stockinged thighs to form a pool on the floor. She hoped desperately that the Master had not seen; of course, he had.

'That is your permitted impropriety, then, Mistress Jana. See to it that you commit no more, or it will go ill for you,' he said pleasantly. 'I bid you goodnight. You and your slave shall be summoned early in the morning, and there are no dress instructions, for you shall attend me naked.'

11

Life Class

'That was a jolly good evening, wasn't it?' said Mimi brightly as she opened the drapes of Jana's and Cassie's bed. 'The Master really knows how to throw a party. He's such super fun! Did he tell you he was a descendant of the Emperor Charlemagne? That would make him Holy Roman Emperor, I suppose.'

Mimi's mood was matched by the bright simplicity of her clothing – a simple white blouse worn without a bra, a pleated, knee-length white skirt, white stockings, and vivid sky-blue shoes which matched her choker of blue crystal.

'Super fun, Mimi,' said Jana, rubbing her eyes. Her dream was dissolving; in her reverie she had imagined the well-equipped dungeon whence Nadia and Waltraut had fetched the instruments of Armintrude's chastisement.

'Well, here's your breakfast – I let myself in, hope you don't mind.' She placed a tray on the table.

'There are no locks in Maldona,' said Jana, half-asleep.

'Maldona?' said Mimi pertly. 'It sounds fascinating and you must tell me all about it. Meanwhile, don't bother to dress, as I believe the Master has instructed you to attend him naked. Shall I run a bath for you?' Cassie stirred.

'Yes,' said Jana, 'we must be cleansed for him.' To her thrilled surprise, she heard herself speak without a hint of irony. 'I have to use the commode first.'

'Oh, don't mind me,' said Mimi gaily from the bathroom. 'My, you go a lot, don't you? I heard about your little impropriety last night. What a lark!'

She watched as Jana squatted on the commode, and held out some sheets of pink paper for her wiping.

'You have a lovely body, Jana,' she said, 'and so does your slave Cassie. We had a bit of a jape together with Gilles last night. Oh well! Now it's daytime, and back to normal, when we must be proper! You'll love modelling for the Master! Nadia and Waltraut are very good at it. I seem to be not quite the right shape, though.'

Cassie entered the bathroom, and put her arms round Mimi.

'You are just the right shape, Mimi,' she purred, 'if I remember last night.' Her hands cupped Mimi's full breasts.

'Oh,' cried Mimi, disengaging, 'you are sweet, Cassie, but don't be improper. The feast is over, until the next one!'

Cassie squatted, too, then joined Jana in the tub, and Mimi watched with curiosity as they went through the ritual of shaving each other.

'Such fun!' she said. 'A bare *down there* is so pretty!'

Jana said she was sure the Master would approve of her doing the same, and Mimi nodded thoughtfully.

'In Maldona, only those above the rank of Adept are permitted to shave,' Cassie blurted. 'Virgins must wear a full mink.'

'Really? You must tell me more about this Maldona,' said Mimi. 'It sounds very strict.'

Jana murmured that it was indeed very strict.

'Then you'll probably find the Castle horribly liberal!'

When their ablutions were finished they proceeded to eat heartily of an English breakfast, typical except that the bouquet of flowers on the tray was fresh chestnut blossom, and beside it was a dish of honeyed marshmallow. Jana smiled. 'Marshmallow again!' she said. 'Do you dare?'

But Cassie's mouth was already full.

'Mmm!' she said. 'Jolly scrumptious, as Mimi would say.'

'I suppose I would,' answered Mimi, who had busied herself flicking imaginary dust from the bedposts and chairs. 'Well, if you're finished, we'll go to the Master. You've quite a full day of training: you'll probably see me from time to time, as I am your Initiator, but I have other girls to attend to, and basically you are on your own until suppertime. And you won't see Armintrude there, Jana! She is a vegetarian – ugh! – and eats alone. I don't think she realises the Master disapproves of eccentricity, no matter how cleansing. By the way, you are allowed to wear shoes!'

Now they went further than the refectory door, and once more Jana cast a questioning glance down the corridor which forked left. The women they passed were all sumptuously robed, but no one seemed to question their nudity. When Jana remarked on this, Mimi said rather apologetically that it was the practice for all new Students to be naked in the daytime during their period of instruction, as it instilled in them the necessary meekness. Jana said that she was proud to be naked, and that in Maldona, nudity, like a clean-shaven fount, was a privilege of high rank. Many of the Parfaites, who she explained were Maldona's equivalent to Elect, went naked at all times. Mimi's eyes and smile betrayed her curiosity.

'Are we Students, now?' asked Cassie.

'Formally speaking, not yet. But I do hope you shall be! Then, of course, you will have to wear your pacifiers.'

'With pleasure,' answered Jana.

'And learn to bow properly. You can practise on me, as I am your Initiator. Silly, but rules are rules. Any infringement of rules,' she added merrily, 'and I'm afraid it's a smacked botty!' she mimed a spanking.

'I shouldn't mind being spanked by the Master,' said Cassie dreamily.

'Not by him – only high-ranking skin is privileged to taste the Master's whip. I'm afraid it's my responsibility to cleanse you. So take care not to be improper, or I'd have the painful duty of reddening those delicious fesses.'

She spoke with a gleam in her eye, as if to suggest that such a duty would not be at all painful to her. Jana asked how many inhabitants the Castle had, and Mimi answered that she did not know. Jana sensed she was telling the truth.

'Only the Master knows exactly how many we are,' she said thoughtfully. 'I think.'

Suddenly daylight flooded the corridor as they turned a corner and found themselves before a panoramic window. The view quite took Jana's breath away; Mimi said they could pause for a few minutes to enjoy it as they were slightly early and the Master considered earliness to be as unpunctual – and therefore improper – as lateness.

They looked out on a landscape of savage majesty, which sloped gently down from the Castle, and whose wild beauty seemed somehow artificial; it was just too perfect to be natural. There was a lake, surrounded by conifers, and, in the background, rolling, forested hills at the foot of a snowcapped crag. The complex of walled and hedged gardens located in the shadow of the Castle was definitely man-made. Mimi explained proudly that the Castle lodged at the top of its mountain, which gave way to a further plateau abounding in game, wild flowers and plants.

'This is the wild heart of the Rhodope,' she said, 'and it belongs to Schloss Enddorf. There is nothing beyond, for boundless kilometres, until the road to Sofia. I don't think even the Master has seen the ends of his domain. We have everything we need here – hydroelectricity from the lake, hunting in the forest, and other food from the fields and gardens. The Master likes to cultivate the more exotic plant species, and you can see some flowers and treetops peeping over the hedges. You will see everything in due course, but I warn you that to know the Castle is so thrilling you will never wish to leave. I certainly don't!'

Jana reminded herself to ask Mimi for her story when she was again in an informal mood. She peered through the glass at the fine detail of the panorama, which seemed almost *too* true to life, with every leaf and wavelet crystal clear through the sparkling glass. Absent-mindedly, she put her fingers out to touch the glass, and recoiled in shock. It was not glass!

Mimi burst into peals of laughter.

'That's right, it is one of the Master's paintings. The view is authentic, as though it were actually a window, but the *trompe l'oeil* appeals to his sense of fun. Don't worry, it fools absolutely everybody. See! Even the corridor lighting is arranged so that it seems to come in through the window. I told you the Master is a perfectionist.'

The next turning brought them to a plain wooden door on which Mimi knocked twice, with a pause of three seconds in between. It was promptly opened by a beautiful young man with cropped straw-coloured hair, who wore nothing but a short skirt of coarse hempen fibre. Jana sensed that she was seeing her first male Student. They found themselves in a large airy room, with bright light from a window that *was* evidently real. The room was filled with the heady smell of fresh paint, and on the stone floor were arranged tables stacked with palettes, canvases, brushes and easels, together with screens, lights and cameras on tripods. It was every inch an artist's studio. Armintrude was there, dressed in a simple white smock and sandals; she smiled very coldly at Jana. Mimi seemed taken aback by her presence, and whispered that she was only there to help the Master.

Sprawled on easy chairs were various males, smoking and chatting; Jana recognised Gilles, and a couple of others from the night before, one of whom she remembered was Michael, a photographer from Hamburg. Their attire was casual, as was that of the Master, who looked chic but incongruous in blue overalls and a white teeshirt flecked with paint. He was busy posing two women: they wore 1930s *femme fatale* gowns that reminded Jana of Garbo or Dietrich. Around them, with pins and tape measures, fussed more slaves, all young blond men wearing identical coarse skirts, their hairless legs and torsos beautifully muscled. Jana had stopped mentally using the euphemism 'Students', for she recognised a slave's demeanour – the downcast eyes and unsmiling lips, and the lithe, supple motion of obedience and efficiency.

The Master did not look round, but called: 'Good morning, Jana and Cassie. Please take your places, I shall be ready for you in a moment.'

151

Mimi showed them to their places, and took her leave after curtseying to the Master's back. Jana and Cassie were left to stand, uncomfortably aware of leering male eyes, as Michael photographed the two models and the Master, murmuring posing instructions, sketched them in pencil.

Jana had time to inspect the paintings, sculptures and photographs which adorned the studio. Many were of nudes, and illustrated the Master's taste for the erotically bizarre – models fantastically well-endowed, hermaphroditic or steatopygous, or simply blessed with a multiplicity of distended organs. One life-sized sculpture at the far end of the studio showed a nearly-nude male and female in matt chalky stone. The woman was bare except for a mini-skirt, each of its pleats artfully sculpted, which was thrown up over the small of her back. She stood with her legs apart and her head lowered, her arms raised in the Castle's strange regulation bow. The male wore only a G-string with a quite extraordinary bulge – delicious poetic licence, Jana thought – and held a thin cane which was resting across the naked fesses of the woman, as though in mid-flogging. His face was grimly serious, and his muscles bulged like whipcord with his exertion, while the woman's expression was dreamy, her eyes gently closed. Jana found the tableau enchanting: a female submissive in subtle command of her male tormentor.

Jana and Cassie watched as Michael photographed the models from every possible angle, under the Master's terse direction. The first frames were classic fashion shots, but gradually the poses grew more outré and openly lubricious: Jana found herself quite excited as the models parted their legs, lowered their panties as though for the commode, squeezed each other's breasts, and even held each other's founts as they exchanged kisses on the lips. The session ended with the burly Michael crouching on the floor and pointing his lens squarely at the naked fount of each girl in turn, as she held her frock up over her torso, as though it had been blown there by a gust of wind.

Both girls had full silky minks and one of Michael's props was a hairdryer which he pointed upwards to blow the hairs and give the illusion of wind. All the time, Gilles led the other males in boastful conversation, most of it to do with the women's bodies and what he should like to do to them, but Jana also caught snatches of shop talk.

'Over there, a conservatory, glass-domed, with the most exotic poisonous blossoms of the rain forest: the plants that eat insects and mice,' said a young male, cherubically handsome, with long silky auburn hair like Armintrude's. 'I want to have real snakes and birds, a river with crocodiles and piranha – a complete fauna in fact! Imagine an improper Student thrown to the river beasts – living sculpture, he said, none too seriously. 'The Master has yet to decide, but it would be a fine adjunct to your palace of arts, Gilles.'

'Yes, where the fauna shall be human, alive, and female.'

'Not all, surely? Female, I mean.'

'No,' said Gilles with a smile, insolently flicking cigar ash in Jana's direction, 'males do have their uses.'

The session over, the models took off their robes, folded them neatly, and handed them to Armintrude with a bow both to her and to the Master. Armintrude told them that Instruction was in one hour, and, nude after the solemnity of their posing, they scampered away with impish smiles.

Jana felt goose pimples as the Master said it was their turn. Casually, he stood before them, neither smiling nor looking them in the eye, and began to feel their naked bodies. The probing fingers which pinched their nipples, parted their cunt-lips, and stroked their bellies and fesses, were not those of a lover, but those of an appraiser of flesh. Jana found the effect very stimulating and, glancing at Cassie, knew she felt the same. They were nothing but slaves in a market, or perhaps beasts.

The Master turned round and spoke to Armintrude, again in a curiously archaic language. Jana sensed that this language expressed some deep bond between them, which explained his indulgence of her awkward personality and her eccentricities. Jana wondered if they were lovers, and dismissed the idea. No, the Master was not fucking Armintrude, despite her evident longing for him, and that was his hold over her. But what was her hold over him? Jana would ask Mimi.

Armintrude now brought dresses – or, more accurately, costumes – for them. Smiling coldly, she helped the two women to dress. Her fingers were light and tender on Jana's bare flesh and, despite herself, Jana felt a thrill as she was touched. There was much pinning, buttoning and zipping, and Jana became giddy with excitement. When the dressing was over, the women were arrayed in the most delicious and most dangerous of contrasts.

Cassie found herself adorned as a rather daring flamenco dancer, in a peach-coloured ensemble which perfectly suited her dark complexion. The flounced skirt was slit to above her waist, revealing a pair of lacy, semi-transparent panties, and silk stockings with lacy tops attached with suspenders to a very tight satin corset. This was laced up at the front, but with the top four eyelets undone, so that her constricted breasts were almost entirely bared. Her shoes had tapering stiletto heels and were a slightly darker shade of peach. Cassie's hair was piled high and adorned with a rosebud on a clip of sparkling stones, and she wore a high choker and earrings to match. The combination of her bright jewellery, the strategically revealing cut of her skirt, the carelessly unlaced corset, and the soft pastel dress made her look feminine and vulnerable rather than aggressively sluttish, as though her lingerie and flesh were exposed by accident rather than design.

Jana's costume complemented her slave's in a way that left no doubt as to the nature of their relationship. It was so tight that she was at first forced to gasp for breath, and as Armintrude applied the finishing touches with grim satisfaction, Jana's fount was soaking in her excitement.

She wore black. Pointed patent leather boots, on heels as high as Cassie's, were seamed to leggings of the thinnest soft latex, coarsely pinned together at the back of her legs, leaving a gap of bare flesh about two inches wide. Each boot had a silver spur, shaped like a starfish. Matching the stocking-boots was a rubber bustier which fitted tightly over Jana's right breast, moulding perfectly to its shape, while leaving her left shoulder and breast naked, save for a silver ring clipped to her nipple. The bustier was decorated with a snake motif, handworked in tiny silver studs, which wound around Jana's back and waist until the snake's head swallowed its tail right above her fount. Above the snake's head was strapped a thick leather belt, also studded, from which swirled an accordion-pleated satin cape, slit at the back as far as the buttock cleft, and sweeping wide open at the front, so that Jana's fount and croup were tantalisingly on view.

Her panties were nothing more than the skimpiest of rubber G-strings, leaving her fesses bared except for a thin strand deep in her cleft. The front of them was a tight sliver of fabric, slit so that her shining vaginal lips peeped out. To each of these was fastened a gossamer chain, from which was hung the larger, heavier sister of her nipple ring, and a third chain was fastened directly on to the protruding nubbin of her clitoris. The slightest movement sent shivers of pleasure through Jana's belly and spine, and her cunt-ring and the skin of her inner thighs were already glistening with the moisture that seeped from her swollen quim.

The Master murmured his directions, and they began to pose, as Michael's camera clicked, with machine-gun rapidity, against the smooth whirr of the Master's video camera. Jana blinked as the lights flicked on and off according to each pose, and she began to sweat in their intense heat. At first, their poses were girlish and tongue in cheek, with Jana 'larking about', as Mimi might have put it, in her role as dominatrix, and Cassie blushing as what she might have termed a slightly 'oopsy' *femme*. Armintrude acted as prop mistress, bringing them quoits, hoops and bouquets. Laughing, and applauded by the male onlookers, they mimed pastiches of rococo paintings by Fragonard or Boucher, somehow maintaining an illusion of coyness as they parted their thighs to display their knickers. The Master had to remind them gently that they were not actors, but models for his dress creations.

Gradually, however, the mood changed. The lights were

dimmed by means of smoky coloured filters, and Jana smelled a pungent incense. The ribald comments from the males quietened precisely as the females' poses rendered them superfluous; Jana and Cassie embraced and kissed, softly touching each other's founts, bottoms and breasts.

'Kneel, Cassie, and kiss your Mistress's cunt-ring,' the Master would intone quietly. 'That's good, now take it into your mouth . . . now put your tongue out and lick her clit. Lift your skirt, bend over and spread your bum-cheeks, I want the cameras to get a good look at that sweet little hole of yours. Jana, your finger in Cassie's anus, please – yes, deep – and touch your own clit. You like your work, don't you? You'll make excellent Students.'

Jana's cunt overflowed with wetness. She had her lips on Cassie's quim, which was also soaking. She pressed her slave and lover to her, holding her buttocks tightly as she licked and swallowed her juices, and smelling Cassie's perfume as the peach dress fluttered against her skin. Then she was on top of Cassie, whose dress she then raised right up to her neck, before unlacing her corset and rubbing herself rhythmically against her, so that her bustier's studded snake motif rasped teasingly over Cassie's naked belly. Then she squatted astride her slave, with her spurs poised at the entrance to Cassie's naked quim, gently and very carefully touching its swollen lips. The studio seemed to be in darkness, except for the pools of hot light which bathed their writhing bodies. Each pose grew more daring than the last, and Jana thrilled at the harsh breathing which surrounded them: they were the centre of attention, and both knew they were no longer acting.

'Oh, Master,' Cassie blurted, 'we desire to be more than students, to be fully initiated –'

'To be slaves!' cried Jana.

She heard the Master chuckle.

'Spank her, then, slave,' he said to Jana, who at once bent Cassie over her knee, lifted her skirt, and pulled her panties right down over her thighs, before starting to administer a hard spanking to her bare fesses.

'Redden her bum well for me,' purred the Master, and

whispered something to Armintrude. Suddenly Jana felt a belt being slid snugly around her waist. It felt heavy and, as Armintrude deftly adjusted it, Jana looked down to see that she had been fitted with an enormous strap-on dildo, fashioned from burnished metal, which passed neatly through her cunt-ring. She thought fleetingly of Damien, his giant metal cock and his hard flesh, and her fount seemed to melt into a pool of gushing hot oil. Her adornment was not over: to her wonderment, Armintrude reappeared with a bulky shoulder-bag of field-grey canvas, from which she took a hideous contraption of rubber, elastic, and scratched goggles. It was a gas mask!

Swiftly, Armintrude looped the gas mask over Jana's head, enclosing it tightly. The garment had an acrid odour, and Jana found her vision blurred and distorted by the scratches on the goggles, as though Cassie and the studio were images daubed on to a misty screen. She could breathe easily, and the sound of her breathing was amplified, echoing raucously in her ears. She felt beautifully detached, a monstrous creation supreme and alone in this soft human world of scented flesh; the chilly beauty of the dildo and the inhuman, grotesque gas mask were her insignia of a Mistress's power.

'Now, rip her panties,' said the Master. 'And her stockings. I want the slut well laddered.'

When Jana had shredded Cassie's panties and stockings, the Master ordered her to raise Cassie's legs and tear holes in her skirt. Cassie uttered a curious moan, as though, by the laceration of her clothing, something deep inside her soul was being torn apart. Jana pulled hard, and heard the fabric rip, her heart exulting in her destructive power. Cassie clutched the tatters of her dress around her legs and exposed cunt, as though to defend herself, but she was helpless against the renewed force of Jana's palms on her bare croup; Jana knew that her moans and squeals of protest were the sweetest play-acting. Cassie wanted to be helpless.

The metal dildo hung low between Jana's thighs, its shining stiffness menacing in the smoky light. She paused in her spanking and caressed the massive shaft. Serenely shaped as a male's cock, with balls sculpted like gnarled walnuts, it was nevertheless a machine, *her* machine, and Jana thrilled at how perfectly in harmony she felt with it. She needed no orders from the Master, now, but jerked apart Cassie's glowing spanked fesses and exposed the pink blossom of her anus. She anointed the tip of the metal cock with oil from her own wet quim, then tickled Cassie's anus, rubbing the metal glans up and down the wrinkled bud, and across the red arse-skin. Cassie's moans were thoughtful: she knew a hard fucking awaited her.

'Mmm,' she whispered. 'You are so big, Mistress.'

Without a word, Jana slid the glans an inch into the tight elastic ring of Cassie's anus. Cassie's buttocks writhed in a sinuous dance as she relaxed, then tensed her sphincter to suck the giant cock into her innermost belly. Jana matched her own hard thrusts to Cassie's squeezing, and Cassie groaned with pleasure as her Mistress's inhuman cock penetrated her up to its very hilt. She stretched her buttocks tight as a drumskin, and Jana began to thrust anew.

'Oh,' moaned Cassie, 'won't the balls go in? Please . . .'

They would not, but as Jana's hips jerked back and forth, ramming the dildo ruthlessly into Cassie's squirming anus, her slave's fingers met Jana's on the throbbing bud of her nympha, and together they pleasured the stiff, swollen clit until their fingers were oily with Cassie's flowing love-juices. Both women were now squatting on their knees, and with her free hand, Jana masturbated her own stiff damsel. Distantly, she heard the still-relentless whirring of the Master's video camera, and heard too a rustling of clothing being removed. She was not surprised, when she felt a hand pulling aside the thong-back of her G-string and parting the bare globes of her buttocks.

The hot tip of a swollen cock brushed her own anus bud, and she sighed in joy as the man's bulb began its penetration of her bucking arse. She knew the cock belonged to Gilles: he was naked on top of her, thrusting his hard penis deep and firm into her willing bumhole even as she was arse-fucking her slave. And her pleasure was enhanced by a delicious tickling in her elastic passage; Gilles, she realised was now wearing a ring, piquantly called a *joug* or yoke, through his pierced foreskin. His hands found her breasts, one bare and one rubber-sheathed, and squeezed her nipples hard until they were trembling and stiff. Then he ripped her bustier until both breasts were bare, and began to knead them mercilessly as he fucked her.

'It is not my only ring, sweet Jana,' he breathed, as his cock rode hard in her anus. 'I have a *guiche* as well –' he pronounced it 'geesh' '– a lovely ring right at the top of my scrotum, just a little way below my perineum. Your cunt must not go unattended, for that would be improper. My friend Michael is here, behind me, and his cock fits so neatly in my *guiche*.'

Jana gasped as she felt a second cock penetrate her, one so long and massive that Michael was able to straddle Gilles and put his cock between Gilles's buttocks, through the ring of the *guiche*, and into Jana's cunt, filling her completely. She began to cry out with pleasure as she felt two massive cocks fucking her, to the rhythm with which she pleasured her own slave's filled anus. And then a third male, the naturalist, came to kneel before Cassie, his naked cock standing high and almost parallel with his belly. Wordlessly, he positioned her head above his swollen glans and without further invitation, Cassie slid the cock's shaft all the way to the back of her throat, and began to suck powerfully. The movements of her head were so vigorous that his tight balls bounced up and down like twin Adam's apples.

'Make my tree bear fruit, sweet lady,' he whispered.

Jana felt the warmth and heaviness of the two naked male bodies straddling her, and the pliant slippery body of Cassie beneath as she fellated the naturalist, all five participants moving in perfect harmony like a single oiled engine of desire. She knew she would not last long before she climaxed; she could feel the urgency in the men's fucking, the brittle hardness of their cocks as their balls prepared to deliver their sweet hot sperm to her belly. Cassie, too, moaned at her plateau as Jana flicked her clit and slammed the dildo into her with fierce gliding thrusts.

Suddenly Jana saw the flash of a curved knife blade against the white of Armintrude's smock. The Master's words echoed in her mind – 'I want the slut well laddered' – as she felt the flat of the blade being stroked over her clothing, and then deft, expert slashes of its sharp edge being used to tear her bustier, her panties, her cape and her stocking-boots to ribbons, without inflicting the slightest scratch on her body. Her train of thought was interrupted by the sound of Gilles and Michael panting, their breathing becoming faster and faster as the first hot drops of their sperm washed her cunt and anus. Her belly glowed, and an electric joy filled her right to the tips of her fingers and toes. The knife blade had ripped her clothing and in doing so had torn away all restraint and all modesty.

She heard Cassie moan deep in her throat as she convulsed in orgasm, felt her quim and belly shudder and heard her swallow her yelping male's seed. Then Jana's males cried out, bathing both her holes in fierce jets of hot sperm. Jana's cries, as she came, were louder even than theirs, for she exploded in a spasm of ecstasy that tightened her throat like the pain and beauty of a whipcut.

When it was over, the lights rose and Jana looked with awed pleasure at the rings hanging from Gilles's pierced cock and scrotum. Her cunt-ring was merely clipped on to her petals: what, she wondered, would piercing be like? The sated males meekly withdrew to sit and smoke their cigars, and the Master approached the women as they lay back exhausted.

'You have performed well,' he said pleasantly, 'and are now admitted as Students of Schloss Ende. But dear me – your clothing is spoiled, and that is improper. I'm afraid there is a penalty for sluttishness.'

'But surely it was meant to happen!' Cassie cried.

Jana hushed her, but the Master smiled and replied: 'Certainly it was meant to happen, but *you chose* to *let it* happen. Mimi, your Initiator, will attend to the matter. Farewell, Students, for now. And Jana, you may keep the gas mask and the strap-on pleasure shaft. They become you.'

Mimi was summoned, and came in an apprehensive flurry to take charge of her new Students. As they left the studio, Jana looked back to admire the marvellous sculpture of the semi-nude female in submission to her male chastiser.

She saw the female's eyes blink.

12

Punishment Cell

'I feel so awful that your Initiation should be *this* way,' said Mimi, 'really I do, Jana.' She brushed aside a tree frond blocking their path through the undergrowth.

'At least you'll get to see a little bit of the garden today,' she added brightly. 'We're nearly at the birch grove – it's fascinating, there are so many kinds of trees, not just birches. Husbandry is one of the Master's passions, and he likes to mingle trees and plants together, to see which will adapt best. He calls it practical evolution, the survival of the fittest.'

'Or the survival of the most exotic,' said Jana drily, looking, as the trio progressed through the fragrant dells, at the strange hybrid plants which seemed to be flaunting their gaudy blossoms.

'The Master is interested in creating, or recreating, a battlefield for survival,' said Mimi. He says that all life is basically soft, and must adapt to this world by developing weapons, shells – in a word, hardness. Look at these gay flowers and berries – they are all beautiful, and all poisonous. Their beauty is either a warning, or a temptation. The shell of a turtle, or the fearsome armour of a crab, have the beauty of pure function, but inside the beast is soft and naked. So it is with humans; we are endoskeletal – the Master is full of big words! – that is, we have our bones inside our flesh, so to survive we must build our own armour on the outside.'

'So to be human, we must become inhuman,' said Jana thoughtfully. 'The Castle sounds like a laboratory.'

'That's a jolly good way of putting it!' cried Mimi. 'The Master sees the whole world as a laboratory.'

The sun was high, bathing Jana's nudity with warmth; all around was the buzz of insects and the air was thick with heady scents. The morning would have been idyllic were it not for the errand that brought the women here.

'This is it!' said Mimi gaily. They entered an arbour where birch, elm, ash and willow trees mingled amid banks of lush wild flowers, and Jana told her that her white dress made her look like a flower herself. Mimi blushed and smiled, and nervously jangled the keyring at the heavy blue belt which so perfectly matched her shoes.

'It is so pretty here,' said Cassie.

'Yes, and we have plenty of time for you to make your selection. The instrument doesn't have to be made entirely of birch twigs, actually. For a Pure Beating it would, and salted and pickled too, for a purer pain. There are plenty of trees and bushes to choose from, and I can help you if you like.' Jana nodded her assent, and Mimi cleared her throat nervously.

'But, Jana, each twig must be at least a metre long, and there must be fourteen of them,' she blurted. 'Oh, I feel rotten, making you fashion a birch for your own body!'

'Don't pretend to feel rotten, Mimi,' answered Jana curtly. 'It's not the first time you've accompanied new Students to this grove. Nadia and Waltraut, for example?'

'Yes,' admitted Mimi. 'I gave each of them their first beating, for separate offences, but this is the first time I shall be beating two girls at once. Oh, Jana, I wish I could go easy on you, but I may not, for it would be improper. I must lash you naked as hard as I can, and – and it must be fourteen strokes, seven each to the shoulders and the buttocks. The Master has decreed it.'

'The Master, or Armintrude?' wondered Jana out loud. 'Never mind. Let us enjoy gathering our twigs, it will give us an appetite for luncheon.'

They passed a pleasant hour at their ominous work, each branch that Jana and Cassie plucked seeming to tremble with the knowledge that very soon it would lace their bare bodies and cause them pain. Mimi warmed to the task, and advised them soundly, so that Jana was able to assemble a bouquet of interesting rods, as well as the faithful birch twigs. At the same time, Cassie picked bunches of sweet-scented flowers, as if to assuage the vengeful power of the punishment branches.

The trees were familiar, but each had a slight variant to the norm: the shape of the leaves or flowers, the thickness of the stem, the bark smooth instead of gnarled. One birch tree had unusual knots that resembled screaming human faces. Mimi proudly explained that this was the same genus of birch whose wood had been used to flog Jacques de Molay, Grand Master of the Templars, seven hundred years before. Jana murmured that she knew something of the Founder of Maldona, and her intimacy with the secrets of the Templar Order.

'I *knew* you'd get on well with the Master!' Mimi cried.

'So well that he has ordered us to be whipped,' growled Cassie.

'You are honoured,' said Mimi primly. 'At least you are not to be flogged!' She gestured at the profusion of flora.

'Here things are sort of experimental. When various species have proved themselves in the wild, they are nurtured in the walled garden. This one is nice, it looks like an ordinary willow, but touch her wood.'

Jana did so, and made a face.

'It stings like a nettle!' she said with amusement, and calmly cut four of the branches to add to her flogging switch.

When the switch was finished, she had six birch twigs, the four of stinging willow, and twigs of ash, sycamore and elm. The total came to fifteen, and Mimi reminded her that that was more than necessary for the switch. Jana responded with a smile that she would take one for luck, because her arrangement of the coloured woods made a pretty rainbow. When this was complete, she took some strong lianas and bound the twigs tightly to make a whip-handle. As they strolled back to the Castle, Mimi said merrily that she was very brave.

164

'Just curious,' said Jana. 'The stinging willow will add a little spice to our tickling. We are of Maldona, and our bodies are not strangers to the whip, Mimi.'

'Oh, Jana, you have never been whipped by *me*,' replied Mimi, and this time her voice was sombre. She instructed Jana to bear the whip in front of her like an offering, and they proceeded with sacrificial solemnity in single file, with Mimi at the rear. The women who passed them politely averted their gaze, but their eyes darted in awe to the beautiful whipping tool in Jana's arms.

After the studio door, then the refectory, Mimi ordered them to turn to the right. Had they been coming the other way, from their room, this would have been the left-hand fork – the forbidden corridor! Jana said nothing, but obeyed, and found herself in a gloomy, ill-lit passage, devoid of pictures or any decoration at all. The floor was bare stone, unpolished, and she was glad she was wearing her shoes. Now they passed padded black doors, with barred lucarne windows set high up in them, and Jana counted four before Mimi told them to stop and fumbled with her key ring. Facing them, at the very end of the corridor, was another, larger, door, occupying almost the whole width of the passage. This door was of bolted steel.

'Won't be a sec,' fussed Mimi. 'Gosh, these keys all look the same! It's been so long since I was last in a cell . . .'

At last the door swung open, and she ushered them inside. They found themselves in a windowless room that was completely bare, save for a single small closet and, in the centre, a long stool like a gymnasium vaulting horse, with a padded leather cushion and six wooden legs, of which the four at its corners were splayed. Each leg had a set of metal cuffs at its foot, and the two centre legs a double set. There was dust everywhere, and Mimi wrinkled her nose.

'Poo!' she exclaimed. 'You can see this one isn't used much, it's not often there is a double whipping. All the cells are for different punishments, you see,' she added help-fully. 'And there isn't really anywhere to hang your clothes, because girls who come here usually aren't wearing any!' She laughed nervously, but Jana merely smiled. Mimi opened the closet, revealing one solitary coathanger.

'That is for me,' she said, 'in case I wish to hang up my own dress. Sometimes it is more comfortable to work naked. In fact, I think I shall, if you don't mind.'

Jana agreed politely and said the heat of the cell was quite stifling: all three women were already glistening with sweat in the dark room, whose only, sinister light beamed in dimly through the bars of the lucarne. Mimi unfastened her belt, pulled her dress over her head, and hung it carefully on the wire, her swelling breasts bobbing deliciously as she did so. Jana noticed that her nipples were as swollen as ripe cherries, and realised that her duty excited her as much as it awed her victims. Her full mink shone with droplets of sweat; Jana felt a sudden urge to shave her as she had shaved Armintrude the night before, and all the more so when Mimi made garlands of their picked flowers and wove them into the lush tresses of both her head and pubis.

'I like to look pretty when I give a whipping,' she said coyly. Well, I expect we'd better get on with it. Hand me the instrument, please, Jana.'

Obediently, Jana handed over the whip she had fashioned, and Mimi balanced it admiringly, then swished it with a fierce crack on to the cushion of the flogging-horse. Jana saw the bounce of her breasts and the quiver of her taut muscles, and on impulse told their Initiator that she was very beautiful, that her body was perfect in its harmony, and that her only regret about taking punishment was that she could not watch it take place. Mimi smiled shyly.

'You'll *feel* it take place!' she replied. 'And don't try and get round me with your lovely flattery! Now, in the closet there are a few accoutrements – gags and straps and hoods, but you don't need to wear them unless you want to. And it will save time if you can take it without being totally bound. Plenty of girls can't.'

'Armintrude, for one,' said Cassie, and Mimi laughed out loud.

166

'Can *you*, Mimi?' Jana asked, and Mimi looked at her with piercing eyes. She did not speak, but bowed her head, and nodded ruefully. Then, businesslike once more, she said that according to the rules, they must bow before taking their places. They made their obeisance, and Jana winced at the unusual position into which her arms were forced by the strange bow, but gained a curious pleasure from the way her pose tightened and stretched her breasts. Mindful of the intricate code of Maldona, she asked if the rules of the Castle were written down, and was told that they were not.

'Teaching is by example and an instinct for what is proper,' Mimi replied. 'Does a crab's claw need a rule-book?'

Then she said winningly that they had instinctively got the hang of bowing. They bent side by side across the flogging-horse, spreading their legs and arms so that Mimi could fasten them in the metal cuffs, which she called restrainers, upon which Cassie blurted that in Maldona that was the same as a pacifier. As her limbs were bound, Jana sensed that Mimi would not respond kindly to any plea for gentleness. By now she was bustling about in a very efficient manner and was every inch the stern Mistress.

'Right,' she said, frowning. 'I think the best thing would be for me to birch you both at the same time, so I'll alternate forehand and backhand strokes, if you agree.'

Jana did agree, and asked that she should start by administering the seven strokes to the shoulders first. Suddenly, from the near distance came a woman's howl, followed by a moment's sobbing, then silence. Jana presumed it was from an adjoining cell, and shivered. Mimi affected not to notice the sound, but fetched her blue leather belt from the closet and placed it lengthways between each woman's teeth. She said that although she was sure they needed no gags and would not cry out, it was better to have something to bite on.

'I whip very hard,' she said gently, and raised the switch with her left arm. Jana and Cassie could not move a muscle, so tightly were they stretched and bound. Their

167

heads hung down, almost touching the floor, and their calves touched, above their ankle cuffs in the centre of the horse. Jana raised her eyes briefly and saw Mimi's blue shoes before her, as the woman positioned herself to lace their shoulders.

'We've lots of time,' said Mimi cosily, 'so I'll give you both a lovely slow fourteen on your bare, and we can have a little chat as I cleanse you.'

'One!' she grunted, as she brought her instrument down on Jana's naked flesh, the stroke followed almost at once by a backhand lash to Cassie's. Jana's whole body jerked as a lance of white-hot pain seared her back. She bit tightly on the belt, glad of it now, and fought back the catch in her throat that made her want to cry out. She gasped at her pain, and shuddered despite herself when she heard Mimi say 'Two', listening for the whip's whistle, and jerking even before the stroke had touched her flesh.

'My,' said Mimi brightly, 'you *are* jumpy. Tight, are they?' Jana nodded, her eyes brimming with tears.

The third double stroke came, and then the fourth. Jana would hear the crack of the lash on Cassie's body almost at once after she had received her own stroke, but the sound was distant to her, alone as she was with her own agony. She felt her body quiver, her every muscle straining against her bonds, and was powerless to control this useless protest. She knew that she would soon reach her plateau, and that at that moment her whole body would be a shuddering mass of pure pain; it would not just be localised to the point of the whip's impact. Only then would she be able to transcend the searing lash: if only she could control herself and not scream in her throat, for screaming only made it worse.

In the distance, she heard the long, drawn-out howl of the unseen female, followed by four or five quick shrieks in staccato succession. What were they doing to that poor woman . . .? Jana's breath was hoarse, and above her own gasps, she could hear Mimi panting from her exertion.

'Gosh, it's hot!' said Mimi. 'This is hard work. *You* seem to be taking it well.' As though, Jana thought, Mimi was

168

the one suffering! Then she felt Mimi pull her hair, and lift up her head to wipe the moisture from her eyes.

'Perhaps not so well as all that,' she said. 'Stings, doesn't it? Five! Now you must tell me all about this Maldona of yours. Six!'

In the delirium of her pain, Jana said 'Mmm' again, meaning that she couldn't speak with the belt between her teeth. Mimi laughed rather cruelly and told her to answer questions by nodding yes or no. She added that while their beating was to consist of only fourteen strokes, the Initiator, according to the Master's rules, had the right to give the stroke over if she judged it had been delivered imperfectly.

'It means that I can beat you all day long, if I want to,' she said gleefully. 'Of course you are free to stop the beating at any time – just shake your head and I'll understand – you would of course have to leave the Castle, but I phoned about your car this morning and it looks as though it will take a long time for the parts to arrive from Japan. And it is a long walk to the nearest town . . .'

There was another outburst from the female in the nearby cell, this time three long cries and half a dozen short ones, like a kind of telegraph code of agony. Jana's own back felt as though glowing coals were being pressed to it, and she no longer experienced the whipping as individual strokes. She sighed as she realised she had reached the plateau, and her glow of pain began to seem almost comforting; a precious possession that was hers alone. She felt pity for her tormentor, who could not feel the same!

'Mmm,' said Mimi. 'Your backs are pretty and red. Now time for your bums. It's nicer to flog a bare bum, she quivers so beautifully.'

She walked behind them and paused, then began to ask Jana about Maldona. Was it, too, a Castle, with its own sacred rules? Jana nodded yes, and heard the whip whistle again, to land this time on the very centre of her outspread naked fesses. She jerked convulsively as her tender croup burned in a flame of agony which seemed more intense than the whipstroke to her hard-muscled shoulders.

And Jana was the supreme Mistress of Maldona? Again, yes, and again the reward of a fierce stroke to the very same point on her bare arse-globes. Mimi tutted.

'Oh, Mistress Jana, your bum is so beautiful,' said Mimi reproachfully. 'It is such a shame, and yet such a pleasure, to mark her thus. You have earned yourself and your slave a repeat of that cut, for although you are a Mistress, you *must* have a Master, supreme over all sluts. You have lied.'

The stroke came again, and again tears – of shock as much as of pain – sprang to Jana's eyes, for it fell dangerously close to her unprotected anus bud. She shook her head frantically as her body jerked, and squealed to indicate that she was telling the truth. The distant cries of the howling woman had now assumed a steady rhythm, uninterrupted, and were rising to a crescendo, which sounded curiously as though the female was in the throes of ecstatic fucking rather than chastisement. Mimi paused.

'Well,' she said slowly, 'I have heard that here in the Castle, there is a supreme Mistress, unseen, and greater even than the Master. But it cannot be true, it is only the rumour of improper Students.'

Jana, despite her agony, felt her quim beginning to moisten, and her belly warming with a glimmer of desire! Mimi was implacable: she would not believe that there could be a society of 'sluts' with no Master, and the cut was yet again repeated, this time landing within millimetres not only of Jana's anus, but also her fount-lips: and again it was the shock that made her squirm so frantically that she thought she would burst her restraining cuffs. The questions continued, Jana finding her predicament rather absurd, as though she were undergoing some exam or test in which one could not speak but had to tick yes or no. Most of her answers, however, satisfied Mimi, although on a few more occasions she was deemed to be lying. Mimi, whose voice was now faltering, and who was gasping as harshly as her victims, seemed to be finding patently absurd excuses to add to their number of lashes, and was no longer even keeping count. Jana was; she knew that the fourteen had been well exceeded, but the fire on her whipped body had spread to her loins, and her quim was now moist, the nubbin of her nympha tingling and hard. It was something to do with the ecstatic screams of the distant woman, and her own thrilled pride in not crying out.

Mimi's shrewd questioning became more and more prurient, as though the interrogation was itself thrilling her, even more than having two helpless bare females in her whip's domain. She seemed to have guessed Maldona's connection with the mediaeval Order of Knights Templar, who when extirpated in England, Germany and France, had found refuge in Spain. Jana was glad of her mute state, as she did not have to speak of her ancestor Jana Ardenne, nor admit that the Order of Maldona had always been female, a part of the Order of Templars – though superior to the male orders – and cognisant of the Templar treasure. Mimi obviously would not have believed such a thing, but murmured that as they progressed they would learn more about the Castle's own Templar lore.

'There are unearthly things in this land,' she sighed. 'I wish I were permitted to know more!'

The questions continued, with feigned casualness. Yes, Maldona had dungeons and an intricate system of rewards and punishment; yes, there was a hierarchy of women with their own male slaves; yes, the females themselves were also trained to absolute submission, absolute obedience, and the absolute freedom of true slavery. This satisfied Mimi.

'Yes,' she panted hoarsely, 'slavery, the natural happy state of sluts. Female is soft, and male is hard. There!'

She delivered two final, ruthless strokes and the birch clattered to the floor, and then Mimi was in front of Jana's face once more, this time squatting as though for the commode. Her breath was laboured, gasping to a crescendo of moans and accompanied by the shrieks of the unseen woman which were becoming shriller and shriller, and which Jana now knew were the shrieks of an approaching orgasm.

'Oh, Jana,' murmured Mimi, 'Oh, Jana . . . did I hurt you terribly? Please say yes.'

Jana looked up and saw that Mimi's fingers were deep in her cunt, whose lips were swollen and gleaming with the oil that soaked her mink and flowed down her inner thighs. All the while, as she had whipped them, Mimi had been masturbating.

Jana smiled painfully and nodded that yes, it had hurt terribly – and at that moment Mimi herself shrieked and her finger was a blur on her red, swelling clit. She ripped the garland of flowers from her hair, and let the petals cascade in the spasm of her climax, and as the voice of the woman in her distant cell soared in a cry of pure ecstasy.

'Oh, Jana, Oh! Oh!' cried Mimi. 'I'm coming, I'm so wet and I'm coming for you! Oh, my sweet Mistress, I'm coming!'

The sight of Mimi's pleasure, accompanied by the crescendo wails of painful ecstasy from the distance, made Jana's fount flow, and she longed to be touched there, to be fucked and to feel tender fingers hard on her swollen nympha. She and Cassie spat out Mimi's belt at the same moment, and it fell to the floor. Mimi picked it up, and looked at their teeth marks. They had bitten halfway through her belt, and she kissed the marks, then rubbed her quim with the ragged leather, whimpering softly in the afterglow of her orgasm. Her face was flushed quite as red, Jana was sure, as her own whipped arse-globes. By Jana's reckoning, she and Cassie had each taken twenty-two whip strokes, and she opened her mouth to beg Mimi to touch her nympha and bring her to the orgasm she craved.

But, before she could say anything, she heard the sound of a key being turned in the lock. The door flew open, and Armintrude stood before them, grinning without friendship. Mimi looked round in surprise, then rose and curtseyed, and obeyed Armintrude's gesture to attend her by the door. The taller woman whispered a few words, inspected Jana and Cassie's bodies with a gloating and satisfied eye, then departed. Mimi returned to the flogging-horse, and glumly began to unfasten the restraining cuffs. She sighed deeply.

'Armintrude brings word from the Master,' she said. 'It

seems that your impropriety was graver than we realised. Not only did you let your costume be damaged, but you, Jana, cravenly failed to act as a Mistress in allowing Armintrude to do it. You showed softness.' She bit her lip. 'I had your initiation and instruction all planned. I wanted to be the one to take you to the –' she checked herself '– to the Master's private art gallery. Perhaps that is still possible, but it is out of my hands.' She shrugged in resignation. 'We must all bend to the will, to *hardness*. Don't worry, you will still be properly instructed, only it'll be a different kind of instruction. Do you see?'

'No,' said Jana and Cassie in unison. Jana thought grimly: I'll show them hardness. I'll have Armintrude, I'll have the Master, I'll have them all . . .

Mimi sighed again.

'It means that you will now go straight to the dungeon,' she said. 'It seems your punishment is only just beginning.'

13

The Dungeon

The dungeon! Jana was too shaken by Mimi's words to resist when two male slaves entered the cell and brusquely seized her and Cassie by the arm. They had the same surly beauty of the slaves in the Master's studio, and were perhaps the same ones. Jana often found that shorn male slaves tended to look the same, so it was difficult to tell.

Her body still glowed with the pain of Mimi's whipping, and she wanted to rest, and eat. She asked Mimi what awaited them at the dungeon, and received her shamefaced answer that she did not know: it was not permitted for her to visit the place, nor even gaze on it. Only the male slaves, whom she called Janissaries, could take her there. It was, as Jana had suspected, the grim door at the end of the passage.

'I am still your Initiator,' said Mimi, 'but my duties are in abeyance until you are released from the dungeon. No one can tell you when that may be. Inside, you will have a Guidress who will instruct you. All I know is that your instruction will be effective but harsh. And when you are released from the dungeon, it is forbidden for you to speak of your experiences, or even to mention that you have been there at all. It is rumoured that dungeon women have secret signs, marks on their body, even, like a clandestine society within the Castle, but I have no way of knowing.'

'Perhaps you haven't been soft enough, Mimi,' said Cassie sarcastically. 'We're going to discover all sorts of things that a good hard girl like you doesn't know!'

'Yes,' said Mimi brightly, 'that's a good way of looking at it!'

The males pulled roughly at their captives, indicating that it was time to leave. Mimi kissed Jana and Cassie full on the lips, and whispered that the two of them would be separated from now on, as friendships were not permitted in the dungeon. They stumbled out of the door, and were marched down the corridor towards the dungeon's ominous portal. Jana found that she was more curious than anxious. She did not believe she would be friendless, as such a state was unknown to her, unless – she shuddered – there was some system of solitary confinement, of hoods, gags and shackles. She knew she could take pleasure in such submission, and at times she even craved it, but whenever she submitted it had to be of her own volition and not because of any obligation. Then she remembered cheerfully that they were free to leave whenever they wished, car or no car. So she was submitting of her own will, after all . . .

She noticed that the male who was holding her was quite comely in a brutal way. He had pretty eyes, and a lovely smooth body with harmonious rippling muscles, as perfectly contoured as her own. He wore the rough slave's skirt, and her eyes could not help straying to his bulge. *Surely* some artifice was involved? She tried asking his name, and got no answer. She tried again, slowly, in German, and told him he was handsome. The male seemed a little taken aback by this, and Jana was gratified to see him blushing.

With adorable shyness, he whispered that his name was Horst, and Jana responded by saying Horst was a handsome name, too: then she took a chance and let her hand brush his penis through the coarse fabric of his skirt. He did not resist or comment, but now it was her turn to blush, for she felt a mass of flaccid flesh, bound by no undergarment, and knew there was no artifice. Horst was massive and, as she allowed her hand to gently clasp the monstrous cock, she felt a tremor as it stiffened slightly, and Horst flushed even more deeply.

The heavy door was unlocked and swung open on noiseless hinges, and then the women were pushed roughly inside the room with Horst and his companion following. The door clanged shut behind them and they found themselves in complete darkness! Jana's heart fluttered as she thought even curiosity could go too far, but the guards seemed to know their way, or else were able to see in the dark, and they were led sure-footedly over a richly carpeted floor. This passage smelled of lavender, jasmine, roses, and a whole host of other lovely scents, in contrast to the dank corridor of punishment cells, and Jana's hopes rose. They stopped again after a very short walk, and Horst took Jana's hand in his. He placed her fingers on the handle of another, smaller, door, and suddenly the two guards loped away. Jana heard the outer door reopen, this time with no need of a key, and called, *'Auf Wiedersehen*, Horst!' with some irony. She heard no reply. The dungeon door clanged shut again, and they were on their own in the darkness.

'Well,' said Cassie, 'do we go in, Mistress?'

'That outer door is not locked from the inside,' said Jana, 'we can escape if we want.'

'Escape? We are honoured guests, remember? Gosh, how my bum stings!'

'Hmm,' said Jana. 'The left fork or the right fork, as it were. But which is which?'

'This has to be the left fork, the dungeon, and more bum-stinging, at the very least!' said Cassie wryly. 'They are expecting us to flee from it.'

'Then we go in,' said Jana, and opened the door. A blaze of light dazzled them, and Jana burst out laughing.

They found themselves in a vaulted hall of white and pink marble, in whose centre was a swimming pool, two whirlpools. All around its perimeter were divans and sun loungers on many of which were draped women, either naked or wearing flimsy silks and satins of bright colours. Jana thought 'draped' the only suitable word for their indolent postures. Even those who were naked still glittered with jewellery, many with breasts and quims pierced for golden rings, and most wore the most outré footwear, either Moroccan *chedik* slippers of yellow or pink leather, or wonderfully sluttish stiletto heels. Jana saw that though many of the women were amusing themselves by applying paint, creams and oils to each other's bodies, none appeared to be shaven: all wore full minks.

The air was heavy with perfume and incense; many of the women were clustered in small groups round the divan of a leader, sipping delicious looking drinks and smoking exotically scented cigarettes, and caressing each other's bodies with playful languor as they did so. Other women splashed in the swimming-pool, without straining themselves by actually swimming; in the corner, wooden doors of Turkish and sauna baths banged open and shut with a naked stream of pink, perspiring visitors. The walls were painted with flowers and birds, all in bright colours, but there was no representation of the human form.

A large picture window dominated the far wall of the chamber, and beside it a door led to a terrace that gave on to the very same view that Jana had admired in the Master's *trompe l'oeil* painting. The sun was high outside, and many of the women had chosen to sunbathe naked. The sun glinted from their body ornaments, and Jana noticed that those with their thighs spread shamelessly wide sported as many as four perineal piercings – symbols of enslavement, she wondered, or of power? This place seemed as far from a dungeon as she could imagine. She gazed longingly at the dark forest beyond the walled gardens, and suddenly wanted to be naked amongst the trees, running wild and dirty, cleansed only by her own sweat, far from this pampered luxury. It was then she observed that many of these women's backs and fesses bore recent whipmarks carefully camouflaged by gaudy *maquillage*.

Her reverie was broken by a sharp female voice.

'You are Jana and Cassie!' it barked. 'Which of you is which?' Jana identified herself, and saw a statuesque female in a severe black skirt and stockings, and a top with large breast pockets, padded shoulders, and military epaulettes. The top two buttons of her blouson were undone, and she looked flustered, as though she had just dressed. At her waist was a red leather belt, from which hung a short leather whip of eight or nine plaited red thongs, each thong tipped with a silver snake's head, with fierce eyes and a forked tongue darting out. Jana thought the artefact very beautiful but doubted that it would make a very practical instrument of correction. The woman was standing behind a white reception desk of curlicued wrought iron, which was laden with papers and flower vases. Her mousy hair was cut in a surprisingly boyish style, and the bulky pockets disguised her evidently small breasts; her skirt, though, clung tightly to her wide hips and her thighs and buttocks were impressively large, the bum almost swollen in her ripeness, Jana thought with an involuntary tingle of desire. She was reminded that she had longed to orgasm under Mimi's whipping; just two or three flicks from a gentle finger to her throbbing nympha would have brought her to a spasm. And she wanted it still: looking at the lounging women, she thought that even if friendship were forbidden in the dungeon, casual dalliances and not-quite-friendships might be possible. And yet their arrival seemed to excite no curiosity in the torpid beauties who adorned the bathing-chamber.

The woman in black now emerged from behind her desk, holding some sheets of paper, and told them to follow her. They did so, Jana marvelling at the sway of her haunches and the tempting roll of her fesses as she walked on black ankle-boots with surprisingly decorative spiked heels. They left the bathing chamber and were suddenly in a quiet, dark labyrinth of twisting, unadorned passages, studded with numerous closed doors.

'That was the dungeon?' Jana said incredulously.

'You will speak when addressed,' snapped the woman. 'I am Gudrun, your Guidress. In here, please.'

She opened the door of a bare cell, which contained a chair and a desk, and had rush matting on the floor. The only other fixture was a bell-rope dangling from the ceiling. Jana and Cassie were ordered to lie down on the prickly rush matting, and spread their legs. Gudrun proceeded to take a stethoscope and a box of medical instruments from the desk drawer. She said, with a glimmer of a smile, that she was a doctor. There followed a most intimate examination of their bodies. Jana felt her nipples being roughly tweaked and her breasts pressed hard, then her vagina and anus were eased open and a cold metal instrument was pushed inside both, as though to measure them. Lights were shone into her eyes and ears, and her muscles were prodded and squeezed with more than a purely medical interest. Jana felt Gudrun stroking her tender arse-globes, her fingers lingering on the red whipmarks as she murmured her appreciation at the thoroughness of Mimi's cleansing. Cassie underwent a similar examination after which they were told to stand and perform various contortions which they did with ease, Jana being reminded of yoga positions.

'Quite good,' said Gudrun grudgingly. 'You have very well-developed musculature and should be admirably suited to . . . your tasks. I notice you are pubically shaved: an interesting practice and, though not strictly improper, it is rare. Mainly, it is males who are shaved, to remind them of their abject status. Most sluts are proud of their fur.'

'In the harem of the Great Sultan at Istanbul, the *odalisque* slave-women who failed to keep themselves perfectly shaven were put in a sack and thrown into the Bosphorus by the Chief Eunuch,' said Cassie rather smugly. 'And your dungeon resembles nothing but a harem.'

'There are many dungeons,' said Gudrun, 'but we do not do things like that.' There was no irony in her chilly smile. 'The bathing chamber is for those who have earned their leisure.' She paused to consult her paperwork.

'Hmm . . . you are new Students, so of course you must be naked for the first two weeks,' she said slowly.

'The *first* two weeks!' Cassie gasped. Jana was silent, but wondered if the elaborate structure of Initiators, Students and the Elect was all a façade for something more sinister. Were *all* Students sent to the dungeon on some pretext of impropriety? Perhaps Instruction and the dungeon were the same thing.

'. . . And you will wear your pacifiers at all times, except when visiting the bathroom.'

Cassie said that their pacifiers were in their room, and asked if they could fetch them. Gudrun answered that their room was out of bounds until they were fit to return to it. She reached into her desk and produced two pacifiers of fearsomely large dimensions, the anal prong being almost as large as the vaginal, and with both prongs of knotted, polished wood fastened to a leather ribbon G-string. Gudrun leered, and Jana was reminded of Armintrude. Hardness certainly seemed to bring promotion in the Castle's hierarchy. Delicately, Jana took her pacifier, noting that it was the slightly larger of the two. Without changing her expression or taking her eyes from Gudrun's, she parted her thighs in a squat and smoothly pushed the pacifier into both of her holes, right to the hilt, before snugly fastening the G-string. Cassie followed suit, and Jana was pleased to see Gudrun flustered by their easy demeanour.

The Guidress then proceeded to ask them questions about their skills and knowledge. Jana admitted that she could cook, could wrestle, could even act and, mischievously, added that her hobby in London had been the manufacture of phallic candles, modelled from life. She started as she realised she had not thought of London, nor of the outside world, for a while: like Maldona, the Castle was a world apart. Jana knew that she would conquer it as she had conquered Maldona – her birthright as the first Jana Ardenne's descendant – and now she shivered with the premonition that perhaps this was her birthright too . . .

'Well!' said Gudrun in conclusion. 'We have no Mistress of Candles, but the Mistress of the Kitchen may want to see you, and the Mistress of *Karagoz*.'

Cassie asked what *Karagoz* was, and Gudrun told her curtly that the Master was fond of puppet plays, with living puppets. Then she pulled the bell-rope.

'Your dormitory slave will take you to your separate sleeping quarters,' she continued. 'Mimi has no doubt told you that friendships closer than a loose association are forbidden in the dungeon. You may not communicate, even outside in the workplace and, as you have already found out, any infringement of rules, any softness in a slut, is severely punished. Your dormitory slave may whip you as he pleases, but for serious impropriety you should be sent to your Guidress.' She smiled with great joy and stroked the thongs of her whip. 'I see your bottoms are well reddened from Mimi's birch-rods,' she said. 'I can assure you that the snake's bite is a wondrous experience.'

She noticed a glint of scorn in Cassie's eyes.

'You think I am joking?' she spat. 'You are impudent!'

Then, suddenly, she turned her back, bent over the desk and raised her skirt to reveal her buttocks. To Jana's surprise, she was wearing deliciously frilly lace panties – red to match her snake-whip – and she pulled them down. Both women gasped, for her naked croup was a mass of sweet crimson blossoms, all of which looked rather recent.

'You see?' said Gudrun proudly.

Two males came through the door, and Jana was pleased to recognise Horst and his companion once more. They curtseyed solemnly to Gudrun's bared buttocks, giving no sign of surprise or arousal at the sight, and when Gudrun had made herself proper again, she consigned Jana and Cassie to their care. The two women touched hands in mute farewell, and Jana was secretly pleased that she was in Horst's charge. They were led out and taken in separate directions, but not before Gudrun had pointed to Cassie.

'That one,' she said to the male slave. 'Whip her soundly straight away. She asks too many questions.'

Jana walked beside Horst through the dim passageway, and was surprised they encountered no one else.

'Aren't you pleased to see me again, Horst?' she said carefully in German. He blushed, and nodded.

'You decided to stay, Mistress,' he said neutrally. 'Hard work. The quarry. You are strong as a male, you will work hard for the Master.'

Jana asked why he addressed her as Mistress, when she was merely a slut, naked and humiliated; he answered that he was a male slave and, though he had the power to punish her, all women were Mistresses.

'Do you like things that way, Horst?' she said, deliberately stumbling so that her bare thigh touched the bulge under his skirt. He looked at her blankly.

'It is proper,' he said.

'Was it proper for you to see Gudrun's bare bum?' asked Jana slyly, and Horst answered seriously that it was normal, since Gudrun frequently required him to whip her.

'She was much punished when she was a mere slut, but she grew to crave the whip on her bare arse,' he said calmly, 'and as a Guidress she may command. Guidresses, too, must be cleansed.'

'And do you enjoy it?'

'I enjoy obedience,' he said, after some thought.

'But the whipping itself, the sight of her bare bum squirming under the power of your arm –' she stroked his biceps '– don't you enjoy that? Doesn't your manhood rise just a little?'

Now, she put her fingertips on the massive cock beneath the skirt, and was pleased to feel it swell.

'Yes – but it is improper.' Jana would not be deterred.

'Horst, when you see Gudrun's naked arse, and her cunt and her anus bud all sweet and bare for you, don't you want to put your manhood inside her, and thrust into her till your spunk comes? A manhood as big as yours, you must have done it many times, and with lots of sluts, too.'

'No!' he cried. 'I know of that, but it is forbidden.'

'You mean you have *never* . . .'

Jana's fingers were now rubbing his stiffening cock quite shamelessly, and Horst gained a temporary respite from his embarrassment by their arrival at the dormitory door. His skirt now raised quite deliciously by his semi-stiff penis, he pushed the door open and admitted Jana to a room foetid with female sweat and echoing to the snores of the dozen or so grimy bodies which lay stretched out asleep on rough palliasses. Some of the women were naked, and some had evidently been too tired even to strip before falling into an exhausted sleep. All around hung garments, washed or unwashed, and mostly rough canvas or denim work tunics, with an admixture of carefully stored pantaloons, blouses and diaphanous skirts which Jana thought were intended for the bathing chamber.

'The morning shift,' said Horst tonelessly. 'They are tired from labour, and when they awake, those that have performed well may be admitted to the baths. You, Mistress, will be on the night shift. It is a pity that you are obliged to be naked, but your work in the quarry will keep you warm. There is your bed, which you must vacate when the afternoon shift returns.'

He pointed to a vacant palliasse by the door; on the bed beside it slept a woman covered in a greasy duvet, with her bottom rather comically upthrust and her pillow clamped over her head to shut out the noise of the talk and breathing.

Jana remembered that she was hungry, and that the promised scrumptious luncheon now seemed a remote prospect. Still, she mentioned it to Horst, who said he would take care of the matter. His penis still stood stiff under his trembling thin skirt, and Jana said that she was hungry for something besides food, again drawing a blank look from Horst. Boldly she put her hand under the skirt and clasped his balls, squeezing them tightly, which made his cock rise to its fullest height.

'No!' moaned Horst, but he seemed powerless to resist. Jana put her fingers to his nipples, and began to stroke them, until they hardened into sweet pink buds.

'When a male says no, he sometimes means yes,' she whispered and bent to lick his belly. 'Do you really mean no?'

His only response was a gentle moan of pleasure, and at this she cupped the nape of his neck and drew his lips to hers. As they kissed, her tongue darting wet against his, she moved her hand from his balls to the shaft of his huge cock and began to stroke it carefully, so as not to touch his engorged helmet, which might have brought him to a climax too soon. She ignored his half-hearted sighs of protest, and asked him gently if he had never kissed a girl before, knowing from his moans that it was so. He was truly virginal. All the time she sidled towards her new bed, intending to make him lie beneath her, but she knew from the trembling of his massive cock that his seed was not to be long in coming.

She whipped the front of his skirt up over his belly to reveal his naked shaft, and gasped at the awesome beauty of it. For Horst was circumcised: no prepuce marred the symmetry of his naked bulb. Her slaves had told her the skin of the glans was so sensitive that vigorous tonguing or caressing could actually hurt, and that this sensitivity was absent in the circumcised cock, the hardened bulk enabling its wearer to pleasure a woman for longer before his sperm came. Jana loved the gleaming smoothness of a swollen helmet, and the contrast between this one and the subtle pink of the rest of Horst's shaft made it especially beautiful in her eyes.

Kneeling before him, she took his stiff prick into her mouth, deep towards the back of her throat, and began to milk him with powerful neck-thrusts as her tongue caressed his peehole. His cock was almost too thick for her mouth, and she was flowing wet in her cunt at the thought of this giant inside her. Her hands cupped his luscious taut buttocks and began to stroke them, but as her fingers strayed to the cleft of his arse, he brushed her aside.

'No ... not there. *Schande!*' he said, with surprising vehemence. She desisted, and concentrated on pleasuring his cock. The first few droplets of his salty sperm began to spread over her tongue, and then he shuddered as she expertly milked him, swallowing every spurt of the creamy hot seed, his gasps of anguished pleasure drowned by the contented noises of the sleeping quarry-workers. He clutched her head to him and, when she was able to look up, she saw tears of joy on his reddened cheeks. A tiny drop of his seed had welled at the tip of his glans, and with this she moistened her fingertips.

'Taste it,' she murmured, pressing her fingertips inside his mouth and laying a film of sperm on his tongue. 'It is your strength, your male essence, and you should know what your essence tastes like.'

He obeyed, licking his lips and swallowing. Now she

took his still-hard shaft firmly in her hand, like a dog-leash. He was docile, whimpering slightly, as she made him lie on his back on the palliasse. She brushed aside some silk blouses, knickers and pantaloons left by another woman, not without the fleeting wish to try them on, and straddled Horst's thighs. She stroked his balls with one hand and, with the other, vigorously rubbed his penis and flicked its massive purple bulb against her stiff clit. Her fount was soaking with love-juice, and she became all the more excited as she watched it trickle, gleaming, down the shaft of his cock. Soon he was stiffer than ever in a perfect lustrous hardness. His protests had ceased utterly.

Jana surveyed the scene of dormant bodies, and said to Horst that they might as well be alone, although she was so wet that she did not care, and indeed relished the notion that someone might observe their fucking. She squeezed his huge cock and masturbated him so vigorously that a lovely smile creased his angular face, and he began to stroke her breasts and buttocks with a sureness surprising in one so inexperienced. Her nipples were swollen and stiff, and she began to masturbate herself, her fingers flicking remorselessly against the hard bud of her nympha.

'Have you been doing this to yourself, Horst?' she said as she frigged his gleaming penis. 'Admit it. Or have you slaves been doing it to each other?'

Now she rubbed her fingertip on the peehole in a circular motion, and he moaned, and nodded yes.

'Like this? Really hard, squeezing and squeezing till the lovely white spunk comes?' Again he nodded.

'*Ja . . . stark reiben . . .*'

'Well, this is lovelier and better,' said Jana and, raising her haunches above him, she removed her pacifier, with a soft little squelching noise, then spread her quim-petals wide and positioned her cunt right on top of his helmet. At first she gulped, for she had a moment's genuine fear that he would be too big for her. But her cunt was so wet and oily by now that it took only the slightest downward pressure for his helmet to slip inside her and, once that swollen tip was in her slit, the rest of his shaft disappeared all at once in a thrust so filling and lovely that she gasped out loud.

Still masturbating her engorged clit, Jana raised and lowered herself on Horst's cock, rising right to the tip before taking all of him inside her again. As she rose, she would squeeze his glans with her elastic muscles, tantalising both him and herself, before she again took the male deep into her womb. He adapted to her rhythm with little thrusts of his own loins, but so heavily did Jana press down on him that he could not jerk his hips far. Sweat poured from them both. This time, Jana knew he would last long enough to make her climax, and knew that she would do so soon: she reached her plateau, redoubled the frenzied caress of her nympha, and squeezed with every ounce of strength on the massive cock inside her. Then she knew the first drop of sperm was in her cunt and, writhing in her pleasure, began to slap his chest and nipples. He moaned louder and more harshly and his cock bucked like a shuddering ramrod, mingling his fierce jets of seed with her hot love juices, and it was then that Jana melted in her own delicious spasm. It felt as though the maw of a glowing volcano were swallowing her loins, her womb, her breasts and her whole self.

When it was over, she sank forward, exhausted, and kissed his lips. Her hands crept unconsciously behind his bare fesses, to press his softening penis into her in one more tender embrace. And at the cleft of his buttocks, she felt – it couldn't be! She had no time to frame the question, for he pushed her away from him and leapt from the palliasse, smoothing his skirt down over his dancing red cock.

'You liked it, my slave?' Jana said softly.

'I – I liked it, Mistress. So that is how the improper thing is done. The Mistress is on top and rides the slave beneath her. That does not *seem* improper.'

'Yes,' grinned Jana, 'that is how it is done. You would like more, sometime?'

'Oh, yes, yes.' His grin was so lovely and soppy!

'Perhaps, if you treat me well, there shall be more. It is

our secret, and no one shall know of it. But if I want to be pleasured, and your *Schwanz*, your lovely thick tail, does not rise for me, it is I, your slut, who shall whip *you*, to make him stand.'

Horst replied that his arse could stand any number of lashes, if it gave her pleasure and made him hard for her. His prowess at taking the pain of cleansing was fully equal to his skill in inflicting it, as Gudrun could tell them. He added rather smugly that only just now, as Jana and Cassie had been receiving their whipping, he had been cleansing Gudrun's naked body in a neighbouring cell. So, Jana realised, the screams of the tormented woman had been those of her Guidress!

'Now I am hungry. For food,' Jana said.

'I shall fetch you food, Mistress,' Horst blurted, and Jana lay back in the glow of pleasure which still washed her, pleased at the knowledge that Horst's giant cock belonged to her, and with it, presumably, the rest of him, including his loyalty . . . The only thing that puzzled her was the little node of skin, adorable and soft, that she had felt at the base of his spine. She wanted to play with it, as you would play with a kitten's whiskers. What had he said? 'Scandal'. But why, what was scandalous about him having a cute little tail at his arse-cleft?

Jana was smiling at this thought when a sudden movement disturbed her. She looked at the bed beside her and saw two bright, mischievous eyes peeping out from under the pillow.

'Aha!' said a female voice. 'I *saw* all of that!'

14

Quarry Women

'I thought everyone was asleep,' said Jana, taken aback. She saw two bright green eyes, which sparkled with points of light and were framed by dark lashes. Equally pretty were the girl's snub nose, red rosebud lips, and smooth, alabaster-pale complexion.

'You thought wrong,' said the girl. 'My, you *have* been improper! I enjoyed it, though – I was diddling myself all the time, and I came just as you did. Bet you didn't hear me squeaking over the noise of all these grunters. I always squeak when I come! I'm terribly terribly jealous of you, stranger. Getting Horst to put that monster inside you, I've always wanted that, but he would never respond, the swine! You never know with these slaves.'

'You do now,' said Jana coolly, her composure recovered.

The green eyes studied her.

'Yes, and I can see why. He must like women with big tits and a big arse. Not skinny little things like me. Men! Still, that gorgeous cock. I'd do anything for a taste, and to sit on top, like you! Mmm . . . Quarrying is hard work, and tiring as hell, but it doesn't half make you horny. This lot generally frig their clits well before they start their infernal snoring.'

'You don't sound very tired, whoever you are,' said Jana.

'I sleep at odd times, and I don't have to swing a pick. I'm Clare, by the way; it's short for Clarissa, but that's a pompous sort of mouthful.'

'Well, Clarissa, I can be terribly pompous,' said Jana, 'so do let me see the rest of you, if we are going to be friends, as I hope. Then I can call you Clare, and you call me Jana.'

Something in the girl's bright impudence made Jana warm to her. Suddenly the dirty duvet was flung away, and beneath it Clare was naked. Jana gasped at the sight. She was reminded of the chain mail that had covered Damien's body on board Caspar's ship. Clare wore no armour, if one discounted the severe, lustrous cap of black hair which coiffed her shining white face, but her body gleamed with metal and stone. Her breasts were small, but her haunches and fesses were superb in their perfect, muscled formation, and the whole blended to a parcel of athletic strength. As tall as Jana, she was in no way skinny, but harmonious as an orchid, and Jana told her so.

'Thank you,' said Clare, with a smile like a sunbeam. 'I've never been compared to an orchid before.'

'It is a compliment,' said Jana. 'Your body is truly magnificent. Your tits, as I see them, are lovely, like little apples. And your bum is absolutely succulent.'

'Apples! Orchids! Why, my tits are so small, they are more nip than tit! I suppose I could enlarge them – I think there are suction devices like men use on their cocks – but I'm far too lazy, and it seems a bit gross.'

Jana said that her nipples were like flowers of apple blossom on her delicate breasts.

'Then you'll want to eat me and smell me, I guess,' laughed Clare, sitting up. And Jana thought that yes, she would like to do both.

'People like orchids because they resemble the cunt,' chattered Clare gaily. 'Did you know that? Same as ginseng, which looks awfully sexy, like balls and cocks and tits all twined together. The Master likes sexy plants. That's why the slaves have big dicks; they use all sorts of potions to rub in them. There's one that they say is a paste of sea anemones, asphodel and Yemen glue, from a sheep's spleen, or there is honey, lavender, musk and pepper, and they rub those on their cocks. Then they say you can mash up leeches with oil, and boil it, then rub *that* in. I doubt

189

that's all there is to it but – ugh! I'm glad I'm not a male! Although I suppose they enjoy the cock-rubbing part. It must smell horrible, but then I have no sense of smell. It has its advantages here; I can be as dirty and smelly as I like and not mind, or have to waste time preening in the baths with those scented ninnies.'

Jana replied tactfully that she was aware of various potions men and women could use. She put her face close to Clare's body, and openly smelled her, smiling at the ripe female odour of sweat and dirt that emanated from her apparently pure skin. It excited Jana: the perfume of womanhood, of earth. She asked how it was that Clare had no sense of smell; Clare told her that she had been born without adenoids, but made up for it in other ways. Jana had never before encountered anyone disabled in this way, but accepted this explanation.

'You really think my body magnificent?' Clare asked, fluttering her eyelids – not coquettishly, but with true, girlish pleasure at Jana's sincere compliment. 'Men say things like that, but only because they want to fuck me. I usually let them, not that one has much choice in this place if one is to be proper, but it's lovely to hear it from you, Jana. Are we friends?' She put out her hand, and Jana took it.

'As my friend,' Jana said, 'you mustn't deny me a look at *all* of your body. She is so lovely.'

'Including my nooks and crannies?' Clare said with pretended coyness.

'Especially those,' Jana replied firmly. Clare grinned and spread her thighs for Jana's inspection.

Clare's body was covered from the neck down in glittering ornament, but the jewels she wore were not slung from chains – quite the opposite. Each of the many golden chains crisscrossing her body was anchored to one of her many jewelled body piercings.

Her navel first caught Jana's attention, for it was extruded, a gorgeous hard plum almost as big as her nipples. Pierced through its very centre was a gold barrette, and from this led two golden chains which ran down over the flat of her belly to her labia. There, the chains split into ten smaller chains, each of them attached to a separate ring pierced through one of Clare's quim-lips, so that each petal shone with five rings, the smallest at the rear, near her perineum, and the largest at the front, peeping out from a splendid mass of black pubic hair.

'A Turkish yoke, it's called,' said Clare bashfully.

Clare pulled on another chain to reveal her nympha, sweet and pink and distended by another ring. Her clitoris was pierced too! This time the operation was in reverse. From the single clit-chain led six heavier chains that framed the navel and yoke, three of them ascending to each of her nipples, where they were attached to a heavy ring.

Her breasts were kept pert and high, by means of a further six chains, three of which ran from a second piercing in each of her nipples, crossed her breasts, passed under the black tufts of hair at her armpits, and criss-crossed her upper back. From there, they looped gently around her neck and ended in two more truly massive rings, through her pierced lobes. The earrings were shaped like snakes, and extended down as far as her collar bone. Hung by their thick forked tongues, they were far weightier than any earrings Jana had seen. This, she learned, was actually a bridle: Clare explained that, as a punishment, the snakes' tails could be lifted and fastened in her mouth, depressing the tongue to form a gag, their tethering chains at the same time stretching her breasts upward, which was less than comfortable.

Jana had seen many bejewelled, ringed and studded faces and bodies at Caspar's 'events' in London, but never one so wholly and beautifully adorned as Clare's. Her forehead bore a star of studded jewels, which she explained was a '*shems*', the Turkish word for sun.

'How lovely to wear him on your brow,' said Jana admiringly, but Clare smiled and said that it was a she: *shems* was feminine in gender. In addition, she wore jewelled studs on her cheeks, and a small one at each end of her eyebrows; suddenly she put out her tongue to show four little studs right in its centre, a jewelled one at its tip, on the underside, and similar ones on the inside of both lips.

Rings circled each toe and each finger, as well as winding snake bracelets a hand's length above each ankle. Similar, heavier bracelets graced her forearms and upper arms, and from her navel barrette a further chain wound round the small of her back to a jewelled stud set right in the cleft of her buttocks, the centre of her *kundalini* energy.

This stud formed the head of a gorgeous red and yellow butterfly, its wings a tattoo which covered the small of Clare's back and her entire arse down to the thigh-fold. From the butterfly's head, a thin chain disappeared into her arse-cleft. Clare bent over and pulled her bare buttocks wide apart; Jana could see the chain threaded through three tiny rings which pierced the very prominent petals of her sweetly wrinkled anus bud. Then the chain passed through, Jana counted, a total of seven tightly packed perineal piercings before dividing to join those through her cunt-lips.

A much heavier chain was clamped all the way up her spine to her necklace, passing, Clare explained, through a stud for each chakra or energy node. Jana was astounded at such devotion to self-adornment, and said so, but Clare chided her that it was not self-adornment at all, but 'energy channelling'.

'And that is not all,' she said gleefully, pulling her cunt-lips apart. 'Look!'

Tattooed on the inside of each petal was a black rose, in vivid contrast to the pink shiny cunt-flesh which swelled around it. Clare suddenly took Jana's finger and placed it against her opened cunt-lips, so that her fingernail was just inside them. Clare was wet, and Jana realised that she, too, was moistening between her legs at this delicious spectacle, all the more so as she thought of such work being done to *her*. Would she have the nerve to go through with it? She jumped in surprise as Clare grunted, and her belly flexed, and Jana's finger was sucked into her cunt as though by a powerful pump. Now her own quim flowed, at the thought of such superb muscle control. Clare's quim had trapped her finger deep inside her.

'There now,' said Clare. 'Feel up there; you've got to the bone, now crook your finger. Yes, Oh! That's it.'

Inside Clare's cunt, Jana felt another bejewelled stud!

'Mmm,' said Clare warmly. 'You know the Grafenburg spot, I expect. I thought, why not celebrate her with a stud.'

'All that beauty must have hurt,' said Jana in awe, expecting Clare to laugh and say that there was no pain at all. But she answered that Jana was right, it had been rather painful.

'It hurts, but you have to *not mind* that it hurts,' she said, 'like a whipping. I did most of this work myself, too.'

'And you said that you were diddling yourself as you watched me fuck Horst?' continued Jana. 'Isn't it rather difficult?'

'Jana,' said Clare, her eyes bright with fervour, 'don't you see? I only have to *move* and I am diddling! People are obsessed with coming, and men, the poor souls, think of nothing but jetting their sperm into a cunt, in one hot flow of passion and wisdom that is gone almost as soon as it arrives. But women, and men too, if they only realised, are blessed with the ability to have a permanent orgasm, a heightened awareness that makes your body tingle all the time. You don't need accessories, although flogging, which must be on the bare bum, is good for heightened awareness. Aware males can pleasure a woman for hours without sowing their seed, and they, too, orgasm as much as their female! If they only *knew*.'

'Your anus rings,' Jana said, blushing. 'They are so beautiful, but . . .'

Clare laughed. 'I need them, because that is where the Quarry Mistress clips my leash, to stop me running away when I have to climb up. I don't work on a regular shift, you see, because I'm an acrobat, for the Master's *karagoz* shows, and he doesn't want me to build up too much heavy muscle. Also, whenever there is a tricky piece of dynamiting to do, or a rock to be dislodged from its crevice, I have to scamper up and do the job, because of my suppleness. I can squeeze almost anywhere! Here, I'll show you.'

Clare uncoiled her slim body like a spring and did a double somersault, landing feet first on the floor. Jana was quite amazed, and all the more so when Clare bent her knees, tensed, sprang up with her arms stretched behind her back and did a double back flip to land on her fingertips and toes, her body arched in the crab; a familiar yoga posture. Then her feet began to inch backward towards her wide-spread wrists, jackknifing her body until she was almost folded in two.

Although she made this display seem effortless, Jana saw that the muscles of her upper arms were corded with the strain of her weight, until, with the slightest of jolts, her toes were free of the ground and Clare was supporting herself entirely on her hands. Her body was then bent further and further until Jana thought she would break. She did not. As graceful as a flower's petal closing for the night, Clare's feet edged further and further through the arch of her arms, until her spine was curved like a coin's rim, and her breasts thrust upwards, straining against her tightened chains.

Jana could not believe her eyes: Clare had curled her whole torso so that the backs of her thighs pressed against her shoulder-blades and her knees cradled her ears, then – as a *finale* – she put her big toes through her nipple rings. She grinned cheerfully at Jana.

Then she began to uncurl, bringing her feet and calves forward until they were stretched straight in front of her, the weight still borne by her rippling arm muscles. Now she bent her legs the other way, curving her spine so that her thighs clamped her head, her chin was almost on her belly-button, and her feet came to rest flat on the floor behind her neck. Her cunt was spread, a delicious wet pink slit gleaming with her jewellery, its black rose tattoos clearly visible.

'This one's the Catherine Wheel. It's a lovely position for fucking,' said Clare casually, 'isn't it?'

Jana was by now hugely aroused and she could not keep herself from kneeling before Clare's spread quim and beginning to lick the hot oil from her fount. The rings felt strangely tingly as she licked, and when her tongue strayed to Clare's clit, the contorted girl gave a yelp of pleasure.

'Clare, you are so lovely,' panted Jana, 'how I wish *I* could fuck you!'

'Why, you can,' said Clare nonchalantly. 'I'd like it too. Just look under the bed again, and you'll find an *obispos*. I have plenty of toys to keep me happy.'

Jana found a strap-on dildo made out of smooth, polished wood. She quickly strapped it on, then leant on her fingers and toes, over Clare's body. The backs of Clare's thighs made a cushion and she seemed happy and comfortable enough as Jana slid the dildo into her tattooed cunt. Jana began to thrust and imagined she were Horst, or Damien, fucking the acrobat with her huge male cock, and that thought made her quite giddy with lust. Her own wetness flowed over Clare's stretched skin and, when she looked down, she saw that the backs of Clare's thighs and her fesses were glistening with it. Gasping with pleasure at the severity of Jana's thrusts, Clare told her to take her hands from the floor and diddle both their clits with her fingers; she would, she said, easily be able to take Jana's whole weight on her thighs.

'These cows will be awake soon,' panted Clare, 'but I don't care if they see us. I want you to make me come and make yourself come on me, so that we can be real friends. And kiss me when you come, sweet Jana. Please? Pretty please?'

Jana obeyed, needing no pleading, as she herself was desperate to climax again, and she told Clare so.

'It's the food,' laughed Clare, 'hadn't you guessed? Of course we'll be whipped if we're caught, but who cares? Oh, yes! *Yes*,' she cried, then screamed even more loudly as Jana's finger connected with her beringed clit. As Jana frigged both Clare and herself, she continued to fuck the girl's pliant cunt with the hardest of thrusts from the huge dildo, until their sweat mingled with the juices that gushed hot from their slits and they both moaned with pleasure. Then, together, they melted in orgasm, Jana pressing her trembling lips to Clare's as both whimpered in ecstasy.

'Oh, Clare,' murmured Jana, slowly disengaging herself from Clare's body, 'how sweet that was.'

She nibbled playfully at Clare's belly and breasts as the acrobat smoothly uncurled herself, and then jumped as a harsh voice interrupted her glowing pleasure.

'Not as sweet as the whipping you'll get for this disgraceful display once we reach the quarry,' said the newcomer, who was carrying a red whip like Gudrun's but with a greater number of flails. These were thicker and heavier and also tipped with metal snakes' heads. She was dressed for the outdoors in sturdy boots and a black denim work skirt and blouse, her numerous pockets bulging with pens, papers and implements. Her hair was pinned up in a severe bun. She was every inch a Mistress.

She passed along the row of beds and used the handle of the whip to prod the snoring women, who awoke with yelps of dismay. Clare watched impassively, and Jana felt herself chill.

'No baths for you yet, you lazy sluts!' cried the new arrival. 'It's back to the quarry!'

'As for you . . .' she sneered at Jana, jealous anger burning in her eyes. 'Pacifier in at once!'

Meek and astonished, Jana obeyed: the familiar feeling of the twin shafts penetrating both her holes was comforting.

'And Clare, you slut,' cried the Mistress, 'bend over, legs wide apart, and touch your toes. I'm going to make that butterfly flap her wings!'

Clare obeyed, and the Mistress raised another whip, a large black leather cat-o'-nine-tails, which had hung from a belt around her waist. Clare took seven lashes on the naked buttocks without a murmur. Jana watched in horrified fascination as the butterfly's wings did indeed tremble beautifully at each shiver of Clare's beaten fesses. Afterwards, she stood up, made a face, and rubbed her flushed buttocks three times. That was all.

Now it was Jana's turn. There was a ripple of excitement as she assumed a traditional whipping position – fingers on the floor and feet raised on tiptoe to increase the pain. Jana took seven on the nates, longing to cry out at the scorching pain which flooded her body. She almost did cry as the last stroke caught the sensitive crease between her thigh and buttock. And her punishment was not yet over; as the Mistress deemed her to be the aggressive party in the improper sexual behaviour, she was ordered to stand and receive three strokes to the naked breasts. She took them without making a sound, although tears filled her eyes.

'Mistress,' said Clare nonchalantly, 'allow me to introduce our new Student, Jana. Isn't she pretty? Jana, this kind and generous soul is our beloved Quarry Mistress.'

'We have already met,' said Jana.

'Yes,' said the Quarry Mistress. It was Robyn.

Jana's first evening of work at the quarry set the pattern for many long nights to come. The work was so back-breaking and overwhelmingly exhausting that thoughts of dalliances in the bathing chamber – which Robyn made sure she was not awarded – soon faded from her mind. The days blurred into a single succession of light, dark, sleep, and work. Food was given at the workplace, in primitive packages like military rations. She saw little of Clare, who was herself kept busy, and when the two were able to snatch a tender embrace, their faces were wan with tiredness. After the whippings from Robyn – and they were many – there was Horst to contend with and, though he looked at Jana with longing eyes, he seemed unable to bring himself to be alone with her. Gudrun was often hovering in the background, and once, exhausted after her night's freezing work, Jana was given a severe whipping, again with a leather cat-o'-nine-tails, which consisted of eleven strokes to the buttocks followed by what felt to Jana like a barely less vicious three on the naked breasts, and all in front of the other girls. Gudrun could hurt.

That first night, she had still been full of curiosity, and everything had still been novel to her. Robyn had arrived early, as it seemed work was behind schedule. Horst brought a bucket of food scraps to the dormitory, and Jana realised that 'mealtimes' were henceforth meaningless. Clare showed her that she had to fight for her scraps with any of the other women who were not too sleepy to tussle for their miserable pieces of meat and potato. Jana managed to get herself some food, largely with the help of Clare who, she saw with amusement, was adept at using her body jewellery as a means of fending off the others. Once they had eaten, they threw their bones on to the floor for Horst to clean up after them: he was, after all, a slave.

He did at least have the decency to make pleading eyes of apology at Jana, for not having brought her the promised delicacies. She nodded with haughty diffidence, but could not help looking at the lovely bulge under his skirt.

Then the women were lined up and chained together with leg and waist shackles, with Jana having the luck to be next to Clare, and the journey to the quarry began. Jana was the only one who was naked, the rest wearing shapeless smocks or pieces of sacking. Time had passed faster than she had realised – already the sun was low, and a chilly breeze made her shiver. On their march, Clare and Jana were able to converse in whispers, above the crack of Robyn's whip. There were thirteen of them in the gang, Clare explaining that, at the Castle, even numbers were considered unlucky.

'That was quite a lacing you got from Robyn,' she said gaily. 'So you've met her already. She certainly knows how to whip. I think she's jealous of my butterfly tattoo – she has a giant cock coming out of her arse, with her bumcheeks as balls!'

'I know,' said Jana grimly.

Jana learned that the work of the quarry was the most onerous of the tasks assigned to Students. Rocks were broken, to be chiselled at the mason's yard into building blocks for the Master's great Palace of Arts, now nearly completed, and which they passed on their way to the quarry. It was at the far end of the walled garden, and connected to them by a decorative footbridge that reminded Jana of the Bridge of Sighs in Venice. She remembered that Gilles, the conceited architect, lived in Venice, and wondered idly if all Venetian cocks were so beautifully pierced.

She could see little of the Palace except a high, sheer seamless wall, which on inspection proved to be of massive blocks separated by hair's breadth cracks. Apparently, no cement had been used to construct this marvel of precision, and above it, soaring like a bird, rose a gleaming copper cupola. The track here was paved with the same smooth blocks, but soon afterwards became a rutted debris of mud and rubble. Jana was again glad of her shoes.

Clare whispered that the Master wanted the Palace finished in time for the great festival of Kurban, which would be marked by feasting and dancing and puppet shows – and, Jana had no doubt, things slightly more lustful. Clare added that at this festival it was customary for a ruler's all-powerful mother to present her son with one of her slaves, an important symbolic gesture. Yet the Master had no mother, unless the Supreme Mistress, whom no one had seen, was his mother.

It seemed that the more resolutely invisible this personage was, the more everyone implicitly believed in her existence: that she was ignorant of the plight of the chained quarry women; that if she but knew, she would free them all and reward them with the band of the Elect, and the freedom of the bathing chamber. Clare laughed knowingly when Jana said that the women in the bathing chamber seemed pretty free already. No, they were just whores, the playthings of the Master and his cronies, summoned on his whim to undergo the most degrading cruelties and punishments, then soothing themselves afterwards with the sensual pleasures of bathing and wine and smoking, to descend into the dreamy nirvana of *kif*, the state of languid idleness. Clare said with scornful pride that they were not tough enough for the work outside. Jana asked what Robyn the banker was doing as leader of a chain gang, and Clare said that though she was a Mistress, she too was tough and 'one of us'. She liked dominating with her whip and had a taste for 'rough trade'. Jana found the expression quaint but apt.

They entered the wildness of the forest, where the gloom and the cold became more intense. Here were no friendly birch groves, just stark, forbidding pines, and Jana was sure she heard the howling of wolves. The track soon left the forest, though, and skirted the trees, so that the great expanse of the lake and its dam was visible to the left. On the other side of the lake, sharp crags rose steeply, and Jana guessed that was where the quarry was. They had to keep to the side of the road, as they constantly passed carts laden with raw building blocks of different shapes and sizes. The carts were drawn by teams of three naked and yoked women, with bridles in their mouths and one whip-wielding driver seated above them.

Far beyond the lake, there stretched fields of bright crops and flowers, but these, too, were flanked by the dour forest. Jana wondered if Freya was there with her wolves now, hunting – bears, lynx, or other, real, wolves? But Clare said hunting took place only at night, and under a waxing or full moon. The quarry was an immense gutted wasteland of naked rock, sandwiched between high jagged cliffs studded with precarious boulders and tortuous caves and crevices. They arrived to find another Quarry Mistress supervising her gang of labouring females; some wielded pickaxes or sledgehammers while others loaded carts, and all were still chained. Jana's heart sank. There would be no escape from here. The new arrivals were greeted with a ragged cheer, and the slaves dropped their tools on an order from their Mistress, and lined up ready for their trek back to the dormitory.

As the other Quarry Mistress passed them, Jana's troupe bowed deeply, forcing Jana to bow along with them. To her horror, this now felt perfectly normal and she was proud of her obeisance. It will not be long, she thought bitterly, before I am broken. Maybe I shall be lucky, and end up like the living sculpture in the Master's studio. She had already given up on the fiction that anyone was free to leave, and wondered if Cassie, wherever she was, had come to the same conclusion. Escape would not be from the quarry, into the fields or forest where Freya's wolves would surely find them. No, it must be from within, using the weaknesses of the slave Horst. She said as much to Clare, who was being unchained from the gang and having a light coiled chain leash locked to her anal rings. The leash was kept tight, and Jana shuddered at the likely result of any attempt to flee. Clare looked at her and giggled.

'Who would want to escape from the Castle?' she said.

That first night, Jana threw herself into the work with vigour, as much to keep herself warm in the darkening cold as to escape the lash of Robyn's whip on her naked back. The procedure was intricately organised: Clare, her pale body glinting in the moonlight, would scamper up the rock face with a goat's agility, carrying a stick of dynamite or just a large wedge like a tyre iron. Her imprisoning chain would uncoil behind her, flapping like a giant shiny tail. Then, when she had squeezed herself into some almost invisible aperture, there would be a crunch or a bang, a shower of huge boulders would tumble down, and the gang would begin hacking them into small pieces with picks and hammers. The food, meagre though it was, gave Jana energy, and her strong muscles adapted easily to the hard work. The other women's smocks were soon drenched with sweat, and she was glad of her cooling nudity. As the night wore on, with a short pause every hour for rest, food scraps and gulps of delicious spring water, she found that she actually exulted in the labour, relishing her strength and the play of her muscles as her pick rhythmically rose and fell.

She sensed the bond amongst these women united in their hardship, and soon she felt accepted as her strength and proud muscles bent to the task and smarted under their Mistress's stinging lash.

Robyn's technique was truly accomplished, and each time she lashed Jana's bare skin, which was every time she passed, tears would spring to Jana's eyes. This whipping was given automatically as an encouragement and not for any specific impropriety, although on one occasion, a woman dropped her pick and was given seven hard lashes with the flail, whose wide thongs could, when properly applied, cover both the back and buttocks at once. The woman was held face down for her punishment by four of her comrades, and the other women cheered as she was flogged. Jana found herself joining in the cheers! Witnessing the punishment was a welcome pause, and Jana felt that the victim had let the team down. Gradually, her tiredness gave way to exaltation, and she felt that her rippling muscles were proud pistons of a great oiled machine. Her back and buttocks were red and smarting, but even Robyn's whipstrokes seemed a necessary lubricant for their machine's unity and smooth operation. Their rockbreaking was interrupted every so often for them to load a cart and, as each cart was drawn away by women of a different dormitory, Jana felt a glow of pride in her strength and prowess, and a superiority over these human drayhorses. When the dawn glimmered in the East and they were marched back to the Castle, Jana felt the elation of achievement and total obedience. Back at the dormitory she touched Clare's hand, smiled at her, then fell on to her palliasse which was still warm from its previous occupant, and fell into a perfect sleep of pure exhaustion and satisfied effort. Her sleep was not entirely dreamless: she drifted off seeing Horst's cock and balls as massive, beautiful pink boulders that it was her task to break up and make into jewels for her own body.

15

The Black Sisterhood

Life in dormitory and quarry assumed a routine whose harshness was broken only by a few amusements devised by the women themselves, and whose very meagreness served to emphasise the monotony of their existence. Day and night became meaningless; there was only light and dark, the food bucket, ruthlessly fought over, and the gossip centring around the arbitrary punishments meted out by Gudrun, Horst, or Robyn. Jana forgot about Cassie, about Mimi, about everything except survival.

Fighting was common: the women were never too tired to come to blows over some imagined insult or the purloining of an extra scrap of meat, even though they knew that fighting would bring about severe chastisement. These skirmishes were watched avidly by all the women, with Jana as enthusiastic as the rest of them, and wagers were placed on the outcome, mostly for food. That in turn led to further disputes and violence. It was almost as if the women courted punishment just to break the monotony and give them chastised flesh to flaunt, whenever they returned from a punishment cell.

What irked Jana was the absence of rules. If only she *knew* how not to transgress! Yet the very arbitrary nature of offence, reward and punishment, seemed in line with this desolate brainwashing, designed to break their spirits with confusion. To this end, the punishments became their entertainment, and the female slaves were brought to take delight in each other's degradation, especially when a beating was awarded in view of all, to cheers and jibes as the offender's flesh was reddened with a whip or cane or leather flail. Thus did the women conspire in their own humiliation.

But Jana found that the regime was also enlightening and strengthening, for she learned to concentrate on deriving satisfaction from the smallest gesture. A smile, a caress, a gift of food, an offence excused when either Horst or Gudrun was in a good mood. Their life was cocooned. There were other dormitories, but they never saw them, nor did they see the corridors ornate with the Master's artworks. Next to the dormitory was their bathroom, a stinking place which had a single cold tap and a row of holes in the stone floor for their evacuations. There were no timepieces, and it was, of course, forbidden to make secret marks to note the passage of the weeks and months. It became noticeably darker and colder, and Jana knew that winter was upon them, but their routine and discomfort did not change. Gradually, she realised to her horror that Clare had been right in not understanding why anyone should wish to escape from the Castle. She was in the bliss of total degradation, total irresponsibility, and the most precious freedom of all – the freedom to obey.

Punishments were varied, unremitting and ingenious. As well as the whip, each of their tormentors had their favoured chastisements. Horst, the male, admittedly, did generally keep to his whip, applying it with a very strong arm and an even more impressive aim. Gudrun favoured combining flagellation with elaborate bondage techniques. Often a girl would have her hands bound tightly behind her back. Another length of cord would then be attached to them, and one end of it slung over a convenient rafter. Then the girl's hands would be raised until she was bent forward at the waist and virtually standing on tiptoe. Gudrun was always careful to ensure that the girl was in no danger of serious injury – to incapacitate a quarry slave when work on the Palace of Arts was behind schedule would be to incur the Master's wrath – but the floggings she then administered were punishment enough. Sometimes Gudrun amused herself by hooding a girl, and trussing her wrists and ankles together so that her back was arched and the front of her body thrust out. Then Gudrun would apply her whip to the hapless girl's thighs and breasts, and sometimes even give the lips of her cunt the tiniest of tickles. This was stimulating rather than painful, but, with her hands bound firmly to her ankles, the poor girl would be unable to bring herself to orgasm. Once the punishment was over, Gudrun would apply a healing herbal balm to all the marks she'd laid on her victim's skin, the only catch being that it stung abominably before it soothed. Once, Jana took such a chastisement, and the smarting of the balm made her eyes water even more than the breast-whipping which had preceded it. She remembered stories of men in locker-rooms daring each other to douse their naked balls with after-shave lotion, and reflected that nothing changes . . .

Robyn's punishments were the cruellest and, in their way, the most exquisite, as she, too, relished incorporating techniques of confinement, bondage, or restriction into them. A woman who had displeased her might find herself invited to place herself in the crab position – bent backwards and supporting herself on hands and feet. Then a chain would be clipped to her nipples and quim petals and she would be forced to hold herself thus for a given length of time, knowing that any slackening of her pose would result in some considerable discomfort. Robyn, who invariably knew just how long a girl would be able to hold out in this position, insisted cruelly that this was an admirable exercise for the back and thigh muscles.

Sometimes she would make her victim labour in the quarry wearing a tight, thick, hooded rubber suit, so that she sweated in appalling heat. One such rubber suit, as an added refinement, had thousands of tiny burrs embedded in its lining. These did not puncture or harm the skin, but prickled and irritated it constantly, driving the wearer to distraction. Even the slightest movement exacerbated the effect, and so a victim who spent the day swinging a pickaxe or a hammer would be sorry indeed by the end of it.

Alternatively, a miscreant might be forced to work naked, save for a rather unusual corset. This consisted of a single sheet of smooth, supple metal, curved tightly around the waist, and to which was attached a thin metal gusset that ran between the cunt lips and buttock-cleft. The fit of the corset forced the breasts up and together, and the naked buttocks were thrust into beautiful, if uncomfortable, relief. This device, which was of Spanish origin, was called the '*cincha*' or saddle, and sometimes Robyn would playfully ride her charge like a horse, whipping the woman's distended fesses as she carried her round the quarry on her hands and knees.

Two of Robyn's other favourites took place in a special cell. One was the customary whipping, but with the added refinement that the victim took her punishment while 'riding the rail' – a term, apparently, from the American South. A frame, shaped like a football goalpost stood at the end of the room, with a ladder at each end of it. The naked victim mounted the ladder with her hands tied behind her back, and sat astride the crossbar, with her back to the ladder. Manoeuvring herself into this position was awkward enough, but the crossbar was so high that her head nearly touched the ceiling, and comparatively narrow, so that when the woman's whole weight was placed on her naked quim, considerable discomfort resulted.

Then Robyn would stand on the ladder and the flogging on the shoulders would begin, with the chastised woman desperately trying to bear the pain of being whipped while balancing on her naked slit, lest she topple to the floor. This, of course, was cushioned to prevent serious injuries, but falling earned the victim double the original number of strokes. It was, therefore, in her best interests for her to steady herself for her chastisement, in order to avoid worse.

The other example of Robyn's ingenuity was 'the pole', the polished trunk of a pine, set, like a fireman's pole, between the floor and ceiling of a different cell. The naked victim's legs and arms were bound around the pole so that her breasts and quim were pressed tightly against the smooth wood. A pulley hung from the ceiling and its rope fastened to padded cuffs around her wrists. The punishment was simply that another slave pulled her right to the top of the pole, then lowered her down gradually. The process was then repeated until Robyn recognised that the friction on her slave's tenderest parts was bringing her to the point of orgasm. Then the punishment would end, and the real torment would begin, as the poor girl was untied and then bound again in such a way that she could not give herself relief. Robyn often disported herself by applying her whip quite ferociously to the woman's back and buttocks while she was within reach at the bottom of the pole, so that the poor slave assisting in the torment felt obliged – or not – to work strenuously in order to hoist her comrade up as fast as she could.

There were rewards, too: occasionally, a good worker would be allowed to visit the bathing chamber, and would return heavy-lidded, perfumed and flushed with pleasure, for the pampered slaves were frequently summoned to service the males of the Master's entourage, or pose in his studio. Jana was never chosen, and was glad, for being plunged back into the squalid uncertainties of a quarry slave's existence only made the women more fretful.

Jana knew that to achieve her subduing of Horst, she had first to make herself the leader of the women, and she achieved this in the simplest way, almost without artifice. She had contrived to make herself a crude razor, from a shard of metal found at the quarry. With this, she faithfully performed her daily ritual of shaving her pubis and underarms, with only cold water as an emollient, and the rest of her body at longer intervals.

Already, her prowess in taking her first hard whipping stood her in good stead, as did her strength at work and her resilience to pain. She knew they sensed in her a Mistress, and hinted that her shaving was the mark of her rank, which indeed it was, according to the rules of Maldona.

Clare was the first to enter Jana's scheme. She had often

207

found a pretext to join Jana in the bathroom, where they would squat together and converse as they cleansed themselves.

Clare would chatter freely about the Castle, the Master, and their history, as well as some of her own. Her knowledge was disjointed but profound, although she thought lightly of the wisdom Jana lapped up so eagerly. Keenly intelligent, it was not that she was unable to understand, but that she did not care to understand.

'All that secret spiritual stuff!' she exclaimed. 'I prefer the here and now – what I can touch and smell and taste. My own body is my world . . . and your body, sweet Jana.'

'What secret spiritual stuff?' Jana asked innocently.

'Oh, about the Master being the Secret Emperor, and the Brotherhood of the Left Path, and his having dominion over the bodies of plants and men and women, and being able to make precious metals from the morning dew! Honestly, we girls do tattle! To me, he is the Master, pure and simple. And one day . . .'

She sighed. Jana pressed her to finish.

'One day, perhaps, when I have proved myself as a slave and when the contortions of my body have given him pleasure, I shall be the one to feel his power within me. You know . . .'

'You mean, that the Master should fuck you?'

Clare actually blushed and nodded yes. Jana smiled.

'I should think the Master has all the fucking he wants. Robyn, Mimi, Armintrude, Freya and Gudrun perhaps, and the girls of his wolf pack, and his servants . . .'

'No!' cried Clare, shocked. 'The Master is pure, he is cleansed, he does not fuck! Nor will he, until a truly cleansed slave is ready for him! Why else would we submit to such purifying pain?'

'And the Supreme Mistress? Is she not his consort?'

Now Clare looked doubtful.

'I cannot believe she exists,' she said, without conviction. 'It is a tale woven by idle tongues.'

She went on to talk of the Rosicrucian philosophy, and the Philosopher's Stone, which had the power to transform base metals into gold, and the wisdom the Templars had learned in the East, which had also passed to the magician Rosencreutz, who had sojourned in the East, in the fourteenth century. He had passed through this territory, and had encountered the Bogomil Sect of the Left Path – who, like the French and Spanish Cathars, followed the Manichaean doctrine that the material world was evil and that only the spirit was good, and that purity could be achieved only when the flesh was utterly subdued by the will, and mind and matter became united in perfect balance.

'But the Persian Mani only wrote down a much older doctrine,' insisted Clare, with strange gaiety. 'It is all as old as Time itself! There was a Golden Age, you know, when humans and nature were in harmony, and the spirit – the female, that is – ruled the material male world!'

'And so the Master is trying to recreate this Golden Age?' said Jana, suspicious but awed.

'If you put it like that, I suppose he is!' cried Clare.

Jana thought of Maldona, the Templar Sisterhood, and her own ancestor Jana Ardenne, whose flight from England in the fourteenth century had taken her to the Greek island of Maldona prior to her arrival in Moorish Spain. It was conceivable that a fragment of her voyage had been lost, and that she had in fact gone as far as Palestine in search of the Templar wisdom. For she had found the treasure of the Templars and, with clues laid across the centuries, had led Jana herself to it. A female's treasure was the mirror of self-knowledge.

But what if there was *another* Templar treasure – a male material treasure, as opposed to the female treasure of the spirit? What if it were here, in the Castle? Jana reflected that self-sufficiency and harmony are made a lot easier if you have gold hidden in a cellar, or in the *Banque Ottomane et de l'Europe Orientale* . . .

'Some say that the Stone is a chemical,' Clare continued, 'or a substance, a food, or even dew, which can dissolve gold, and thus gold can be distilled from it! Some say it is purely an idea. But I don't care. I live to submit, and that

209

is all – because we slaves are the base metals that the Master transforms into gold!'

Jana then said that all occult sciences had a *grimoire* or book of rules and procedures.

'No! The rule is within the Master, like it was within other Masters before him! The secret is handed down from Master to Master. The Emperor of this world is unseen! If there were a book, then the Castle would not be eternal, for rules can be changed, and a book rewritten or replaced.'

'So the Master is this secret Emperor?' Jana said.

'*He doesn't know!* The truth waits to be revealed, and no one knows how or when! Even the Master must obey silently, follow the rule that is within him.'

'Him,' said Jana slowly. 'How do we know that this secret Emperor is a him?'

'Only a male has the sacred penis and balls, the tree of life and the fountains of seed and knowledge. We females bear and nurture, we must rule by submitting!' said Clare.

'No,' said Jana firmly, 'the male may have the power to create, but we have the power to rule and destroy. The male is finite, the female infinite, and to be worshipped. Have you never heard of the Indian goddess, Kali the Destroyer? There are four *yugas*, or yokes, that is, four ages of the world. The first was the Age of Gold, after which each age has been baser, until the last, when all baseness shall be cleansed.'

'And what age is this?' asked Clare.

'This *is* the fourth and last age, the Age of Kali,' said Jana. 'And let us take advantage of our privacy and devote ourselves to the timeless female art of pleasure.'

So saying, she placed her fingers on Clare's mink, then on her clit and open cunt-lips, and smiled.

It was rare that Jana and Clare were alone at commode, but when they were, they would compare whipmarks and cuddle and kiss and masturbate each other as they squatted. These hurried caresses were less than perfect, but satisfactory none the less. Neither woman had any prudish shame, but it was in deference to the supposed shame of the others that they remained discreet. The inevitable eventually happened, and they were surprised by one of the other women, who watched in awe as Jana's naked cunt was caressed by Clare's fingertips, then asked if she could join in. This was permitted, and Jana felt two pairs of hands on her body, the new girl, whose name was Sibel, cooing with pleasure at the silky feel of Jana's shaven mons.

Gradually, others, too, came to participate in this mutual, affectionate, relief from the tensions of their existence. Niket, Ebru, Hulya, Candan: all melodic names to match the dusky beauty of their owners, who Jana guessed to be Turkish in origin, like Mokka. Origins did not seem to matter; they were of the Castle, and that was all, although Clare let slip one day that she too was English, 'sort of'.

'What does "sort of" English mean?' said Jana.

'Irish, of course. A raven-haired colleen!' laughed Clare, 'though I went to an English college for girls, St Fausta's. She was the patron saint of needles and pincers, for she was pierced to death! They didn't pierce us there, though they beat us a lot on the bare, skirts lifted and panties down. Ooh!'

Jana told her she was the most beautiful of colleens, pierced or unpierced.

Eventually, Jana learnt that all of the girls, like Clare, shared an acceptance and even an enjoyment of their harsh fate. All longed to be favoured by the Master, and firmly believed that the more punishment they took, the more favour they would ultimately enjoy.

Shaving Clare was the first step in bending them to her will. She did this when they were alone at commode, and Clare was overjoyed at the result. She made a puddle of water on the floor and stared for ages at her reflection in this imperfect mirror, stroking her naked fount and shorn legs and armpits with purrs of delight, like a child with a new toy. The other girls were envious and begged to borrow Jana's razor, but she refused, saying a little fancifully that the skill of shaving safely had to be learnt, and that only she could do it for them. There would be a small price to pay, though. If they wished to improve their womanhood, the improvement must start with their hair, their clothing, and their deportment. Ragged though they were, a bob or a bow here, a flounce artfully introduced to a shapeless coverall, would make all the difference. Mirrors were not necessary, indeed mirrors were forbidden in Maldona, as they encouraged the imperfection of vanity: a woman must be perfect and know herself to be so.

As the weeks passed, and the weather grew even colder, a change came over the quarry women. Even in the bleakest weather, they would walk to work jauntily, with little bows fashioned from rags in their hair, or an artful knot transforming their coverall into a bodice or skirt. Horst did not really notice what was going on, but Gudrun did, and Robyn at once sensed that something was changing. She, however, was not always at the quarry; her duties frequently took her back to the Castle, or to Switzerland.

Her place was invariably taken by Gudrun, whose whip was just as active. Jana organised things so that mealtimes became an orderly procedure, and appointed Sibel as Manciple, or, playfully, Mistress of the Bucket. She was thrilled to have a rank, and other appointments followed – Mistress of the Bedchamber, Mistress of Cleansing, Mistress of Combats (for disputes were now settled, as in Maldona, by bouts of *pankration* wrestling), Mistress of Dalliance, and so on. Jana had meant them to be tongue-in-cheek, but all the women took their titles with utmost seriousness.

Jana enthralled them with stories of Maldona, the greater Castle, her intricate system of ranks, duties, pleasures and punishments and, above all, her book of rules. A Castle with rules written down! At first, they could not believe that anything so complicated could possibly be condensed in print, any more than the subtlety of female-ness itself could be. But, after a while, Jana saw that she had planted seeds of unrest: if Maldona could function thus, then why not Schloss Ende?

Jana said that it would be improper and inadvisable for

her to found a new Sisterhood of Maldona within Schloss Ende itself, but that now they were all ranked in a slender hierarchy, they must have a name and an identity.

'Let us be the Black Sisters of Kali the Destroyer!' cried Clare suddenly. 'Only because my hair is black,' she said bashfully, and blushed.

Jana was secretly delighted, but pretended to ponder the matter, then nodded her approval. It was agreed.

'We must have a mark of belonging,' she said.

'A tattoo? Or a special cunt-ring?' said Clare eagerly.

'Perhaps. But we have not the means here. For the moment, a clean body, and one that is entirely free of all hair except on the head, shall be our mark and our pride.'

This was greeted with enthusiasm. Soon everyone was shaved in a ceremony by which they swore obeisance to Kali and Jana her Priestess – Clare's suggestion – after which Jana prostrated herself before each in turn, to lick and kiss their feet and bared founts. Gudrun viewed the women's newly smooth bodies with suspicion, but did, or was able to do, nothing. Had she not told Jana that shaving was not forbidden?

As well as the sacramental shaving, Jana said that she would devise a proper initiation ceremony. She had noted that, above all, the women complained about the lack of males.

'Cuddles are all very well, said Sibel one evening, as she and Ebru openly masturbated each other while at full commode. 'And Clare's toys are lovely –' Clare, as well as being Jana's lieutenant, was slyly named Mistress of Artefacts '– but what I want is a man's cock in my cunt! It has been such a long time, I have almost forgotten that lovely hot fullness – Oh, I'm going to come just thinking about it!'

'Yes,' said Candan wistfully, 'that Horst would do very nicely, but he never takes his skirt off, even when he goes to bed. And we've all tried to excite him, haven't we?'

'He must be "like that",' said Hulya, making a lewd gesture. 'That's why he's a slave, like the eunuchs of old.'

Jana did not mention her own unrepeated dalliance with Horst, nor that she knew he pined for more of her favours. She decided that now was the moment to attack.

Every day they passed the looming bulk of the Master's Palace of Arts, and were confident it would be finished in time for the Festival of Kurban. None of the women knew what this festival entailed, and tremulous rumours went around of human sacrifice, of female slaves being barbecued alive, or being racked until they broke, or flayed on the wheel. Jana sternly ordered that any girl who spread, or believed, such nonsense, would be stripped of her title, whipped, and forbidden to shave. Whipping meant little, but the other threatened punishments quelled any disobedience.

Excitement was in the air: there were numerous less morbid rumours that some role or another was planned for the dormitory women in the celebration of Kurban, and the inauguration of the Palace of Arts. Horst became edgy, alternately joyous and sullen, and Jana saw that his cock trembled whenever he saw her, and especially when he took frequent opportunities to whip her. Jana, too, missed maleness inside her, but was glad she had bided her time. When she explained her plan in detail to the women, they were avid and excited.

On the appointed day, they made sure to be on their best behaviour, so that they would not be interrupted by the need for punishment. Horst brought the bucket of food, and watched them eat, bemused at their impeccable manners and courtesy.

'What has happened to you girls?' he said in his dialect German. 'You shave your bodies, you are clean, you are polite to each other.'

'A lady is a lady even when she must eat from a bucket,' said Jana smoothly. 'And as for your question, *this* has happened.'

She nodded to Candan and Sibel, who seized Horst by the arms, while Niket and Hulya pinioned his ankles: Ebru had the pleasant duty of ripping off his skirt to reveal his naked cock. Clare's hand was firmly clamped around his mouth to gag him. At the sight of his massive virility, there was a sigh of pleasure from the dormitory women which almost drowned his cries – of confusion and surprise, rather than of fear – and their sighs became shrieks of glee when they saw the pretty little tail that adorned the base of his spine.

'Now, Sisters,' said Jana sternly. 'You know our procedure. After myself and Clare, each of us in turn, according to rank and beginning with the lowest. Horst, I shall order my lieutenant to release you from being gagged, but if you make a sound, your punishment will be doubled.'

Horst nodded, terror in his eyes, and Clare removed her hand from his mouth.

'What will you do?' he babbled. 'This is improper! I shall have you all flogged!'

'No you shan't,' said Jana grimly. 'What will happen is that you are going to assist us in our impropriety, so that if we are to be flogged, so shall you be. Flogging is extreme, though: a tickling should get you in the *proper* mood.'

Horst was spreadeagled while Niket pinioned his ankles. Jana took Horst's leather whip from the belt of his skirt and swished it fiercely in the air.

'It won't hurt me a bit,' he mumbled, ashamed of his submission. His head was buried in Jana's pillow.

'You can smell me in my bed, can't you, Horst? Smell my sweat and my dirt.' She knelt beside him and lifted her robe to reveal her naked cunt, whose lips she parted and pressed to Horst's cheek. She had not washed, and she saw his nose wrinkle, then heard him breathe deeply of her perfume.

'Would you *like* it to hurt, Horst? Would you?'

Horst moaned and shook his head. Roughly, Jana thrust her hand under his belly and seized the bulb of his cock, which she then squeezed quite roughly. She felt his penis already stiffening, as she had known she would, and smiled.

'Your cock tells me you would like it to hurt, slave Horst, and so it shall,' she said softly. 'Ten light ones on your lovely bare arse, to get you ready for the Initiation of Kali's Sisters.'

She raised the whip and cracked the stiff thongs sharply

across his bare buttocks, which clenched pleasingly as the sudden colour appeared. He moaned, but made no further sound as the whip danced on his squirming naked arse-flesh, leaving streaks of crimson that were sweet to Jana's eyes. She took him low, being careful to avoid the little tail, which she thought might be too sensitive to be beaten; she was right, for to gasps of pleased astonishment, the tail trembled and swelled in a semi-erection!

'That is what boy slaves want, isn't it, Horst?' panted Jana as her lash descended on his bare. 'A proper chastisement from a stern Mistress. Isn't it?'

'Yes, Mistress,' moaned Horst brokenly. 'Oh, yes . . .'

'Ten!' cried Jana, and Horst sighed in relief. 'But I forgot, even numbers are unlucky,' she added.

Grasping the whip with both hands, she raised it and delivered the most powerful stroke of all, which sent such a spasm through the male's bare squirming arse-globes that his whole body shuddered with the force of it. Jana ordered that he be released and turned on his back, where he lay moaning. As she suspected, his cock was ramrod stiff.

'Now you are proper,' she said, 'we may proceed with the ceremony.'

'Ceremony? No!' His hands flew to protect his cock and balls, rather comically, as they could scarcely cover the massive organ. Jana laughed, and told Horst he need not worry, they were not going to cut his balls off. 'No lady would harm the thing she loves most,' she said.

Jana was the first to mount him, and she would be the last as well. While Clare sat full on Horst's face, with her powerful thighs straddling his neck and shoulders, Jana lowered her already moist cunt on to the bulging helmet, whose peehole seemed to beckon her with little puckered lips. She sighed with pleasure and relief as she took the massive engine right to her womb's neck, and with her strong sphincter muscle, began to squeeze the distended cock until she felt it tremble with Horst's rising seed. She saw his pink tongue flickering on Clare's exposed nympha as she queened him, her love juices shining on his chin and throat, and then Jana knew the first drop of sperm was there inside her, and began to bounce up and down on Horst's belly as he moaned in the first throes of his orgasm.

Jana did not intend to come herself, but was content to let him bathe her with his hot seed, her cunt-muscles milking him of every creamy drop as Clare pursued her own pleasure. When Horst's cries had subsided, the two women changed places; Jana thrilled as she squeezed Horst's face with her naked thighs and felt his tongue on her swollen clit, while Clare expertly masturbated his slightly softened cock until it stood tree-firm again. Now Clare mounted him, and rode him as though he were a rodeo horse, bucking and twisting and pulling his cock hard up with her prehensile slit as though it were a puppet or rag doll. Jana thought that Clare would tear the man's cock from its balls, seeing the force with which she was pulling on it with her cunt.

Horst groaned and writhed, bucking upward to match Clare's rhythm, and she began to slap his belly and nipples.

'Come, Horst, come!' she cooed. 'I want all your spunk from those big hard balls!' And with that, she began to massage his balls, gently at first, then astonishingly hard, her squeezing interspersed with little slaps. Jana thought these must be painful, but they appeared to increase the frenzy of Horst's writhing; it seemed that the more roughly Clare was handling his testicles, the more he howled deep in his throat, and Jana knew instinctively that he had made sperm for Clare.

Thereafter, all the women took turns to mount Horst, first queening him and then taking their pleasure from his cock. They took him in ascending order of rank, and were permitted to ride him for as long as they chose to. Some of them achieved orgasm after orgasm, for after two more climaxes, Horst's ball-sac had been drained of sperm, and Jana knew he had attained the happy if painful state of priapism by which his numbed cock would, indeed had to, stand indefinitely, to pleasure any number of women.

The pleasure the women felt, as they rode Horst's massive, red and doubtless aching cock, was almost indescribable, and as Jana and Clare watched the joy on their sisters' faces, they embraced and kissed. Their hands soon found each other's naked founts, and they began a tender, slow mutual frigging until each felt her clit swollen and tingling with spasms of pleasure. Then they stood facing each other, with Clare's bare feet upon Jana's, and rubbed their breasts and thighs and mounts together. Soon, their hard clits were pressed together and moving in delicious tribadism until they both shuddered and cried out with the joy of orgasm. At once, Jana sank to her knees, and, clasping Clare's buttocks, pressed her face to her fount and kissed her crimson cunt-petals, then lapped up every drop of the love-juice which she had caused to flow down Clare's trembling thighs.

The other women abandoned themselves to the same lustful gamahuching, and then asked Clare's permission to delve under her bed in search of love toys. Happily, Clare smiled her agreement, and soon the whole dormitory was a mass of writhing bare bodies, penetrated by dildos and pacifiers, the women gasping in their respective ecstasies as anus and cunt were filled, kissed and licked, and the juices of their loving shone on wet thighs and lips.

Jana lost count of the number of bodies she clasped, the number of fingers and fists which plunged into her soaked slit and her joyously pulsing anus, and of the number of tongues which licked her to climax after climax. Sometimes her bottom tingled with a gentle spanking, and sometimes her mouth kissed two wet swollen cunts at once as her anus bud was tickled deliciously by stiff nipples. When every woman had sated herself with the pleasure from Horst's ramrod, it was time for Jana, as Mistress and Priestess of the Sisterhood of Kali, to take the final drop of essence from the male. Her cunt dripping with her oils, she mounted Horst once more, sliding his cock easily into her stretched silky cunt. This time she had him to herself. He was not queened, but Jana bent forward and took his lips gently in her teeth, tasting the love juices with which the previous queenings had anointed him. His face was red and glistened with the women's oils, and Jana licked up more of the juices and kissed him on the lips, making him swallow the mingled essence of the Sisterhood as her tongue slid into his mouth.

'Now, Horst my slave, you must come again for me,' she whispered. 'I am Kali the Destroyer, the Avenger, and I shall not let you go until I have every last drop of your spunk in me. Every creamy hot jet of your maleness shall be mine. I shall ride you forever until I get what I want. I want your balls, Horst, I want all your manhood.'

Horst groaned, but such was the severe tenderness of Jana's fucking that she knew his balls had made sperm for her, and would deliver it. She was bathed in sweat and her love-oil cascaded on to Horst's hard shining balls, as she tickled and slapped them. His orgasm took a long time to build, but, as her squirming rhythm grew fiercer and fiercer, she felt it coming: his cock trembled, and became even more gloriously stiff, and then she felt a superb jet of seed washing her womb, and she herself shook in a final orgasm so intense she thought she would melt in its hot glow.

'The initiation ceremony is complete!' Jana gasped. 'We are the Black Sisterhood of Kali the Destroyer!'

At that moment the door flew open, and Gudrun stood glowering at the scene, her whip in her hand. Her expression made it obvious that she had seen and understood what had been going on, and that she was furious. She cracked her whip, gazing contemptuously at the exhausted, trembling body of Horst.

'So!' she spat. 'The most disgusting impropriety, and the – the rape of the slave Horst! There will be punishment for this as you have never dreamed! The Master shall be informed at once, and he shall decide your fate.'

'Wait!' said Jana quietly. 'I am the Priestess of our Sisterhood.'

'Your Sisterhood? What nonsense is this?'

'No nonsense, Gudrun. We are strong, and could make a slave of you, here and now, as we have made a slave of the male Horst. But, while we despise you, we are loyal to the Master. I alone shall take the punishment for us all –

if *he* decrees it. And if that means thirteen floggings, then so be it. I am ready.'

There were murmurs of dissent, but Jana quelled them with a wave. Gudrun stroked her chin, then smiled cruelly.

'Yes, I accept, Jana. But you shall not be flogged. Oh, no. Instead, you shall accompany me to Mistress Freya's chambers. Tonight is a full moon, and she leads her wolf pack in the hunt. It is fitting that you should be her prey. Sisterhood indeed! You shall come with me at once, after you have said a final goodbye to your sisters.'

16

Hunted

Jana was blindfolded by Gudrun, her wrists cuffed behind her back, and ignominious shackles were fastened to her legs. Thus Gudrun marched her down a series of winding corridors, until a door opened and she was admitted to a chamber where women's voices hushed on her entry. Her blindfold was removed, and she heard Gudrun rapidly withdraw, as though in fear. No words were exchanged. She gasped with awe and terror as she looked upon Freya's lair, but did not forget to bow. She was alone with Freya in the chamber, and there was a door leading to an anteroom, whence the women's voices recommenced their muted, ominous chatter.

Freya's lair was small and candlelit, with a bare stone floor; she was surrounded by a meticulously displayed and labelled assortment of whips and flails, and instruments of restraint and correction, which in less hurried circumstances Jana would have pronounced wondrous. There were also swords and armour, and what seemed to be mantraps.

'You are honoured to be admitted to my chamber,' said Freya lazily. 'Even my wolves must wait in the drawing-room. But I am told that you, Jana, are somehow special. Only a very few lay their eyes on my treasures; none tells of them, although rumours abound, as rumours will. I believe my collection is honoured by a rather grandiose title.'

'The Museum of Correction!' cried Jana.

'Yes. It was this you came here to see, wasn't it? I am afraid we have no time for a full tour, as my wolves are restive and want their sport. But look around.'

Through the slit window, Jana saw that snow had fallen outside, rendering the landscape white and ghostly in the light of the full moon. Naked, she shivered, although the cold in Freya's chamber would seem mild once she was outside. Her horror at her possible fate was mollified by the fact that Freya's disciplinary collection seemed entirely antique. She thought longingly of her Castle in Spain, her apartment in London, and her sunny Greek island, where she was Mistress. She wished, suddenly, that Cassie were with her.

Freya coolly informed her that she was lucky to be the prey for tonight's hunt, or 'the Master's entertainment' as she put it. Jana was to be naked, and barefoot, and would receive a generous three minutes' start before Freya unleashed her wolves. Freya explained that she would be glad of her nudity, once her running began to heat her body; indeed, it would give her an advantage over her huntresses.

Jana stared at Freya in silent awe, but a question was forming in her mind: Gudrun had not consulted with Freya before delivering her up as the wolves' prey. Why? It was as if Freya had expected her; as if Gudrun had somehow known she would catch the Sisters of Kali at their lustful initiation ceremony. A more cynical explanation was that Gudrun was envious of Jana's dominion over Horst's magnificent circumcised cock, and had been scouting for any opportunity of jealous revenge. And yet . . . She was about to speak, when there was a knock at the door, and it opened without Freya's summons. Clare entered, with a brief curtsey.

'I came to wish you good luck, Mistress Jana,' she said, 'and to congratulate you on your honour.'

She prostrated herself, and kissed in turn Jana's feet, her cunt-lips, her nipples, and finally her eyes and lips.

'Nine kisses, for luck,' she trilled in her sweet voice. 'I knew you were the one, Mistress Jana my beloved. I just had to see you again before you go. How I envy you! It is so exciting, and I'm so proud to love you!'

'You have done well, Clare,' said Freya. 'Of all the Elect, I think you merit the sacred band the most.'

'I serve the Master,' said Clare, dreamily. Then she smiled at Jana, curtseyed again and departed, her beringed naked body flashing so prettily and so temptingly as she closed the door behind her. Jana was chilled with astonished sadness at Clare's betrayal of her.

They passed to the bare anteroom, which was nothing more than a cell. The wolves at once bowed, hindered by their cumbersome clothing. There were twelve of them, Nadia and Waltraut smiling in their midst. Waltraut bore a heavy garment folded in her arms. Twelve gold chains hung from a single ring bolted to the wall, each one connected to a bracelet around the ankle of a wolf, tethering her. Jana noticed that the wall-ring had a slip fastening, which would allow Freya to release all of them simultaneously. Freya reiterated that the wolves would be released three minutes after Jana's naked flight, then added, with a smile, that wolves were furry animals and must remain furred at all times.

The wolves wore heavy coats of black sable, and balanced on deliciously high stilettos, with sheer black stockings underneath. They were immaculately groomed and jewelled, with necklaces, earrings, and brilliant red lip gloss. Jana, always curious about apparel, wondered what they wore beneath their coats, and was rewarded with a fleeting glance, courtesy of Waltraut, as she opened hers to wrap it more firmly around herself – black knickers and a suspender belt, and a very fetching black waspie corset, which Jana found herself longing to try on, despite her apprehension.

In an attempt at humour, she said that the wolves looked like they were dressed for a party. Freya smiled with icy politeness and said that they were. All held long coiled whips, which Freya explained could lasso a fleeing victim at twenty paces, 'as well as delivering quite a warm chastisement to her bare skin'.

Freya herself wore a simple smock, incongruous with her large fur-lined boots, but, at her nod, Waltraut unfolded the garment she had been holding and robed her Mistress. It was a fur coat like those of the wolves, but with a hood and collar of mink. Then Freya barked an order, and the wolves held out their hands for her inspection, looking for all the world like schoolgirls being checked for ink stains. Jana was going to laugh, but stopped herself, on seeing that the wolves' red-painted fingernails were outrageously long and honed to razor-sharp points. Their eyes, as they watched their prey, were as hard and cold as the icy sky.

'Good!' said Freya. 'The party may commence, as soon as the pack leader has joined us.' She unfastened Jana's handcuffs and shackles, explaining that, though she was tempted to leave them on, Jana was 'special' and it would therefore be more sporting and more entertaining for the Master to trap her unfettered.

'Most sluts choose either to run as fast as they can through the forest, or else hide in a cave at the quarry, but I'm sure you are ingenious enough to think of something else. There may be mantraps in the forest – I don't advise you to go looking for them – and it is unlikely that you will reach the edge of the Master's domains. As for a cave, we know them all, but anyway it is healthier to run than to hide.'

'How long have I got, Mistress Freya?' said Jana, plucking up her courage. 'I mean, before I have won, before the wolves are called off.'

Freya seemed astonished by this question.

'Why, as long as it takes them to capture you,' she said.

'You mean, no time limit?'

'That would spoil things.'

'And what will happen when – *if* – they do?'

'Whatever the hunt leader deems fitting,' said Freya with a shrug. 'I hope she is not unpunctual, and thus improper. To hunt with an even number is unlucky. Ah, here she is.'

The anteroom door opened, and a magnificent creature robed in black fur entered, her dark face bearing a superb *maquillage*: flames like the sun's rays spurted from her mouth and eyes, giving her the aspect of a vicious celestial avenger. Her lustrous black hair was piled in a tight military bun, and her eyes were as cold as the rest of the wolves'. It was Cassie, Jana's beloved slave, now carrying a snake whip and a hunting horn.

* * *

Freya had been right: the panic of the chase, the mad dash through thorn and bracken, and over sharp stones and boulders, made Jana glad of her nudity. Soon the sweat was pouring from her buffeted body as she pelted through the dark forest. The light caress of the snowflakes cooled her body, but she cursed the layer of snow which made her powerless to cover her tracks. First, the path past the gardens and the completed Palace of Arts, now illuminated by searchlights at its base. Moonbeams played on the burnished copper of its cupola, which seemed to Jana for the first time like a beautiful woman's breast pointing at the sky. After that, she plunged away from the quarry track, and into the unfamiliar terrain of the forest's rough path.

For the Mistress of Maldona to hide herself in a cave would be imperfect, but she was frightened of the man-traps. What sort were they? Toothed or spiked? Were the wolves waiting for her screams – their cue to come and take their easy prey? She tried to scan the track in front of her, but the shade of the trees blotted out the moonlight, and at last she gave up on the idea of staying on any recognisable track, preferring instead to bruise her feet amidst the thorny undergrowth, in the hope that the trap-layers would not have ventured there. She began to run parallel to the track; in the distance, the utter stillness was broken by the bloodcurdling shriek of Cassie's hunting horn. Cassie! Her true love! What had they done to her? And Clare's duplicity – if it was duplicity. The beautiful Irish girl actually seemed to think she had done Jana a favour.

She had no time for any further thought, for she heard another sound, a howl that she knew must be a real wolf. She shuddered but did not slacken her pace, until she saw in front of her two red, glaring eyes, and smelled an overpowering stench of dogflesh. There was a growl, and the wolf launched itself at her. She turned and began to flee to the left, but knew that the wolf could outrun her. The slender lower branches of the firs would not easily hold her weight, and by the time she had slithered to the stout middle branches it would be too late.

Suddenly, there was a mighty slithering whoosh and a strangled yelp from the wolf, followed by shrieks of lupine despair and frustration. Jana stopped and turned, and smiled, almost bursting into laughter, so great was her relief. The wolf had triggered a tripwire, and had been bagged by a net suspended between two treetrunks, in which he was now dangling helplessly. Jana sped on, mindful of tripwires and feeling reassured, until she came to a metal trap in which one of the wolf's fellows was snared. It was not howling, knowing that howls would bring its hungry and unsentimental fellows, but whining piteously to itself. There were no spikes, just two giant metal jaws like clamshells which would clamp a woman by the thighs, and held the wolf across its belly. The red eyes glinted viciously at Jana, her only points of light in the glimmering moonglow that swathed the forest. Then she did something which seemed curious to her.

She reached into the jaws of the trap and found that, though she could not pull them apart, there was a system of gears and cogwheels at its base, out of reach of the trap's victim. She reached down, wryly noting that this was not the first time she had presented a wolf with the moons of her naked bottom, and unfastened the lock. The jaws sprang open, and the wolf gave a little yelp, like a male coming to orgasm, then disappeared. Jana followed the saved animal, running at full speed and just managing to keep up with it; he would be her guidance through the minefield of traps. In the near distance, the hunting horn sounded, as though in disappointment.

She came to a clearing and ahead of her gleamed the lake, covered in ice. An idea began to form in her mind and she headed towards it, still following the obliging wolf. Suddenly an agonising pain lanced through her left side, and she gasped to a halt with a throbbing stitch. The hunting horn sounded again, further away now: Cassie was leading them in the other direction: Jana sank down at the base of an elm tree, a sad dying thing forlorn in the cold, and felt a carpet of limp blossoms under her buttocks.

Panting with her exertion, she looked up at the moon,

then at the icy lake ahead of her, and thought of her loneliness, her betrayal by Cassie and by Clare, and the hopelessness of her plight. What awaited her? A whipping, the various instruments in the Museum of Correction, then the slow flogging itself? And for the Master's entertainment. No doubt Gilles and Michael and Robyn and Mimi would be there too to enjoy her torment. Her heart swelled suddenly with desire and gladness, and her desperate icy solitude seemed the most beautiful thing on Earth.

There was a strange smell in the frosted air, and it seemed to be coming from the whorled flowers which cushioned her bare bottom. She shifted and looked down: they seemed a kind of orchid, purple in colour, and she picked some in her sudden gaiety of despair. She put them to her nose and sniffed, then suddenly felt a surge of wild energy, an erotic shiver which transfixed her belly, tingled up her spine from her lower back to her neck, and made her clit throb as the very petals of her cold fount became warm and moist.

She looked at the strange dying flower, her petals swirling like fold upon fold of fragrant cunt-lips, and knew indeed why the orchid was a flower of romance. She looked out again on the frosted landscape, and knew that it was no enemy, that it was hers. The hunting horn sounded again, nearer this time, and hurriedly she gathered all the flowers, then squeezed them into a tight cylinder. Droplets of juice were extruded from the blossoms and she rubbed this essence into her breasts, her hair and her belly, with the last drops saved for her feet and cunt-petals. Then she thrust the cylinder tightly into her slit, whose warmth expanded the petals until they filled her like a pacifier: not with the harshness of cold steel, but with a feeling of joy approaching ecstasy as she knew the glory and beauty of her female power.

She remembered Mimi's talk of an 'early purple orchid', found at the roots of dying elm trees, *Orchis mascula* or something, and much sought after. She had refused to say why, though she had blushed. Well, with the snow on the winter ground, this orchid was certainly early.

The pain of her stitch subsided, and Jana started off again, towards the lake. The horn sounded again, very near this time, and she could hear excited female voices. She quickened her pace and emerged from the cover of the trees on to the flat open scrubland abutting the icy lake shore, where clumps of reeds were frozen in delicate immobility, stopping abruptly a few metres out: there, the water must suddenly deepen.

Jana smiled, seeing that her idea would work perfectly. The ice was thin, and broken in many places, perhaps by unlucky wolves, so that her passage would not be apparent. She padded out over the ice, being careful not to trample the frozen reeds, and came to the deep water, where she selected the largest hole in the ice, took a deep breath and eased herself into the lake.

The shock of the freezing water on her unprotected body took her breath away. Gingerly, she immersed herself completely, and found herself swimming amongst shoals of tiny fish whose caress of her naked skin would have been erotic and lovely under different circumstances. She swam powerfully out towards the centre of the vast lake, holding her breath – a secret technique she had learned on her Aegean island – and, when she judged that three minutes had passed, she let herself drift upwards until her lips touched the ice. There was, as she had known there would be, an inch of air between the ice and the water beneath it, and as she heard the howls of her pursuers coming closer and closer, she suspended herself like a frozen stalactite in the water, and tried not to shiver.

After a while, the discomfort of the cold turned to a kind of burning, not unlike the pain of a prolonged whipping. Her nerves were registering some kind of sensation, but were, it seemed, unable to discern exactly which kind, so overwhelmed were they by its intensity. Jana hung motionless, her breathing shallow, now aware only of the tickling of the fishes on her naked body, and the powerful flowers of warmth and love hidden inside her quim. It was strange that her slit was so hot and moist, while her outside skin was on the verge of freezing. She listened intently, and heard noises that sounded like disappointment.

At first, she thought that if she could get to the edge of the Master's domain, she would reach the road to Sofia, and surely any Bulgarian truck-driver would happily give a lift to a naked honey-blonde female . . . Then, suddenly, the warmth of the orchid blossoms inside her cunt began to suffuse her entire body, and she knew that she had to take the Master. If she could hide, and elude the wolves until daybreak, they would, she knew, have to return to their duties at the Castle and admit their failure, and no doubt receive some very harsh punishments, which it pleased her to imagine. Then the coast would be clear for her nonchalant and astounding return. The last thing they would expect would be for her to go back to the Castle. *Or would they?*

Her reverie was broken by a caress of her ice-stiff nipples, belly and fount-lips, that was not the caress of the fish. She started and looked behind her. It was Cassie, her slave, smiling ruefully. She knew the mind of her Mistress, had known exactly what she would do. Jana bowed her head in submission. Cassie kissed her on the lips, very hard, almost in valediction, and the bubbles of air from their sucking mouths fluttered up through the water to form one large silvery bubble beneath the ice. Then Cassie punched upwards and broke the ice. Jana was captured.

She accompanied her slave back to the shore, where the posse of befurred wolves awaited, arms linked in a semi-circle and whips at the ready. Jana shuddered at what was to come, but knew it would be hopeless to flee.

'Cassie,' she pleaded, 'Cassie . . .'

But her slave stared at her stonily and did not answer, as she clasped Jana's neck tightly and thrust her forward. Jana knew she could fell Cassie with one chop, but there were too many wolves for her to escape. Instead, she reached down and withdrew the bundle of orchid blossoms from her cunt.

'Oh, Cassie, my love,' she said sweetly, and suddenly pressed the orchids to Cassie's lips.

Her captor and slave jumped in surprise as Jana quickly smeared her mouth with the orchids' juices, before concealing the roll of petals in her palm.

'Oh, Jana!' cried Cassie, as though seeing her for the first time. 'Mistress! What . . . ?'

'You recognised me under the ice, Cassie,' said Jana softly. 'And now, at the touch of a flower, you recognise me again. What do your wolves plan to do with me?'

'I don't know! I lead the pack, but Freya controls them. And when their lust is up, then – whipping you, sweet Mistress, till you can take no more, and then – Oh, God, how giddy and foolish I have been! Freya's caresses were so sweet that I became her slave.'

'Well,' said Jana resignedly, 'a slave must obey her Mistress. If I am to be whipped and flogged, then so be it.'

Freya, resplendent in her fur coat, looked on gloating, her arms folded. The wolves released each other's arms and raised their whips – heavy bullwhips, with thongs long enough to reach Jana's body from where they stood. Jana opened the bundle of flowers and unrolled the oily petals.

'Here,' she said. 'Give one to each of the wolves, on your orders as pack leader. It shall heighten their pleasure at my torment. Rub a petal on their lips before they begin to whip me. I am ready.' She stowed the remaining petals back inside herself.

Cassie curtseyed, then took the petals and passed along the line of wolves, rubbing the lips of each before handing her the petal. The effect was magical; as soon as each woman had tasted the orchid juice, she took the flower and threw open her fur, thrust her hand into her black panties, then rubbed the petal frantically against her quim-lips. Jana watched as coolly as she was able to, for the sight of these befurred huntresses pleasuring themselves made her moist in her own cunt. It was not long before the whips had fallen, to lie curled like black snakes in the snow.

The wolves thrust open their furs, to reveal their stockings, knickers and tantalising waspies. These were feverishly removed, the intricately laced corsets ripped from their bodies as though they were hot coals, and cast down to the snow.

'Not your furs!' cried Cassie, joining the throng of naked bodies. 'Without fur, you are not wolves!' Then she gasped in surprise as a hand slid roughly in between her thighs and

230

tore off her panties, and others feverishly unlaced her corset and threw it aside. Jana watched from the lakeshore as the pack of wolves writhed befurred on the snow, their coats speckled with the still-falling snowflakes as they rubbed their naked quims and breasts together, pleasuring each other with tongues, clits and fingertips in fervent tribadism. Nadia reached for a fallen bullwhip and began to stroke Waltraut's buttocks with it then raised the whip and brought it down hard on the naked flesh. Waltraut quivered and cried out for more, and the bullwhip began to rain its harsh blows on her bobbing nates.

The scene was repeated, with Cassie amongst the jerking, moaning throng of tribadists, who sighed and howled not with the hunt, but with the frenzied pleasure of their whipping and gamahuching. The moon shone pale on the squirming mosaic of black fur and white skin, like a chessboard of lust come to life, and Jana suddenly shivered – not with desire, but because she realised she was cold. Freya alone stood aloof, but Jana saw that her coat was open, and her smock lifted, and that she was strongly masturbating herself at the spectacle of her orgiasts. Jana darted to her side, but so intent was Freya on pleasuring herself that she scarcely noticed. Jana took the orchid petals and swiftly rubbed them on Freya's lips and cunt, then held them hard against her nostrils, and suddenly Freya moaned and broke loose. Soon the Mistress of the Hunt was writhing on the snow amidst the caresses – and the lashing whips – of her wolves.

Calmly, Jana walked amongst the writhing bodies, avoiding the hissing whipthongs that caressed the air, and the fingers which reached out to stroke her thighs and breasts. The effect of the flowers, she knew, would not last forever, and when the orgiasts were sated, they would recommence their pursuit. She stooped to pick up Cassie's waspie, awarding herself one souvenir of her chase, and then, grinning, began to run back towards the Castle. She knew where she could hide. The howling of wolves pursued her all the way to the Master's garden.

* * *

231

The walled garden, and the 'Bridge of Sighs' connecting it to the palace, loomed above Jana as she shivered. She had laced herself in Cassie's corset, for the minimal warmth it provided, and felt pleasantly silly as she began to scale the steep, smooth walls. Handholds were few, but she reached the halfway mark, looked down, and knew she must not let herself fall. Snow-fringed leaves and branches peeped over the top of the wall, as though inspecting the new arrival. The climbing warmed her, and when she reached the rounded parapet, she slid thankfully into the branches of a welcoming tree, whose bright foliage had no right to be blossoming amidst such snowy bleakness. Carefully, she made her way back down to the ground, relishing the cold embrace as she slithered through the caressing branches.

The garden was larger than she had realised, and its vegetation was wholly shrouded in snow, the various shapes giving it the look of a white mask in crumpled rubber. At its end stood a gatehouse – much more than a handyman's shed, for it was a charming facsimile in miniature of the Castle itself! Jana was not sure if she should risk staying there, but she would at least shelter for a while, and perhaps find some warm covers, to reprise Mokka's experience as a stowaway on Caspar's boat. How long ago it all seemed! She shivered; her flesh was translucent and blue. Jana began to trudge along the flat surface of the path, and at the touch of her body, the garden came to life.

She was astounded as the doleful bulk of a tree began to quiver and shake the snow from itself! It was a kind of weeping willow, but with branches that were much longer and thinner than Jana had seen, and were more like tendrils or whipthongs. As she passed it, the tendrils shook as though overjoyed at her arrival, and she felt a sudden warmth in her heart; a certainty that the garden was her friend.

One of the tendrils reared up like a dragon and flailed the air, then cracked across her body like a whip, not painfully, but winding itself at lightning speed round and round her legs, buttocks and torso, until she was tightly and fully bound from neck to ankles. At first she was frightened, but the tendril was warm, and she felt the tree's warmth seeping into her freezing body. She realised then just how cold she had become, and that the tree had sensed a body in distress, and was warming and nurturing her!

Nevertheless, her instinct was to try and disentangle herself, and she tried to prise the tendril free, but it was stuck fast. She had no choice but to stand where she was, bound as though for chastisement, watching as the snow at her feet melted. The puddle that formed uncovered a plant of broad, shapeless leaves rather like a squashed lettuce. These leaves began to vibrate, and raised themselves to form little envelopes which wrapped themselves around her cold feet and began to pulsate, massaging them into warmth.

Jana had read of sentient plants that snapped shut on small creatures and ate them, but here she had found a sentient garden, which seemed to be actually friendly! The willow's fronds were trembling and making little skips as though for joy, and the slipper plant seemed to be purring with satisfaction as Jana's body returned to its usual temperature. It was as though these flora fed not off the carcases of animals but off the aura of happiness their warmth provided. She began to feel that the Master's penchant for biological oddity was not all malicious.

She thought of Horst's sweet little tail, of the Master's living nude sculpture – human bodies, pretending to be stone – of all the piercings and tattoos she had seen, of Freya's pack of women furred as wolves, and of Clare's transformation into a beautiful creature of shining metal. Clare had spoken of Rosicrucians and Templar alchemists and the Philosopher's Stone that would turn base metals into gold. Was the Castle a single laboratory of transformation, in which the elements of life, once separate and alone, fused into a single, holistic entity?

When she was glowing with warmth, the willow tree began to unwind its tendril from her body, and the slipper plant gently released her feet. The garden was awake, now: as she walked towards the gatehouse, myriad bright plants waved flowers and fronds at her, and tickled and caressed her body as human lovers would. She saw a tree whose leaves resembled lips, and another whose flowers looked like eyes, and wondered if the cold had forced her into a delirium. She pinched her warm flesh, and decided that she and her sensations were real enough.

All around her, stamens and pistils took the form of human penises, breasts or testicles, and fruits that of women's fesses. Flowers blossomed like pert nipples or lovely dimpled belly-buttons, or else fingers and toes, or slender calves and thighs, and clumps of moss grew like the tender sprouting of a girl's mink. Jana's heart swelled with pleasure and she saw herself as a goddess, bringing the cold Earth to life. She stroked the plants as she would a lover's penis, fount or breasts.

Before the door of the gatehouse, instead of a moat and drawbridge, was a giant golden anemone with waving fronds, glossy as her own hair, which was flanked by trees. There was no way around it, and Jana was obliged to step on to its bared throat – a carpet of delicate golden penises. At her first touch, the cock-blossoms writhed and began to swell.

Delighted, Jana stopped and watched them stiffen into a very realistic semblance of male erections, and saw that the seed-pods beneath them took the form of lovely soft testicles. She gasped in wonder, and suddenly the waving fronds of the anemone glued themselves together to form a sheer wall which clamped shut around her, like a Venus fly-trap. Her arms were trapped: the anemone had closed just under her breasts, which now rested on the silky fibres.

Then she felt a stroking pressure on her fount, and another on her fesses and legs. Gently, the plant's penises coaxed her thighs apart, found her nympha and began a soft caress of her whole body which, despite her foreboding, made her quiver with pleasure. The touch of the lovely stiff cocks was so sure, so tender, so ... human. She jumped as she felt something tickling her nipples, and saw that the mouth of the giant anemone had formed itself into a perfect woman's fount, the lips gleaming and golden and

234

swelling in a soft undulation. And her breasts were being caressed by a clitoris of truly gorgeous proportions, a stiff golden rod that swayed back and forth over her firm orbs, and seemed to glow with pleasure.

She could not move; such were the sensations of pleasure that coursed through her body that she was obliged to surrender herself to them. Her cunt flowed with wetness, and she heard lovely little gurgling sounds as the penises drank her essence. Gradually, the plant began to hum, as though in pleasure itself, and its humming grew louder until it was a moan, like the howling of the wind or a wolf or a banshee. The plant was stroking itself to orgasm! Jana was not far from her own plateau, and when the plant suddenly shuddered and clasped her with an almost painful tightness, as though it were out of control, her own thoughts were interrupted by the opening of the gatehouse door. A beam of yellow light poured on to the snow, and a figure appeared in the doorway.

As the anemone softened and began to release Jana's trembling body, a whip snaked out from the doorway and wound its biting thong powerfully around her breasts, trapping her.

'Good!' said Armintrude. 'I am glad you have not evaded capture after all. Please come in, slut.'

17

Jana Bound

'Well!' said Armintrude as she surveyed her captive. 'You must be cold – we'll have to warm you up!'

Jana was helpless in the tight whipcoils which squeezed painfully around her breasts and said that she was not cold.

'I insist,' said Armintrude, and cracked the whip with lightning speed, so that it lashed every inch of Jana's body, making her skin glow a warm shade of crimson.

Then Armintrude coiled the whip around Jana's upper body again, pushing her arms to her sides. Laughing, she then tugged on the handle, forcing Jana to her knees on the luxurious carpet. As the leather tightened around her flesh, Jana looked around and saw that she was in a small, cosy chamber, equipped with comfortable armchairs, tables and cabinets, and a crackling fire.

'You admire my furnishings?' said Armintrude. 'It is comfortable, though I have other rooms that are not so comfortable. This place is mine, by gift of the Master: the House of the Elect.'

'And what do the Elect do here, when they're at home?' asked Jana sarcastically.

'They don't do anything,' Armintrude replied. 'They have things done to them. Things that will be done to you, Jana.'

There was menace in Armintrude's voice, but Jana detected a strange tenderness, too, even pride.

'What if I say no? What about this rule that any inhabitant is free to leave the Castle at any time?' she said, bitterly.

'Why, of course you are free to go, Jana,' replied Armintrude, genuinely astonished by her question. 'Just say the word, and I shall unleash you. But once made, the request may not be taken back, and you must go. Why, your car is ready for you here in my forge.'

'My car! But Mimi said . . .'

'Hmm! Mimi tells tall stories verging on impropriety. But as you know, the means justifies the end!'

Her words seemed to Jana to be the wrong way around, but she let it pass, and Armintrude continued, telling her that Stephan the innkeeper had brought the car from the village with his tractor, and that she herself had fixed the damage the very same day.

Jana replied that she had no choice but to take Armintrude's word for it, but added that if Mimi was not to be trusted any more than Clare, another member of the Elect, then how could she possibly trust Armintrude, their Mistress?

'You have a choice, Jana,' said Armintrude fiercely. 'Everyone always has a choice. And before you know what is to happen to you, it is necessary for you to choose: do you stay, and face your destiny, or leave us? The hard left-hand or the easy right-hand path? Remember that you are here not because you were lured here, although lured you were, but because you want to be here. You are in the Castle, and *of* the Castle. We have our disputes and our rivalries, but we are one, in our submission to the Master. Please stay.'

Before Jana could reply, Armintrude suddenly ordered her to bend so that her chin touched the floor, and her naked fesses were thrust upwards. Armintrude laughed cruelly and parted Jana's buttocks with her whip handle.

'While you think about it, I'll give you a proper trussing. Then there is a special pacifier I have made just for you. It is the biggest and hardest in the Castle.'

From a cupboard, she took a truly gigantic pacifier, the two wooden prongs joined to form the shape of a snake whose body was carved with intricate striations and studded with smooth bright hillocks of seashells. It was a work of art, fearsome in its beauty, and, smiling, Jana said so. The orchid flowers in her quim, and the stimulation of the penis-plant which had nearly brought her to orgasm, still worked their lustful magic. She craved sensation, and if the sensation were to be chastisement, then something deep in her trembling body longed to accept it. In truth, her earlier excitement at Armintrude's slim body had returned; she wanted to touch and be touched by her mannish beauty.

Armintrude wore leather and metal: a pair of sumptuous high-heeled black thigh-boots, with spurs, and a corselet with two shallow golden cones covering her slender breasts, the metal nipples protruding with grotesque loveliness. At her neck was a wide leather choker adorned with a single golden stud, and she also wore the skimpiest of G-strings, which scarcely covered the swelling of her fount. Jana noticed that, since their first encounter, Armintrude had kept her mons beautifully shaved, and asked, in an ironic tone, if that was in her honour.

'Of course, damn you!' snapped Armintrude.

'It is as though you knew I was to arrive here, Armintrude,' Jana murmured.

'Why, the whole Castle knows! You are special, slut Jana. You *are the one!*' Voices in Jana's heart cried out to her to leave, to say the simple words. But she could not. She, the Mistress of Maldona, wanted to give herself in ultimate submission, for her own perfection and for the joy of her others – Cassie, Mimi, Armintrude, sweet Clare . . .

'Yes, I accept my fate,' she murmured. 'I take the left-hand path. I stay.'

Armintrude reached down and roughly pulled the bundle of orchid petals from Jana's cunt, then pushed the pacifier to half its length inside her now empty slit and anus. Jana gasped at the size of the lovely artefact, at the tickling, painful pleasure of the striations and smooth shells, and at the probing of the snake's tongue at the neck of her womb. The anal prong was as big as the cunt-prong, and she had to relax her sphincter as much as possible in order to allow the device's ingress. The cunt-prong had a second, smaller snake's head jutting from the neck, like some mutant hybrid, and this clamped firmly on to Jana's now stiffening nympha.

Armintrude pushed relentlessly, until, in a blissful spasm of release, Jana's anus gave way to her pleasure, and the plug slid smoothly in as though magically oiled, filling her to its hilt. Armintrude ordered her to hold the pacifier tightly, and now Jana was obliged to clench the muscle she had just relaxed. She shivered at the harsh pleasure of her fulfilment, a willing prisoner of her own desires. She wanted anything and everything to happen to her!

Armintrude sniffed the orchids, and sighed.

'What are these?' she said. And what were they doing in your cunt, my sweet slut?'

'Keeping me warm,' said Jana mischievously. She watched as Armintrude breathed deeply of the flowers' fragrance which was by now suffused with Jana's own sex scent, and then began to lick them as though gnawed by hunger. Armintrude's face flushed and her eyelids became heavy with desire. Suddenly, she reached down and pulled aside the thong of her G-string, pushed the bouquet deep inside her own cunt, and then began to thrust it in and out like a dildo.

'You have come to me,' she gasped as she masturbated in front of her trussed captive, 'as it was known you would, sweet slut! You have brought me the *satyrion*, the sacred *obispos* of the forest, the petals that make a woman captive. Oh, how I have dreamed of avenging my humiliation at your hands, Jana! And now that you have given your word that you will stay, I may unbind you, in preparation for a sweeter restraint. You may stand.'

Meekly, Jana did so, and Armintrude began to flick her whip, uncoiling the lash until Jana was once more unbound, her buttocks tightly clenched as she maintained the pacifier in her nether holes. Armintrude's masturbation with the flower-dildo grew more and more rapid, and her fingers delved between her glistening cunt-lips, to diddle her swollen pink clit. She groaned, and closed her eyes, then suddenly stopped.

'Oh, you sweet slut!' she moaned. 'The *satyrion* is the

most powerful of aphrodisiac flowers, and these petals are also imbued with *your* essence and power! We must proceed to your chastisement at once, before I forget myself. I have dressed for you, and perfumed myself: the occasion must be perfect.'

'Am I to expect a spanking, then, like the one I awarded you, Armintrude?' said Jana, in a friendly voice.

'More than that,' said Armintrude. 'Follow me, with your hands behind your back and your head bowed.'

Jana obeyed, though it was awkward to walk with the pacifier so snugly inside her. She followed Armintrude through a door and into another chamber, the sight of whose sinister appurtenances quickened her pulse. Armintrude seemed so excited that, trembling on her high heels, she looked about to fall. Jana took her arm to steady her.

'There, Mistress Armintrude, I am yours to chastise. So let's get on with it, and the quicker it is over, the quicker I shall learn my ultimate fate.'

'Yes – yes . . .' stammered Armintrude.

The chamber was a true dungeon, containing every conceivable instrument of correction – Jana recognised the rack on which she had fastened Armintrude some months earlier. There were shackles and whips and chains, strange padded thumbscrews, bridles and branks. There was a pillory, and a mediaeval stocks, and various whipping frames, including a correction chair, which was a sturdy wooden throne with stout armrests, and shackles for the wrists and ankles, but with the seat cut away like a commode, so that the tormentor might have access to the intimate parts of her victim. Finally, there was a table, with straps for restraining the victim. Jana thought of her own dungeon back in London, and longed to exchange it for this magnificently appointed one.

A small door at the far end opened on to a shining array of needles and tubes, not a dungeon so much as a laboratory or surgery. Jana shivered as she asked what kind of subtle tortures could be inflicted there, the intricacy of surgical torment seeming somehow much more terrible than the open lash of whip or cane.

'Oh, that is no torture chamber,' said Armintrude. 'That is the Altar of Adornment. Please rest assured that torture is not practised anywhere in the Castle! The Master values the style, but is repelled by the hideous substance. Imagination can be so much more powerful than reality! Now, I have so looked forward to this, slut Jana, but I – I am quite at a loss as to where to begin.'

'I should begin by bowing to you, and addressing you as Mistress,' said Jana.

'Yes, that would be proper.'

Jana bowed and whispered, 'Mistress, take me.'

Armintrude sighed.

'I should be bound,' said Jana in a brisk tone.

Armintrude nodded apprehensively.

'The sight of your bare flesh is almost more than my desire can stand,' she murmured.

Jana's fount became very wet as she thought of the fierce whipping she could expect from her vengeful new Mistress, and at her desire for the touch of Armintrude's hard body on hers.

Meekly, but with her heart pounding, she positioned herself on the fearsome rack. Armintrude shook her head in refusal.

'I insist, Mistress. The Duke of Exeter's daughter shall remind me of my homeland! And I might grow a little . . .'

Armintrude gulped, as though terrified of her task, but proceeded to prepare her captive for punishment.

'You seem afraid, Armintrude,' said Jana gaily. 'Why, you must be hard-bitten to floggings and – well – all sorts of other terrible things. A mere rack is scarcely frightening.'

'Oh,' said Armintrude, biting her lip. 'Most of these things are just for show, unless they've been adapted for use as instruments of restraint, like the thumbscrews you saw and that crushing press over there. They are not, though, as I said, used for torture; all that belongs in the past. It's just that the Master likes us to know what women and men are *capable* of inflicting upon each other. He thinks that the idea is more voluptuous than the thing itself, just as the beauty of the day becomes apparent in the stillness of twilight. The body whipped, bound, pierced and ringed, or adorned with the tattoo is a symbol of submission and power, and hence of naked purity. When is a woman truly more naked than when she is clad entirely in rubber, steel or leather?'

'I have always been whipped naked,' said Jana. But for you I choose to be bound in rubber, leather, *and* steel.'

Jana directed her own bondage; when she was finally trussed, she lay hooded, bound and helpless on the rack. Around her waist she wore a tight rubber corset which, loosely fastened, was at least two sizes too small even for her slender midriff, but which, when properly laced, was almost impossibly tight. Her breasts were pushed up in delicious oval swellings, but these too were confined by a conical metallic brassière, like Armintrude's – Jana was touched by the thought – which again was slightly too small, so that her nipples were compressed against the smooth moulded cups. Her panties were black leather, as tight as her corset, and held her enormous pacifier inside her cunt and anus even more deeply than she was able to with her sphincter alone.

Her legs were sheathed in sheer latex stockings, opentoed, and on each of Jana's toes Armintrude fitted a tight steel thimble in the shape of a snake's head. Over all this Jana wore a sheer black rubber catsuit which moulded itself to her body like a second skin. The catsuit extended from her neck to her toes. When Jana asked to be gagged properly, the tremulous Armintrude demurred, and they agreed on a snug leather blindfold hood which left only Jana's nose uncovered.

Jana felt hugely aroused. She had never felt so serenely trussed, so secure in her warm solitude. And when she felt Armintrude fasten her wrists and ankles in strong cuffs, her belly fluttered in joyful pleasure. The cuffs were not all; her waist, already constricted by the rubber corset, was now bound by a metal cincher to the crossbar of the rack. Her swooning pleasure was brought to a climax as, unseeing, she felt the thongs of Armintrude's whips being wound around her buttocks, and the full length of her arms and legs encased in the tightest of carapaces.

'I can't move a muscle!' she cried in delight. 'I've never been whipped through rubber before, but I feel so beautifully naked! You can't lace my breasts, though, Armintrude, so my bottom will have to take it extra hard!'

There was a creak, and Jana felt herself being stretched ever so slightly as the rack tightened. She felt no pain, but, instead, a sensation of sensuous helplessness, like falling, as her body was pulled. She felt like a goddess, in thrall to this inhuman engine, whose plaything her stretched form had become.

'That's enough, I think,' said Armintrude nervously.

'No!' cried Jana. 'More! Honestly, Armintrude, anyone would think you had never administered chastisement before. It hurts so! Don't be afraid of my pain!'

In truth, it did not hurt at all, but, rather, gave Jana a sense of wonderful lightness, like an intricate yoga pose. When she heard the rack creak a little more, and Armintrude panting, she judged it time to order herself whipped.

'And lay it on hard, Armintrude,' she ordered sternly, relishing the hot breath with which each word caressed her hooded face. 'Revenge is sweet, remember?'

The first stroke of the whip, which landed squarely across Jana's tightly sheathed buttocks, was indeed hard, and she thrilled as her involuntary jerk was stifled by the tightness of her bonds. The pain, now, was building, as Armintrude's strokes came thick and fast, each whiplash seeming to find the precise spot of a previous one. Armintrude lashed her fesses so hard that, at each stroke, Jana's sphincter tightened in a spasm, and squeezed her pacifier.

She lost count of the number of strokes she took, knowing only the searing delight of her pain. Every nerve ending in her body seemed to soar with life as the whip touched her second skin and, as her body quivered, she felt the pacifier deliciously loving her filled holes, and the stiff bra cups tenderly caressing the breasts and nipples they squeezed so exquisitely. She heard Armintrude panting and suspected that the heaviness of her breathing was not entirely due to her physical exertion.

'Are you masturbating as I squirm for you, Armintrude? Answer truthfully,' she said. There was a pause, and an especially severe stroke caught her at the tops of her thighs.

'Yes, damn you, yes,' hissed Armintrude. 'Oh – Oh – It's enough, now.'

'My back must be laced properly,' said Jana, gasping with pain. 'And the rack cranked a little tighter. Do it, Mistress!'

'Please . . .' whimpered Armintrude.

'Do it!'

As Jana felt the whip descend on her stretched shoulders, she asked Armintrude if she were the Mistress responsible for the adornment and piercing of bodies. Yes, Armintrude was trained as an artist, and in charge of tattooing and ring-piercing.

'The very best! Trained in my home in Lapland, then in Africa and South America. That is why the Master searched for me, and brought me here. He insists on perfection.'

'So that is your hold over the Master,' said Jana.

'It is not the only reason. Oh, I have said enough! I can take this punishment no more!'

'Whip me harder, *slut!*' cried Jana fiercely. 'Whip me until I beg for mercy.'

Armintrude obeyed and maintained the rhythm of her flogging but said that it was she who was begging for mercy.

'Release me from my revenge, Mistress Jana!' she pleaded. 'Revenge is too hard for me to stomach! I can take pain, but I hate to inflict it, even though my Master says it is pure. I am masturbating, I want to come for you, and that is true purity! The pain of a tattooing or a piercing results in art and beauty, but there are so many hideous things that humans have devised to inflict on each other.'

'But a true whipping or binding, given and taken with love, is poetry,' said Jana firmly. 'In adorning ourselves with pain, we conquer it. Don't stop, I command you! Nature is a cruel goddess. What humans can do is impose rules on her disorder. In my Castle of Maldona, we have intricate rules. Why are there no rules here except unspoken ones? Why no rule book? Answer, slave!'

'Oh ... there is a rule book. I found it! The Master knows of it, but I have never revealed where it is hidden, even under his lash. In any case, it is useless, for it will remain locked until the chosen one comes. Only she may open it. *That* is my hold over the Master. He hates me for it, but I would die if he expelled me from the Castle. It is my life. Please, Mistress, let me stop the whipping! I cannot bear your pain any more.'

'Not until you agree to show me where the rule book is. Whip me, lovely slut, and pleasure yourself as you do it. I want to hear you spasm, and spasm again.'

'Oh ...'

Neither woman spoke as Jana's chastisement continued and the silence of the chamber was broken only by the crack of the whip and the harsh breathing of Armintrude as she masturbated herself frantically. At last she cried out in orgasm, but Jana would let her stop neither the chastisement nor her own masturbation. She climaxed twice more before sobbing brokenly that she was defeated, and that she now submitted herself to Jana's will. She would show Jana the rule book.

Jana then ordered Armintrude to unbind her and, when her shackles and bonds had been stripped from her, she saw that her rubber suit had been torn to ribbons by the whipping. Her shoulders and back flowed with a warm smarting pain, and her bare nates were fiery to her touch as she rubbed them gingerly. Armintrude was kneeling before her, her eyes wet, and she bowed to kiss Jana's feet. Jana stroked her hair, and said softly that, before she saw the rule book, she would have to pay Armintrude back.

'Pain, Mistress?' said Armintrude, looking up with tear-stained eyes.

'A little,' said Jana, smiling. 'I'm going to warm your Arctic bottom for you.'

She positioned herself over Armintrude's back, straddling her like a horse, and slapped her buttocks.

'To your chamber, my pony!' she cried gleefully, and Armintrude obediently moved in a shuffling canter back to the chamber, where Jana ordered her to stand with her back to the fire. Armintrude did so, leaning her elbows on the mantelpiece as Jana knelt down before her, and pulled the G-string from her cunt to reveal her glistening wet clitoris. This was already distended, swollen and pink and, hungrily, Jana fastened her lips on it, cupping her tormentor's buttocks as she feasted on her flowing love-juice.

'My croup is so warm,' moaned Armintrude.

'I am roasting you, slut,' said Jana, 'as we do in our English schools. Cold bottom to warm fire!'

'Oh, I am going to come once more, Mistress,' cried Armintrude. 'Oh, yes! Roast me with your lovely hot tongue!'

Jana's fingers crept to her own damsel and she frigged herself joyfully as she felt Armintrude's belly flutter in her spasm. Then Jana, too, reached her plateau and plunged into a sea of warmth and swooning pleasure that seemed to engulf her whole tingling body. She reached down and removed her pacifier, which was gleaming with her love-juice, and pressed it firmly into Armintrude's wet cunt and tight anus, pushing the orchid bundle firmly against the neck of her womb, and securing the device in place with the strap of her G-string. Armintrude gasped with surprised pleasure.

'Thank you, Mistress Jana,' she moaned. My bum is so lovely and hot and naked before the flames of my desire – I have never been filled so sweetly.'

'Now we are even,' whispered Jana as she embraced Armintrude. 'Pleasure for pain. So you may take me to inspect the rulebook.'

Armintrude robed both Jana and herself in fur coats, and gave Jana warm fur slippers, as they had to walk through the snow to reach the hiding-place of the rule book. As they passed through the garden, the foliage and flowers trembled again at Jana's passage, as though in obeisance. Armintrude said that the plants recognised Jana as their Mistress and were bowing to her. Then she began to talk in a low, passionless voice, as though recounting a story learned by rote and kept for the appointed time.

'You have heard of the Crusades, the great migrations of armies and peoples in the Time of Tumult. Much seed was sown here then, just as in the time of the Turks, the Romans, Greeks, Macedonians ... when were the Balkans not in tumult? I myself, from the snowy North, am just part of the new blood which has nourished this Earth through the ages. The Crusader Gottschalk, having been beaten in Hungary, came here with the remnant of his crew and sowed their seed, and the Castle became Enddorf, and to this day the villagers speak their old German of the Middle Ages. But the Castle has never been conquered. It has always absorbed those who came to it, and absorbed their ways. The Turks brought much – their perfumes and spices, and the great sacrificial ceremony of Kurban, the slaying of the lambs, although now the sacrifice is of a different kind ...

'The Castle has always been here, but not as we see it. In the Old Days, Enddorf had a name only in the Old Language which, legend has it, came from the stars. You have heard the Master speak of it, and you shall learn it yourself ... it is like no known earthly language.

'A princess came from the stars in a wondrous ship, which alighted in our Rhodope, and she was taken for a sorceress by the uncouth natives. Her ship was made of gold, which they craved, and they put her through terrible torments to make her tell them where more gold was to be had. She would not, she was racked, whipped and flogged, but said only that all life was one, that the sea and sun and stars and moon were one, and that pain was the same as love, and submission the same as joy.

'She was whipped with a nine-thonged flail whose points were stars, until her tormentor fell faint with exhaustion, and let fall his whip, and the peasants fell before her at this sign of grace. There she told the awed peasants that they should build a castle, with her whip as its foundation. The peasants obeyed, and she became the queen of the village and gave birth to a race of prodigious menfolk, with the virility of the stars.

'She ruled for hundreds of years, teaching them skills and arts, the adornment of the body and the cultivation of wondrous plants which could prolong life, before she took her golden ship and returned unseen to the stars, one night during a snowstorm. And to this day the peasants worship the stars known as 'the Snake', because the nine points of her star-flail form the body of a serpent in the heavens.

'In the fourteenth century of our era, there was a great plague all over the world, called the black plague, and there were marauders and warriors pillaging abandoned cities. One such, named Decius, came to the Castle and spoke of being cast adrift by a sorceress, and enslaved by Barbary corsairs, whose Master he had subsequently become through his superior lore and wisdom. He was burnt by the sun, and his voice was of the North. He had with him a band of dark-hued ruffians, and took possession of the village and its Castle, but was soon enslaved anew. The dark men learned the art of the tattoo, and were captured by it. Their cocks and breasts were adorned with snakes and roses, until they became *of* the Castle. The village women spoke with awe of the virility of the men and the size of their members, some two handspans, for what woman will not admit to her delicious awe in the face of a mighty cock?

'While Decius was Master, another princess came, alone and from the East, with a chest on her humble packhorse, and carrying a many-thonged white whip encrusted with jewels. The slaves of Decius wished to enslave her in turn, but she confounded them by disrobing and revealing her naked body, which awed them with its power, for she had the perfection of tattoos. Her body glowed with sun and stars, snakes and fish and butterflies and birds – truly all the secrets of this world. Her tattoos were her knowledge.

'Her cunnus was shaved bare like her whole body, and in front and back she was adorned with a rosebush, the stems growing from the valley of her fesses and from her mons, so that her breasts and shoulders were garlands of rose petals, blood-red kin to the amaranthus of eternal life. Snakes entwined her thighs and calves, devouring their

248

own tails, and between her bare fesses and on her mons were rosebuds, from which the stems sprang, so that her body was a symbol of life eternally giving birth to itself, and devouring itself. Decius recognised her as the sorceress who had marooned him, and he was going to put her to death, but she bewitched the men of the Castle.

'Naked, she lay in the snow and opened her thighs, and bade them come to her. Nine times nine mighty cocks she took in her cunnus, and still begged for more, taunting them that they had not enough seed for her. She drained them of every drop of strength and manly essence, and then they recognised her witch's power and made obeisance to her. Decius was punished for his insolence, by taking nine times nine strokes on his bared nates with her white jewelled whip. He was then made her slave, and robed, perfumed and shaved as a woman. He was happy at last, for he was now a true slave and learned the secrets of women, the making of perfumes and sweetmeats, and the joy of submission in opening his thighs to the embraces of others.

'She left behind a golden treasure and a book of rules. The treasure is kept by the Master's Comptroller, a sacred function, and the book of rules was hidden at the place where she was swived by the Castle's men. Legend said that no snow shall ever fall on the imprint of her body where she lay, and I found this place, by accident, at the base of a tree sacred to me. That knowledge is my power.'

They came to a huge red tree, whose like Jana had never before seen. Its base was a massive double core of hard red wood, like a male's balls, with red blossoms sprouting like little hairs from it, and this tapered to a smooth, shining trunk, topped with a bulb of waving red petals. Armintrude smiled and stroked the shaft, and told Jana that she called it her penis tree, and that she came here to pleasure herself when she felt the spirit of the princess fill her. She kissed the penis-shaft, and murmured, 'Does the root serve the tree, or the tree the root?'

'Who is the Comptroller of the golden treasure, and where is the treasure kept?' asked Jana. Armintrude began to dig at the base of the tree, under the core, its testicles . . .

'Currently, Clare is the Comptroller!' she said. 'I am forbidden to know where the treasure is kept.'

Jana thought of the chest Clare kept under her bed. Then Armintrude unearthed an oilskin containing a leather pouch, which she opened. Inside was a book bound in red leather, its pages yellowed with age, and locked with a golden clasp. Armintrude's face was very grave as she handed it to Jana.

'As you can see, it is not an ordinary lock,' she said. 'That is why the rule book is useless to the Master, though he does not know it. The princess, who called herself Maldona, said that only when she, the One, returned to the Castle, would the rules be known. The lock is a hole into which will fit only the little finger of the One's left hand. If you are the One, Jana, then your finger will fit the hole, and the book will open. Should that be the case, you must be presented at the Festival of Kurban, when the Palace of Arts shall be inaugurated. If not, well, you may still be presented there, but not in joyful sport.'

Jana shivered, and then shrugged, and placed the little finger of her left hand at the lock's opening. Armintrude turned her face away, saying that she was afraid to look.

Then Jana took a deep breath and pushed her finger into the oiled aperture. It fitted perfectly, and the book sprang open in a flutter of creamy pages. Jana promptly closed the book again, and told Armintrude she could look.

'The book is mine,' she said, and Armintrude kissed her joyfully. Jana did not tell her that the pages were blank.

18

Kurban

Armintrude escorted Jana back to the quarters which had
been allocated to her when she had first arrived at the
Castle. Jana was costumed in a simple black robe which
covered her from neck to ankles, and barefoot, and her
long blonde mane hung loose and uncoiffed. Under her
robe she was naked, and her breasts swung full and soft
against the loose fabric, making her feel strangely self-
conscious. She carried her rulebook demurely at her waist,
and the women bowed to her swiftly as she passed them in
the corridors. They *knew*!

Once in her quarters, she found everything as she and
Cassie had left it, and immaculately tidy. Armintrude
expressed her appreciation of the luxurious apartment.

'The bridal suite,' she said softly. 'It is fitting. As soon
as you arrived, the Master knew.'

Jana sat down, quite tired now, and said that she wanted
to bathe, eat and rest. Armintrude promptly went to
prepare her bath, and then telephoned for a meal to be
brought. Soon, Jana was soaking in a hot tub and heard
the door open, as a Student delivered her meal. After her
bath, Armintrude anointed her with perfume and oils,
wrapped her in a silk kimono, and then joined her at her
meal, at Jana's insistence. There was champagne, and
dishes of oysters, quails' eggs, duck and suckling pig,
salads, and others containing fruits and cheeses. Jana's
plate was adorned with a single long-stemmed rose, which
she thought touching, and she was even more impressed by
the provision of a fresh packet of French cigarettes and a

gold lighter. As she ate, Jana mischievously decided to test her new-found power.

'The bridal suite,' she said thoughtfully, between mouthfuls of duck and cranberry, 'you must explain, Armintrude.' Armintrude laughed nervously.

'I must obey, of course, Mistress,' she said, 'although all things will become clear during your training.'

'And that, too, you must explain fully,' replied Jana. 'But first I wish you to take a couple of oysters, and a spoonful of this delicious duck.'

Armintrude the vegetarian blanched, but obeyed, first swallowing the oysters quickly, following Jana's example, then hesitantly taking a mouthful of duck and chewing it with surprising zeal. She swallowed that, too, and blushed.

'Mmm! I enjoyed that,' she said with a guilty grin.

'Then have some more. *And* some suckling pig. I want to see some meat on your lovely bones, my slave, and see your tongue lick the grease from your lips.'

Soon, Armintrude was eating as though she had not had a proper meal for years, which Jana thought was no less than the truth. And, as she lit her post-prandial cigarette and luxuriated in smoking it, she congratulated herself that power has its benign uses. Next, she said that Armintrude must give her the promised explanations, and Armintrude became nervous again. Jana touched her hand to comfort her, but she drew back.

'No,' she said sadly, 'it would be improper for us to touch. You must be chaste, Mistress, the Purified, and the Purifier.'

'More riddles!' cried Jana, lighting another cigarette.

Armintrude told her of the Festival of Kurban. The inauguration of the Palace of Arts was to be the most wondrous Kurban in all memory, with *karagoz* performances, feasting, dancing, and all manner of entertainments. The Sisterhood of Kali would play an honoured part, as would Freya's wolves.

'Lascivious entertainments, I hope,' said Jana, impishly blowing smoke at her guest, 'as long as Freya's wolves haven't eaten each other by now.'

'Lascivious is scarcely a proper word,' said Armintrude, 'but you know the Castle's ways, and its ways are pure, free of the repressed darkness of ordinary mortals.'

'Where do *I* come into all this portentous stuff?' said Jana impatiently.

'In the old days of the Ottoman Turks, the Sultana, or Emperor's Supreme Mistress, was the real power behind the throne. It was the custom, at Kurban, that the Sultana would show her favour by presenting him with one of her slaves, to be his concubine. The slave was attended by her bridesmaids, and purified for seven nights and seven days, after which she was presented to her new owner.'

'I still don't understand,' said Jana, smoking furiously, because she was indeed beginning to understand.

'More than this I cannot tell you,' said Armintrude tonelessly, 'for I am not permitted to know more. You will stay here for seven nights, and your bridesmaids will attend and cleanse you. They shall bring you to me for your adornment, after which you shall be finally purified for the festival, on the seventh day. For *your* festival, Mistress.'

Jana was not allowed to be alone, even in bed, when there was always a bridesmaid in wakeful attendance. Otherwise, she was escorted by one or many of her bridesmaids. These were Mimi, Clare, Cassie and Gudrun. She saw Freya and Robyn from time to time, and there were many visits to Armintrude's chamber of adornment.

She was taught wifely duties, or had to prove herself adept at them. A single day labouring in the sumptuous kitchens proved her capable of creating the most elaborate dishes, which she was then permitted to serve at the Master's table. As his waitress, she wore the same uniform as the other servants, a frilly French maid's concoction with the laddered stockings which were *de rigueur*, but she was hooded, either because the Master was not permitted to see his bride's face, or to hide her identity from him; she was never sure which. She acquitted herself superbly at her menial service, ignored by Gilles and the other braggart males who tossed their bones and scraps on to the floor for her to pick up, crouching on her hands and knees. Sometimes the Master would slap her raised buttocks, which were usually bare, or clad in the thinnest silken panties, and order her, in his mild voice, to hold her hands behind her back and pick up the scraps in her lips.

This she did without a murmur, and she felt a real glow of pride at the approving grunts which came from the menfolk. If Gilles or Michael knew she was the model they had fucked all those months ago, they gave no sign. Neither did they touch her body; the occasional bum-slap was for the Master alone, and she was moist at the thought that soon she would be his property. She found it piquant and proper that, as the future Princess, as the 'One', she must learn the arts of submission to the Castle in order to rule it, just as English public schools taught their charges to obey in order that they might learn how to command. She thought of her ancestor Jana Ardenne coming to this remote outpost centuries ago, and conquering it by giving herself to all its menfolk. That thought, too, made her quite wet – to be the plaything of all those beautiful hard cocks. A doll for their pleasure! She wondered if such a submissive treat awaited her at Kurban.

In her room, she was taught deportment and manners by her bridesmaids. Each treated her with formality, calling her 'Mistress', and always bowing low in greeting, but was peremptory in her role as tutor, rather like the sergeants at officers' training colleges who made life hell for their cadets, but still had to address them as 'sir'. At first Jana rebelled: she was, after all, Mistress of Maldona, and said she should teach *them* about manners, but at such outbursts none of them hesitated or raised so much as an apologetic eyebrow before ordering her to bare herself for chastisement. She was never whipped or caned, her punishment being a bare-bum spanking with bare hand: but the spankings were deliciously hard – of at least two hundred slaps – and the resulting sore bottom invariably reminded her to behave properly.

One day she was robed in fur, and became one of Freya's wolves for a hunt, pursuing a hapless Student

254

through the snowy forest. The Student was less successful in evading them than Jana had been, and they found her suspended in a trap net, whereupon Jana was instructed to bind her naked to a tree and whip her mercilessly with a flail of heavy lianas. When the girl sobbed for mercy, Jana granted it, and Freya commended her for her wifely skill at whipping, and her kindness in ceasing the chastisement when the girl's back and fesses had been correctly reddened. Jana wondered whom she would have to whip as the Master's wife.

Mimi was especially fond of devising subtle exercises in deportment and proper behaviour. She would make Jana strip, then blindfold and gag her, and cuff her hands behind her back. Jana had to dress herself fully in this awkward position, with a spanking her reward if she fumbled or was not speedy enough. Alternatively, her hands would be left free, and she would be paraded naked in front of all her bridesmaids, who would bark orders at her in rapid and confusing succession, telling her to squat, put her hands behind her head, sit down with her legs spread and her tongue out, and put her fingers in anus or quim, or bend forward to take her toes in her mouth.

Often, she would be handcuffed and gagged, and ordered to remain squatting as though for the commode, without moving, while her bridesmaids left the room. Such was the manner of their leaving that Jana was unsure if they had left at all and, on one occasion when she moved to ease herself after an unconscionably long time squatting, she found that Mimi had been there watching her all the time. She was duly rewarded with a bare spanking of a hundred slaps from each bridesmaid, and never repeated her mistake.

She would often, too, be obliged to wash her bridesmaids' entire bodies with her tongue, while they were naked and she was cuffed and blindfolded. Otherwise, she might be made to squat under the table and lick each of their bare feet in turn while they chatted gaily at tea, or to kneel and present her back as a footstool, usually while one of her merited spankings was being

255

administered. Sometimes she was given a hairbrush and ordered to spank herself in front of a mirror while maintaining a perfectly motionless expression, and sometimes she was made to beg humiliatingly for a spanking, confessing her improprieties until one or another of her bridesmaids consented to touch her flesh. Jana put all her effort into these entreaties, finding that she genuinely wanted to persuade them to spank her, and feeling disappointed on those occasions when she was deemed unworthy. That was *real* punishment . . .

She was forbidden to touch or pleasure herself, even though she was obliged to watch in frustration as her bridesmaids playfully and openly masturbated, eyeing her contemptuously as they fingered their nymphae. More often than not, they would make the torment worse by forcing her to lick their clits until they orgasmed. She was constantly observed, especially when at commode, and Gudrun would delight in ordering her to hurry up, or allowing her only one piece of pink paper for afterwards. Mimi again revealed her cruel streak by allowing Jana to go to commode when she was quite desperate, but refusing to let her evacuate until she had squatted for a long time in discomfort and frustration. Jana was obliged to attend the others at commode, apply the pink paper, and wash their fundaments afterwards. Sometimes after washing the founts of her bridesmaids, she had to give them an extra cleansing with her tongue and lips. And every morning, she received a thorough hot and cold cleansing in both anus and quim from the gleaming irrigation machine in her bathroom.

At night, Jana's bridesmaids would amuse themselves by making her wear a bridle, bit and *cincha*, and then ponyriding her through the deserted corridors, her knees and feet encased in soft felt padding. Clare was particularly fond of this, and seemed to relish giving playful slaps to Jana's croup even more than usual when she could punctuate them with whoops of 'giddy up!' She had, apparently, done a lot of horse-riding as a girl, and had also raced motor-cycles and sports cars. She had, she said, even tried free-fall parachuting, and Jana's theory was that, lacking the all-important sense of smell, Clare compensated by taxing her other senses to their very limits. Jana liked it when Clare rode her because the sensation of Clare's body jewellery on her bare skin was very arousing.

Jana's training was interrupted by frequent sessions with Armintrude in her chamber of adornment. In a stern white top, and a rather daring black skirt with a frilly white petticoat, and black fishnet stockings beneath it, Armintrude looked – and was – half nurse, half artist. The piercing and tattooing procedures ranged between the uncomfortable and the rather painful, but Jana loved the sensation of beauty flowing on to her naked self. On the third day, when the bandages covering the first tattoos came off, the mirrors were removed from her room; she might not look at herself until her adornment was complete, lest she demur. But the tingling pain of a freshly etched tattoo gave her a good indication of what images adorned her: she could feel the shapes that now marked her forever. She felt she had always worn such beauty. The thought of abandoning her adornment or training was as distant as the stars themselves.

At last, the day came, and Mimi brought a full-length mirror for her robing. All her bridesmaids, and Freya and Robyn, too, were there to admire her as she took her first look at her fully adorned naked body and, when she gasped in delight, all their faces, too, were wreathed in smiles, and they applauded, then showered her with kisses and hugs. Jana's body glowed with the beauty Armintrude had bestowed upon her, and she felt like a goddess: it seemed that every inch of her skin had been pierced and ringed, or painted in tattoos of the brightest and most serene colours.

Her breasts and buttocks were roses, and at the base of her spine a butterfly, like Clare's, fluttered from its lair of rose-petals, its thorax elongating and metamorphosing into a massive penis which followed her spine. Each bony node of power or *chakra*, was adorned with a smaller blossom, until the flowered penis culminated in a beautiful shining bulb which almost covered her shoulders. Her forehead wore a sun and moon surrounded by stars, snake-rings hung from her pierced ears, nose and lower lip, and small sun-rings adorned the points of her eyelids. A gleaming serpentine fish, pink-tongued, and also unmistakably a penis, sprang from her cunt-lips, which were enlarged by tattoos of two scalloped pink shells. The peehole of her fish-penis was the beast's gaping mouth, a dark sweet crevice from which the roses on her breasts grew, and all around this leviathan were fluttering birds or twined flowers. Halfway up the shaft of her belly-cock, her navel was transformed into a single eye and this blinked whenever she moved her hips.

Her arms and legs were quite bare, and Armintrude said that no adornment of these muscled limbs had been necessary. Their essential beauty lay in the way they functioned and was best compared to, say, the beauty of a supple machine, rather than to that of something which was essentially decorative.

'Adornment is for parts which do not move or function,' she explained. 'I know some men, like the Marquis Gilles, sport the *joug*-ring on their cocks, or as in your England, the more saturnine device of the Prince Albert, but I prefer the humble *guiche*, coyly peeping from atop the balls, a lovely hint of the inner function.'

And outside, Jana's tattooed body glittered with rings and jewels which were glorious whispers of the beauty that was within her. The lips of her scallop-shelled quim were a sheer flank of broad cunt-rings, leading unbroken to tiny perineal rings which extended from her cunt all the way to her anus, the exterior bud of which was pierced by no less than three rings. The phalanx of gold now bifurcated into twin rows which framed the cleft between her buttocks, and then formed spirals and whorls which decorated the wings of her tattooed butterfly. From her mount, the rings snaked up and over her belly to form an orbit around the eye of her navel, before continuing upward to join the cluster of giant rings hanging from each of her pierced nipples. Her toes and fingers were not pierced, but shone

258

with rows of rings like golden gloves. The webbed flaps of skin between them were pierced, however, and set with tiny metal hoops.

Her breasts were pierced, and not only through the nipples but also on their undersides and, above each of her teats, another line of rings led up to a chain secured to the multi-stranded golden choker around her neck. This was fastened at her nape by means of a gleaming pearl clasp, to which another chain connected an artfully placed ring, which appeared to be piercing the glans of the huge penis tattooed on her back. But the most beautiful ring on Jana's entire body was also the smallest – the miniscule gold band which pierced her clitoris.

Jana pirouetted and posed in delicious shamelessness in front of her looking-glass, her whole body dancing with pleasure.

'I am Beauty,' she whispered in awe, as her bridesmaids set about preparing her for the festival.

First, she was given a long, hard cleansing with the irrigation machine, and a variety of fragrant oils and potions was pumped into her willing cunt and anus. There was no mercy for the bride-to-be, and she was made to squirm until Mimi knelt to lick her two holes, and judged her thoroughly cleansed. She was shaved until her skin was as smooth as porcelain, and then bathed and perfumed. She returned, fragrant, to her bedroom and was corseted with an ultra-tight crimson waspie, fringed in brocaded écru lace, which flattened her rings against her skin; their bite made her feel tingly and snug. Below the waspie, a suspender belt of the same fabric held crimson stockings of the sheerest translucent latex.

There were no panties, and the garments were a pretty frame for the naked amaranth lips of Jana's quim. Her hair was garlanded with roses, and then long chains were looped around her waist and breasts, and threaded through her many rings to form a shimmering petticoat and corselage. A golden snake bracelet was fastened tightly around her left thigh, just above the red rubber stocking-top, and a similar one was placed around her left ankle.

Soft Persian slippers with curled pointed toes and high stilettos were fitted to her feet, and were as perfect as a second skin. Her eyes were painted with dark kohl, and her lips, nipples, anus bud and quim-petals with a crimson unguent.

The crowning beauty of her costume was applied by Cassie.

'Remember this, Mistress?' she murmured. 'At Caspar's party in Lennox Gardens, so long ago?'

'It looks like a strap-on rubber cock,' said Jana.

'It is a punishment harness of a Parfaite of Maldona, Mistress. See? The base of the dildo fastens *here* –' she slipped one end of the soft rubber dildo firmly into Jana's slit, and secured it with a gossamer chain '– and when you squeeze on it with your quim muscles . . . well, you'll see.'

The pleasure of being filled by the dildo was heightened as Jana squeezed it tightly between her vaginal walls, only for its tip to suddenly burst into a wondrous rainbow of peacocks' feathers. These formed an ovoid fan, which covered the front of her body from her breasts to her thighs, but she soon found that by changing the pressure on the dildo inside her she could adjust the fan to almost any shape, and be as coy or as daring as she pleased.

'It is perfect, Cassie!' she cried. 'But as I remember it, at Caspar's party I had two fans; one, like this one, in my quim, and another in my bumhole!'

'Ah,' smiled Cassie, 'I think it is proper, here, that you should content yourself with just the quim-fan, Mistress. Your anus rings would make ingress of the other shaft rather difficult.'

Finally, a fire was lit in a copper brazier, filling the room with fragrant smoke. Mimi explained that it was the sacred *fumée d'ambergris*, a mixture of sandalwood, myrrh, frankincense and other precious spices, with which the princesses of old Mokka, Turkey and Persia would perfume their bodies, and in particular their sacred orifices of cunt and arse, for their menfolk. Jana said that she wanted to make a last visit to the commode, to collect her thoughts, and asked permission to be alone for that. Mimi

260

said that the Master's bride no longer needed to ask such permission on her wedding day, and Jana duly squatted – though not before retrieving the rulebook, wrapped in its protective oilskin, from within the cistern where she had hidden it.

After commode, she wiped and cleansed herself, then replaced her dildo, squeezed her quim muscles and opened her peacock fan. She hid her rulebook securely behind its iridescent feathers, and returned to squat once more over the glowing coals of the brazier. She breathed in deeply as she felt the oily smoke penetrating her, sliding into her nether holes and over her breasts like the caress of a lover's gentle fingers, and perfuming the fan-feathers trembling at her fount. Her body glowing with the power and pleasure of her robing, Jana was carried, shoulder-high on carpets of rose-petals, through the Castle and outside to the Palace of Arts.

From her balcony, Jana and her bridesmaids could see down on to the vast floor of the palace, but were shielded by filmy gauze drapes from the eyes of the throng below. Her bridesmaids were all dressed in white, save for their fingernails, lips, and toes, which were painted crimson to match Jana's apparel. They went barefoot and had white chestnut blossoms in their hair, the pungently sexual scent of the flowers perfectly complementing Jana's own fragrance. All had completely shaven bodies, and were naked under their robes. Their swelling founts gleamed against the tight flimsy silk of their short mini-dresses, the cut of which left bare their arms and stockingless legs. Their only other adornments were golden chokers, the band of the Elect around their upper thighs, and thin chain belts from which hung pretty white whips with half a dozen snake-head thongs.

The marble walls of the palace soared aloft to a shadowy vaulted ceiling. Above the shadows gleamed the burnished copper of the cupola's interior, like a giant star above a night sky, with the thronged bright Earth beneath. There was an astonishing array of sculptures, paintings and photographs, some bearing the hallmark of the Master's art, and some recognisable as Old Masters – Botticelli, Fragonard, Poussin – but tableaux which were hitherto unknown to Jana. She could not tell if they were skilful pastiches, or true purchases of hidden masterpieces. All the paintings were powerfully erotic, and on the floor the guests conversed brightly amid daring nude sculptures, which Jana guessed to be the Master's cherished living statues.

The guests were arrayed in finery so gorgeous or bizarre that they seemed to have stepped out from the canvases they were admiring. Jana recognised Gilles, and Michael, who was proudly showing off his work – sweetly explicit portraits of Jana herself at pleasure during her modelling session. Maids circulated discreetly with trays of drinks and sweetmeats, and came on to Jana's balcony to serve her and her train, with their heads lowered. Jana smiled as she saw their stockings to be laddered with uniform precision. She saw Robyn, wearing an outfit of straps and buckles and very little else, her near-naked body gleaming proudly in the light of a hundred chandeliers, and wished she could mingle with the throng. Cassie whispered, however, that she must wait for the *karagoz* show, and then her ceremony.

Jana sipped her champagne, and held Cassie's hand chastely for comfort. Wine flowed amongst the enlivened guests, but suddenly there was a hush, and Cassie said that the *karagoz* puppetry was to begin.

'And then I shall be the Master's bride,' she said, still not quite believing it. 'Somehow, it seems imperfect to gain power without conquest.'

She felt herself to be almost a puppet, a plaything in the hands of her far-seeing ancestor. A wild, rebellious thought reared in her. Down below she could see Freya's wolves, and the Sisterhood of Kali, minus Clare, huddled together. Horst was at their head, not in his usual slave's tunic, but resplendent in full *maquillage*, jewels, and a glittering sequined ballgown, which did not however hide the beautiful bulge of his manhood. If she rebelled at the very last moment, and ordered her Sisters to join her and subdue the

262

Master exactly as they had subdued Horst, then perhaps Horst and the other slaves would join their revolt! Would Cassie and her bridesmaids obey her? Or could she take to her heels and flee out into the snowy forest once more, to be tracked by Freya's wolves . . .? Cassie shook her out of her reverie and said, 'Mistress, we are your willing brides-maids, but there is much we do not know. Armintrude, Mistress of the Elect, commands, but does not tell all. We do not know if you are to be the Master's bride, or the bride of Kurban itself: *if you, Mistress, are to be the ritual sacrifice.*'

The chandeliers were extinguished, and electric spot-lights began to flicker around the dimmed and expectant crowd. Oddly, the little stage in the hall's centre was not illuminated, but Jana suddenly saw reflected in the spot-lights myriad little silvery wires which descended from the vaulted ceiling. As one, the living sculptures began to move as the wires trembled – a puppet show with living marion-ettes! Jana saw that Freya's wolves, and the women of her Sisterhood, were also governed by these wires. Moving in and around the guests, the living puppets began their mimed performance, touching and caressing the guests so that it became impossible to distinguish guest from puppet.

'You will recognise some of the stories from the old legends,' whispered Mimi, applauding the clever dances and mimicry. There were males dressed as females, females as males: female gods of thunder and lightning, male goddesses of love and fertility. Despite her anguished presentiments, Jana found herself drawn to the spectacle, and reassured herself that sacrifices and torment were things of the past. Had Armintrude not assured her so?

She found herself laughing and clapping at Sinbad the Sailor, Aladdin and his Wonderful Lamp, and various episodes with magic carpets. There was more to the per-formance than just tales from *The One Thousand and One Nights*, though, and gradually the playlets became more openly erotic and more sombre, and the movement of the puppets was punctuated by sinister drumbeats. There was the story of the Golem, the man of clay made in Prague,

263

who died because he could not love a woman. There was that of Leda, wife of Tyndarus, who was impregnated by Jupiter in the form of a swan while she bathed, and that of Hero and Leander, drowned in the Hellespont for their love of each other. And there was that of Queen Boudicca of Essex, flogged by the Roman conquerors and leading her Britons to a hideous, lustful revenge. Then, in what Jana sensed was the grand finale, there was the story of Thracian Orpheus, the poet whose words could move rocks to tears, and women to unbridled passion. When his wife Eurydice was taken by death, he journeyed to Hades, the Underworld, and so charmed its ruler Pluto that he agreed to release the woman back to Earth, on condition that Orpheus did not look back before they had reached Earth. He set foot on Thracian soil, and thoughtlessly looked back, whereupon Eurydice vanished forever. Then he prowled the Rhodope, mute and mournful, until its loveless, angry women lost patience with him, cut his body into pieces, and consigned his head to the river.

Jana marvelled at the lighting effects which helped bring the scenarios to life, especially in the terrifying story of Orpheus: subtle glows illustrated the gloom of Hades and the rippling of the river – his watery grave, while brighter bursts mimicked the flash of the women's swords. Jana comforted herself that the dismemberment was not real – though where *had* the actor gone? – just as she was sure the whipping of Boudicca had been very real indeed. She had, however, no further time to reflect, for Robyn burst on to her balcony, bowed rapidly in the customary manner, then barked an order in the mysterious Old Language. The bridesmaids seized Jana by her wrists and ankles, and she was raised above their heads. She did not even try to struggle, knowing that she could not overpower them all, but felt only an overwhelming sadness that she had been betrayed.

'Why the deception?' she asked Robyn, bitterly. 'Why all the training? The adornment of my body? Just for this ...?' She looked down the stairway at the crowd of smiling, eager faces, and saw that the floor of the little stage was now furnished with a high, skeletal frame, with restraints like those on a flogging horse.

'There is no deception, Jana,' said Robyn, the Swiss banker, who now seemed to be in charge. I suppose money talks, thought Jana.

'You are to be the sacrifice of Kurban. You are to emulate your ancestor Jana Ardenne, and return to the stars.' Jana's blood froze in her veins. According to the legend, her illustrious predecessor had been roasted alive and devoured by those who worshipped her.

Contemplation of this horror prevented Jana from making any sound except for a low moan of sadness and despair. She was carried to the dais where, swiftly and efficiently, she was trussed to the flogging-frame, which she saw had a turning device, like a spit. Freya and Armintrude joined Robyn in supervising her bondage, and Armintrude took a special delight in making sure her wrists and ankles were properly secured. Jana was unable to move. Then she felt warmth and light play on her body, as beneath her coals began to glow. She shuddered: she was indeed to be this gruesome feast!

Armintrude held a thick gag and blindfold at the ready. Below her, Jana could hear the hungry excited murmuring of the crowd, and this soon reached a crescendo of lustful frenzy. She craned her neck to look, and saw that already the guests were jettisoning their clothing and jewellery, and that bared bodies were intertwining in kisses and embraces. Just as the women of Thrace had needed to dismember poor Orpheus to regain their lustful female prowess, so it seemed that the sacrifice of the Master's bride was now necessary, that desire might be rekindled, in this bleak snowy winter, and new life and ardour given to the age-old beauty of the Castle. Jana suddenly felt a strange serenity. Her sacrifice would see her life essence and her female power shared amongst the lustful, and give new life to their own seed and their own wombs. From her pain would flow love.

'You *do* have a choice, you know, Mistress,' said Robyn, and Armintrude nodded. 'You may meet your destiny as the One Awaited – or you may turn your back, say the word and be cut from your bonds, then go back to your world and disappear from the Castle forever. The left path, or the right.'

Jana thought calmly, I am Mistress of Maldona, I have ruled, loved, and taught, taken and given pain. What more is there if I am alone and shunned by those I love? The Castle is my world.

'I choose the left path, and stay,' she said softly, then added with new urgency, 'but wait, I am the One, and you must submit to me, for I have the rulebook!'

She moved the only muscles she could, which were her cunt-muscles, and her peacock fan sprang back into its cylinder, revealing the hidebound rulebook nestling on her belly.

Robyn smiled and fondly stroked Jana's hair.

'I know all about the rulebook, Mistress,' she said. 'The pages are blank. But you have chosen, now! Your sacrifice may commence. You must first take the nine times nine.'

Now Jana felt the heavy blindfold and was gagged with her own rulebook, fastened into place against her teeth by a strong band. Plunged into mute darkness, she felt the fire grow slightly hotter. Its heat was not yet uncomfortable, but enough to make her sweat profusely until she knew her body glistened with moisture. Crazily, she felt a pang of regret that she had never got to see the Lamartine Museum, and the poet's line sprang into her mind, that one soul is absent, and everything is desert. She would be that soul.

Worse than anything was the suspense; having chosen, all she wished now was for her torment to be over and done with; and yet the fire grew no hotter. She wanted to cry out bitterly that they should not tease her thus but finish the job, when she heard the frame creak, and felt her legs being slowly spread apart, as though it were necessary that the flames should sear her fount. Then she felt a tickling sensation all over her body, heard the rustle of hair, and smelled the powerful scent of chestnut blossoms: her bridesmaids had shed their garlands and scattered her body with an offering of white petals. Suddenly she jerked, as the dildo of her fan was slid out of her quim, leaving her feeling quite naked, and was replaced, to her gasping astonishment, by a stiff, massive limb . . . a man's cock!

The cock began to pump swiftly in and out of her slit, which, despite her agony of uncertainty, quickly moistened at the power and beauty of the mighty engine. She *knew* that cock! Behind her gag, she cried a muffled 'Horst!' and heard the slave reply that he was honoured to be the first. She felt herself enveloped by a sweetly scented cloth, and remembered Horst's sequinned robe – she had longed to wear it, and her wish was granted.

'So beautiful, so pure . . .' groaned Horst, and she felt his cock tremble before he cried out and washed the neck of her womb with a beautiful hot jet of creamy sperm. She felt his lips kiss her nipples, belly and clitoris in thankful homage, and then his cock slid from her, to be replaced at once by another, just as poweful. At each stroke, her pierced clitoris tingled with fierce pleasure, and she forgot where or who she was, knowing only the joy of her utter helplessness – a bound woman filled. She recognised Gilles's cock, and Michael's; her cunt flowed hot and wet, and she lost count of the number of cocks that pleasured her, knowing only that after the third, each fucking heightened the continuous orgasm she was experiencing until her whole body drifted glowing in a golden sea of joy.

'Isn't this what you have always dreamed of, Mistress?' whispered Robyn in her ear. 'To be fucked into oblivion?'

Jana felt her thighs cascading with sweet cunt-oil, her body flowing in hot sweat, and nodded fervently, *Yes! Yes!*

After an age of pleasure, Jana heard Robyn whisper again that she had taken her final stroke, and that her pain must now be soothed, as was proper. Once more, Jana felt the unbearably sweet tingle of orgasm as gentle tongues licked her cunt – female tongues, nine times nine of them, cooing and kissing with tender lips as they brought her to a giddying plateau of ecstasy. Jana was trembling, swooning uncontrollably and felt herself melting with the joy that seared her body.

She scarcely noticed the roll of drums which grew louder and louder, snare drums rattling fervently with stark punctuations from bass and tympani, until suddenly the sound was quelled, and replaced with the beat of a single tom-tom.

'The Master comes!' whispered Robyn.

The flogging-frame moved again, and now Jana's legs were forced up and back, until her open fount was pointing at the ceiling and her cheeks were cradled by her calves. She felt her blindfold and gag being removed, and blinked as she opened her eyes. Around her stood a circle of naked young males – her erstwhile lovers – all of whom she recognised as the slaves of the Castle. They stood solemnly, their hands clasped to cup their balls, from which sprang a serried forest of huge red cocks, all erect, and all neatly circumcised. Jana thought she had never seen anything so beautiful. Behind each male knelt a female Student, clad in a bra, skimpy knickers, a suspender belt, shoes with fantastically high and pointed heels, and stockings which were, of course, beautifully laddered . . .

Craning her neck, she looked around; the guests were, by now, mostly naked, and abandoned in their ecstatic embraces, with couples, threesomes and foursomes in intricate variations of fucking, tribadism or gamahuching. There was the pleasing crack of whips and swish of canes as implements of correction were applied gaily or fiercely to reddening, squirming fesses. Jana saw Clare, bent double in one of her backwards contortions, being fucked in both holes by Gilles and Michael. Simultaneously, she was fellating a third and fourth male, with two cocks in her mouth at once, as her fingers masturbated two other men who knelt beside her. The air was thick with the sweet perfumes of lust. Jana craned again, this time to look below her at the fire on which she was roasting, then burst out laughing. There were no coals, just a gentle kaleidoscope of laser lights waving like flames, or a rainbow of warm penises. I am, she thought, a human *son et lumière*!

And she saw that the blond male slaves with their gorgeous stiff cocks were further accoutred, for at the cleft of each man's buttocks, a little tail grew, just like Horst's. These tails were not soft and pliable, but cartilaginous, and stood erect like furry little penises! When Robyn saw that Jana's eyes were open, she gave a signal and the kneeling females, as one, lowered their heads and took the tails of the male slaves deep in their mouths. Their heads began to bob up and down as they fellated the tails, and Jana saw the males' eyes close as they moaned and sighed in evident pleasure, as though their tails were more sensitive even than their penis helmets!

The male slaves' cocks trembled and stiffened until they seemed to be on the point of bursting and, after a short time of this strange tail-sucking, their moans became deeper and hoarser. Suddenly Jana saw white cream appear at the tip of each peehole, and then, to her wet delight, the males spurted as one! Thick creamy jets of hot seed bathed Jana's skin, until her whole body glistened like a nacreous pearl in the shimmering light. She was wet in her cunt, and her skin was washed in the most powerful of lotions, a male's essence; she breathed deeply of the scent of the chestnut blossoms adorning her, and floated joyfully in their seed-bath.

The drum continued, and now Jana was mounted by each of her bridesmaids in turn. Clare was already breathless from her sport on the floor, and her mouth and inner thighs gleamed with the sperm she herself had taken. Each woman rode Jana like a horse, pressing their naked cunts and clits together in fervent tribadism, and pushing Jana to a higher plateau of orgasm. She climaxed with each of her bridesmaids, and her heart swelled with love and happiness, for the Castle and everyone in it. For *her* Castle . . .

So this is how I am sacrificed, she thought, giving the joyful gift of my body to every one of my – *slaves!* She did not complain, and nor was she surprised when the machine creaked again, this time tilting her into a vertical position with her trussed limbs outstretched as though for a flogging. Cassie reverently brought her a white nine-thonged whip to kiss, and Jana saw that the whip was studded with diamonds. She touched her lips to each thong, and murmured her gratitude, as the whip was lifted and the first stroke lashed her bare buttocks. She jumped in shock, for the pain was surprisingly acute, and that first stroke was followed swiftly by a second, from a different hand. Jana could not see who was flogging her, but she guessed that every female and male in the Castle was awarding her squirming body one lash. So it was; when the whipping stopped, her back, thighs and buttocks were a sea of golden flames, and the glowing floor of the dais sparkled with the diamonds that had fallen from Jana's body. And in the centre of this diadem gleamed the red cover of her fallen rulebook.

Now, every light was suddenly extinguished, except for the firelight from the dais, which grew in intensity and then began to shoot upwards like dazzling flowers, climbing to the ceiling until the inner cupola was illuminated like a giant star that cast its warm glow on the whole shadowy chamber. Jana was gently released from her whipping frame, and, without being bidden, stood transfixed by the beam of light, which seemed to bathe and penetrate her like a cock. Her skin glistened with the droplets of sperm, as though she were Aphrodite risen from the ocean.

Doors opened, and Robyn announced the approach of the Master. A single spotlight detached itself to shine on the doorway, and the Master appeared. He was alone, dressed only in a black silk cloak emblazoned with stars, and his head was shaven smooth. He bore stars and moons on his face, whether tattooed or painted it was impossible to tell, and his eyes and lips were painted dark crimson. There was total silence as he walked slowly towards Jana, knelt before her and kissed her feet, then stood and threw off his cloak. The company gasped in awe. The Master was naked, his body devoid of hair and painted like Jana's, though he bore no rings. And Jana saw that his naked penis was massive and erect, bigger even than Horst's and, like his, circumcised. A tail grew halfway up his spine, thicker and longer yet than his stiff sex organ. Jana gasped as she looked, for it was more than a tail: to her eyes, it was a second sex organ, a twin penis, and growing not from the base of his spine like Horst's but from far deeper, as though the Master's balls had sprouted two giant horns. All thoughts of rebellion against the Master wilted in Jana forever, as she looked on the power embodied in those giant twin cocks.

She moaned in joy as, silently, the Master took her, standing up. His cock pushed at the lips of her wet quim, then with a swift motion sank inside her to his balls. With strong, gentle hands, he clasped her, and Jana raised her thighs until they pinioned him by the waist, and her ankles were tightly cupping his face. He stood motionless as she fucked him, sliding up and down on that massive naked engine until her love-juice was a torrent on his thighs. Then she brought herself rapidly to orgasm, once and then again, thrusting and squeezing his power as though to milk it of its every drop of essence. Yet, as Jana sighed and shrieked in the slippery joy of her climaxing, the Master did not yield his sperm! She squeezed and milked him, but no cream came for her, until he bent forward and whispered in her ear: 'Mistress Jana, my bride, my sacrifice, the Supreme Mistress comes to bless us!'

Through the doors came a female resplendent in golden robes, her black hair piled up in a thick, lustrous knot on top of her head and sparkling with gold and diamonds. She approached the dais and the two entwined lovers, then dropped her robe and stepped up to them. Jana froze with shock, for she recognised the Supreme Mistress. It was Mokka.

Mokka gave no word of greeting, and no sign of recognition, save to touch her naked cunt with her fingers, then press them to Jana's lips. Their eyes met, and Mokka's eyes were diamonds of joy and desire. Wordlessly, Mokka clasped the Master's shoulders, and with lithe agility ascended his back until her bare, shaven quim was poised above his massive hard tail. In one smooth motion, she took this second cock all the way into her slit, and Jana saw that her thighs, too, glistened with her own love-oil. She lifted her legs until her feet touched Jana's, and then the two women commenced their fucking of the

271

Master, who was now helpless in their powerful embrace. The Master's strong muscles rippled under their combined weight, and he closed his eyes. As Mokka fucked him from behind, Jana felt his penis tremble in her cunt, and knew that he would spurt soon.

'Yes,' she whispered, 'you are coming for me, my Master! Give me your seed, make me whole!'

At these words, Mokka redoubled the power of her fucking, and Jana approached her orgasmic plateau as she felt the first warm drop of sperm deep at the neck of her womb. Mokka moaned, her eyes tight shut and her breath heavy and hoarse, and then Jana felt the Master's cock buck and shudder, and climaxed herself in a long, swooning golden orgasm as her womb was washed with a hot flood that seemed like lava from the Earth herself.

As lithely as she had mounted the Master, Mokka detached herself, and with strong arms lifted Jana from his body. As she held her, Mokka pressed her mouth to Jana's cunt and licked up every drop of her love-oil, and with it potent rivulets of the Master's sperm. She swallowed all of it, and then licked every inch of Jana's soaked body, savouring her like a succulent morsel of food, until all the seed which had washed her had been consumed. Then Mokka gently placed Jana on her feet.

'I have drunk of my Castle,' said Mokka so that all could hear, 'and now, as is fitting, I give a slave to the One who is my Purifier and my Mistress.'

She placed her hand on the Master's shoulders, and made him kneel before the astonished Jana, pressing his lips in obeisance to the swollen fount to which he had so recently given the tribute of his male essence.

'Take him, Mistress Jana, for he and all the power of the Castle are yours! You are Supreme!'

And Mokka, the Supreme Mistress, picked up the rulebook and handed it to Jana, bowed in the now familiar manner, then knelt beside the Master, joining him in his fount-kiss. The pages of the rulebook fell open, and Jana saw that they were covered with handwriting in faded ink, as though awakened from a long sleep by the warmth of

272

her body. The great hall was still, and Jana saw the naked bodies frozen in silent embraces. She thought the Master would be superb as one of *her* living sculptures . . .

Jana pressed the rulebook to her belly, atop the heads of her two worshipping slaves.

'My slaves,' she said loudly and firmly, 'I bring the most precious of gifts. I bring you the rules of Maldona!'

Envoi

From the Rule Book of Maldona

When all is said and done, after all argumentation, gifts, sweet words and kisses, the only way to bring a female to her senses is to perfume and robe her properly in frilly things, and give her a sound thrashing on the bare. This applies even more so to males.

NEXUS BACKLIST

All books are priced £4.99 unless another price is given. If a date is supplied, the book in question will not be available until that month in 1998.

CONTEMPORARY EROTICA

THE ACADEMY	Arabella Knight		
AGONY AUNT	G. C. Scott		
ALLISON'S AWAKENING	Lauren King		
AMAZON SLAVE	Lisette Ashton	£5.99	
THE BLACK GARTER	Lisette Ashton	£5.99	Sept
THE BLACK ROOM	Lisette Ashton		
BOUND TO OBEY	Amanda Ware	£5.99	Dec
BOUND TO SUBMIT	Amanda Ware		
CANDIDA IN PARIS	Virginia Lasalle		
CHAINS OF SHAME	Brigitte Markham	£5.99	July
A CHAMBER OF DELIGHTS	Katrina Young		
DARK DELIGHTS	Maria del Rey	£5.99	Aug
DARLINE DOMINANT	Tania d'Alanis	£5.99	Oct
A DEGREE OF DISCIPLINE	Zoe Templeton		
THE DISCIPLINE OF NURSE RIDING	Yolanda Celbridge	£5.99	Nov
THE DOMINO TATTOO	Cyrian Amberlake		
THE DOMINO QUEEN	Cyrian Amberlake		
EDEN UNVEILED	Maria del Rey		
EDUCATING ELLA	Stephen Ferris		
EMMA'S SECRET DOMINATION	Hilary James		
FAIRGROUND ATTRACTIONS	Lisette Ashton	£5.99	Dec
THE TRAINING OF FALLEN ANGELS	Kendal Grahame		
HEART OF DESIRE	Maria del Rey		

ANCIENT & FANTASY SETTINGS

THE CLOAK OF APHRODITE	Kendal Grahame		
DEMONIA	Kendal Grahame		
THE DUNGEONS OF LIDIR	Aran Ashe		
THE FOREST OF BONDAGE	Aran Ashe		
NYMPHS OF DIONYSUS	Susan Tinoff		
THE WARRIOR QUEEN	Kendal Grahame	£5.99	Dec

EDWARDIAN, VICTORIAN & OLDER EROTICA

ANNIE	Evelyn Culber	£5.99	
ANNIE AND THE COUNTESS	Evelyn Culber	£5.99	
BEATRICE	Anonymous		
THE CORRECTION OF AN ESSEX MAID	Yolanda Celbridge	£5.99	
DEAR FANNY	Michelle Clare		
LYDIA IN THE HAREM	Philippa Masters		
LURE OF THE MANOR	Barbra Baron		
MAN WITH A MAID 3	Anonymous		
MEMOIRS OF A CORNISH GOVERNESS	Yolanda Celbridge		
THE GOVERNESS AT ST AGATHA'S	Yolanda Celbridge		
MISS RATTAN'S LESSON	Yolanda Celbridge	£5.99	Aug
PRIVATE MEMOIRS OF A KENTISH HEADMISTRESS	Yolanda Celbridge		
SISTERS OF SEVERCY	Jean Aveline		

SAMPLERS & COLLECTIONS

EROTICON 3	Various		
EROTICON 4	Various	£5.99	July
THE FIESTA LETTERS	ed. Chris Lloyd		
NEW EROTICA 2	ed. Esme Ombreux		
NEW EROTICA 3	ed. Esme Ombreux		
NEW EROTICA 4	ed. Esme Ombreux	£5.99	Sept

NON-FICTION

HOW TO DRIVE YOUR WOMAN WILD IN BED	Graham Masterton
HOW TO DRIVE YOUR MAN WILD IN BED	Graham Masterton
LETTERS TO LINZI	Linzi Drew

Please send me the books I have ticked above.

Name   ....

Address   ....

                       ....

                       ....

                 .... Post code.......................

Send to: **Cash Sales, Nexus Books, Thames Wharf Studios, Rainville Road, London W6 9HT**

Please enclose a cheque or postal order, made payable to **Nexus Books**, to the value of the books you have ordered plus postage and packing costs as follows:

UK and BFPO – £1.00 for the first book, 50p for the second book and 30p for each subsequent book to a maximum of £3.00;

Overseas (including Republic of Ireland) – £2.00 for the first book, £1.00 for the second book and 50p for each subsequent book.

If you would prefer to pay by VISA or ACCESS/MASTER-CARD, please write your card number and expiry date here:

....

Please allow up to 28 days for delivery.

Signature   ....
